I Am Vidocq

Other Books by Vincent McConnor

THE FRENCH DOLL
THE PROVENCE PUZZLE
THE RIVIERA PUZZLE
THE PARIS PUZZLE

I Am Vidocq

Vincent McConnor

Dodd, Mead & Company
New York

Copyright © 1985 by Vincent McConnor

All rights reserved

No part of this book may be reproduced in any form
without permission in writing from the publisher.
Published by Dodd, Mead & Company, Inc.
79 Madison Avenue, New York, N.Y. 10016
Distributed in Canada by
McClelland and Stewart Limited, Toronto
Manufactured in the United States of America
Designed by Erich Hobbing

First Edition

Library of Congress Cataloging in Publication Data

McConnor, Vincent.
  I am Vidocq.

  I. Title.
PS3525.A165312   1985   813'.52   85-4578
ISBN 0-396-08716-7

This romantic novel of crime and dedication is dedicated, with admiration and presumption, to Honoré de Balzac. Without his generous assistance it would never have been conceived or written.

One evening long ago, on the terrace of a café on Place Dauphine, he introduced me to his friend—François Eugéne Vidocq.

I Am Vidocq

PARIS—1823

CHAPTER 1

Vidocq's eyes darted from side to side, missing nothing.

Paris was the most beautiful city he had ever seen. Even *les touristes*—English, German, and Russian—said it was.

That was a popular new word in recent years. *Touristes* . . .

The most beautiful city in the world, but if you were a policeman it was, at the same time, sordid and evil.

Of course he hadn't as yet seen other large cities. One day he hoped to visit London, New York, and especially Phil-a-del-phia . . .

He relaxed, leaning back against the leather-cushioned corner of the carriage, as his coachman guided the bay mare through the familiar streets leading from his home on rue de l'Hirondelle to 6, Petite rue Sainte-Anne.

They followed a different route each day to prevent inquisitive eyes from noticing the unmarked black carriage two days in succession.

He enjoyed sitting like this, out of sight, glancing from side to side, holding his silver-headed cane with both white-gloved hands, face shadowed by the wide brim of his gray summer hat, an anonymous blur in a pale gray suit of lightweight English cloth, trousers tucked into calf-length black boots. Today his hair was its natural chestnut color. Yesterday it had been black, but tomorrow it might be gray.

The carriage turned left down rue Git-le-Cœur, away from the river, then right on rue Saint-André-des Arts.

Not so hot as yesterday, but it was certain to get warmer this afternoon. July was always uncomfortable.

Many of the old mansions he was passing had their shutters closed. The wealthy, whenever possible, fled to their country estates for the summer months, leaving Paris to the poor, *les touristes,* and, of course, the criminals.

3

Some starved-looking dogs, running in a pack, were hunting in the dusty gutters for food. Probably abandoned by their owners, who didn't care to take them in a crowded diligence to some distant province.

Early morning was one of his favorite times of the day, winter and summer, especially this brief ride to his office. A peaceful interlude with none of the problems he might face later.

Sunlight washed the dirty cobbles where fat sparrows were screaming over their breakfasts. Greedy rascals! They nested in the trees, but dined and died in the streets. When they flew above the city, their sharp eyes probably saw only the passing horses leaving their next meal.

As his carriage turned toward the river again on rue Dauphine, he glanced at a familiar mansion where years ago he had cornered that scoundrel Varcolle, who enticed innocents newly arrived from the country down to his cellars, where he tortured and poisoned them. No one would ever know how many young girls had vanished.

Many streets had such personal memories for him. Landmarks where he had tracked down or captured every variety of criminal.

This morning he had stayed in bed later than usual. He'd had trouble sleeping last night because of the heat.

At breakfast he had sensed that this might be one of those special days when an important investigation would develop that only he could handle.

Yesterday brought an end, without scandal, to the Marquis de Luynes inquiry. The only case this week that had involved him personally.

He hoped there wouldn't be another murder until Vignon returned to duty. Breaking his arm in that ridiculous accident! Now there wasn't anyone to make sketches at the scene of a murder, and Vignon wouldn't return for several weeks.

He wondered where Calamatta was today. At this instant! Was the villain in France, or had he escaped long ago to some foreign land? He thought about Calamatta nearly every day . . .

Breakfast had been a fresh brioche with a bowl of black coffee. His mother had taught their cook to make brioches almost as delicious as the ones his father used to bake in Arras. With the brioche there had been fresh country butter and a jar of his mother's raspberry confiture. King Louis, in his fine palace, didn't eat any better.

Before leaving home, he'd gone up to his mother's suite, where, because of the heat, she was having her coffee in bed. Kissed her on the cheek and escaped, avoiding a flurry of questions about his work, which would be unanswerable. Had continued down the corridor to Jeanne-Victoire's suite. Observing that his wife was asleep in her ivory and gold bed, he had closed the silken curtains, shutting out the light without waking her.

How satisfying it was that he could give his dear mother a life of comfort after all those bad years, following the death of his father, when she had possessed so little but had given him so much. Taken him in and welcomed him each time he returned home without warning, after another escape from prison or desertion from the army.

And it was good that he was able to provide everything for his delicate wife.

He was, at last, a comparatively wealthy man. Not rich like a banker, but he had quite enough.

Living like a king at home and acting like the king of his Brigade.

That was his personal kingdom! The Brigade de la Sûreté Nationale, known more familiarly—especially to the criminal world—as Number Six.

Sunlight shafted across his knees as his carriage shot out from the shaded street and rolled over the Pont Neuf.

He peered toward Nôtre-Dame in the distance, its facade in deep shadow above the huddle of shacks and low buildings that crowded the open Parvis.

Blue sky overhead, but the Seine was the color of stale coffee. Carriages and carts clattering in both directions across the bridge, hooves pounding with a hollow sound, combining into one thunderous rumble. Footpaths along both sides thronged with hurrying people. He watched them unnoticed, guessing at their secret lives.

This was a favorite pastime, driving across any Paris bridge, and he had to cross at least one to reach his office from any part of the city.

He studied the face of every beautiful young woman. Who were their lovers? Were they happy? Or were they virgins . . . That ugly girl walking alone! Did she have someone to caress her? There were always men, of course, who were attracted by ugliness.

He wasn't one of those. An exquisite face had baited the sexual trap for him from the first. That English girl who stayed overnight with her family at an Arras inn when he was thirteen. He ran errands for the foreign guests and knew every bedroom. What a brouhaha that had caused!

The stench from a cart removing a load of night soil made him cover his nose as his attention was caught by a familiar weasel face. Where could that rascal be going at this hour? One of his accomplices must be on trial, and he would be heading for the Palais de Justice to learn the verdict. Many friends and relatives of criminals showed up outside the courtrooms, if at the moment they were not being sought for some crime of their own.

First thing today, after glancing through the morning reports, he would have his assistants in for their morning meeting to discuss criminal activity in the city during the past twenty-four hours and make plans for the day ahead.

After the staff meeting he'd been requested to see the Minister of Interior, probably to discuss his budget for the Brigade. He would be questioned again about his division, but he would outwit the Minister, whatever it was, without difficulty. That pompous politician!

Unless something unforeseen came up to take him from his desk this afternoon—and he hoped something would—he planned to spend the remainder of the day studying the dossiers and reports that had been piling up while he was involved with the de Luynes business.

He would have lunch upstairs in the staff dining room, or if the day turned out to be as warm as yesterday ask Madame Babelay to serve something at his desk.

They were bumping along the Quai de l'Horloge, the mare trotting briskly, past the ominous stone bulk of the Conciergerie. Smart animal. She knew they were approaching their destination.

Should he have dinner at home this evening? He'd dined at Le Grand Véfour last night with his mother—first time in weeks—but his wife still wasn't feeling well enough to venture out.

Perhaps he would eat alone tonight, in one of the smaller cafés, make a brief tour of the boulevards, and have supper with some little actress or visit one of those luxurious apartments on rue de la Chaussée-d'Antin, where there was always a buffet of exotic dishes with an amusing company of wealthy men and ravishing young women.

Les grandes courtisanes . . .

His carriage entered the alley and slowed through open gates into the rear courtyard of Number Six, where one of the older coachmen lounged in front of the stables and a stableboy was grooming a horse.

He saw the uniformed guard recognize his carriage, straighten, and salute.

One of the younger guards would be watching for him from an upstairs window—he wasn't supposed to notice—and spread word that the Chief had arrived.

Flinging the carriage door open and disregarding the step, he jumped to the ground before the wheels slowed to a stop or anyone could reach for the door handle. Glanced up at Jean in his light-gray summer livery seated on the box. "I'll be dining out tonight. Take your orders from Madame Vidocq today."

Jean smiled. "Which Madame Vidocq?"

"Both! As always. Perhaps they'll ride in the Bois this afternoon to escape this heat." He turned to face the guard. "Good morning, my friend."

"Morning, Chief."

He strode across the open courtyard as his carriage rolled out through the gates into the alley.

There was no sign anywhere to indicate that this was the famous Number Six.

He hurried up the worn marble steps to the rear entrance, past another saluting guard, into the marble-floored entry. Pushed against a paneled section of wall, which swung in, revealing a spiral iron staircase. Closed the panel behind him and started up the steps.

His day had begun.

CHAPTER 2

Pausing on the dim first floor landing, Vidocq sniffed the air.

A delicious aroma was drifting down the steps from the second floor. Veal cooking with garlic and basil.

Madame Babelay must be preparing a roast to serve cold throughout the day whenever any staff member became hungry, which was a continuous situation. She was an excellent cook and housekeeper, who with the help of a maid kept the entire building reasonably clean. Her husband was one of the night guards, and the Babelays lived in a small suite between the kitchen and the locked rooms where official records were stored, across from a dormitory for staff members who had to remain on the premises overnight.

He grasped a leather handle and, swinging a panel of the wall open, stepped into a long central corridor that extended to the front. Closed the door again and strode down a bright aisle of light from a row of overhead skylights.

Most of the doors on both sides of this corridor stood open, and as he passed he could glimpse his assistants at their desks. He never looked directly into their offices but could see them from the corners of his eyes without turning his head.

This morning several doors were closed.

The third door, on his left, stood open, and that office was empty. Ronquetti must be sleeping late again.

Allard's door, across the corridor, was closed. Charles Fouché, third in command, had the office next to Allard. He was slumped behind his desk reading a morning paper. The mass of his great body seemed to have collapsed. He looked up as Vidocq passed and set his paper aside. Opposite Fouché, on the left again, André Goury—his second in command—looking tall even when seated, was studying a dossier and scowling with his customary intensity.

Continuing on past Goury's door, he nodded toward the guard at the distant inquiry desk, who saluted without rising, and ran his eyes over the waiting people, seeing familiar faces but giving no sign of recognition. He had learned years ago how to look directly into any crowd, yet never let anyone catch his eye and detain him.

He approached an unmarked pair of open doors—his name was nowhere visible in the entire building—and entered his private suite.

Aubé, general secretary of the Sûreté, occupied the first office. He sat at a desk piled with red-ribboned official documents, stacks of reports and dossiers, his back to open windows facing a side alley, surrounded by shelved walls holding leatherbound boxes packed with correspondence. He was, as usual, making notes on a ruled pad. Aubé knew all the secrets of the Sûreté and was constantly jotting down his precise notations with a freshly sharpened quill. Those notes were what kept the Sûreté running smoothly.

"Good morning, my friend."

Aubé looked up, his balding head and spectacles reflecting light from the windows. "Good morning, Chief. You're late."

"Overslept. We'll have our meeting in ten minutes."

"I'll tell everyone."

"That confidential matter concerning the Marquis de Luynes was resolved yesterday. Didn't have a chance to tell you."

"Congratulations!"

"If you made any notes either time his daughter was here, destroy them. I want nothing in our files and nothing sent to the Préfecture." Continuing through the antechamber beyond Aubé's office, he saw that no one was waiting on the small sofas intended for important visitors. In the faint light from a window overlooking another alley, he glanced at the framed portraits of former Ministers of Interior and recent Préfects, most of their faces displaying extravagant mustaches. He had found them in an attic and rescued the lot when he moved into Number Six. As was his daily custom, he studied the faces of two Préfects, Comte Dubois and Baron de Pasquier. One played an important role in his joining the police and the other helped him achieve his present success.

He went through the open doors into his private office. Looked toward the open windows beyond his desk, across the Cour de la Sainte-Chapelle, toward the peaceful old church. It was the color of ivory in the bright sunlight.

He rested his hat upside down on the polished surface of a table placed against the wall near the doors, put his cane beside it. Pulled off his white cotton gloves and dropped them next to the cane.

As he sank into the black leather armchair at his impressive Napoléonic desk, he noticed that Madame Babelay had left a small crystal vase holding four yellow rosebuds. He selected the smallest and snapped its stem. Tossed the wet part through the nearest window and tucked the bud into his lapel after inhaling its delicate scent.

For a moment before he opened the dossier marked PRIVÉ, which Aubé always left in the exact center of his desk, he glanced around the handsome office with pride. This was something he did frequently, as though he were seeing everything for the first time.

All this furniture had been brought from his home or purchased especially for the office. The wall on his left was lined with crowded

9

bookshelves, mostly volumes on crime along with a few novels, partially hidden behind a large map of modern Paris suspended from the ceiling. On the opposite wall, above the black marble fireplace, was a favorite painting of happy roisterers in a medieval tavern. To the right of the doors was a large framed etching, by an unknown engraver, of François Villon.

His eyes were held briefly, caught by the sly face of that rogue and master thief. There was a criminal he would have enjoyed pursuing! Probably the greatest rascal who had ever lived in Paris. Legend said he vanished through the snow one winter's night, but nobody knew for certain what happened to him.

He opened the leatherbound PRIVÉ dossier and began to read each document and report and finally a page of notes in Aubé's neat script, commenting on the major crimes in the city during the previous twenty-four hours. The reports were from his staff, detailing their individual activities. All were brief and contained little that was new.

Before he had finished reading, Vidocq sensed Aubé come in silently and sit in the same chair, to the right of his desk, that he occupied for all meetings. Was aware of the others filing in one by one at intervals. Without looking up, he knew each man from the sound of his footsteps, the rhythm of his stride, the way he pulled a leather armchair from its place against the wall, carried or shoved it toward the desk, and sat down.

He closed the PRIVÉ dossier and handed it to Aubé. "Good morning, my friends!" Smiling, his eyes sweeping across their familiar faces—Goury, Fouché, Allard, and Cauler—as each responded. "And where is the Duc de Modena this morning?"

"Late," Fouché's voice boomed. "As usual."

"He went to the new gambling club last night," Goury added.

"Probably still there!" Allard laughed. "Or in bed."

"If he's in bed he won't be alone!" Cauler, the youngest, exclaimed with admiration.

Vidocq chuckled. "Paris was tranquil again last night, according to your reports. Perhaps we should all take a vacation."

Allard shrugged. "It's the heat. Although, when I was a gendarme walking the streets, every hot night seemed to have its crime of passion."

"People aren't so passionate anymore," Fouché muttered. "Or does it only seem that way because I'm getting older?"

"I'm not that old." Vidocq raised his eyebrows at the idea. "And pray I never shall be. Paris could never survive without passion. But what about this suicide in Montparnasse?" He looked at Cauler. "Could it be murder?" he asked, hopefully.

"There was no evidence," Cauler responded, "to suggest murder. The young woman had frequently spoken of taking her own life."

"Have another look into her past. Her lovers. Ask questions in the neighborhood." Vidocq moved from case to case without consulting the dossiers again, remembering every detail, raised points he had wondered about as he read their reports, and made suggestions for additional lines of inquiry to explore.

Aubé leaned forward during a pause in the conversation and whispered in Vidocq's ear. "You have that other meeting at ten."

Vidocq glanced at the ormolu clock on the mantelpiece. "That will be all for the moment, my friends." Getting to his feet as they rose from their armchairs. "I have been summoned across to the Préfecture, once again, to defend our budget."

Several groaned, Fouché's voice deeper than the others.

"Never fear! I shall argue with courage and vehemence." He moved between them to get his hat from the table, leaving gloves and cane behind. "If anyone sees the Duc de Modena, tell him I expect a full report, in writing, on his adventures last night. Everything!"

Their laughter followed him into the corridor.

CHAPTER 3

Vidocq crossed rue de Jerusalem through scorching sunlight, following his customary route to the Préfecture.

It had been several weeks since he'd been summoned by the Minister.

He was in an excellent mood, in spite of the heat, and would not lose his temper.

His stride was careful in case he was observed, because any man who ever wore leg irons could be recognized by the way he walked. You never lost that for the rest of your life, limping slightly and favoring one leg. He had taught himself though, years ago, how to disguise it.

The guards saluted as he entered.

He knew all the corridors of the Préfecture, had climbed every staircase and explored each narrow passage in his first years with the police. He had quickly discovered all the shortcuts.

These days he avoided the ancient building unless it was necessary to visit the Préfect or the Minister, because there were always criminals waiting in these endless corridors. Most of them, fortunately, had never seen him without a disguise, but there was always the chance there might be someone—of the thousands he'd arrested, many had vowed to kill him—who might remember him.

These walls were painted an ugly yellow that had faded long ago to a hideous mustard unlike any color known to man. Caused, some claimed, by the poisonous air which escaped from distant prison cells.

One gendarme came toward him. He saw that it was Jaminet, who hoped one day to join the Sûreté. The young gendarme saluted. "Could I speak to you, Chief . . ."

Vidocq paused. "Of course."

"Something you might want to know." Dropping his voice. "There was a murder last night. I hear the Préfecture isn't reporting it to the Sûreté."

Vidocq restrained his temper. "Why not?"

"They say it's not important enough."

"That's for me to decide. They've been told I want to know about every murder in Paris. You heard the victim's name?"

"It was the whore. Clochette . . ."

"Little Clochette? Where did this happen?"

"Her apartment on rue Bréda."

"How was she killed?"

"A bullet in the heart."

"And the murderer?"

"They're saying it was a prowler."

"This is not being reported to me?"

"No, Chief. That was an order."

"You're a bright young man, Jaminet. Wasted here. I won't forget."

Jaminet grinned, saluted again, and turned back to his handcuffed prisoner.

Vidocq strode on, down the crowded corridor, his rage growing.

Little Clochette murdered! He'd known her since she arrived in Paris

12

seven or eight years ago. She had been called Clochette because of her azure blue eyes. Like those blue bellflowers. Clochettes . . .

His anger increased as he bounded up more marble steps.

Clochette had been kind to his wife before their marriage. Had come to visit Jeanne-Victoire after she became ill, but then her visits had stopped and he had thought nothing of it.

In those days she had a more fashionable address than rue Bréda.

Poor Clochette. Shot in the heart by a prowler . . .

He must never tell Jeanne-Victoire.

Climbing the final staircase, he reached a deserted corridor leading to the office of the Minister of Interior, passing through a spartan ante-room where a sour-faced assistant motioned him toward the inner office. Vidocq knocked sharply and swung the door open.

The Minister, seated behind his desk, looked up from a pile of letters. "Ah, Vidocq! Come in! Come in . . ."

"I received your note. That you wished to see me this morning." He closed the door and crossed the office—larger but not so elegant as his own—toward the desk. "If you hope once again to try and convince me that I should open our books at the Sûreté for examination, my answer will be another firm refusal."

"No! No. . . ." The long-fingered aristocratic hand gestured toward an armchair. "Sit down. Sit down."

"I'm well aware that I must report now and again to the Préfecture." Sitting as he talked, resting his hat on the faded carpet. "But, as you well know, the instructions from the Préfect, Comte Dubois, contained in his official directive establishing our Brigade were extremely vague and subject to interpretation."

"I know. I do, indeed, know . . ."

"I shall protest any further attempt to cut my staff, reduce their salaries, or pare my budget."

"Of course! Of course . . . How many do you employ at the moment?"

"As many as our work requires."

"Dear me! Dear me . . ." He scowled. "There have been rumors recently that your staff has grown to more than a hundred persons."

"I wouldn't be surprised. There's a need for every one of them. And more!"

"Are you still hiring reformed criminals?"

13

"And why not! I've done that from the start. Aubé was a forger and Goury a swindler!"

"How many would you estimate are now female?"

"That stupid question again! Won't those antiquated police officers downstairs ever learn how useful a smart young woman can be in their work? They get into places to ask questions where no man could hope to venture."

"I'm told that some of these females in your employ are former— prostitutes."

"Who could know the evils of Paris better than a whore!"

"Ah, yes! Who, indeed?" The Minister chuckled, but his lack of experience made the sound more like a series of small coughs.

Vidocq's temper exploded suddenly as he remembered Clochette. "I've learned that the Préfecture neglected to report to the Sûreté that there was a murder last night in rue Bréda."

"I received a brief report on the matter this morning. Some . . . whore . . . was shot by a prowler."

"They're supposed to report all murders to me."

"They didn't wish to bother you with such an insignificant incident. Impossible to find a prowler. They're letting the matter drop."

"Letting it drop! But . . ." His anger seeped away as he felt an urge to laugh at those fools in the Préfecture. He would look into Clochette's murder on his own.

"After all, my friend, we both know there are certain matters you at the Sûreté are supposed to report to the Préfecture, which frequently are not reported . . . "

That was true. He rarely bothered sending reports to the police. As the Minister continued in a more placating tone, Vidocq began to relax, aware that this wasn't going to be as serious as their last conversation. He studied the lean face with its red-veined nose, suggesting more than a casual fondness for fine cognac. A distinguished man with silver hair. Must have something up his sleeve, leading to a trap he was about to spring. He admired the old man for his apparent candor but had never trusted him.

". . . and I was remembering only this morning what Paris was like before you entered our police service. That would be ten years ago . . ."

"If you mean the Paris police—which I joined as an informer—it was fourteen years ago."

14

"Is that possible! Well, well . . . I recall, in those days, it was unsafe to walk on the boulevards after dark. Respectable citizens were assaulted in our parks. Dozens of houses robbed every night!"

"That was, in part, because Napoléon had taken all the young men off into his army. Leaving only middle-aged gendarmes to guard the city. My first project was to retire them and recruit younger men."

"What an uproar that caused! Not only did you use former convicts but you put them to work without giving them any uniforms."

"They were the foundation of my plan for the future. Many of them were serving prison terms but had their sentences canceled when they agreed to work for the Sûreté. Their success was immediate because, without uniforms, nobody knew they were policemen. Many criminals—the worst element—fled to Italy or Germany. And the files I instigated at the Sûreté—complete records for all known criminals—led to hundreds of arrests. Crime in Paris has been reduced more than forty percent!"

"They could use your talents outside of Paris." The Minister picked up an official looking letter. "For instance . . ."

Vidocq twisted his head slightly but was unable to decipher the writing, upside down, from where he sat.

"I've been informed by the local authorities in Blois that the great château of Chambord was desecrated and robbed last week."

"I too had a report on this incident."

"What are the true facts? Is this that same gang of brigands which has been robbing castles throughout the valley of the Loire?"

"So it would seem."

"Who is their leader? Does anyone know?"

"He's called Le Diable Noir! The Black Devil . . ."

"And who the devil is he?"

"As yet, nobody has ever seen his face. He's said to wear a black mask, black scarf around his head, and black clothing under a black cloak. He's killed at least a dozen innocent people in addition to the guards at various châteaux."

"How does he manage to evade capture?"

"They claim he's like an eel. Escapes from every trap. Those old castles have only a single caretaker on guard. Most have been locked in a cellar unharmed, but if they attempt to resist they are killed. The Black Devil apparently heads a band of a dozen or more ruffians. They've

15

been glimpsed riding through remote villages or galloping across distant fields in the moonlight."

"What, precisely, do they take?"

"The owners of those châteaux either lost their heads to the Widow during the Terror or have returned from exile and are living in Paris. These scoundrels take everything of value that was left behind."

"But that would require heavy carts to remove their plunder!"

"It has been observed that perhaps half an hour after Le Diable and his horsemen ride through a village there is a sound of thunder like the passing of a storm. Farmers cower in their beds. Those who venture to a window observe a parade of charrettes rolling past. These carts rendezvous with the band of horsemen at each château. They have removed treasures valued at many millions of francs. Paintings by famous masters. Furniture that once belonged to kings. Some of these châteaux were the property of former royal mistresses. Fortunately none of these robberies have taken place within our jurisdiction."

"What do you suppose becomes of all these treasures?"

Vidocq shrugged. "I would think they're being sold in foreign countries. The Russians, for instance, pay high prices for French antiques and ask no questions. There are forty roads leading out of France and our borders are easily crossed."

"I pray this Diable Noir never comes any closer to Paris."

Vidocq chuckled. "I've been wondering when he'll ransack Versailles or Fontainebleu."

"That of course would be a matter for the government. Not the Paris police."

"Then there's the greatest treasure of all, not far from where we are sitting, waiting to be plucked. The palaces of the Louvre!"

"*Mon Dieu! Mon Dieu!* Don't even suggest such a possibility." The Minister's face paled at the idea. "You've heard nothing to make you suspect this villain would attack Paris?"

"Not yet. But that would certainly be a logical move for him to make in the future. He's running out of châteaux in the provinces."

"You're jesting, of course! I refuse to worry, as long as he continues his operations elsewhere." He waved his hands, fingers fluttering, as though to brush the unpleasant thought away. "To a more immediate matter. I've a favor to request of you, my friend . . ."

"Anything within the power of the Sûreté is at your service."

16

"This is a personal favor I must ask of you—not your office."

"And what is that?"

"I remember some years ago when you did a great service, at my request, for the Comte de Grandeville ..."

"A simple matter of removing a certain person from Paris."

"The Comte had most indiscreetly become involved with a ... a ...."

"A *courtisane!* One of the more notorious."

"You managed, with great discretion, to persuade her to depart."

"Only by suggesting she take her charming person to Peru, where her various talents might be more appreciated. The Comte was pleased to provide a purse of louis d'or to pay for her journey, with a generous amount left so that she could start some kind of business after she arrived. By now, I should think, she is mistress of the most profitable bordello outside of Paris."

"I only brought up the matter because there's another task that requires your discreet attention."

Vidocq smiled, knowing that he was finally about to learn the reason for this meeting. "And what is that, Monsieur le Ministre?"

"Yesterday I had a most urgent request from the well-known banker, Monsieur de Fontanelle ..."

"I know him by reputation. Another lady off to Peru?"

"No! No! Certainly not. This concerns two visitors from the city of New Orléans in the United States ..."

"Americans?" Vidocq leaned forward expectantly.

"They arrived last week. I presume you speak English?"

"Only a few words, unfortunately."

"No matter. The gentleman is a wealthy businessman who, I'm assured, speaks excellent French. As does his young daughter. They're staying at the Hôtel Belvedere."

"What is his difficulty—this American—that he needs my attention?"

"It is apparently a matter of tremendous secrecy, which even Monsieur de Fontanelle wasn't told. Only that his friend expressed an urgent desire to meet the famous Monsieur Vidocq and seek his advice." Checking a notation on a fold of paper he produced from an inner pocket, "His name is Monsieur Penny-packaire ... "

"An American Indian?"

"I couldn't say. And there's nothing more I can tell you." Handing

17

the slip of paper across the desk. "You have all the information I was given."

Vidocq folded it into a pocket, then picked up his hat from the carpet and got to his feet.

"I'm grateful to you, my dear friend." The Minister rose and held out his hand.

Vidocq shook the outstretched hand. "I will call upon the American at his hotel."

"I shall inform Monsieur de Fontanelle."

Vidocq was crossing the anteroom before he realized that he hadn't asked for an increase in his budget so that he could take on more assistants at Number Six. *Eh bien!* Another time . . .

CHAPTER 4

Vidocq followed a different route through the side corridors of the Préfecture. Down an abrupt staircase to the first floor where, as usual, there was a throng of whispering people. Criminals of every profession. He could guess, with a glance at each face, which crime had brought them here. Petty thieves mostly, pickpockets, prostitutes, and drunkards.

Wooden benches were crowded with drunks pulled off the streets and quais during the night who were waiting to be questioned. Some were asleep, others stared into space, their empty eyes unfocused. These were the dregs of Paris! His department had nothing to do with this sort.

He noticed a youth in a blue denim smock, patched trousers, and scuffed boots crouched on the floor, sketching an old woman slumped in a drunken stupor on a bench. Her toothless mouth gaped. The boy was too young to be here, but someone must have given him the necessary permission. He was a healthy provincial type with a heavyset, muscular body, curly black hair, rosy cheeks, and a small nose shaped like a plum.

Vidocq peered over his shoulder at the drawing and saw that it demonstrated genuine powers of observation. As he watched, with a few quick strokes of the crayon, one wrinkled hand came alive on the page of the sketchbook.

The boy was so engrossed he wasn't aware of being watched.

"That's very good. You have talent."

The youth looked up. "Monsieur Vidocq!"

"You know me?"

"Anyone who comes here knows the Chief of the Sûreté."

"How would you like to work for me?"

"I wouldn't mind. Are you joking?"

"There's a member of my staff, does sketches for me . . ."

"Vignon? I've heard about him. Makes drawings of murder victims."

"He fell the other day, pursuing a suspect. Broke an arm."

The boy set his sketchbook on the floor and stood up to face Vidocq.

"If there's a murder while Vignon's unable to work, how would you like to sketch the cadaver?"

"I could do that. Even better than Vignon."

Vidocq chuckled. "Confident of yourself, aren't you?"

"I am an artist."

"How old are you?"

"Fifteen."

"You make a living selling your sketches?"

"Not yet. I have a job most afternoons at a bookshop in the Palais-Royal, but mornings I'm free to wander through the city and sketch what I please."

"You have a home?"

"I live with my parents."

"Born in Paris?"

"Marseille."

"Your name?"

"Daumier. Honoré Daumier . . ."

Vidocq pulled a pad and pencil from his pocket. "Write your name and address for me."

"Yes, Chief." He took them and began to scribble on the pad. "You will pay me to make these sketches?"

"Of course."

"How much?"

"The same amount I pay Vignon."

The youth grinned as he returned the pad and pencil. "When do I start?"

"When we have another murder. I will send for you, Daumier. I promise."

Vidocq smiled as he continued down the corridor. Followed a side passage to a narrow staircase that led down to a busy corridor on the ground floor with a door that brought him to a side street and another shortcut back to Number Six.

Reaching his own suite, he saw that Aubé was checking through a stack of official forms. "Where's everyone?"

"Pursuing their morning assignments. What was the old man's mood today?"

"This time he wanted something from me. Another private matter he asked me to undertake personally. I'm to pay a visit to a certain American gentleman this afternoon who's staying at the Hôtel Belvedere. Another one to keep off our records."

"I understand."

"No word from the Duc de Modena?"

"It's a little early."

"Anything new while I was gone?"

"No. It's unusually quiet. However, if you recall, it was like this last year in July. Nothing happened for days, and then there were all those murders on rue de Clichy."

"I do remember." Vidocq pulled the pad from his pocket. "Keep this name and address." Handing the pad across the desk. "A young artist I saw sketching a prisoner in the Préfecture. He might be useful until Vignon comes back."

"Right. Will you want lunch today?"

"I suppose. It's too warm to venture out." He continued on toward his office. "Tell Madame Babelay I'll have a slice of cold meat with a glass of wine. Nothing more."

The air was slightly cooler in his office because Aubé had closed the heavy curtains, but he preferred the light.

He removed his hat, set it on the table again next to his cane and gloves, then opened the curtains. Felt a rush of hot air as he swiveled his leather armchair and sat facing the windows.

The carved stone of Sainte-Chapelle in the distance was blurred by the sunlight, as though someone had wiped a cloth across an unfinished painting.

He was intrigued by this wealthy American visitor with a problem requiring his attention. What could it be this time? Would the daughter be plump and attractive or like one of those angular British females he'd seen on the boulevards, walking in pairs as though for mutual protection from the natives?

Late this afternoon he would pay a visit to the Hôtel Belvedere. He'd discovered that most foreigners could be found at their hotels late in the day, exhausted from shopping and sightseeing.

Turning slightly, he glanced at the book waiting on his desk. Perhaps he would have time to read more of Bretonne today. He enjoyed novels about crime in the last century. People didn't change. Even criminals!

He smiled, remembering Monsieur le Ministre's anguish at the thought of Le Diable Noir and his band venturing closer to Paris.

He'd heard of them first more than a year ago and had instructed Aubé to begin a special dossier listing every robbery along with any items of information about them, reported or rumored.

Perhaps the center of their operation might be located by checking every village the procession of charrettes had passed through in one night.

Impossible to undertake such an extensive search from Paris. That would require an army of investigators moving from village to village. With gendarmes from each local Préfecture.

Which reminded him that the Préfecture across the street hadn't bothered to notify him about Clochette's death.

Should he do something about that? Look into her murder on his own, without telling anyone at the Préfecture . . .

Staring at the sun on Sainte-Chapelle, he considered twin questions of murder. Those brutal murders in the Loire valley when the Black Devil and his band pillaged another château and the murder of a single whore last night in Paris. Poor Clochette . . .

He turned back to his desk and spent the remainder of the morning on reports that had been delivered while he was with the Minister.

Someone tapped lightly on one of the open doors.

He smiled, recognizing the sound. "Enter, Madame!" He looked up as a plump woman wearing a white apron over a neat gray dress entered bearing a napkin-covered tray.

"Good morning, Chief . . ."

"Madame Babelay!"

"Aubé said you wanted only a slice of meat with your wine."

"I was aware, when I came in this morning, that you were roasting veal today."

"That nose of yours! Babelay brought it from the market before dawn, after he'd finished guard duty for the night." She deposited her tray in front of him. "You don't eat enough." Folding the napkin and placing it within his reach.

He saw a slice of lean meat in the center of the plate, freshly baked bread with a small pottery crock of butter, and a glass of red wine. "This is all I need for such a warm day."

"I'm serving cold veal to everyone."

"How's your husband?"

"Babelay's complaining about the heat. like everybody else. They should all stand over my hot ovens! Which is why I did the baking first thing today. Will there be something more?"

"No, Madame. Thank you." He watched her depart, leaving the doors open, before he unfolded his napkin and picked up the heavy silver knife and fork, which felt warm to his touch. He sliced through the tender meat and broke a morsel of bread, which he popped into his mouth with the first bite of meat. The veal was redolent of garlic and basil. He raised the glass of wine and studied its color before letting it flood across his tongue. One of the Burgundies he'd bought for his private cellar. Either the 1809 or the 1812 . . .

He had finished eating and was enjoying the last swallow of wine when there was another knock on one of the open doors. The rhythm was familiar, sharper than Madame Babelay's tapping. "Come in, Monsieur le Duc!" He looked up to see the slim Italian clutching a bowl of steaming coffee carefully in one hand.

"Am I disturbing you at lunch?"

"I've just finished." He put his empty glass aside.

Ronquetti glided like a cautious dancer, careful not to spill his coffee, and sat in one of the armchairs facing the desk.

"And how is the Duc de Modena this afternoon?"

"Afternoon? I suppose it is . . ." He sighed and took a large swallow of coffee.

"From the elegant though rumpled silk evening suit you're wearing and the traces of beard on that unshaven chin, I would say you're heading home from a long night's work on the boulevards."

"Monsieur, as usual, observes everything." He gulped more coffee.

"Business or pleasure?"

"Both. Business first."

"How were they?"

"The official matter for Number Six was disappointing." He shrugged. "The pleasure—afterward—more satisfactory."

"A few details, if you please." Vidocq observed his associate with affection.

"Permit me several more swallows of this coffee . . ."

"By all means." Ronquetti was the most amusing member of his staff. The Italian had come from the slums of Naples but somewhere had picked up the manners of a Roman aristocrat. Vidocq always called him the Duc de Modena in their more relaxed moments together. That was the name Ronquetti had used when he first turned up in Paris and attempted to outwit the owners of the fashionable gambling establishments. Word had quickly reached Number Six of the handsome gambler who was rumored to be a genuine duke. From the first Vidocq had suspected the title was false, but Ronquetti had won so consistently at cards and had so charmed the owners of every club—in addition to the beautiful women, young and old, who played at the tables—that he had offered him a job at Number Six. The rascal had immediately confessed his true name was Ronquetti and accepted the offer. Because of his incredible skill with cards, he was placed in charge of supervising all the gambling houses in Paris. Later he'd been given more discreet investigations, especially those involving women. Ronquetti had proved to be one of the most successful choices of the many Vidocq had brought into Number Six from the criminal world.

The Italian had to be in his middle thirties, but looked half a dozen years younger. Studying him now, Vidocq was aware of the sleek black hair and the luminous brown eyes under long lashes. Sensuous Latin lips, white teeth, dark skin. No wonder women adored him. Most of all, he was conscious of the gambler's hands with their delicate fingers.

Ronquetti rested his china bowl on the desk.

Vidocq saw that it was empty. "I assume there will be no written report on your adventures last night."

"Is that absolutely necessary?"

"When was the last time you bothered to fill out a report?"

"Perhaps a year ago. Or was it longer?" He flashed a smile. "About last night! *Primo* . . . The new gambling establishment on Boulevard des Capucines appears to be in the clear. I visited each of their elegant rooms and played at several tables. Roulette and cards. No evidence of anything irregular. Of course they probably knew who I was and were expecting me. I shall return tonight with the enchanting Violette on my arm, an attractive mustache covering my upper lip, and a neat beard to hide my dimpled chin. Perhaps even a monocle!"

"Always a good effect."

"The lady and I will appear to be enjoying too much champagne, and we will be careless with our money. If their wheels are controlled or their dealers use marked cards, I shall learn the truth tonight."

"Have you made your arrangements with La Belle Violette?"

"I plan to stop at the lady's apartment as I drive home from here. *Secundo* . . . There are two young women waiting and gossiping at this moment in my office—the delicate Nun and the boisterous Rat, wondering if you require their services today."

"Not at the moment. In fact, I plan to spend a few hours this afternoon reading. Waiting for something interesting to put an end to my ennui."

"What you need is a fresh and puzzling murder to investigate!"

"Which reminds me, I'll be going out later. Tell the ladies they will come with me. I can use both of them."

"They'll be delighted." He picked up the empty coffee bowl as he got to his feet. "Any messages for La Belle Violette?"

"Only that she can keep her winnings tonight, in addition to the usual fee she always receives."

"I shall inform her." He headed for the open doors.

"You'd better get some sleep this afternoon."

"That's my intention."

Vidocq swiveled his chair to face the windows again.

He must see that American around five o'clock. Before that he would stop by Galerie Marchadier and look at the painting they were holding for him.

He would wait until the middle of the afternoon, until the sun had moved across the city, before ordering a carriage.

Take the Nun and the Rat along with him.

His first stop would be Clochette's apartment.

CHAPTER 5

The gray staff carriage, drawn by a pair of gray horses, clattered over the cobbles in a shimmer of sunlight.

Vidocq sat facing forward, the Rat and the Nun on the opposite seat, all silent as they drove through the empty streets.

The afternoon sun was keeping people indoors.

Before leaving Number Six, he had told the two young women what he wanted them to do this afternoon. They would go from house to house on rue Bréda, while he visited Clochette's apartment, and learn what they could from the neighbors and shopkeepers. They were old hands at covering a neighborhood and picking up facts. He would drive on after he finished there and would meet them at Number Six later.

He casually studied this unlikely pair.

The Nun had thrust herself back into a corner of the seat, away from the light. With her pale skin, blue eyes, and cropped blond hair—hidden at the moment under a gray cloth bonnet—white-gloved hands folded in her lap, she appeared to be a member of some secular branch of the church. She frequently wore a sort of habit and veil, but today—perhaps because of the heat—she was in a plain gray dress with white collar and cuffs. To emphasize the effect of a *religeuse,* a small crucifix hung from a silver chain around her neck. Neat black slippers, worn but polished, peeped from under her skirts. She claimed to be in her early thirties and looked even younger.

The Rat leaned forward, peering through the carriage windows. Black locks of hair, twisting like tails, encircled her round face with its skin coarsened and darkened from exposure to the elements. She had a sharp nose, above full red lips, which were in constant motion. Talking, laughing, or singing. At the moment she was humming softly to herself. Her clothes looked as though they had belonged to several other people, and her heavy shoes, barely visible below her dusty skirts, must have been cast off by one of her lovers. She was younger than the Nun, by several years, but looked older because of her eyes. They were large and brown and had seen everything. Many times.

Both young women had worked for him with great success after he removed them from the Paris streets.

He saw that the Rat was leaning forward as the carriage wheels slowed. "You each know what to do."

They nodded.

"I will get out first. Wait for a moment, then leave the carriage one at a time and take opposite directions." He opened the door, leaving his cane on the seat, and stepped down onto the cobbles. Glanced up at his driver on the box. "Keep out of the sun. Yourself and the horses. I'll be inside for half an hour."

The coachman from Number Six touched the brim of his hat.

Vidocq peered up and down rue Bréda. This was one of the most unsavory streets in Paris.

Aubé had found the address in Clochette's dossier. She had apparently lived here for the past two years.

The last time he had visited her apartment, it was in a more fashionable street.

This dark entrance hall was filthy.

Clochette's apartment was number five, on the first floor.

He started upstairs, aware of threadbare carpet on the wooden steps.

The first floor corridor was lighted by open windows at each end, which permitted enough light for him to find number five. There was no placard with a name, only the painted number, but the door was ajar.

He entered a narrow hall and saw that the few pieces of furniture were shabby. Not like Clochette's apartments in the past, which had been richly decorated. He paused in the open doorway of a small salon. Windows stood open, but the air was musty. All the furniture looked secondhand. Upholstery on the sofa was faded and torn.

He continued down the hall to the next pair of doors. "Anybody here?" His voice echoed through the silent rooms as he entered a small boudoir with trees visible through open windows. There was a gilded bed with a white satin cover. The bed had not been slept in.

Crossing to the foot of the bed, he saw that the white satin bedcover had been torn and patched, one leg was missing from a chair. Powder scattered across a dressing table, where bottles had been knocked over and shattered. He could smell the cheap perfume that had spilled out. The gilt dressing table chair had fallen backward onto the floor.

"What are you doing in here?"

He turned to see an old woman poised in the doorway. "This was Clochette's apartment?"

"Madame's dead. She was murdered last night. I was her maid."

He saw that she was small and thin, with straight gray hair and sharp eyes. "Where did she die?"

"There at the dressing table. I found her body on the floor—that chair knocked over. She was lying there when I came back with a bottle of wine."

"You'd gone out to buy wine?"

"Did that every night. They wouldn't give Madame credit anymore. I always had to pay cash. Got back around nine o'clock and found her . . ."

"Did you send for a doctor?"

"Why would I do that? I knew she was dead."

"How could you know?"

"She wasn't breathing. And there was blood on her chemise. I've seen death before. Many times."

"What did you do?"

"Went to the windows and screamed. Somebody sent for the gendarmes. Why are you asking all these questions? The police questioned me last night. Are you from the landlord?"

"I am Vidocq."

"Vidocq?" She came toward him now. "I've heard Madame speak of you. You're the head gendarme . . ."

"I am Chief of the Sûreté."

"Madame said you were her friend."

"Where are the other servants?"

"They left weeks ago. When she couldn't pay them."

"Do you have any idea who killed her?"

She shrugged. "I told the police nobody had been here to see Madame in months. When things get bad, your friends leave you alone. The gendarmes said Madame was shot. Whoever it was, he only fired one bullet but it went into her heart."

"They found the gun?"

"No. And they searched every corner. I looked around this morning, but all I saw was where her blood had dried on the floor."

"Did the gendarmes return today?"

"Nobody's been here but the creditors. After their money. I told them I haven't been paid in months . . ."

"Who do they think killed her?"

27

"They said it was a prowler, off the streets. This is a bad neighborhood . . ."

"How'd he get in here?"

"I leave the door unlocked when I go out. Madame lost the key."

"Did the prowler take anything?"

"Only the little cross Madame always wore around her neck. She was very religious. Went to church every morning. She was a good girl. Poor thing . . ."

"When did you realize the cross was gone?"

"Right away. When I found her body . . ."

"You told the gendarmes?"

"Yes, but I told them it was worthless. Madame had sold everything of value. She said to me many times the cross was a fake. The diamonds were only glass. She'd have sold it long ago if she could've gotten a few centimes for it . . ."

"I want to look around here. See if I can find anything that might reveal the identity of the murderer."

"Of course, Monsieur." She turned wearily back toward the hall. "I'll be in the kitchen . . ."

"Don't tell those gendarmes that I was here."

"They won't come back again. Told me they don't have time to look for a prowler."

"Don't they!" He watched her shuffling, in her felt slippers, into the hall before glancing around the room more carefully.

Poor Clochette! To end her life here . . .

She had been a beauty when he first met her. Those dancing blue eyes the color of bellflowers.

He studied the cheap bed as he remembered the large carved bed in which he had enjoyed her soft pink flesh. To think that she would die like this! Deserted by all but one of her servants.

As he circled the dressing table he saw the dried bloodstain on the floor.

Those gendarmes weren't interested in the death of a prostitute. Shot by a prowler who had taken nothing of any value. This was why the Préfecture hadn't notified him of Clochette's murder. They had no intention of hunting for her killer.

He began to go over every part of the boudoir. Slowly and carefully.

After half an hour he had found nothing.

He pulled a handkerchief from his cuff and mopped his forehead.

28

Retrieved his hat from a chair and set it on his head as he went down the hall. No point in asking the maid more questions.

As he reached the entrance he heard a baby crying, muffled by distance, probably upstairs.

CHAPTER 6

Vidocq walked down rue Saint-Honoré, cane in hand, as his carriage headed back to Number Six. No one was likely to recognize him here. Even without a disguise, he would appear to be a resident of the Faubourg out for an afternoon stroll.

He had tended to several personal matters. Waited in the carriage near Place de la Grève while his coachman picked up the sacks containing his profits from the taverns he owned in the neighborhood. He did this every week, but only collected them himself if he wore a disguise. All the taverns were meeting places for criminals who didn't realize that at least one waiter in each was a Sûreté agent. He had bought his first tavern nearly ten years ago, and they had been the means of catching many a criminal—although no one was ever arrested on the premises. Criminals felt safe there, and his profits were pleasant.

His driver was taking those sacks back to Number Six, where Aubé would lock them in the small vault hidden behind a paneled wall of his private office.

After his visit to Galerie Marchadier, it would be time for him to see the American gentleman, Monsieur Penny-packaire . . .

This was the hour when elegant Parisian women ventured out to do their shopping. Riding in open cabriolets, shading their delicate complexions with parasols. Most of them wore bonnets trimmed with flowers matching the pale colors of their summer gowns. When one stopped in front of a shop, the footman jumped down and lowered a step, then extended his white-gloved hand to help the lady descend.

Vidocq sniffed their perfumes appreciatively as they swept past. The essence of exotic blossoms he was unable to identify.

These were the respectable women, wives and daughters of wealthy men who remained in Paris for the summer months.

The others—*les grandes courtisanes*—wouldn't show their lovely faces in public until dusk, when all these women would be dressing for dinner. That was when their husbands' beautiful mistresses would drive up the Champs-Élysées in their even more expensive landaus, heading for the Bois to escape the heat. The two groups, wives and mistresses, never met and only glimpsed each other from distant boxes at the theater.

Vidocq turned down rue Saint-Florentin where he glimpsed workmen in the distance, near the Tuileries, destroying still another fine old mansion. It was a scandal the way whole streets were vanishing.

Paris was no longer as beautiful as it had been when he saw it for the first time over twenty-eight years ago and fell in love with the miraculous old city.

He remembered that first day. Arriving tired and dusty in the creaking diligence. Bone-weary after the long journey from Brussels, where an attractive widow had presented him with fifteen hundred francs, even though he refused to marry her . . .

He'd lived like a prince for a few days after his arrival, then lost every sou to the first whore he met. He had been barely twenty . . .

Money gone, he'd departed for Lille where he met still another charming lady. He'd forgotten her name and her face. Only recalled her plump body . . .

GALERIE MARCHADIER: the sign in gilded letters on an oval plaque was small and discreet.

He hurried up the marble steps and went inside.

A woman with a young man, both fashionably dressed, was gazing with apparent rapture at a large painting of peasants standing in an open field watching a flight of pigeons against a sunset sky.

No sign of the attendant in charge of casual visitors who wandered in from the street.

All the galleries were hung with gray velvet, but this first one was unfurnished—not a chair— and always displayed Marchadier's most ordinary offerings, the sort that would be admired by members of the bourgeois class who had risen in the world but never lost their fondness for rural scenes.

Vidocq walked on, his footsteps silenced by the thick carpet, toward an arched passage that extended beyond the inner galleries.

He moved through pools of light from the hanging oil lamps with glass globes that provided the only illumination. Today they made the gallery uncomfortably warm.

The young attendant was in the second gallery—this one had a few comfortable chairs and displayed more intimate paintings—explaining the qualities of a large framed canvas to a bearded gentleman. There didn't seem to be anything about the picture that required explanation. A pink-fleshed cow of a nude. Imitation Rubens!

He nodded at the attendant and continued on into the adjoining gallery.

This one had more globed lamps suspended from overhead and several handsome pieces of antique furniture but no paintings on display. A large wooden easel, the kind used by professional artists, was placed in the center of the far wall facing a red plush sofa. This easel, as always, was empty.

He removed his hat and, thrusting his cane under an arm, pulled a fresh handkerchief from his cuff to dry his forehead.

The air held an unmistakable smell of dust.

He was certain that he was being watched. Somewhere among those folds of gray velvet were peepholes through which every customer was observed. In another moment Monsieur Marchadier, in person, would appear. He would bow and exclaim, "Ah, Monsieur Vidocq! I had no idea you were waiting . . ."

"Ah, Monsieur Vidocq! No one informed me that you were here . . ."

Vidocq faced him, smiling in anticipation. "Monsieur Marchadier . . ."

"You received my note?"

"Last week. But I was too busy to look at pictures."

Marchadier shook his head sympathetically. "The great Vidocq is always occupied protecting the honest citizens of Paris from the criminals of Paris! I have several canvases for you to inspect."

Vidocq sank onto the sofa, resting his hat and cane beside him. He knew that somewhere behind these walls three paintings were being pulled from racks and presently would be displayed, one after the other, by an attendant without any apparent instructions from Marchadier. Which proved that his arrival had to be observed. There were always three pictures for him to consider, but the final one would be the prize.

". . . delighted you were able to stop in today," Marchadier was saying, "because I'll be joining my family in Rambouillet next week, for our annual vacation. Will you be leaving Paris this summer?"

Vidocq grunted. "I've not had a vacation in years."

"I always return refreshed, and of course, while I'm away, I visit

31

many painters. Arrange to handle their latest canvases next winter for the new season. Paris is boring at the moment with my wife and children gone. They left in June to open our villa. Took the cook with them, so I must dine out every night. Mostly at the Midnight Club."

"Midnight Club?"

"We have an excellent chef. You must join me one evening for dinner. In fact, you should become a member yourself."

"I have never been attracted to private clubs."

"But this is the most elegant club in Paris! Some of our leading bankers are members."

"Much too rich for me!"

"They also accept businessmen like myself."

"But you too are a wealthy man."

"Not as wealthy as I might wish to be." Marchadier shrugged. "But then, who is? Ah! Here we are ..."

A uniformed attendant crossed the gallery with, as Vidocq had anticipated, three framed canvases. He rested two of them against the velvet-covered wall, lifted the smallest onto the easel, and stepped out of the way.

Vidocq saw that it was a lustrous nude. Long golden-red hair flowing enticingly across a delicious body. The color of the hair reminded him of Ève, who at the moment was said to be the most beautiful woman in Paris.

"The flesh tones, as you observe, are exquisitely painted!"

"You know I seldom buy nudes."

"But this one is very special ..."

"I still prefer my nudes in the flesh."

Marchadier laughed and snapped his fingers.

The attendant removed the painting and set another framed canvas on the easel.

A view of strange bulbous-roofed buildings in flames, the sky a mass of smoke with a sun—or was it the moon?—barely visible.

"This shows the destruction of Moscow ..."

"So I suspected."

"It was found by one of Napoléon's soldiers, who brought it back to Paris. There's no signature, so we'll never know whether the artist was French or Russian."

"Whatever his nationality, he was an amateur. It's not for me."

"I thought you might be interested because of Napoléon."

"I've never been involved with politics. Emperor or King!"

"Very wise." Marchadier snapped his fingers. "This next one's a masterpiece!"

Vidocq waited with mounting curiosity as the Moscow canvas was replaced by a larger painting in a carved frame. He craned to see what it was, knowing this was the one Marchadier hoped he would buy.

"A true work of genius!" The dealer's voice was hushed as he presented his final offering. "Notice the delicacy of the brush strokes. The knowledge of anatomy. The rather shocking subject!"

The attendant backed away, and the canvas was revealed.

Vidocq stared, startled in spite of himself.

"I've kept this one especially for you, Monsieur. Knowing your interest in criminal matters."

His eyes were held by the painting, and he didn't bother to reply.

He had, in his time, seen many incredible scenes where death was involved but never anything like this. The details were realistic, the colors fresh but muted because light seemed to come from a distant window, except for one shaft of sunlight cutting across the pool of blood on a black and white tiled floor. "Who is the artist?"

"Again, unfortunately, the painting is not signed."

"Where'd you find it?"

"This came from the private collection of a famous Viennese physician. His widow has only recently offered it for sale."

"Then the artist is Austrian?"

"Possibly. Although I've discovered no proof. There are no marks on the back, but I would judge from the condition of the wooden stretcher and the canvas that the painting is at least a hundred years old. Probably Dutch . . ."

Vidocq continued to study the picture. "How much are you asking? I want the painting. Give me your lowest price."

Marchadier smiled, displaying sharp canine teeth. "Since it is you, Monsieur Vidocq . . ." He hesitated. "Forty thousand francs."

"Thirty thousand!" Vidocq snapped, picking up his hat and cane as he arose from the sofa. "In cash."

"I will have it delivered as usual, to your residence."

"This afternoon?"

"Certainly."

"And covered. So no eyes but mine will see it."

"Of course, Monsieur."

He turned to leave. "I'll send you the money."

"At your convenience, Monsieur."

Vidocq paused, facing a large flat-topped red lacquer desk set against the wall, which he hadn't noticed when he entered. "That's a handsome piece of furniture."

"An extraordinary item. This *laqué rouge* finish is extremely rare, and the desk, as you see, is palace-size. I suspect it could have belonged to Pompadour."

"Where'd you find it?"

"Well, I . . ."

Vidocq was aware of his hesitation.

". . . obtained it from a private source. They prefer to remain anonymous."

He was obviously lying. Could this be part of the loot stolen by Le Diable Noir?

"Actually, I will tell you—in confidence—this desk came from the Baron de Chabrillat's mansion in Paris."

"Oh?"

"Offered to me personally by a member of the family."

He was overdoing his explanation to cover up the truth.

"I've several other fine pieces from the same collection." Lowering his voice. "The family's in desperate need of money. This desk is a bargain."

"Don't tell me the price. I could use a desk at home, but I can't afford this one." He glanced back toward the easel. "Not until I recover from buying that painting!"

The dark pool of blood seemed to shine with a life of its own, as though it would never dry.

CHAPTER 7

Vidocq stepped down from his hired fiacre in the crowded courtyard of the Hôtel Belvedere and instructed his driver to wait as he glanced out toward the street.

The rue de Richelieu had many old mansions identified with important events and personages in addition to Richelieu.

This was one of the newer hotels. Created by combining two private mansions.

He hurried up the white marble steps and crossed the dim entrance hall with its rows of dark-green marble columns reflected in mirrored walls. Approaching the desk, he saw himself reflected many times, as though a dozen Vidocqs were hurrying toward him and he was about to collide with all of them.

The concierge, an old man in a gold-braided uniform, rose from the desk. "Monsieur?"

"I wish to see Monsieur Zeb-u-lon Penny-packaire."

"Ah! Monsieur Penny-packaire only returned a moment ago. You'll find him in the Salle Anglais." Coming from behind his desk, ramrod straight, obviously a relic of Napoléon's army. "I will escort you there, Monsieur."

Vidocq followed the erect old man between the marble columns, toward a murmur of women's voices coming from an arched doorway.

"Many of our guests enjoy the English ceremony of tea at this hour." The concierge paused in the archway, eagle eyes inspecting the spacious room where open windows overlooked a green sweep of garden. "It's the gentleman with a large mustache, sitting alone near the windows."

Vidocq slipped a coin into the white-gloved hand, removed his hat, and thrusting his cane under an arm, started across the high-ceilinged room. A dozen tables were occupied by guests, mostly female, all of whom seemed to be talking at once in languages he didn't comprehend. The women were attractively dressed but seemed much thinner than French women and appeared to be less healthy. They were drinking tea from china cups and eating *pâtisseries* served by waiters in pale-blue satin liveries.

Beyond the windows he glimpsed terraced gardens with the distant summerhouse for which the hotel had been named, where Marie Antoinette was said to have watched *les fêtes champêtres*.

Approaching the American's table, Vidocq saw that he was a younger man than he had anticipated, possibly in his early forties, with curly light brown hair and impressive darker brown mustaches. He was sipping a brandy as he studied what appeared to be a sheaf of letters. "Pardon. Monsieur Penny-packaire?"

The American looked up, frowning. "Yes?"

35

"I am Vidocq."

"Monsieur Vidocq!" He got to his feet, smiling, dropping his letters onto the table. "A great honor! I've been hoping to hear from you. This of course can't be a coincidence. Our meeting . . ."

"The Minister of Interior informed me that his friend Monsieur de Fontanelle had suggested I might be of assistance to you in some confidential matter."

"I certainly hope so." Indicating a chair. "Do sit down . . ."

Vidocq rested his hat and cane on another chair as he sat facing the American whose face was now revealed in sharper detail. His skin was tanned but unwrinkled, his eyes blue, his manner cordial.

"What will you have? They are famous here for their English high teas, but I, for one, prefer a brandy at this hour."

"A brandy would be excellent."

Pennypacker gave the order to a waiter.

"I was informed that Monsieur is American, but your French is excellent. Fortunately! Since I speak little English."

"I learned your language years ago, when my father decided I should come over here every summer to replenish our stock."

"Stock?"

"Paris gowns, hats, and gloves. All the latest styles for the ladies. Shirts and cravats for gentlemen. Even fine antique furniture and paintings! My family owns a large and well-known establishment—Pennypacker's—in New Orleans."

"Ah, yes! That is in Louisiana . . ."

"We call our shop a dry goods or department store, but some of our customers describe it as a palace of merchandise. Somewhat larger than your famous Ville de Paris. After the death of my father, I became president of our company. I visit Paris each summer to confer with our suppliers and inspect their latest products. My father, for many years, did this himself. Here's your brandy . . ."

The liveried waiter set the glass in front of Vidocq, who raised it toward the American.

Pennypacker lifted his in response.

As they drank, Vidocq saw that the American's tanned hands were those of a man who had never done any manual work. No rings on his fingers. Wearing a white suit, not so fitted as one made by a French tailor. A diamond stickpin in his black silk cravat.

"I spoke to Georges de Fontanelle the other night during dinner.

Told him there was a certain matter that required a discreet investigation, but I did not wish to involve the French police or the American Embassy. I've heard about you frequently, Monsieur, during my previous visits. Especially ..." glancing at the chattering women nearby as he lowered his voice "... how you recovered a diamond necklace for Napoléon himself and prevented a public scandal."

Vidocq shrugged dramatically. "I have never officially confirmed that such an incident ever happened."

"I admire your discretion. I've been told confidentially that the Emperor rewarded you handsomely for your secret service on his behalf. There've been rumors about the incident in the United States."

"I had no idea!"

"Oh, yes! Your name's well known back home. Frequent stories in the leading newspapers, and of course I've read of your investigations in the Paris papers during my annual visits and heard my French friends discuss your recent exploits in the world of crime. I had hoped that Georges might know you personally, but he didn't."

"We've never met."

"He offered, however, to speak to some influential acquaintances who would get word to you privately that I needed help in a matter of some delicacy."

"And here I am, Monsieur! How may I be of assistance?"

"This involves my daughter, who for the first time has come with me to Paris."

"Her age?"

"Nineteen. And, I must tell you, extremely innocent for her years. Which is, I suppose, part of my problem. She was educated in a convent and has no knowledge of the evils which infest this modern world. No experience, whatever, with men."

"Her mother?"

"Deceased. She had been in precarious health for many years, unable to bear a second child. Only Belinda ..."

"Belinda? A charming name."

"She is my joy! My very life ..."

"You Americans, it is rumored, do not have mistresses."

"That's not entirely true! I have many friends in New Orleans who do. But I've never looked at another woman since the day I met the young lady who became my wife. What about you, Monsieur?"

"I ... ?"

37

"You have a wife? Children?"

"A wife. No children."

"I hesitated about bringing my daughter to Paris. She's been shielded since birth, and I intend to keep her like that. Belinda is, of course, a virgin."

"Indeed?" Americans apparently were more direct than the French in discussing such personal matters with a stranger, although they seemed to have less to discuss.

"I want her to remain untouched until her wedding night. Like her dear mother! I had hoped she might meet a young Frenchman during her first visit to France, perhaps at one of the dinner parties my friends have arranged in our honor. Some youth from an excellent old family who would be happy to live in the United States. My daughter doesn't know this, but I've purchased a fine house for her—whoever she marries—in an excellent residential area of New Orleans."

"And Mademoiselle Belinda has already met a young man at a dinner party and now she's in love?"

"She met a rogue and says she's in love with him, but I know this is not possible in such a short time!"

"It is always possible to fall in love, Monsieur, when one is young. Especially in Paris."

"This young man is a rascal and, I suspect, a thief! Belinda met him while strolling in the gardens of the Palais-Royal."

"There are many unsavory characters there—male and female—every night. Visitors in Paris should be cautious after dark."

"This meeting took place in broad daylight! Belinda promenades in the Palais-Royal every afternoon. That's where she's walking at this moment most likely. She goes there to meet him."

"Many young couples walk in the Palais-Royal every afternoon. It's a favorite spot for them to rendezvous. You wish me to find out about this young man? His name and background . . ."

"Belinda's already told me his name—Lucien Revol!"

"Then she's spoken to you about him?"

"She told me about him after their first meeting."

"You want me to investigate his family? His income?"

"Much more, Monsieur! I wish first of all to know if he has a criminal record."

"We began to keep records of all criminals ten years ago at the

Sûreté, but I've never heard of a Lucien Revol. Of course that could be a name he's assumed recently. What makes you think he is a criminal?"

"He's stolen a diamond bracelet valued at fifty thousand francs!"

"From your daughter?"

"I bought it for her shortly after our arrival."

"From whom?"

"The famous jeweler—Monsieur Tessier—on rue Taitbout. I've been purchasing jewelry from him for many years, my father before me, to sell in our jewelry department at Pennypacker's. Each year Monsieur Tessier designs special pieces for us. Rings and bracelets of the finest quality. Years ago I bought a Tessier necklace for my dear wife and, on Belinda's eighteenth birthday, I gave her a Tessier ring. She was of course delighted to meet Monsieur Tessier and visit his elegant showroom. It's more like a salon in a private mansion. That's when Tessier—that crafty fox—brought out, among more elaborate items, a simple diamond bracelet on a black velvet tray. I saw at once how Belinda's eyes sparkled when she saw it, and I purchased the bracelet for her next day. I've never told her its true value. Only that I bought it to celebrate her first visit to Paris."

"She doesn't know what the bracelet cost?"

"That's what makes it difficult. I never want my daughter to desire anything because of its price. I would rather have her admire things for their beauty."

"Where was your daughter when the bracelet was taken?"

"She has no idea."

"What do you mean?"

"She hadn't realized it was missing until she wakened the other morning and couldn't find it. When I questioned her—as casually as possible—she couldn't remember whether she'd worn it the previous evening or not. And neither could I!"

"Where had you been? The previous night."

"We dined at the Café de Paris, but I've no recollection of the bracelet on Belinda's wrist during dinner or afterward as we walked along the boulevards before enjoying an ice at Tortoni's. The evening was warm, and we returned here in a fiacre."

"The bracelet could've been removed from your daughter's wrist while you were on the boulevards. A clever thief—and there are hundreds prowling every night—can release the catch on a lady's bracelet and remove it without her knowledge."

"No! I'm convinced it was taken by this young man, Revol, when he was with Belinda in the Palais-Royal!"

"Have you told her what you suspect?"

"Certainly not! I've no proof. And no intention of saying such a thing, antagonizing my daughter, unless I do have proof. That's what I want from you. Proof that this scoundrel, Revol, took her diamond bracelet!"

Vidocq set his empty glass down. "I will get you that proof, Monsieur." He rose from the table, snatching up his hat and cane as the American got to his feet. "Or proof of the young man's innocence."

"I promise you he isn't!"

"How long will you be in Paris?"

"At least until the middle of next month. Except for a few days we must spend in the country. My daughter and I are to be guests at a private estate. I'm waiting for word from our host as to when our visit will be convenient. We'll be staying at this same hotel when we return."

"And I must get back to my office. Good day, Monsieur Pennypackaire."

"Zebulon Pennypacker! Call me Zeb . . ."

Vidocq bowed. "Monsieur Zeb . . ." Placing the hat on his head as he turned toward the arched entrance.

The Rat and the Nun would be waiting at Number Six, but he wanted to have a quick look at Mademoiselle Pennypacker.

CHAPTER 8

Vidocq strolled, apparently without purpose, down one of the long central paths of the Palais-Royal, casually swinging his cane.

His eyes observed the small children playing around the great circular fountain, their uniformed nursemaids watching them from nearby benches.

Impossible to glimpse the shops and cafés in shadow under the pillared Galerie Montpensier, because the sun had already dropped behind the western wing of the palace. The tall windows of a gambling club on the second floor stood open, and he could see servants moving about preparing for the evening. Attractive women, fashionably dressed and carrying small parasols, darted back and forth across the gravel paths toward favorite shops.

No sign of any young couples. They would be sitting under the old trees that extended in rows down the length of the garden, on both sides, where they would be hidden from prying eyes.

He turned off the central path and, still moving slowly, headed for the deeper shade beneath the trees.

Several benches were occupied by shabbily dressed couples who worked in the neighborhood and had managed to steal a few moments to meet here. Most of them looked like shopgirls and waiters. All their faces were hidden because they were embracing.

Only one couple, the girl better dressed than any of the others, sat side by side without embracing but holding hands. At least the young man had reached out to clutch the girl's white-gloved hand as it rested on the bench between them.

Vidocq knew at once that this would be Mademoiselle Pennypacker and young Revol.

He slowed his steps as he approached, noting every detail of their appearance.

Mademoiselle Pennypacker looked out of place here. She had an exquisite face, with blue eyes like her father's and delicious lips. Blond curls visible under a summer bonnet of pale-green lace, which matched her green and white striped dress and the green satin slippers peeping out under her long skirt from a froth of petticoats. Her eyes were filled with adoration as she listened to her handsome companion.

The youth had curly black hair, brown eyes, and the sort of audacious face that would always be ready to laugh. At the moment he was only smiling as he talked. Clothing of good cut but worn, and he needed a new pair of boots. His hat rested beside him on the bench. Face and hands pale, as though he worked in an office or shop.

Vidocq edged closer as he passed them, his presence unnoticed, to hear what they were saying and discovered they were speaking French. Mademoiselle's folded pale-green parasol was propped next to her at the end of the bench. He looked away from them toward the fountain, ears straining to catch their words.

". . . like to take you in a fine carriage with a pair of matched horses,"

Revol was telling her, "to a picnic on the grassy bank of some country stream. Only I have no fine carriage or horses . . ."

"I would much rather sit in this charming garden and talk to you. Our garden."

"It belongs to King Louis, who graciously permits us to enjoy his beautiful flowers. But he doesn't own the air, and the birds singing in the trees recognize no king. They also think the garden belongs to them."

"And so it does! I'll wager your King Louis has never stepped foot here."

"Will we meet again tomorrow?"

"If I don't have to drive into the country with Papa."

"You're leaving Paris!"

"Only for a few days. I didn't tell you before, but I've known since we arrived. There's an important personage—Papa won't tell me his name—he must see on some business matter. We're waiting for a letter to tell us when we're expected. Papa thinks we won't leave before the end of the week. So I should be here tomorrow, at this same time."

"I'll never see you again!" He lifted her hand and pressed his lips against the white-gloved fingers.

Vidocq smiled. They sounded like lovers in an Italian opera.

"I promise you I'll not be away for more than a few days. When we return you'll meet Papa. I want you to be friends . . ."

Vidocq could no longer hear their voices.

Mademoiselle Pennypacker was quite certainly in love with this young man.

And Revol seemed to adore her—understandably. But was he only deceiving her with his charm? One of those Parisian scoundrels—there were hundreds of them—who sought out young women as their victims? Especially young women with rich fathers . . .

He quickened his steps across the garden toward rue Saint-Honoré where his fiacre was waiting and told the driver to take him to Number Six.

CHAPTER 9

As he anticipated, at this hour the entrance corridor at Number Six was almost empty.

The guard at the inquiry desk saluted, as Vidocq strode past with his cane held in readiness for any stranger who tried to approach. Dashed up the marble staircase and passed the upstairs desk, where another guard saluted and released the gate in the wooden balustrade for him to enter. He headed straight for the open doors of his private suite.

Aubé, quill in hand, looked up from a letter he was writing.

"No staff meeting tonight. Much too warm. Anybody in?"

"Only Goury."

"I've a job for him. And bring your notebook . . ."

"I'll get Goury." Aubé put his quill aside and rose from the desk.

Vidocq swept off his hat as he entered his office, placing it on the table with his cane again before sinking into his black leather armchair and swiveling to face the open windows.

The clock on the mantelpiece at that instant began to chime the hour, its tinkling obliterated by the shimmering bells of Sainte-Chapelle, which were joined by a dozen other bells from distant churches.

Five o'clock . . .

He began to sort out what he had learned this afternoon.

The American girl had no idea what her missing bracelet was worth . . .

Her father must be an extremely wealthy man! Who could he be visiting in the country? Was he going somewhere to buy merchandise for his emporium in New Orléans? Antique furniture? Treasures stolen by Le Diable Noir and his band of brigands?

Had the daughter misplaced her diamond bracelet? Or had young Revol slipped it off her arm unobserved as they embraced?

Tomorrow he would pay a visit to that jeweler. Tessier . . .

He was aware of two persons entering, recognized their footsteps, Goury's firm tread followed by Aubé's light steps. He turned to see them sinking into their usual armchairs. Aubé beside the desk, notebook on his knee and pencil in hand. "We have a fresh problem to consider, gentlemen. Prominent people are involved, so everything must

43

be kept absolutely private." Glancing at Aubé. "Another confidential dossier. With no copies to anyone."

Aubé nodded and made a notation.

"This is why the Minister wished to see me this morning. His friend the banker Georges de Fontanelle requested I contact an American gentleman—Monsieur Zeb-u-lon Penny-packaire . . ." He smiled as Aubé, scowling, wrote the name. "I talked to the American at his hotel—the Belvedere—learned that he'd recently purchased a diamond bracelet for his young daughter from the jeweler, Tessier, in rue Taitbout. The daughter, Belinda, is with her father. Her first visit to Paris. He claims she's a virgin."

Goury exploded with laughter. "She won't remain one very long in Paris."

"She's already met a young man with whom she has a rendezvous every afternoon."

"You see?" Goury was still shaking with laughter.

"Real diamonds?" Aubé asked.

"Monsieur Penny-packaire claims he paid fifty thousand francs for the bracelet."

Aubé pursed his lips, and Goury whistled softly.

"The American gentleman is apparently extremely wealthy. You might check on him, André . . ."

Goury nodded.

"He claims to own a large department store in New Orléans. He's come to Paris on business but is taking his daughter somewhere into the country for a few days, to some private estate. Penny-packaire wants me to find that bracelet. See what you can learn about a young man named Revol—Lucien Revol—who meets Mademoiselle Belinda late every afternoon in the Jardin du Palais-Royal. The young lady is blond. Very pretty. Revol has curly black hair. Follow him tomorrow afternoon and find out where he goes. Probably back to some office. He may have stolen the bracelet. Or he may not . . ."

"Where was it stolen?"

"Monsieur Penny-packaire doesn't know. And his daughter isn't certain when she wore it last. She has no idea of its value. Her father gave it to her as a present and didn't tell her its worth."

"Fifty thousand francs . . ." Goury sighed, shaking his head.

"Warn all fences to watch for the bracelet. Question the staff at the

Hôtel Belvedere about both of them—the American and his virginal daughter—as well as the bracelet. Hotel maids and valets know everything about a guest. But use discretion. Monsieur Penny-packaire has very influential friends and wants no scandal." He turned to Aubé. "Anything else, my friend?"

"No one's working tonight." Slipping pad and pencil back into their respective pockets. "Only Ronquetti."

"Hot weather never bothers the Duc. He's from Naples. See you both in the morning."

Goury and Aubé got to their feet.

"This is going to be another night when Paris won't be able to sleep because of the heat. I only hope the criminals won't have the energy for any mischief." He turned his armchair to face the open windows again.

And immediately began to think about little Clochette . . .

CHAPTER 10

Hat in one hand and cane in the other, Vidocq crossed the rear courtyard of Number Six where a groom was giving one of his charges a final brushing for the day. The nightguard was on duty at the gates which would be closed and locked after dark.

The uniformed coachman lounging beside a pair of carriages, their horses harnessed, straightened as he heard heels on the cobbles.

Vidocq nodded toward him as he stepped forward, touching the brim of his hat. "You're on late duty?"

"Until midnight, Chief."

"Take me to Nôtre-Dame first. I'll be there half an hour, as usual. Then I'll drive out through the Bois while I decide where to dine."

"My pleasure, Chief." He opened the door of the smaller carriage.

Vidocq climbed in and, as the door closed, sank back against the cushions. The black leather felt unpleasantly sticky and warm to his touch.

Gusts of warm air came through the open windows as the carriage rattled across the island. Twilight was settling over the city, turning the old buildings gray and silver under a hot sky washed in scarlet by the last rays of the sun.

This morning there had been no important projects to occupy him, but now there were two.

The American, Monsieur Pennypacker, whose daughter's diamond bracelet was missing. Lost or stolen? Her lover, young Revol, didn't appear to be a criminal type. Only there was no special type for any crime.

And the death of little Clochette!

Why would a prowler kill her for a worthless cross? Couldn't he see the diamonds were false?

The Rat and the Nun had returned to Number Six, their assignments for the day completed, with little to report on any of them. They had learned that Clochette was liked on rue Bréda, but nobody had any idea who could have shot her. Everyone accepted the fact that it was a prowler. There had been several recently in the area. They did learn that she had a lover, but nobody had seen him in months. Not since Clochette had her baby. The other whores thought she was a fool to fall in love and an even bigger fool to get herself pregnant. Nobody knew what had happened to the baby. Probably somewhere in the country. With a relative ...

He remembered suddenly he'd heard a baby crying as he left the apartment. The sound had seemed to come from upstairs ...

His carriage, he realized, was slowing to a stop in front of Nôtre-Dame with its rising tiers of carved Gothic figures. Vidocq flung the door open and, leaving hat and cane, jumped down as the coachman reined in his horses. "Wait for me, my friend ..." He went toward the northern corner of the cathedral and knocked on a low wooden door.

It was opened by an aged man who was wiping his white mustaches with a bandanna. "Monsieur Vidocq! Wasn't expecting you in this heat. Although our steps aren't too warm. They never see the sun ..."

Vidocq dropped a coin into his wrinkled palm as he noticed the crude wooden table holding bread and cheese with a nearly empty bottle of red wine. "I won't be long."

The narrow steps twisted up through gradually cooling air into a haze of faint light seeping through vertical slits of windows. Lanterns, hung at irregular intervals, had not been lighted.

He reached the final step, perspiring slightly, and stepped out onto

46

the top of the tower. The sun had gone, and the sky was darkening toward the east.

First thing he saw, as usual, was the twisted remains of the old belltower which had been destroyed during the Revolution. Walking to the edge of the parapet, facing west, he looked down between the stone gargoyles into the open Parvis directly below, crowded with a low mass of crudely built shops and ugly shacks between streets barely wide enough for the passage of a carriage.

Raising his head he gazed across the city.

This island was the heart of Paris. Surrounded by villages that stretched in every direction. High to his right were vineyards ringing the village of Montmartre, and straight ahead, toward the west, was the distant village of Chaillot beyond tall trees lining the Champs-Élysées. Continuing to turn his head, he saw the dark forest of the Bois and, nearer at hand, the great trees in the elegant gardens marking the village of Saint-Germain.

He leaned forward, over the parapet, to look down at the Pont Saint-Michel and saw that the bridge was clotted with small dark figures scurrying for home at the end of this hot day. Walking and riding. Crowded into carts or seated alone in fine carriages.

The faceless people were like frantic mice from this height, hurrying to reach their dark holes for the night. Their miserable attic rooms and small apartments would be stifling. Even the rich would find their great mansions uncomfortable.

Vidocq glanced toward the other island to the east. The buildings on Île Saint-Louis were a blur of gray and violet shadows.

Facing north again, he noticed the jumbled mass of low structures covering the rising slope of Montmartre. Thousands lived in those streets and alleys twisting up to the top of the Butte. Fires glowed where lime-cutters worked in their quarries.

He peered at the lower half of the distant hill. That was the center of crime. The evil heart of all Paris!

Soon the dark creatures of the underworld would be stirring and waking. Crawling from their hiding places. Ready to kill.

He wondered what mischief they were planning for tonight. Which of their crimes would he learn about tomorrow? Some would never be reported and, if they were, would get lost in the red tape of local police headquarters. Few would be important enough to reach Number Six.

Before dawn some of those creatures would lie dead in a dark alley.

As he circled the top of the tower, avoiding scattered timbers left behind by workmen, he wondered if he would run into Balzac tonight. He'd been talking recently about changing his name to Honoré de Balzac. Probably only talk. Writers enjoyed talking when they weren't working. Trying ideas on you which they planned to use in a book.

Last week at Café Procope Balzac had questioned him about his use of disguises, and he had reluctantly agreed to let him see his collection of wigs and costumes.

But which collection? The one at Number Six was a salmagundi cramped into a small room on the top floor but the larger collection was in a dressing room at home with everything properly hung and kept in order. His wigs in boxes, each carefully labeled. He would take Balzac home with him one night and let him see everything. That should silence his questions. The crafty devil was undoubtedly going to write about disguises in one of his potboilers.

The first lights were appearing, yellow pinpoints in the dusk.

Lamplighters with wooden ladders would be climbing up to turn on the street lamps.

He could barely make out the cupola of les Invalides or the Vendôme column in the deepening twilight.

As he watched, tiny flames came alive across the entire city.

This was a magic moment! He waited for it every time he came up here.

Standing like the King of Paris surveying his kingdom.

His kingdom of crime!

He wondered how many Parisians had ever seen the lights of their city blossom like this at the end of a day . . .

Turning from the parapet, he made his way toward the open door which led to the steps.

As he started down, he saw that the candles in the stone lanterns were casting circles of light on the curving staircase. One of the street boys from the Parvis must earn a few centimes for lighting them every night. Certainly the old man couldn't climb this many steps.

He descended even faster than he had climbed, stealing past the porter who was asleep at the table, his wine bottle empty, without waking him and within moments was seated in his carriage and heading for the distant Bois.

The air in the streets seemed warmer than before.

He picked up his hat and placed it firmly on his head, pulling the brim down to hide his face. Leaned back against the cushioned corner, where no casual glance would notice him.

This was another part of his method of relaxing at the end of a hot summer day. This evening he was trying both methods. Sacred and profane! The glorious view from the top of the cathedral, followed by a drive beyond the city to enjoy the amusing spectacle of the great whores—*les grandes courtisanes*—gossiping in the Bois.

The Avenue des Champs-Élysées with its rows of old trees on either side was unpleasantly sultry. He could see a faint breeze stirring the canopy of dark leaves overhead but felt no trace of it on his face.

The lights of the old Panorama exhibition glowed on his left as they crossed La Rond-Point and started up the sloping avenue toward Le Montagne du Roule, which marked a city boundary.

All the shops were closed for the night, but he glimpsed the Jardin d'Hiver with its display of tropical plants and the private mansions behind high-walled gardens.

The site at the crest of the hill had long been marked for an important monument, and Napoléon had finally decreed the construction of a triumphal arch to commemorate his victories. The first stones were laid years before, but the monument had never been completed. Napoléon was dead, and his unfinished arch looked like a ruin.

At the Étoile de Chaillot a guard on duty at the barrier was an old acquaintance, and when Vidocq leaned into the light, he was waved on without showing his passport.

The horse sensed they were leaving the city and quickened his pace as they rolled through the Bois. The ancient forest was dark, their route barely lighted by an occasional street lamp and a few lanterns suspended from posts.

The air felt cooler under these towering oaks and elms.

His carriage continued on for several minutes before he glimpsed a dimly lighted glade between thick tree trunks.

The small window opened above his head. "How far do you want to go, Chief?"

"Circle the carriages, but don't stop. Then back to the city."

The window snapped shut.

As they came closer, Vidocq saw the familiar open space in a circle of trees, where three shiny landaus had stopped in a circle of light from hanging lanterns and a pair of street lamps marking where the road led into the forest.

Two expensive black broughams waited at the edge of the grass, the coachmen holding the horses' bridles while their wealthy owners stood in the center facing a trio of beautiful women relaxing in luxurious landaus.

Coachmen also held their horses, and a liveried footman stood beside each door. This group was younger and more smartly uniformed than the two older coachmen, as the three women were younger than the middle-aged men who stood gossiping with them and, from the sound of the women's laughter, making witty remarks.

The female voices had the exotic sound of tropical birds, and their costumes always made Vidocq think of plumage. They were dressed in lacy, pale summer gowns and, at this hour, displayed no jewels. Flowers in their exquisitely arranged hair instead of bonnets, which might hide their beauty. The men's faces were not familiar, but he recognized the three beautiful women.

Ève, Apolline, and Maya! Apolline was getting fat again.

He pulled his hat brim lower as his carriage circled the oval of trampled grass.

All the faces turned toward the intruder, but as he passed they resumed their interrupted conversations.

The younger coachmen and footmen were uniformed in colors matching their employers' landaus, which also matched their hair. Scarlet for Ève, black for Maya, and yellow for Apolline, whose hair was pale blond. Ève's footman also had scarlet plumes in his hat. Her golden red hair seemed to glow in the twilight. Its color, he knew from personal observation, was natural.

He wondered if she had recognized his carriage. Not likely.

There were, at the moment, perhaps twenty *grandes courtisanes* in Paris, but these three—Ève, Maya and Apolline—were among the most successful. He had a dossier on each of them at Number Six. Everything back to their birth, if that event was ever recorded. They amused him, and he had slept with each of them.

He was smiling as his carriage started back through the dark forest heading out of the Bois.

Ève, Apolline, and Maya! Those enticing blossoms who only came alive at dusk and flowered, again and again, until dawn. *Les fleurs de nuit* . . .

Ève was the most beautiful of them all!

Ève with her monstrous, black-scaled serpent bed, a huge gold apple suspended above your head between its pointed fangs.

There was a rumor that, if a lover became too demanding, she could press a release hidden somewhere in the carved ebony bed, and the golden apple would fall and crush his skull.

He had his own theory about that apple. It would be as light as a bubble, probably only a gilded hollow shell, and Ève permitted it to fall for certain wealthy clients who enjoyed playing childish games in bed.

There'd been no need for games of that sort when he visited the lady.

CHAPTER 11

He dismissed his carriage for the night on the corner of rue de la Chaise and walked down rue de Grenelle toward a glow of light from the lanterns hanging in front of a restaurant. *La Petite Chaise.*

Legend said that The Little Chair had existed at this same address since the seventeenth century.

He glanced at the graceful wrought iron grille on either side of the entrance as he went inside.

The interior was uncomfortably warm but pleasantly empty.

"Monsieur Vidocq! Welcome . . ."

Many restaurant owners knew him, but this one was especially friendly because they had both come from the province of Artois.

Following *le patron* to a secluded table, he glanced up at the tiny chair hanging above the bar.

It was said that Louis XIV had noticed the first patron, many times, sitting in the open doorway of his restaurant. One day he had stopped the royal coach and presented him with a new chair. Judging by its size, that early proprietor must have been a dwarf! The chair had hung there for more than a hundred years.

As he sat next to an open window, he noticed a copper tub of pink and white flowers in the open fireplace. "Peonies! They remind me of Arras. We had peonies every summer."

"And they remind me of Écurie." *Le patron* smiled as he glanced at the huge blossoms. "We also grew them there."

"Impossible!"

"Why do you say 'impossible'?"

"*Écurie* means 'stable,' and you can't grow peonies in a stable."

Le patron laughed. "Horse manure grows the finest flowers!"

"Then roses should bloom in every Paris gutter!"

Avoiding the handwritten menu, Vidocq discussed what to order for dinner. He decided finally on a *pâté de fois aux pruneaus* then cold *boulettes* with a glass of Burgundy, to be followed by an apple tart.

And, in spite of the heat, he ate everything.

The pâté with its plump black prunes reminded him of a pâté his mother made when she did her own cooking. The *boulettes*, like succulent small cannon balls, were made with veal in a cold herbed sauce. He finished his wine before the apple tart was served and ordered hot black coffee to end the cold meal.

The proprietor would not permit him to pay, but he left several coins for the waiter.

Walking toward the river, he decided not to go home just yet. He wasn't so exhausted since his drive through the Bois and knew he wouldn't sleep for hours if he went to bed this early.

The air coming from the Seine reeked of decay, and the sewers stank. Hot weather brought out the worst in both.

He hailed a fiacre and ordered the driver to take him to Boulevard des Italiens.

Produced a fresh pair of white cotton gloves from a pocket and held them in his left hand, cane in his right, as he stepped down from the carriage and paid the driver.

Hesitated at the corner of rue de la Chaussée-d'Antin, pulling a glove onto each hand. Many of *les grandes courtisanes*, including Ève, had their apartments here. She should be home now, preparing for the evening.

He looked down the wide boulevard toward rue de Richelieu, wondering if Monsieur Pennypacker and his daughter were dining on Boulevard des Italiens again tonight.

More likely they would be guests at some private mansion.

Strolling on, he glanced at the people seated at tables on the sidewalk terraces. A few were dining, but most were only having cool drinks. He overheard snatches of conversation in many languages as he passed, peering at the shimmer of candles inside each restaurant.

He considered an ice at Tortoni's, but the café was too crowded.

The air, as he walked, was oppressive, but in spite of the heat the sidewalks were thronged with people. Street urchins, sharp-eyed and filthy, lurking in every shadow. An old man selling fried potatoes from a wood-burning stove on rickety wheels. Nobody buying them in this heat. He noticed a pickpocket walking close to a group of laughing people and winced as the rascal's hand darted. Pickpockets weren't his problem, and, as usual, there were no gendarmes visible anywhere.

Leaving the boulevard he visited several theaters. He was known to every manager and attendant who bowed in welcome as he entered each lobby. The doors had been left open, and the actors' voices and snatches of music could be heard from the street. He liked to stand at the rear to watch the performance for a moment, looking for familiar faces in the audience—friends and criminals—before going backstage. The thought of the high temperatures in the cramped dressing rooms prevented his visiting any of his favorite actresses tonight.

The manager of the Gymnase appeared as he crossed the deserted lobby. "Ah, Monsieur! Your friend Dumas is here tonight."

"He would be! The heat never bothers him."

"With another animal friend."

"Yes? Where'd he go?" Peering through the open doors, at the actors on the brightly lighted stage.

"To visit Mademoiselle Joly, of course!"

"I'll find him." Vidocq continued on around the perimeter of the auditorium, his eyes on the noisy audience, toward a velvet-curtained door that led backstage.

Theaters were more dramatic since gas lighting had replaced the old Argand lamps and auditoriums could now be darkened while the curtain was raised.

Pushing the low door back, he stepped into a blast of heat. Closing the door quickly, he started down a narrow corridor past the open doors to a row of tiny dressing rooms. The first two were empty, but waves of perfume poured out from each, a combination of scents from the bottles and jars on every cluttered dressing table plus the familiar smell of the same theatrical makeup he used for some of his disguises.

Through the third doorway he saw a young actress slumped on a chaise, sound asleep in full costume. He remembered her from the first night of the play. She had a small part—an inquisitive shepherdess in the second act—and must have fallen asleep waiting for her cue.

The final dressing room, nearest the stage, belonged to Mademoiselle Joly, blond and enticingly beautiful.

Looking inside, Vidocq had to restrain a burst of laughter.

Dumas sat at the dressing table staring into the hinged mirrors, candles guttering on either side, making extravagant faces at himself. Then he saw the "animal friend," a wrinkled simian face watching Dumas in the mirrors and making frantic grimaces of its own.

"Which of you is Mademoiselle Joly?" Vidocq asked.

"Vidocq!" Dumas had seen his reflection and rose, the tiny black monkey springing onto his shoulder, its long tail thrashing. "I was trying to teach Marmosetta a new expression. She has only two at the moment, angry or happy, and they have become boring. I'm considering sending her to the great Talma for lessons in pantomime. Mademoiselle Joly would not be amused to hear you think she looks like Marmosetta!"

They embraced affectionately, and Marmosetta leaped onto Vidocq's shoulder, clutching his ear with delicate black fingers.

Vidocq looked up at Dumas as they exchanged greetings, feeling, as usual, a pang of envy for the younger man's height, his broad shoulders and slim body, although he had put on weight in the past year with his social life. The women of Paris adored his striking appearance. The crisp purple-black curls and small beard. His clear blue eyes seemed more intense than anyone else's because of the dark skin that made his teeth even more impressive, white, and perfect between the full red lips.

"Marmosetta likes you!" Dumas lifted her to his own shoulder with one hand, causing her to screech.

"Doesn't she suffer in this heat?"

"She thrives on it! We both have tropical blood in our veins. My father came from San Domingo, and I flourish in such weather. Been working all day in a wretched airless office, but I shall spend the night with Mademoiselle Joly!"

"Have you seen Balzac?"

"Honoré rarely comes out in hot weather."

"I haven't run into him all week. How does he get food? Is there some woman living with him?"

"He's too busy for women! Except to write endless letters to his beloved. Such a fool! Agonizing over a married woman old enough to be his mother. I shall never make that mistake." Fondling the monkey as he talked. "He gets his dinner from a baker who makes him a special dish which is delivered hot every evening. In the summer he never gets dressed unless he ventures out after dark. Works day and night at his writing table, wearing that filthy monk's robe and sandals."

Vidocq realized, as Dumas talked, that there was no trace of sweat on his handsome face, saw that the little monkey had curled up on his shoulder. "What do you feed your beast?"

"She's not a beast, my friend! Marmosetta is a lady who eats tropical fruit and nuts. She eats well in the summer, but winters are more difficult. For both of us!"

"You're waiting here?"

"Until Mademoiselle Joly finishes her performance. Then, after supper somewhere, she will give a private performance just for me."

"What will you do with Marmosetta?"

"She's an excellent audience. Always applauds at the proper moments."

"How's your writing going?"

"Not much time for that. I'm still copying letters all day in the secretariat of the Duc d'Orléans. But I've started a new play. Work on that nights and weekends, but tonight it's too hot in my small apartment."

"Everything's too hot tonight." Vidocq turned toward the door. "I'm heading home."

"Any delicious crimes in this weather?"

"One or two." Glancing back. "We'll have dinner soon."

"You can tell me about your latest murders." Dumas sat before the mirrors again, the monkey peering at her reflection like an actress searching for new wrinkles. "I need fresh ideas for my writing ..."

As Vidocq hurried to leave the oppressive heat of the theater, he considered his two friends. Balzac and Dumas ...

Rascals, both of them! Yet so completely different.

Dumas slaving in an office every day. Something Balzac had tried but given up after several miserable years to start writing his potboilers.

Balzac must be twenty-four now, Dumas was only twenty-one.

He'd known them for more than a year. Balzac had introduced himself one night at Café Procope and joined him for dinner. Within the month Balzac brought Dumas to his table, and he had invited both of them to dine with him.

He had admired writers since his first years in Paris because they had inquisitive minds, much like policemen.

Dumas and Balzac were forever picking his brain, but he, at the same time, had learned many things from them. Trying out new ideas on them. Confirming his personal theories by their immediate and frequently violent reactions.

Perhaps one day he would start his memoirs. His early days in and out of prisons, his escapes from the galleys. The duels he had fought and the women he had loved. The hundreds of criminals—more like thousands—he had tracked down and caught . . .

"Ah, Monsieur Vidocq! What luck! I was hoping to encounter you this evening."

Vidocq was crossing the lobby toward the open entrance doors as Magistrate Mourric was entering from the street. "Magistrate! You too on the boulevards this warm night?"

"I could not sit at home in this heat and listen to my dear wife recite her familiar litany of miseries." The old man lowered his rasping voice. "Would it be possible for you to let me have a thousand francs? Without inconveniencing yourself."

"Certainly!" Vidocq reached into an inside pocket for his wallet.

"At the same low rate as usual?"

"Of course!" He removed a thousand-franc note, handed it to Mourric and thrust the wallet back into his pocket.

"I probably won't need all of this but one never knows . . ." Placing the folded note in a pocket. "I'm planning to invite Mademoiselle Joly out for supper. Delightful little hussy. Not yet grasping or greedy like some of these actresses."

"She'll learn. Before another winter."

"Nothing for me to sign?"

"I never forget what I lend."

"They tell me you possess one of the finest memories in Paris. Especially when it comes to recognizing the face of a criminal."

"As Chief of the Sûreté, I strive for an infallible memory, Monsieur. Enjoy your supper with Mademoiselle Joly!" As the Magistrate tottered into the theater, Vidocq continued on his way. Old Mourric had no chance against the charms of young Dumas and his Marmosetta. That should be an interesting encounter.

A fiacre was waiting at the corner.

He gave the driver his address and climbed in, removing his hat and resting it with his cane on the leather seat before pulling off the damp white cotton gloves and stuffing them into a pocket.

As the fiacre started down rue de Gramont, he noticed a pair of young whores waiting on a corner.

Too warm for passion tonight. In spite of Mourric and Dumas.

Or was he getting old? Mourric was at least thirty years older!

No. It wasn't age. This continuing hot weather had drained him of energy. He would be rested after a good night's sleep.

He looked forward to the fresh linen sheets on his bed. Before retiring, he would sponge himself with cold water as he'd learned to do years ago when he was sentenced to that Toulon galley in hot weather much worse than this.

Dozing briefly, he was wakened as the fiacre slowed to a stop.

He snatched up his hat and cane. Jumped down, tossing a coin up to the driver.

"Hot night, Monsieur Vidocq."

"You know me?"

"I've driven you home before."

"Can't see your face in this light."

"You're early this evening."

"Too hot to wander on the boulevards." He watched the fiacre roll on toward the arched entrance to Place du Pont Saint-Michel and saw that the sky directly overhead was trembling with stars.

Bringing out his key ring and, with his fingertips, finding the door key, as he climbed the marble steps in the glow from a pair of antique lanterns.

He glanced up at the trio of salamanders carved in stone above the entrance. They seemed to be crawling, tails waving, in the flickering light. Slipping his key into the bronze lock, he pushed the door open.

A breath of cool air came from the depths of the mansion.

He was home.

CHAPTER 12

The old mansion was silent. One oil lamp was lighted in the high-ceil-inged entrance hall, set in the center of an Empire console table against the wall, its flame steady under an etched-glass globe.

He hesitated briefly after closing the door, looking toward the deep shadow at the top of the impressive marble staircase with its wide strip of dark-green carpet.

Everything in this mansion had been his personal choice, paid for with cash. The entrance hall was sparsely furnished, but only because he liked open space with room to move about. There was a long Au-busson rug in the center of the polished parquetry floor with a small sofa on his right, beyond the lighted lamp, a pair of chairs directly op-posite. Large framed paintings on the paneled walls. Peaceful rural scenes he had selected to please his mother, knowing they would re-mind her of the country around their native Arras.

Slipping his keys back into the same pocket, he walked on toward the staircase and was surprised to see young Jean in the shadow, slumped on the sofa, still in the summer uniform he wore evenings when he served dinner. His high collar was open, white cravat hanging loose. Something must have happened for his mother to order the youth to wait up for him. Reaching the console table, he saw a folded sheet of notepaper near the lamp.

He snatched up the note and unfolded it to read the familiar old-fashioned handwriting.

> *I had another note from my dear*
> *sister. Will tell you about it at*
> *breakfast.*
> *Also Jeanne-Victoire isn't well*
> *again.*
> *Perhaps it was only because of*
> *this heat.*
> *Which didn't bother your loving*
> *mother.*
> *Sleep well . . .*

He folded the note and slipped it into a pocket. His mother's mes-sages were always precise, never informative. He wondered what had been wrong with Jeanne-Victoire? And what was this note from his aunt?

"Jean?" He whispered the name, touching his shoulder carefully in order not to startle him.

The youth opened his eyes instantly and struggled up from the sofa. "Sorry, Chief. I fell asleep."

"So would I, on such a night. Why aren't you in bed?"

"Because of a parcel that was delivered late this afternoon."

"Parcel?"

"The man said it was valuable." He indicated a large rectangular shape covered with burlap, propped against the wall.

"Ah, yes! I bought another painting."

"That's what Madame, your mother, thought it must be. She told me to wait and carry it upstairs for you."

"Could've done that myself." He went toward the staircase. "Come along, my friend."

Jean picked up the carefully wrapped painting, holding it in both muscular arms, and followed, his weight making the floor creak.

"Quietly! Everyone's asleep." Vidocq started upstairs, walking lightly on the carpeted steps, the youth following.

His family had separate suites on the first floor. The cook, both maids, and Jean were in attic rooms.

He glanced back at the young man in his pale-gray uniform. "Your room must be hot on a night like this."

"Not too bad."

Jean was one of his recent discoveries. He'd found him last year when he visited Bicêtre to observe a group of prisoners in chains being prepared to leave for the galleys. He did this every few months, walked unguarded and unarmed through the central prison yard where hundreds of other convicts watched the departure ceremony. Some of those standing in the front rows to observe the ritual were serving time for minor offenses. Others behind them were hardened criminals, even murderers, who had been given long sentences. A few, usually young men with spirit, always stepped forward to hand him a note for a relative or mistress. Some even asked him to help them.

This youth had stepped out of the crowd and said, "I am innocent."

In the moment he paused to talk with him, he had learned his name and why he was in Bicêtre, but promised him nothing. Jean had been arrested at the age of seventeen, for stealing from a shop in Montmartre where he worked as an assistant, and convicted on the testimony of an older employee. One of hundreds from the slums of Paris who were serving lengthy terms for the most minor offenses.

He had assigned Cauler to Jean's case and learned that the testimony of his fellow employee had been false. The older man had been jealous because the shop's owner took a greater interest in the boy after his daughter fell in love with him. The merchandise had been stolen by a woman customer as the other clerk watched, but he had told their employer that Jean was guilty. He acknowledged his false testimony when Vidocq confronted him, even though he'd married the shop owner's daughter, and he was now serving a prison sentence for perjury.

Jean had come to work at Number Six as an apprentice and, after proving his worth and loyalty, was assigned to be Vidocq's personal protector in the guise of valet, coachman, and factotum. Another year and he would be promoted to the junior staff at Number Six.

His mother had no suspicion that the procession of young male servants who worked for her through the years were members of the Sûreté.

Vidocq continued ahead, down the wide upstairs corridor, where another oil lamp was lighted. His mother and wife had their suites on his left, but the entire first floor on the right was his private domain. Bedroom, dressing room, *salle de bain,* and picture gallery, as well as the big room where he kept his disguises.

The first door led to the gallery.

Vidocq brought out his keys again, fingering them without looking, and selected the correct one. "Put that down. I can carry it now."

Jean rested the covered painting against a Louis XVI table. "Can I light a lamp for you?"

"I'll do it." He was amused, knowing that the youth still hoped to see inside the gallery. "Get to bed. And I hope you can sleep."

"I always sleep. Learned that in Bicêtre."

"I, too, know about sleeping behind bars, in spite of the heat or the sounds from the wild animals." He unlocked the door and pushed it open.

"What time in the morning?"

"Better wake me at seven." He left his hat and cane on a table near the door. "Good night!"

"Good night, Chief." Saluting and continuing on down the corridor, toward the servants' stairs in the rear.

Vidocq picked up the covered painting with one hand and carried it inside. Nudged the door shut and paused for a moment peering across the dark gallery. Facing a pair of tall double windows standing open onto the side garden, through which after a moment he glimpsed a blue glow of moonlight. As his vision cleared, he was able to make out the big wooden easel standing between the windows.

He crossed the bare floor, his leather heels thudding in the silence— all rugs had been stored in the attic for the summer—and leaned his new purchase against the easel. Lighted an oil lamp on a nearby table before removing the rough burlap and lifting the framed canvas onto the easel.

Turning to get a chair, he glanced at the other paintings hanging on the paneled walls. In this light he could barely make out two of his favorites, large canvases in heavily carved frames: the death of Jeanne d'Arc, flames reaching up toward her anguished virginal face; and the beheading of Jean le Baptiste, blood spattering the hands of Salomé as she caught his severed head.

He moved a small armchair to face his latest acquisition. Sat down, suddenly weary again, and studied the painting more carefully.

The nude body of a woman, against a white cloth that partially covered a wooden table, was completely mutilated. He had thought earlier that this was the result of an accident or murder, but now he began to suspect the cadaver had been dissected by a skilled surgeon. At least that was what the artist, whoever he was, wanted you to think. A sharp knife rested beside one severed arm. The blade was an odd shape and length, probably the kind of scalpel used years ago. His eyes darted over every part of the canvas, seeking a clue to the origin of the painting and nationality of the artist. There had to be some evidence hidden here that would reveal in which country it had been painted. He discovered several things. The flesh remained darker than usual after death, in spite of the lost blood, which suggested that the woman might have been Latin or had spent long hours in the sun. Her head was missing, so it was impossible to know the color of her hair. Probably glossy black. One hand rested close to the edge of the table. The fingernails were cracked and broken, her wrist thick and muscular. She must have lived on a farm or been a servant. The artist could have obtained the body from a medical school or morgue. Or had he murdered her himself?

One lovely breast, barely visible, was that of a young woman.

This painting gave him much pleasure. It was the startling arrangement of anatomical specimens, like vegetables on the stark white cloth, with bloodstains soaking down to the scarlet pool on the floor. He had never seen blood painted so realistically, already darkening at the edges of the puddle where it had begun to dry.

Tomorrow he would hang the new canvas in a place of honor.

He rose and, after a brief glance at his other treasures, blew out the light, avoiding the armchair in the dark as he went to the door. Locked it again and continued down the long corridor to his wife's suite on the opposite side at the far end.

Opening and closing her door silently, he crossed a shallow foyer lighted by a single candle toward the open double doors of her bedroom. Pausing in the doorway, his eyes, as usual, went first to his wife in the delicate gold and white Louis XVI bed. He had selected it for her, like everything else in this suite, the week before their marriage.

She was, as he anticipated, sound asleep. Head turned away from the shaded candle on the bedside table.

The only sound was her gentle breathing.

This was how it usually was, each night, when he came in here before retiring to his own bedroom.

He tiptoed to the foot of the bed and looked down at her lovely face.

The sheet was tossed aside, and her body, not much larger than a child's, was covered only by a nightgown, her pale flesh visible through the sheer material. Long golden hair spread across the pillows. Hands folded together like one of those touching statues carved on Gothic tombs.

In a few moments his presence would waken her.

He turned from the bed toward the row of tall windows open onto a balcony and stepped outside, standing in deep shadow, to look down at the moon-drenched gardens. He enjoyed analyzing the scents rising from below. Especially the rose and lemon. He couldn't see the rose garden, only moon-pale rows of lemon trees in large white pots, the fruit hanging like ornaments against their dark green leaves.

A choir of *cigales* was chirring in the shrubbery, and from the trees came a soft trill of melody from a nightingale, answered by another and another.

Turning abruptly, he went inside and sank onto a *fauteuil* facing the bed as the bells of Saint-Séverin muffled by distance rang the hour. He was earlier than usual tonight.

Seated like this, he had two different views of his wife. The back of her head with its silken yellow hair, and in a tall mirror on the far side of the room he could see the shadowed oval of her face against the white pillowcases. *Chère* Jeanne-Victoire . . .

They'd been married three years now, and, after a fashion, their marriage had worked. Unlike his first! He had deserted Louise in Arras, when he returned home on leave from the army and found her in bed with an officer of the Eighteenth Chasseurs. Had nearly killed him before the constables arrived and he was forced to flee for his life. Louise had gotten a divorce years later, when she wanted to marry someone else. He would always wonder how she'd selected one man from so many!

He'd never loved Louise. Only married her because she claimed he'd gotten her with child and because her father was chairman of the Terror in Arras and could have ruined his father. She had been lying, he soon discovered, about the child.

Jeanne-Victoire had been different from the start. He had adored her immediately the first time he saw her delicate face.

There had been nothing romantic about that first meeting.

He was trailing a gang of cutthroats, most of them remnants from Napoléon's campaigns who had organized themselves into a band and were terrorizing the private bankers of Paris. Killing couriers as they delivered gold to a government official or important business firm. A number of people, including one prominent banker, had been murdered. The gang's blunders eventually led him to a notorious tavern on rue des Marais. It was in that tavern, with its evil and rowdy customers, that he first glimpsed Jeanne-Victoire.

She was seated at a table with several members of the gang, and her eyes had touched his several times from across the noisy, low-ceilinged room. He was disguised that night as Jules, one of his favorite impersonations, a rough brawler who was well known in such unsavory spots. Jules wore a straggly beard and walked with a limp, which he told everyone was the result of an injury at Waterloo.

Next time he saw her, she was coming out from the same tavern as he entered. Again their eyes had touched.

The following week she had been seated alone, in shadow, at a corner table. She had seemed so thin in her plain white summer dress, probably waiting for some of the gang, not even a glass of cheap wine in front of her. As he drank his raw Burgundy, he studied her intently, careful to keep his eyes moving in case anyone was watching. She became aware of his continued glances and smiled briefly, then looked away. It was the most forlorn smile he'd ever seen. Furtive and shy.

As he tossed off the last of his wine, he had been aware of her rising and hurrying toward the door. Several hands reached out to clutch her, but she smiled and avoided all of them. As she passed his table, she hadn't looked at him. He didn't move until the door had closed behind her, then got to his feet and slowly limped in pursuit.

The street had been dark with one street lamp flickering at the corner of rue de Paradis. She would have taken the other direction, away from the light. He peered up the street, searching both sides, checking the shabby houses and shuttered shops. Then he saw something move. Her white skirt. She was standing in the shadow of a doorway. Once again he checked the street, but there was no sign of life except for an old man collapsed against a wall, an empty wine bottle in one filthy hand. He had been sprawled there earlier.

Moving quickly, no longer limping, he hurried up the street.

As he joined her, he saw that she was trembling in spite of the warm weather, thrusting both hands out as though to protect herself. He still remembered her face in the moonlight, her frightened voice, the first words she had whispered.

"Who are you, Monsieur?"

"I am Vidocq." He had never before told his name to anyone while wearing a disguise.

Her eyes had widened with shock. "Vidocq!"

"Have no fear, Mademoiselle. I intend no harm."

"You're arresting me?"

"Certainly not. I would like to talk to you." He reached to take her hands, but she pulled them from his grasp. "We can't stand here. Someone will notice us."

"They would kill me. If they saw me with you." She glanced toward the tavern like a frightened rabbit listening for distant hunters.

"You know that old church around the corner?"

She nodded, unable to speak.

"Meet me there. But we must go in opposite directions."

She nodded again, darted out from under the arch and hurried up the cobbled street, keeping close to the shuttered buildings.

He waited until she disappeared around the corner. Would she meet him, or was she already turning into the first alley that would let her escape?

Limping again, he went down the street past the tavern. By the time he reached the church, she could be far away. If she reported to a member of the gang that Vidocq was watching them, they would never show up here again. He'd been stupid to tell her his name. When he reached the church, there was no sign of her.

"Monsieur . . ."

He whirled to see her step from behind a tree at the far side of the church. Forgetting his limp, he hurried toward her.

"Why do you want to talk to me?"

He didn't answer but took her in his arms and kissed her on the forehead. Felt her body shivering under the thin dress.

"You can't force me to answer your questions. I will never tell you anything about my friends."

"I know quite enough about them, Mademoiselle. I only wish to question you about yourself. Who are you? What's your name?"

"Jeanne-Victoire Guerin." She said her name like a child reciting it for a teacher.

"How long have you been in Paris?"

She frowned. "It must be—three months . . ."

"Jeanne-Victoire!" He bent to kiss her forehead again. "I'm going to marry you."

She looked up, unbelieving, into his eyes. "What did you say, Monsieur?"

"How old are you? The truth!"

"Twenty-one. Why would you wish to marry me?"

"Because I love you."

"Nobody's ever told me that before . . ."

"Have you been in trouble with the police?"

"No, Monsieur. Never."

"Not that it matters. If you have a dossier at the Préfecture, I will destroy it. How did you get involved with these rascals?"

"They noticed me in the street. I had no place to sleep, no money or friends, and they took me in. They've been kind to me. That's why you mustn't ask me about them, because I'll never tell you—or anyone else—anything I know."

65

"I respect your loyalty. And I will never question you. Within the week they will all be behind bars."

"Oh, no!"

He held out his hand to her. "Come!"

"Where are you taking me?"

"To my home, where my mother will welcome you."

"You really do mean what you've been saying?"

"We'll be married at the Bureau of Registry."

She reached out timidly and took his hand.

"None of your former friends will ever realize that you are Madame Vidocq. They won't recognize you in the fine new clothes I'll buy you." He kissed her lightly on the hand. "You are as beautiful as a flower, and I am removing you from the dunghill of Paris. An innocent virgin who has survived among thieves and murderers."

"I am not a virgin, Monsieur."

"No matter! Virgins are as scarce as unicorns!"

She giggled as they walked, hand in hand, away from the church.

When he told his surprised mother that he was going to marry Jeanne-Victoire, she had embraced the frightened girl and asked no questions.

"Who are you, Monsieur?"

Vidocq, startled from his reverie, gazed into the mirror as he heard the familiar whispered question. His answer was always the one he had given her that first time. "I am Vidocq . . ."

"And you still love me?"

He saw, in the mirror, that her blue eyes were wide open. "I shall always love you, *chérie.*"

"Always?" She turned toward the light and faced him.

"Always will not be long enough."

She smiled. "I stayed in bed today."

"Were you ill again?"

"This hot weather tires me."

"I hope you were able to eat some dinner."

"Enough. Cook prepared a lovely custard with cold meringues. Angels in the snow . . . Where did you have dinner?"

"La Petite Chaise."

"With your friend, Monsieur Balzac?"

"I dined alone tonight. Haven't seen Balzac. Dumas says he won't venture out in this heat."

"Where did you see Monsieur Dumas?"

"Backstage at the Gymnase. Waiting to take Mademoiselle Joly to supper. With a monkey, called Marmosetta, perched on his shoulder."

"I've never seen a real monkey!"

"I found a note from Maman just now as I came in. Saying she'd heard from my aunt. Was it anything important?"

"Maman didn't tell me. Only that there was a letter in the post from her sister." She hesitated. "The doctor was here again . . ."

"Today?"

"I begged your mother not to send the maid for him."

"What did he say this time?"

"Same as before. I must rest and eat more to regain my strength. I did rest all day but I can't force myself to eat . . ."

"You're not feeling worse?"

"Of course not."

"And you're certain that's all Doctor Morain said?"

"He tells me nothing, as usual. What time is it?"

"Just past eleven."

She rearranged the pillows and sank back against them again as she talked. "Your mother said you've bought a new painting."

"Yes."

"Someday I'd like to see your picture gallery."

"Those paintings are not for your eyes. I may bring Balzac home one evening. He keeps asking to see my collection of disguises."

"Couldn't I meet Monsieur Balzac? And Monsieur Dumas?"

"When you're feeling better."

"You never let me meet them when your mother and I used to dine out with you . . ."

"Didn't know them then."

"Those wonderful dinners! All the fine ladies in their pretty gowns. I haven't dined out since last year."

He realized that her voice was fading. "You miss dining out?"

"Oh, yes . . ."

"Why don't we have dinner here one night, in your room. The two of us! Cook will prepare something special, and I'll fetch a bottle of champagne from the cellar . . ." As he talked, letting his voice drop to a whisper, he had a sudden and surprising premonition of death. Was it because her flesh looked so pale in this light? He whispered her name. "Jeanne-Victoire?"

There was no answer.

Vidocq got to his feet and silently circled the foot of the bed to look down at her face against the golden hair spread across the pillows. Her eyes were closed. He leaned down and kissed her cheek.

"Vidocq . . ." She barely whispered his name, but he heard it.

He sighed. Few men knew the pure love of a beautiful young woman who knows she is going to die.

Turning to leave, he was aware of that nightingale singing in the garden.

CHAPTER 13

"Good morning, François!"

"Good morning, Maman." Vidocq leaned down and kissed his mother's plump cheek, breathing the familiar scent of lilac powder, avoiding the gray curls peeping out from under a lacy nightcap.

"Another warm morning, although it's pleasant enough here on our terrace." Pushing back the beribboned sleeves of her peignoir as he sat across from her at the small breakfast table. "I'll ring for fresh coffee." She picked up a silver bell in her jeweled fingers and shook it briskly. "Didn't change the color of your hair this morning?"

"I've nothing planned that should require me to work in disguise."

"I like your hair when you leave it alone—its natural chestnut color—like your dear father's. Isn't that a new suit?"

"Had my tailor make it last month. First time I've worn it."

"Light tan becomes you. I heard you hammering just now upstairs."

"Hanging a new painting." He looked around as the maids hurried out through the open dining room windows. "Good morning, Rosine! Good morning, Prudence!"

The two young voices responded as one. "Good morning, Monsieur!"

He watched as Rosine put the Sèvres coffeepot down and Prudence set a plate holding a brioche in front of him, reached for the coffeepot as they returned inside. "More coffee, Maman?"

"Not this morning, *chéri*. Doctor Morain has ordered Jeanne-Victoire to drink goat's milk for breakfast." Folding her napkin. "He wants her to eat more fish and vegetables. I've told cook . . ."

He poured black coffee into his Sèvres bowl and took a large swallow before breaking off the top from the brioche. Aware that, as usual, his mother was about to give a detailed account of everything that had happened since they breakfasted together yesterday. He dug into the sweet butter with his knife and spread it on the warm brioche, spooning confiture onto that, glancing at the shaded garden directly below the terrace and the clear blue sky overhead. At the same time hearing every word his mother was saying.

". . . and cook's feet are troubling her again. Just like last summer. I've told her not to stand so much, but she does as she pleases. You found my note when you came home last night?"

He nodded, mouth full of brioche, wondering if that nightingale was sleeping late this morning.

"My dear sister wrote to say that her daughter will be arriving in Paris this week. Tomorrow, as a matter of fact. Remember? We invited her to stay with us."

"She'll be company for Jeanne-Victoire. How old is she now?"

"Let me think! I believe she was born in—1807—which makes her . . ."

"Sixteen."

"I'm having the maids prepare the bedroom next to mine. Far enough from Jeanne-Victoire not to disturb her."

"What's her name? This young cousin of mine?"

"Fleuride. You saw her, last time we were in Arras."

"She was dark as a Spaniard. Black curls and brown eyes. A little beauty!"

"I've always thought my brother-in-law, Monsieur Maniez, has Spanish blood, though my sweet sister denies it. She says he's Basque. Something of that sort . . ."

"Basques are Spanish."

"They claim they're not."

"He looked Spanish to me."

"Fleuride will be here for several days. Perhaps a week . . ."

"You must show her something of Paris. Her first visit . . ."

"I plan to take her shopping every afternoon and buy her some

69

lovely dresses. As well as gloves and shoes. The sort she can't find in Arras."

"One night we must go out for dinner and to the theater."

"Something a sixteen-year-old would enjoy . . ."

"At sixteen, I enjoyed everything!" He poured more coffee and finished the last of his brioche as they talked.

"A sixteen-year-old from Arras is still innocent. Her mother would not wish her to see anything in bad taste."

"I wasn't innocent the first time I came to Paris."

"You were twenty. And you weren't innocent even at sixteen."

He sipped the hot coffee, remembering that first day he arrived in Paris. He hadn't known anyone. For about an hour. Her name was . . .

"You were only fourteen the night you went off to Calais with that little actress. Came back after she'd taken all your money! Walked all the way home. No longer quite so innocent."

"We were sailing to America. To Phil-a-del-phia . . ."

"Jean can find out this morning, after he drives you to Number Six, what time the diligence arrives from Arras tomorrow. I must be there to welcome Fleuride. It might frighten the child if I wasn't waiting. The journey will tire her, so we'll dine at home tomorrow night. Will you be free?"

"I doubt it."

"Jeanne-Victoire wasn't feeling too well yesterday. I sent for Doctor Morain. He thinks her condition may be more serious than he suspected last month . . ."

"What does he think is wrong now?"

"He says a specialist should be brought in for consultation."

"Did you tell him to get the best?"

"I did. He's bringing another man this afternoon."

"Perhaps I should come home."

"That won't be necessary. In fact, Jeanne-Victoire might become disturbed if you did. She would think it's more serious than it is."

"Obviously Doctor Morain thinks it's serious."

"He says she's not regaining her strength, and it could have something to do with her spine. That's why he suggested a specialist."

"Tell him to get half a dozen if he wishes!"

"I've thought myself that Jeanne-Victoire wasn't improving these past months."

"Why didn't you say so?"

"You have so much already to worry about. New problems every day at Number Six."

"Damn it, Maman! I should've been told. Jeanne-Victoire's my wife."

"I love her, too. And I would do anything to make her well again. Prevent her suffering . . ."

"Is she suffering?"

"She won't tell me." Rising from the table. "It's as though she doesn't wish to walk anymore. She only leaves her bed for a few hours in the afternoon." Bending to kiss him on the brow. "I'll go up and sit with her while she has breakfast. She seems to eat a little more when I'm there. Will you be home for dinner?"

"Not tonight."

"Then we'll talk again tomorrow morning."

"I'll stop by and see Jeanne-Victoire when I finish here." He watched her go toward the open dining room windows. "Leave me a note this evening. Let me know what the doctors say."

"Of course, *chéri.*"

He faced the gardens again.

Once more he felt the same premonition of death that had troubled him last night.

Jeanne-Victoire was much too young to die . . .

CHAPTER 14

Vidocq snapped a fresh yellow rosebud, leaving its stem in the crystal vase with the other roses, thrusting the bud into his left lapel buttonhole. He glanced at the few members of his staff—Goury, Fouché, and Allard—seated on the other side of the desk, which was covered with fresh documents and the morning's reports he had just read, the PRIVÉ dossier in the center. "Good morning, my friends!"

"Good morning, Chief!"

Today their response came almost in unison, Fouché's basso rumbling under the others like a viol.

"I've read your reports and agree with the action you're taking in each instance." Organizing his thoughts, Vidocq glanced over their heads at the etching of Villon on the wall behind them and smiled, as though at an old and understanding friend. "Aubé . . ."

"Yes, Chief?" Aubé, seated beside him, had his pencil poised.

"Inform Madame Babelay I won't require any lunch. I plan to be out most of the day." He peered at Goury. "What did you learn about that American gentleman?"

"The Préfecture had no record of him in their meager files."

"They seldom interest themselves with foreigners, unless they're political spies."

"I'll be asking questions around the Palais-Royal today, about Lucien Revol."

"Don't frighten him away."

"I've heard a little more," Fouché growled, "about Clochette's murder."

"Yes?"

"A gendarme from Pigalle headquarters, who was at the scene, got a description of that cross the murderer took from her body. Imitation gold and false diamonds. He says Clochette was having a bad time. She owned nothing of any value."

"An amateur with no knowledge of jewels. He must've been frightened and, in his panic, shot her. Stupid! To take a life for nothing. Poor Clochette . . ." He glanced toward the open doors as Ronquetti, his hat set at its familiar jaunty angle, came through the empty antechamber. "Ah! The Duc de Modena has arrived!"

Heads swiveled, faces smiling in anticipation, as Ronquetti paused in the doorway to bow.

Vidocq turned to Allard. "Check all the pawnshops. The killer may try to sell that cross. Also the American girl's diamond bracelet. Ask about both of them."

Ronquetti pulled an armchair forward to join the others, arranging his long body against the leather cushions. "Isn't that a new suit you're wearing, Chief?"

"You're most observant this morning."

"Looks cool."

"It may be. I'm not."

The others laughed.

"What did you learn last night, Monsieur le Duc?"

"La Belle Violette and I spent a charming evening at the new gambling club." Ronquetti removed his hat and balanced it on a knee. "She, of course, never wakes at this unfortunate hour—as you well know—so I will report for both of us."

"Proceed." Vidocq always welcomed the presence of Ronquetti to lighten staff meetings.

"We dined at nine. They have an excellent chef but their prices are a scandal." Glancing toward Aubé. "I shall give you the exact amount spent in the course of our evening and, if you survive an attack of apoplexy, I shall expect immediate remuneration."

"Never mind about your dinner," Vidocq ordered. "Are their wheels crooked?"

"La Belle Violette played roulette while I tried the card tables. Violette lost, but she always loses at games of chance. She saw no evidence of the croupier doing anything dishonest. I, on the other hand, had an amazing run of luck at every table I played. We observed nothing suspicious all evening and departed, after midnight, with my winnings."

"Which should be turned over to the Sûreté," Aubé grumbled, "inasmuch as we would've had to pay your losses."

Ronquetti smiled. "Fortunately there's nothing in the Code that says I must relinquish my winnings."

Vidocq laughed. "Pay them another visit next month, when they won't be expecting you." He fingered a pile of reports on his desk and slipped one free. "Here's something curious that turned up this morning from the Commissaire of the Montmartre police. Seems one of his more notorious criminals—and he doesn't lack for them in that district . . ." Raising his eyes from the report to see that his assistants were listening with interest. "I presume all of you remember Goron . . ."

"Goron?" Young Cauler whispered the ominous name.

"Prince of Pickpockets!" Fouché muttered.

"King of Cutthroats!" Goury exclaimed. "They have many names for the rascal."

"He's also known as Crépuscule," Vidocq added. "The Twilight Owl who appears after dark."

"They warned me about Monsieur Twilight, when I was a young gendarme," Allard murmured, looking around at the others, "walking the streets of Montmartre and avoiding the alleys. We were offered a bonus if we could get Goron's description, but none of us ever saw him. He was said to have killed dozens of people!"

"They used to say hundreds." Vidocq shrugged. "Everything grows smaller in time. However many there were, Crépuscule was never put behind bars for murder or any other crime. I saw him once years ago and have never forgotten his evil face. Nobody's seen him in months!"

"I used to know Goron's wife," Allard announced, quietly.

"Did you, Pierre?" Vidocq turned to him with interest. "When?"

"Before she married Goron—if she ever did—she was a waitress. Worked in the taverns on the Butte."

"Was she aware that you were a policeman?"

"I never told her, and in those days I don't think she was mixed up with criminals. She was living with a young musician."

"Locate her," Vidocq ordered. "Find out if she knows what happened to Goron."

"I'll make a tour of the Butte tonight."

"By the way, Chief," Aubé interrupted, "We've warned every fence to contact us if that diamond bracelet turns up."

"Something tells me it won't, or Clochette's cross. André, I'm paying a visit this morning to the jeweler who sold that bracelet to Monsieur Penny-packaire. His establishment's on rue Taitbout. When I finish there, I'll pay another call on that American at his hotel."

"I've questioned some of the staff at the Belvedere but learned nothing," Goury responded. "The Americans are rich—as you already know—and give generous *pourboires*. They occupy a suite of rooms on the first floor, and the father has had a number of visitors who appear to be businessmen. The hotel valet says the Americans go out every night. Mostly to private dinners, from what he's overheard. None of the staff saw the missing bracelet."

"*Eh bien!* That's all for this morning." Vidocq pushed himself back in his leather armchair. "I see the Duc de Modena is having a nap. Leave quietly, my friends, so as not to disturb him."

Young Cauler came toward Vidocq's desk as the others filed out. "I must report, Chief," he whispered confidentially, "that suicide in Montparnasse was only a suicide. I questioned everybody a second time and checked all the evidence again. Everything points to suicide."

"I much prefer murder. Suicide is so banal. So useless."

"Yes, Chief." He backed away awkwardly and hurried after the others.

Vidocq saw that Aubé, as usual, was leading them through the antechamber. He smiled as Ronquetti straightened, roused by the departing staff members, and peered at their empty armchairs.

"I seem to have dozed for a moment . . ."

"At least half an hour."

"Impossible!" He set his tall hat firmly on his head. "Did I miss anything?"

"Several matters of importance. None of which, however, concern you, my friend. But I do have something rather special to occupy your talents for several days. A matter concerning an American heiress."

"I knew one of those in Venice. Rich but elderly. Ugly as the Queen of Spades!"

"This one's young and beautiful. You will take a suite of rooms—a small suite—at the Hôtel Belvedere for the next week, as the Duc de Modena. Better do that this morning. Along with your customary elegant luggage. The Americans are father and daughter—Monsieur and Mademoiselle Penny-packaire."

"Penny-packaire?"

"The young lady is blond with blue eyes. Her name is Belinda, and her father claims she's a virgin."

"Many American women are, until they visit Europe."

"You're to find out if his claim is correct."

"Am I? Well . . ."

"With your ancient title and extraordinary charm, it will be a simple matter for you to meet them casually."

"Nothing could be easier!"

"They will be traveling in the country for a few days. I want you to find out when they plan to leave and where they're going. Also the reason for their trip. The American gentleman bought a diamond bracelet for his daughter after they arrived in Paris last week."

"Diamond bracelet?" Ronquetti was fully awake.

"Bought it from Tessier. Claims he paid fifty thousand francs for it."

"Narcisse Tessier? He's well known. Even in Rome! Designs expensive jewelry for royalty—crowns and that sort of thing—as well as for those who are only very rich."

"This bracelet seems to have disappeared."

"Stolen?"

"That's what we must learn. Monsieur Penny-packaire wants no official reports made. He suspects, I gather, that the daughter may have lost it herself, or misplaced it."

"Misplaced fifty thousand francs in diamonds?"

"It's a small bracelet, and Mademoiselle had no idea what it cost."

"You mean she could've given it to a beggar woman in the street! Or lost it down a sewer?"

"You're asking questions, my friend. I want answers."

Ronquetti rose with dignity. "I will find answers for you after I move into the Hôtel Belvedere."

"Remain there until they return from the country."

"My pleasure!" Bowing and leaving. *"Arrivederci . . ."*

Vidocq smiled, watching the elegant young Italian head straight for Aubé's desk to report his expenses for last night. Aubé would question every item.

He realized, now the staff meeting was over, that the presence of so many perspiring bodies had made his office even warmer.

His new summer suit was not as cool as that obsequious English tailor had promised.

Rising from the desk he snatched up his hat and cane.

First stop this morning would be that jeweler—Tessier . . .

CHAPTER 15

Vidocq yanked the elaborate bronze pull and heard a discreet bell respond inside with each tug he gave. Stepping back, he looked up at the facade of the elegant stone mansion, which in the last century had belonged to the mistress of a king. The upstairs windows were open but shuttered inside, and open double windows on the ground floor were curtained with what appeared to be golden brocade draperies. There was a high brick wall around the entrance courtyard with side gardens visible beyond wooden gates. The only thing to suggest this might be a commercial establishment was a small plaque with TESSIER to one side of the double doors.

"Monsieur?"

He turned to see that one of the heavy doors had been partially opened by a tiny old man wearing an old-fashioned powdered wig, dressed in a gray satin livery over a ruffled white shirt with a richly embroidered waistcoat. "I wish to see Monsieur Tessier."

"You wrote for an appointment?"

"No. I am a friend of the American gentleman. Monsieur Penny-packaire."

"Ah! Monsieur Penny-packaire!" He swung the door back and bowed.

Vidocq entered, tucking his cane under an arm without looking back at his waiting carriage. Today he had ordered the finest black cabriolet from the stables of Number Six, with a sleek black gelding and a uniformed coachman.

Wise old eyes glanced appraisingly at his expensive new suit as the majordomo motioned for him to follow across the surprisingly cool lobby, where a marble staircase rose in the center and branched to the next floor. The old man bowed him into an intimate salon with small sofas placed against paneled walls hung with paintings, and light came through narrow openings between the brocade curtains he had glimpsed from outside.

"If you would wait here, Monsieur . . ."

Vidocq remained standing, watching the old man go up the broad staircase. When the majordomo disappeared from sight, he glanced at the paintings in their carved frames. Copies of Watteau and Fragonard. Or were these authentic? Doll women and toy men in laces and satins dancing under feathery green trees. He preferred the paintings in his private gallery at home.

He became aware of a faint humming sound. Some sort of machinery, in the depths of the mansion, muffled by distance. He was trying to decide what it might be when he heard footsteps descending the stairs, but he did not look around until he heard them crossing the marble-tiled lobby.

"Monsieur Tessier will receive you."

He followed the aged majordomo up the marble steps through a spill of light from a circular skylight high above. Reaching the first floor, he continued behind the old man down a wide corridor with open windows far ahead.

The majordomo stopped in front of a pair of closed doors and knocked before opening one, stepping inside, and bowing. "The friend of Monsieur Penny-packaire . . ."

Vidocq removed his hat as he entered a large and sunny salon where a gaunt, gray-haired man sat facing him in a massive armchair behind a Louis XV desk. The walls were covered by *boiserie,* the room furnished with fine antiques.

"You are a friend of Monsieur Penny-packaire?" The voice was that of a salesman, silken and persuasive.

"That is correct." He saw that the jeweler was elegantly dressed—ruffled white silk shirt under a light summer jacket—and surprisingly tall when he rose from the desk. His long fingers sparkled with gems. Intelligent eyes and a prominent nose above thin lips.

Tessier motioned toward a *fauteuil.* "Sit down, Monsieur."

Vidocq rested his hat and cane on a table but remained standing as Tessier lowered his lean body into the armchair again. "I am here on a confidential business matter for Monsieur Penny-packaire. The American recently bought a diamond bracelet from you."

"Yes."

"He claims to have paid you fifty thousand francs."

Tessier grimaced. "One never discusses the price of an exquisite item of jewelry."

"I'm afraid, Monsieur, this is not a matter for casual discussion. I want to know how much Penny-packaire paid for that bracelet. The precise amount."

"Why should I disclose such information to you, Monsieur?" He scowled. "Who the devil are you?"

"I am Vidocq." He said the words quietly.

Tessier's thin face paled even more as the blood drained away.

Vidocq smiled. "So you've heard of me."

"Everyone in Paris knows your name, Monsieur. Honest people, as well as criminals. And, of course, hope never to meet you. Why are you questioning me about Monsieur Penny-packaire's gift to his exquisite daughter?"

"The bracelet seems to have vanished."

The eyes narrowed. "Stolen?"

"That's what I must find out."

"How did the Sûreté become involved?"

"Through the Minister of Interior. . ."

"Minister of . . ."

"Whose friend, the banker Monsieur de Fontanelle, suggested we undertake a discreet investigation for the American gentleman."

"I know Monsieur de Fontanelle, of course. He has frequently purchased jewels for his enchanting young wife."

As they talked, Vidocq was aware of that continued humming sound in the distance. It would stop and start up again, then stop once more. He observed that the blood was returning to Tessier's face.

"And how can I be of assistance to you, Monsieur Vidocq?"

"First, let me repeat my question. What did you charge the American for that bracelet? Was it actually fifty thousand francs?"

"Most people, especially wealthy foreigners, like to say they paid more than they actually did for a piece of jewelry. I've done business with Penny-packaire for many years and, prior to that, with his late father. Whenever these gentlemen come to Paris, they buy jewelry to sell in their great 'department store' in the city of New Orléans."

"You have not, as yet, answered my question."

"Since this bracelet was to be a gift for Mademoiselle Belinda, rather than merchandise for his store, I gave Monsieur Penny-packaire a slight discount on the price."

"How slight?"

"I charged him only . . ." He named the amount with obvious reluctance. "Forty thousand francs."

"Forty thousand?"

"Of course, if Penny-packaire ever sold that bracelet he could realize at least sixty thousand for it. Those diamonds are perfect stones, the gold setting an original design by one of my best artists."

"Did Mademoiselle Penny-packaire know what her father paid?"

"The price was never discussed in her presence. In fact, her father asked me not to mention it in front of her. That was when he came in without her, to tell me he wanted a gift to celebrate his daughter's first visit to France. So nothing was said about the price of anything I showed her."

"She looked at other items before she made a selection?"

"Oh, yes! Mostly necklaces and bracelets. I suspect she picked this particular bracelet because it was so simple. She thought, no doubt, it was the least costly, when actually it was designed to display seven of our finest diamonds."

"Do you have the artist's design? It would be a great help if I could see that."

"Certainly. All my artists work on the premises." Rising again from his armchair. "I will take you to our atelier, which clients are never permitted to visit."

"I am honored, Monsieur."

"Each design is filed for future reference, in case the purchaser wishes to have a duplicate made or, as today, if the article of jewelry should be lost. Or stolen . . ." He turned toward a section of the *boiserie* behind his desk. "Through here, Monsieur Vidocq . . ."

He followed as Tessier touched a part of the molding, which released a hinged section of the carved paneling.

Tessier pushed it back and stepped through the opening.

Vidocq went after him, into an endless and deserted corridor sparsely furnished with antiques.

Now the humming sound was more distinct.

This must be the wing of the mansion where the jewelry was made. There would be furnaces for melting gold and silver, grinding wheels, and polishers.

Tessier opened a door, motioning for Vidocq to follow him inside.

He found himself in a long room where three men sat at drawing tables facing a row of open windows. They were perched on stools, working silently, wearing blue denim smocks over their suits. The humming sound did not come from here.

"These are my artists," Tessier whispered, motioning toward them with a sweep of his hand. "They design every piece of jewelry that's made by our craftsmen." Lowering his voice even more as he led the way toward a solid wall of antique wooden cabinets. "I won't tell anyone that you are Vidocq. No point in alarming members of my staff." He opened the doors of a cabinet. "Our original designs are kept here in alphabetical order. These are all the important ones we've created in the past five years."

The cabinet's interior consisted of rows of wooden compartments holding cardboard tubes. Some cubicles were filled, while others contained only a few. Above each compartment a single letter was carved in the wood.

Tessier reached into a compartment, under the letter P, which held dozens of the dark-gray tubes. He selected one and turned, tube in hand, toward the nearest unoccupied table. Unscrewed the metal cap and tapped the tube against the palm of his hand.

A roll of white paper slipped out.

Vidocq glanced around the room as the jeweler unrolled the sheet of heavy paper, holding it delicately between the tips of his long fingers. One of the artists, a dark-haired young man, had risen from his stool and gone to a table where an older man was working.

"Here you are, Monsieur Vidocq! The Penny-packaire bracelet . . ."

He looked down at the drawing spread flat on the table.

"Exquisite! Don't you agree?" Tessier sighed with pleasure as he studied the design. "Such delicacy!" Handing it to Vidocq. "But see for yourself."

Vidocq held the drawing toward the light and saw that it was a deceptively simple design for a bracelet. Two views, back and front.

"This is, of course," Tessier explained, "several times larger than the actual bracelet. The artist does that to show every detail."

Each of the seven diamonds was indicated with meticulous care as well as the delicate garland of twining leaves that joined them together. "May I borrow this for a few days?"

Tessier looked startled. "Well, I—I suppose . . ."

Vidocq rolled the sketch quickly as he talked. "I will return it, Monsieur, after I recover the missing bracelet." He picked up the tube and thrust the sketch inside, noticing PENNYPACKER-BRA-23 lettered in green ink on a label pasted across the metal cap.

"Remember this is our only copy!"

As Vidocq twisted the cap onto the tube, he saw that the black-haired youth was turning away from the older artist, laughing at something the other man had said, glancing at the intruders as he returned to his own work table.

It was the young man who had been in the garden of the Palais-Royal with Mademoiselle Belinda.

He had found Lucien Revol.

81

CHAPTER 16

Vidocq, the cardboard tube under his arm and cane in hand, hurried through the entrance hall of the Hôtel Belvedere, as the same concierge rose to greet him. "I was here yesterday. Monsieur Penny-packaire . . ."

"The American gentleman is in his suite with Mademoiselle, although I believe she did mention they might be going out for lunch. Suite number two on the next floor. The staircase will take you almost directly to their door." Leaning forward to point toward the stairs. "You're in luck! Here's Monsieur Penny-packaire now. With the young lady. Another moment, you'd have missed him."

He turned and saw the Americans coming down the red-carpeted marble steps, laughing and talking. The father was wearing a wide-brimmed pale yellow straw hat, white trousers with a light-brown jacket, ruffled white shirt, and dark-yellow cravat. His daughter's blond curls were visible under a straw bonnet trimmed with pink rosebuds. White frock with sprigs of embroidered pink roses and a ruffled pink parasol in one white-gloved hand.

As he walked toward them across the columned entrance hall, he saw everything—the Americans and himself—repeated countless times in the surrounding mirrors and, at the same instant, noticed a gentleman seated in the shadows. It was Ronquetti!

Vidocq glanced from side to side, but it took several moments for him to find which was image and which was real.

"Ah, Vidocq!"

He turned to face the Americans. "Monsieur Zeb!"

"Were you looking for me?"

"I was, indeed."

"May I present my daughter, Belinda . . ."

"Mademoiselle!" Vidocq bowed as she extended a gloved hand.

"Monsieur Vidocq!" she exclaimed. "I've heard about you. Even in New Orleans! We get all the news from Paris in our newspapers."

He took her hand and raised it to his lips, aware of her delicate perfume, conscious that she spoke French even better than her father.

"Papa told me he's arranged for you to find the little bracelet I seem to have misplaced . . ."

"He has, indeed, Mademoiselle. And I've just come from seeing Monsieur Tessier."

"Did you learn anything from him?" Pennypacker asked.

"Very little. He did show me the design for the bracelet so that I now have an idea of what it looks like."

"Splendid!"

Vidocq saw that Ronquetti was rising from the shadow into the light. "Ah! Here's an old acquaintance of mine! The Duc de Modena . . ."

"A real duke?" Belinda turned, wide-eyed, to see him but was confused by the mirrored images.

Vidocq raised his voice. "My dear friend! When did you arrive in Paris?"

"Only this morning." Ronquetti came toward them, smiling, confidently handsome. "What an unexpected pleasure!" Embracing Vidocq and kissing him on both cheeks. "I thought it was you but didn't wish to intrude . . ."

"Permit me! The Duc de Modena, Monsieur Penny-packaire and his daughter, Mademoiselle Belinda, from New Orléans . . ."

"From the United States? I've met many of your countrymen in Rome." Bowing to Belinda. "Mademoiselle! I am enchanted."

She extended her gloved hand, and he kissed it.

"You live in Rome?" Pennypacker asked.

"I keep a small villa there, but I frequently come to Paris on business, Monsieur."

The two men shook hands formally.

"I've never met a real duke before!" Belinda exclaimed, as Ronquetti edged her away, imperceptibly, from the others. "How long will you be staying here?"

"Perhaps a week, Mademoiselle. Possibly longer . . ."

Vidocq, grateful for a moment of privacy with Pennypacker, pulled the cardboard tube from under his arm. "I have the design for that bracelet here, and I would like you to identify it, if you will."

"Of course."

He opened the tube as he led the American to a marble-topped table. "Also, I would like to know whether you or your daughter ever visited the atelier at Tessier's where his designers work."

"I have, but not my daughter. She saw the bracelet, with several other pieces, in Tessier's salon."

"Who brought them?"

"A uniformed footman—an old man—I've seen him many times in the past."

Vidocq had unrolled the sheet of paper as they talked and spread it flat on the table. "Is this the missing bracelet?"

"That's it!"

"And this was not designed especially for you but was among a number of completed pieces Tessier showed you?"

"Quite right! He always has a selection of finished items to show visitors who are in Paris for a brief visit."

"I understand." Vidocq rolled the sheet of paper and returned it to the tube, twisting the metal cap into place. "You said you'll be leaving the city for a few days?"

"I'm still waiting for confirmation of the date we're expected in the country. Should arrive at any moment, and we'll be off at once."

"You told me yesterday that you buy antique furniture for your 'department store' in New Orléans . . ."

"Oh, yes! Every time I come to France."

"Will you be looking for some while you're in the country?"

"I'm always searching for treasures to take home with me. Americans, you know, like fine antiques. Preferably French. That's because your country was our ally when we fought the British . . ."

"Papa!"

They turned as Belinda came toward them with the smiling Ronquetti.

"The Duke's agreed to join us for lunch."

"Excellent!"

Vidocq thrust the tube under his arm as they walked toward the entrance. "And I must return to my office."

"You live a charmed life, Vidocq!" Ronquetti observed. "Always in danger with your pursuit of criminal types. And always surviving! I trust we'll meet again while I'm in Paris."

"I'm certain we will, Monsieur le Duc. It is inevitable."

"Can I drive you anywhere, Monsieur Vidocq?" Pennypacker asked, as they stepped out into the hot sunlight.

"Merci. I have a carriage."

"Thought we might have lunch at the Tour d'Argent. How will that suit you, Monsieur le Duc?" Pennypacker led his daughter and Ronquetti toward a waiting carriage.

Vidocq was smiling as he crossed the courtyard to his cabriolet. He had managed Ronquetti's meeting with the Americans in the simplest way. Now, having been introduced by Vidocq, they would never suspect the Duc de Modena worked for Number Six.

The coachman touched his hat and reached down to open the door.

Vidocq climbed in, sank back against the seat, and watched the others getting into a fiacre. "Back to Number Six!"

CHAPTER 17

Late in the afternoon, realizing that the light was fading, Vidocq turned his chair to face the windows and saw that the sunlight had vanished. Clouds must be scudding overhead.

He wondered if his mother had gone to meet her niece . . .

There had been no one to welcome him the first time he arrived in Paris. He had stared at every strange building and unfamiliar street, wondering what each building was and where every street would lead. Never suspecting that one day he would be head of the Brigade de la Sûreté Nationale—which, at that moment, didn't exist—and would know every street.

Those doctors must have seen Jeanne-Victoire. Doctor Morain and the specialist he was bringing to examine her. Pray God, they wouldn't find her condition more serious. She was going to die, certainly—he'd always been aware of that—but not just yet . . .

He hoped his little niece, with her laughing brown eyes and Spanish blood, would bring fresh life and laughter into their home. It would be good for Jeanne-Victoire to have an amusing young companion for a few days.

Sensing someone behind him, he swiveled and faced Aubé, white envelope in one hand and several documents in the other.

"This just came." Handing the envelope across the desk and setting the documents in front of him. "These are today's final reports. Nothing of any importance. Shall I light your lamp?"

"That would only make it warmer. I can see."

"Allard's waiting. When you're free . . ."

"Let me read this first. Tell Pierre I'll see him in a moment."

"Yes, Chief." Aubé headed back to his office where Allard was waiting.

As Vidocq ripped the envelope open he saw Hôtel Belvedere embossed on the flap.

A communication from Monsieur Pennypacker?

He pulled out a folded note and recognized the flowing Italianate hand.

> *My dear Chief . . .*
> *Monsieur Pennypacker departed this*
> *afternoon for the country.*
> *Mademoiselle Belinda tells me he*
> *received a communication when they*
> *returned to the hotel after lunch.*
> *She claims not to know where her*
> *father has gone.*
> *The charming young lady, at the last*
> *moment, decided to remain behind with*
> *her new friend, the Duc de Modena.*
> *We will spend the evening together*
> *and I plan to question the beauteous*
> *Belinda about her father and his*
> *urgent trip to the country.*
> *I shall keep you informed.*
>
> *Ronquetti*

Vidocq chuckled. If Mademoiselle Belinda was truly a virgin when she arrived in Paris, she was in for a delightful experience tonight at the hands of a master.

He folded Ronquetti's note and dropped it on his desk. "Come in, Pierre!" Motioned toward an armchair. "What have you learned today?"

"Very little." Allard lowered his muscular policeman's body carefully and began to arrange several pages of notes on the leather arm. Studied the top one, clearing his throat. "In the matter of that American girl's missing bracelet . . ."

"Yes?"

"It hasn't been offered to any of the fences."

Vidocq grunted. "Perhaps one of them bought it and decided not to report diamonds of that value. What about Clochette's cross?"

"Nothing."

"The murderer must have discovered it was worthless. Tessier tells me the diamonds in that bracelet are worth forty thousand francs. Warn every fence to report any loose diamonds they're offered. A single stone or any number up to seven. It may be a woman trying to sell them. Jewel thieves often travel with female companions. They might be staying at the Hôtel Belvedere. Check on any couples who turned up there after the Penny-packaires arrived and departed in the next few days . . ."

"In the matter of a certain Lucien Revol, believed to be a friend of Mademoiselle Penny-packaire . . ."

"Yes?"

"I inquired in the Palais-Royal area—the shops and offices—in case he worked there. Nobody recognized his name."

"He works on rue Taitbout."

"You found him?" Allard's face showed his surprise.

"Quite by accident. Revol works for Tessier. Designs jewelry for him."

"Designed the missing bracelet?"

"I don't know yet. Haven't talked to him. Want to arrange a meeting away from rue Taitbout."

"Shall I pick him up and bring him here?"

"Perhaps later on." He watched Allard turn to his next slip of paper. "You know, Pierre, your days as a gendarme have influenced you for life."

Allard looked up, face flushing. "What do you mean, Chief?"

"Everything precise and exact. Careful notes on separate pages for each investigation . . ."

"They keep my thoughts in order while I talk to you and later when I write my report. Otherwise some important fact could slip from my mind."

"I doubt that! Some day, when I'm no longer head of the Brigade de la Sûreté . . ."

"You're not thinking of leaving?"

"I've already stayed longer than I intended or anticipated."

"But you're the Chief. You're secure here."

"There's no security in this world, my friend. Even kings and emperors lose their thrones. If not their heads."

"We've certainly seen that happen."

"I could die tomorrow. Many criminals have sworn to destroy me, and in the early days several tried. When I leave the Brigade, alive or otherwise, your early police training—your attention to detail and your inquisitive mind—will make you an obvious choice to succeed me."

"Not I, Chief. Never!"

"You, my friend. Remember I told you so."

"I refuse to think about your leaving. The Sûreté wouldn't survive."

"It will survive long after you and I have departed."

"Meant to give you this earlier." Aubé placed a dossier in front of him. "You said this morning you wanted to see our file on Le Diable Noir."

"Ah, yes . . ." Vidocq pulled the dossier closer but didn't open it.

"There's a new report there. Came in this afternoon." He turned back toward his own office.

Vidocq looked at Allard again. In addition to his other excellent qualities, he was one of the most loyal members of his staff. There had over the years been frequent examples of that, and he'd forgotten none of them. He realized that Allard was waiting for him to speak. "You've something more there?"

"In the matter of the missing criminal, Goron . . ."

"Yes?"

"I found his wife last night. Only she tells me she never was his wife."

"Where'd you locate her?"

"With some friends in a tavern on the Butte. I remembered in the old days she liked to go from tavern to tavern every night. She didn't recognize me at first, until I told her my name."

"And she never married Goron?"

"Seems he wasn't much for marriage. Told me she doesn't want to see the bastard again. He was a wild man. Always beating her. Broke her arm the night he disappeared."

"A farewell present! Does she have any idea where he went?"

"He wouldn't tell her, but for a long time before he left he'd been talking about living in the country."

"Find out where Goron was born. When criminals leave Paris, they often return to their native village."

Shuffling his notes together, Allard rose to leave. "Anything more for me?"

"I've nothing planned for this evening. Get yourself some rest. When it's this quiet, I always anticipate we're heading for an explosion of crime. An unusual murder, hopefully." He glanced at the piles of unread documents Aubé had left on his desk, as Allard left, and picked up the dossier resting on top of the others. There was a label pasted in one corner: L'AFFAIRE DE LE DIABLE NOIR

CHAPTER 18

Vidocq closed the dossier and revolved his armchair to face the open windows again. Saw, to his surprise, that it had started to rain.

Rising and moving to one of the windows, he realized that it was only a gentle drizzle, which had done nothing to cool the air. He leaned forward in order to peer at the sky about Sainte-Chapelle and glimpsed a churning mass of black clouds.

The new information contained in the dossier had been a report saying that another château in the Loire valley had been robbed of its treasures. At least Le Diable wasn't moving closer to Paris.

This was not as yet his problem, but he was becoming increasingly more inquisitive about Le Diable and his roving band of cutthroats.

Was it possible that Monsieur Pennypacker had left for the country to buy some of those treasures? Had he been waiting for word that another château had been robbed before he departed? Would he ship them off to New Orléans?

The United States of America! Would he ever realize his dream to go there? Maybe after he retired from the Sûreté! He wanted above all, to visit that city they called Phil-a-del-phia . . .

What about that *laqué rouge* desk at the Galerie Marchadier? Had it come from one of those châteaux?

Was Marchadier's story true, that he'd bought it from the Chabrillat Mansion? Not likely! That was overdoing it. Trying to make the deal appear legitimate.

He would like to see a bill of sale. Check the name of the person who sold the desk. Only way he could do that would be to visit Galerie Marchadier at night and have a look at their records.

There was a distant growl of thunder, and the rain appeared to be getting heavier.

He turned from the window and went back to his desk. Snatched up the cardboard tube he'd taken from Tessier this morning, unscrewed the metal top, and let the rolled drawing slip out. Flattening the sheet of paper on his desk, resting the volume of Bretonne on one edge, and placing the vase with the dead rosebuds on the other, he studied the design again.

Running his eyes over it as he wondered where this bracelet with seven perfect diamonds could be at this moment. Resting in a dark hiding place or clasped around some lovely wrist?

As his eyes moved down the sheet of paper, he discovered an almost invisible line of printing at the bottom.

Printed in black ink, but he couldn't make out the words. "Aubé!" he shouted. "Where's my magnifying glass?"

"I have it here, Chief. I'll bring it."

"And light this lamp."

There was another rolling grumble of thunder.

Aubé hurried in with a small magnifying glass on a leather-covered handle that he passed across the desk before removing the painted glass globe from the oil lamp. He lit the wick then set the globe back in place, turned up the wick until there was a circle of light on the desk, and hurried back to his own office again.

Vidocq held the magnifying glass over the writing in the lower right-hand corner under the bracelet design, saw it was composed of a printed row of tiny letters and numbers. Some kind of code? He picked up a pencil and copied each letter and numeral onto a pad: 7-DI-BRA-7-23-PE-RE

What did they mean? Perhaps he should ask Monsieur Tessier?

He became aware of Aubé hovering in the doorway. "Yes?"

"Inspector Damiot would like to see you."

"What's he want?"

"Wouldn't say. Only that it's a private matter."

"Wife having another baby?"

"He's not married."

"That's right. He isn't." Vidocq put the magnifying glass aside and looked up at Aubé. "While I'm seeing Damiot, send word downstairs I'll want a carriage tonight. One of our oldest and least conspicuous. Is young Cauler on the premises?"

"Came in before the rain started."

"Tell him he'll be my coachman. He should wear a nondescript livery nobody will notice."

"What time?"

"Shortly after dark. Say—seven-thirty? And tomorrow morning I want a map of the Loire valley with every château circled in red that Le Diable and his band have plundered."

"I'll get one and mark it for you."

"Send Damiot in. Then I'll look through these other reports."

"Yes, Chief." He headed back toward the dim outer office.

Vidocq smiled. Aubé never lighted his own desk lamp until it was too dark for him to see what he was writing.

He glanced at the clock on the mantelpiece as a flash of lightning illuminated its face. Not yet three o'clock? He had thought it was much later.

A crash of thunder, directly overhead now, made the ancient building tremble and groan.

Young Damiot came out of the dimness, through the open doorway, into the light from the desk lamp.

Vidocq saw that he was wearing a cheap suit. With his heavyset body and shock of dark hair, it gave him the look of a provincial. His appearance was deceptive. Damiot had a cunning mind and during his three years on staff had proved extremely useful. Smiling now as he came toward the desk, a smile so completely ingenuous that Vidocq had more and more frequently assigned him cases involving attractive young women, but of a lower class than those involved with Ronquetti.

"Sorry to bother you, Chief . . ."

"What's the problem?"

"Well, I—I've put off coming to see you because I didn't know how I should say what I have to say . . ."

"You're in some kind of trouble. Women? Money . . ."

"Oh, no! Nothing like that. First of all, I want to tell you, I've been very happy here at the Sûreté . . ."

"You're leaving."

"Yes, sir."

"How soon?"

"Not right away. Maybe the end of September."

"That's much too soon!"

"I'm sorry, Chief, but I . . ."

91

"One of the new men will have to be moved up to take your place. Don't tell anyone for the moment that you plan to leave. Not until I decide on your replacement. Somebody's offered you a better job?"

"I couldn't find a better job anywhere! In fact, I must tell you, my life's completely changed since that day you came to my trial and told me I wouldn't be sentenced if I'd agree to work with you. Took me to a tavern and fed me a good meal, while I made up my mind. I've never known why you did that . . ."

"Because I was sure you weren't a criminal."

"I was a thief because I needed money to keep from starving."

"So did I when I was young, but I never got caught. At least not for robbery! I selected you to join the Sûreté because you had an honest face, and that's useful when you work here. You still haven't said why you wish to leave!"

"To return to my home. The village where I was born . . ."

"It saddens me when any member of my staff leaves. You're from Provence?"

"The village of Courville. And the more I see of Paris, the better I like Courville. My people and the way they live . . ."

"You have a family there?"

"My parents and two brothers. They have a farm outside the village."

"You'll help them on their farm?"

"Oh, no! I'm going back to get married."

"Ah! That's the best reason of all."

"Rosette and I have been in love since the day I first saw her, years ago, at the village fair. We write every month, but I miss her, more and more. The girls of Paris are too fickle for me. Too grasping. Not gentle and loving like Rosette."

"Her parents have agreed to your marriage?"

"Oh, yes! They own a small inn. That's where I'll be working."

"As a chef?"

"I'll only be a waiter at first. Rosette's the waitress. Her mother helps, but she's been ill."

"And her father?"

"He's the chef. Cooks the true Provençal style. That's why his inn's such a success. The village is on a coach road to Marseille, so travelers stop overnight."

"As a waiter, meeting many different people, you'll be able to use some of the knowledge you've acquired with the Sûreté."

"I've thought of that. One day my wife and I will inherit the inn for ourselves. That's what her parents want. For it to stay in the family. Rosette's father is going to teach me how to cook. Everything he knows!" His eyes brightened at the thought. "I'll like that. Nobody will ever suspect I was a thief in Paris and, thanks to you, became a policeman."

"I hope everything works out for you. Take my good wishes to Rosette and kiss her for me on your wedding day."

"With pleasure!"

Vidocq got to his feet. "And if you ever return to Paris . . ."

"I never will."

"There'll always be a job for you here. We'll have another talk before you leave." Holding out his hand. "Good luck, my friend."

"Thank you, Chief."

They shook hands across the desk.

Damiot turned abruptly and hurried out of the office.

Vidocq sank back into his leather armchair, aware that Aubé had at last lighted his own desk lamp.

He would miss young Damiot . . .

No way to keep him in Paris with a wife waiting in Provence.

Perhaps Damiot was picking the better life . . .

Eh bien! That was not for him. He still loved this aged bawd of a city and continued to be fascinated by his work.

There was another flash of lightning, followed by an explosion of thunder that made the windows rattle.

He glanced toward the outer office and saw a police messenger handing an envelope to Aubé, who had risen from his desk to accept it.

Vidocq straightened in his armchair, watching Aubé open the envelope as he came toward him.

"Just arrived by hand, Chief. From the local Commissaire de Police, rue Taitbout headquarters . . ."

He sprang to his feet. "Read it to me."

Aubé began to read aloud in his flat clerk's voice. "He says, 'Suggest you come at once. Prominent jeweler, Narcisse Tessier, found murdered in his residence, rue Taitbout. Apparently you questioned him earlier today' . . ."

Vidocq was already crossing the office to snatch up his hat and cane as he barked orders. "Have Goury meet me downstairs. Also Fouché and two other men . . ."

"I'll get them." Aubé hurried past him toward the corridor.

"And send someone to bring that young artist. His name is Daumier. You have his address. Have him brought to rue Taitbout! I'll order carriages and wait for Goury and Fouché. Hurry!"

CHAPTER 19

There was a small bullet hole in the center of Narcisse Tessier's forehead.

Now that the salon had been cleared of people, Vidocq stood in the center and studied the dead man seated at the desk.

The bullet's impact had thrust Tessier backward against his massive armchair. It was difficult to see the details of his features—the previously impressive nose and thin lips—behind the veil of blood that had flowed from the wound and dried into an ugly brownish mask.

Blood covered the front of his ruffled, white silk shirt and had soaked through the black velvet collar of his jacket. This was nothing like the living man he'd seen earlier, except for the jewels on his fingers.

Whoever killed him had not removed his rings.

He must have been shot as he talked to the murderer, unaware of what was about to happen. The killer had sat in the *fauteuil* he himself had occupied this morning. Suddenly pulled out a pistol and aimed across the desk. No wonder he hadn't missed.

It had been a small pistol, because the bullet hole was barely visible under a clot of blood in the mouth of the wound.

No humming vibration from the depths of the mansion now. The only sound was the scratching of a charcoal stick on paper, as young Daumier, perched on a tufted velvet stool facing the desk, sketched the dead man.

From time to time in the distance there were diminishing rumbles of thunder, like angry growls made by a mastiff after a fight with another dog.

All the windows were open, and the air was not so humid since the storm had passed over the city.

This salon had been crowded when Vidocq arrived, with a talkative group from local police headquarters. Commissaire, doctor, and several

94

gendarmes. He had cleared them out as quickly as possible, in order to go over every corner of the room himself.

Goury was rounding up Tessier's staff and servants with the assistants he'd brought from Number Six, while Fouché, with a pair of gendarmes, had gone to search the gardens for evidence of an intruder.

Only the young artist remained, working swiftly, as Vidocq moved around the salon.

The room appeared to be in order, exactly as it was when he had been here earlier, nothing changed or moved.

He paused to look at several letters on the desk in front of the dead man. Apparently nobody had touched them because one of Tessier's hands was resting upon them.

Vidocq slipped the letters from under the cold hand. The top one was spattered with blood. A business communication from a firm in Zurich, quoting prices on gold and silver bullion with a list of possible shipping dates. The second letter, only faintly marked by blood spots, was written in violet ink and came from a comtesse inquiring about an emerald necklace she wished to have designed for the winter social season. He lifted the letter and saw a brief note underneath, written in green ink on expensive paper, unmarked by blood.

> *My dear Narcisse . . .*
>
> *It has been many months since you dined with me.*
>
> *I've found a new chef who has created many delicacies which should tempt your palate.*
>
> *I can promise you the company of some ravishing young beauties and several wealthy gentlemen who, I suspect, would be willing and eager to spend money on them.*
>
> *We dine, as usual, at midnight.*
>
> *Affectionately . . .*
> *Ève*

So Tessier had known the voluptuous redhead!

He thrust the note into a pocket before slipping the two letters back where he had found them, under the jeweled hand.

Moving around the salon again—slowly, missing nothing—opening every drawer and cabinet, taking random books from shelves, flipping pages for anything that might be hidden inside. Checking under the Aubusson rug and behind each framed painting.

Pausing finally to look over Honoré's shoulder, he saw that the picture of Tessier was nearing completion. "That's very good, my friend."

Daumier only grunted.

"They let you leave that bookshop where you work?"

"When I told them Vidocq wanted me to do some sketches. They were happy for my good fortune . . ."

"When you finish that you can make several sketches of this room. Showing everything in relation to this desk and the body."

"You want a map of the place?"

"Exactly! Come downstairs when you've finished."

"I'll be another hour."

"Take your time. Although, in this heat, that cadaver's beginning to stink."

"I've smelled death before."

"Have you?" He went toward the open *boiserie* panel and stepped through it into the remembered corridor.

Striding down the empty corridor, he opened each pair of doors on either side, discovering nothing of interest in the handsomely furnished rooms. No sign of life anywhere. Even the atelier where Tessier brought him to see the design for that missing bracelet was deserted.

The only sounds came from the gardens beyond the open windows, where rain was striking against the leaves of the tall trees.

At the end of the corridor, he found a wooden staircase down to the empty kitchen, where pots steamed on an old-fashioned stove and two chickens were roasting on a spit in the fireplace.

Followed a long hall toward the front of the mansion, passing a pair of doors that stood open onto an elegant formal dining room. The closed doors directly opposite opened to reveal a large salon. He passed other doors, which he didn't bother to open, and reached a marble archway leading through a cool passage under the main staircase to the entrance lobby, where clusters of people were gathered.

Goury and Fouché were in a group with the Commissaire and Doctor Pingard, old friends from local police headquarters. Behind them were two gendarmes standing apart near several men from Number Six.

Crossing the marble-tiled floor, his heels echoing sharply, he noticed Lucien Revol, looking troubled, with the two older designers on the other side of the lobby, along with the household staff.

Everyone noticed his arrival.

Goury, aware of heads turning, looked around and hurried to meet him. "You've finished upstairs?"

"For the moment." He kept his voice low. "What have you learned?"

"Nobody heard the shot."

"These walls are much too thick to hear anything, even in an adjoining room. What about Fouché?"

"No trace of an intruder in the gardens. The rain would've washed away any footprints."

"Do these people know who I am?"

"I thought you'd prefer to surprise them, as usual."

"I'll ask a few questions. We'll compare notes later as to how they react."

Goury moved toward the people on the far side of the staircase. "If you please! The Chief wishes to ask you some questions."

Vidocq stepped forward, slowly but deliberately, into the gray light from the overhead skylight. His eyes darted from face to face, finally pausing on the chef, a grease-spattered apron around his ample belly, dwarfing the old man in gray satin livery and powdered wig who stood next to him.

Young Revol, beyond them, was observing him with interest but without any sign of apprehension.

He paused at the foot of the marble staircase, facing them for a moment before he spoke. "I am Vidocq."

There was a faint intake of breath from some. Like a sigh.

"My assistants or your local police may have already asked these same questions, but I would like to hear your answers for myself. The doctor informed me when I arrived that Monsieur Tessier had been dead at least two hours. Did any of you hear the shot that killed him? Raise your hand, please, if you did." No one moved. "Which of you was the last to see Monsieur Tessier alive?"

One hand was lifted timidly by a young maid wearing a white apron over her gray uniform. "I was. I think . . ."

"When did you see him, Mademoiselle?"

She giggled, nervously. "When I went upstairs to get his lunch tray."

"Upstairs?"

"He always had lunch at his desk."

"Was he irritable? Seem upset or nervous?"

"No, Monsieur. He was laughing and joking."

"Was he?" Vidocq's eyes moved on to the old man in livery. "We met earlier today. You're the footman?"

"Monsieur Tessier called me his majordomo."

"Did you hear any unusual sounds after I was here? Voices raised?"

"I heard nothing, Monsieur."

"He's deaf." The chef laughed, his chins trembling.

"Nothing wrong with my ears!" The little maid again. "And I didn't hear a thing."

"None of us heard anything." This from the middle-aged housekeeper. "We were together, all the servants, eating our lunch in the kitchen."

"Were there any visitors after lunch?"

"Nobody," the majordomo answered. "I would have answered the bell."

"Where does it ring?"

"There's one bell under these stairs, another in the kitchen."

"Where were you?"

"After lunch I always come to the small salon." He motioned toward the open doors of the salon where Vidocq had waited on his first visit. "I can hear the bell ring and admit the caller at once."

"If you're not asleep!" the chef exclaimed.

"Did you fall asleep this afternoon?" Vidocq asked.

"No, Monsieur, I did not."

"Which of you discovered Monsieur Tessier had been shot?"

"I found him."

He turned to see a middle-aged man with a thin, sallow face pitted by smallpox—sharp-eyed and neatly dressed—standing apart from the others. "Yes, Monsieur? Who are you?"

"Alcidor Drumont, at your service. I have, for the past five years, been in charge of Monsieur Tessier's affairs. The bookkeeping and all the other details of his business. I take a sheaf of papers and letters in to show him every afternoon after lunch."

"Where do you eat lunch?"

"Usually with Monsieur Tessier, but today I was out all morning, tending to business matters. When I returned, I went straight up to see him."

"What happened?"

"He didn't answer my knock, and when I entered I saw at once that he had been shot."

"What did you do?"

"I came downstairs and told the others he was dead. Sent one of the gardeners to summon the police."

"Do you have any suspicion, Monsieur, who might have killed your employer?"

"None."

"Did he, to your knowledge, have enemies?"

"Every man of importance has enemies. Monsieur Tessier was sharp in business matters, but his clients were his friends and his staff was happy working for him."

"That's true!" Revol motioned to the two men standing beside him. "We're the designers who create the Tessier jewelry, and these ..." indicating a pair of aged men in denim work clothes, "... are the master craftsmen who turn our designs into reality."

"Tell me, Monsieur Revol, did Tessier pay you well?"

"Better than most Parisian jewelers," Revol answered. "Monsieur Tessier was an excellent employer. Providing us with a sunny atelier in which to work. Having his chef serve us lunch every day ..."

"Monsieur appears to have been an agreeable man." Vidocq glanced from face to face. "And yet somebody shot him. Do any of you have a suspicion who his murderer might be?" There was, as he anticipated, no reaction to this question in any of their eyes. He turned back to Drumont. "Is there one person who owed your employer a large amount of money?"

"In the jewelry business—dealing with the wealthy and the famous—there are always people who owe you money."

"Some who refuse to pay?"

"Nothing like that, Monsieur."

"Was anything stolen at the time of the murder? Are jewels missing? Either finished pieces of jewelry or unmounted stones?"

"I can't answer that until I do an inventory. All the jewels are kept in a locked vault. Which hasn't been opened today. It's never unlocked until Monsieur Tessier orders me to do so."

"I will come with you, along with the Commissaire, to see this vault opened."

"Certainly, Monsieur."

"Have you ever been robbed in the past?"

"Never!"

"Very well! You can open the vault, and we'll see if anything's been taken."

"If you'll follow me upstairs . . ."

Vidocq turned to Goury. "Come along, André. And you, Monsieur le Commissaire." He paused as Drumont led them toward the marble staircase, lowering his voice as he spoke to Doctor Pingard. "I want that bullet from Tessier's skull."

"Unfortunately, as you well know, autopsies are not permitted."

"Who said anything about an autopsy? Just do as I tell you. Dig the bullet out! Before anyone suspects what you're doing."

Pingard shrugged. "I will do it for you, but no one else. Only Vidocq!"

"I will show you my gratitude in the future." He turned toward Fouché. "Let everyone return to their duties, but for the moment nobody will leave the premises without permission."

"Right, Chief."

Vidocq bounded up the marble staircase ahead of Goury and the Commissaire, following Drumont to the first floor.

"This way, gentlemen . . ." Drumont, reaching the top, motioned toward a side corridor.

This was a wing of the mansion Vidocq hadn't seen before. More closed doors.

"You will be the first person to visit our vault, Monsieur Vidocq. Even the staff doesn't know where it is." Drumont swung a door open and went inside. "This is my office. Visitors are never permitted here."

As Vidocq entered, he saw that it was a large bare room with daylight coming through open windows facing distant trees dark with rain. There were no curtains, probably removed for the summer. One wall had shelves crowded with leather letter boxes. There was an old desk piled with papers, two uncomfortable-looking chairs.

Drumont had gone straight to the mantelpiece above a small marble fireplace, bare except for an ugly metal candlestick encrusted with drippings of wax from a stub of candle.

As the bookkeeper lifted the candlestick down, Vidocq saw that the drippings were gray with age. There was a candelabra on the desk holding three half-burned candles that had been used more recently.

"Since you gentlemen are from the police . . ." Drumont held up the heavy candlestick as he talked. "I will show you how we enter our vault. There's nothing here in my office that would attract a thief. Including this cheap candlestick, which, however, was especially designed. Voilà!" He clicked a hidden spring, and the metal base swung out. Fumbling inside the shallow space, which had a velvet lining, he pulled out a key before setting the candlestick back on the mantel. "I keep this key at all times. Monsieur Tessier had a duplicate, but I've no idea where he kept it."

Vidocq followed as, key in hand, Drumont moved away from the empty fireplace. "Did Monsieur Tessier tell you I was here this morning?"

"I've told you I was out all morning." Drumont faced him. "May I ask the purpose of your earlier visit?"

"To inform him that a diamond bracelet he'd sold recently to an American gentleman—Monsieur Penny-packaire—was missing. Either lost or stolen."

Drumont went toward a large armoire set against the wall, but turned to look at Vidocq. "You think that missing bracelet has something to do with Tessier's death?"

"That's possible."

"The Penny-packaire family has been buying jewels from Tessier for many years."

"Does Penny-packaire, to your knowledge, owe money to Tessier?"

"Not a centime! The American pays in full every summer before he returns to the United States. As his father did before him. I've heard Tessier say many times he wished he had a dozen customers like the American gentleman." He turned back to the armoire, slipped his key into the lock, and turned it. Removed the key and dropped it into a pocket before swinging the armoire door open.

Vidocq saw that there was nothing inside except a bull's-eye lantern resting on the wooden floor.

Drumont picked it up, lit and adjusted the wick, then shot the beam of light onto the wooden ceiling of the armoire. Reached up and fingered a section in one corner.

There was the faint whirr of a mechanism, and the rear of the armoire opened into a dark void.

Vidocq felt a rush of cold air against his face.

"If you'll follow me, gentlemen." Drumont aimed his lantern beam into the darkness and, stooping slightly, entered the vault.

Vidocq felt the wooden floor of the armoire give beneath his weight as he bent to pass through the opening. He heard a loud protest from the wood as Goury and the Commissaire followed and was aware he had reached a hard surface, which felt like stone under his feet.

Drumont was flashing the lantern from side to side.

They appeared to be in a high-ceilinged space formed by rough stone walls with wooden shelves holding velvet-lined trays of jewels.

Diamonds blazed in the moving ray from the lantern. Emeralds flashed, sapphires gleamed, and pearls seemed to glow. Other gems, which Vidocq didn't recognize, sparkled and glittered. Gold and silver ingots were stacked under the shelves.

He heard Goury and the Commissaire gasp as they glimpsed this incredible display.

Moving on, peering from side to side, he passed trays with elaborate necklaces, tiaras, bracelets, and rings. Still other trays were piled with more loose stones. "You keep an inventory on all this?"

"Oh, yes! There's also a small card under the velvet linings listing what's on each tray. Nothing appears to be missing." Drumont continued to direct his lantern beam from side to side. "I'll have to check every tray, but I would notice at once if a single piece of jewelry was gone. The loose stones, of course, must be counted." He moved deeper into the darkness where water could be heard dripping in the distance. "It will require several hours for me to do that."

"Could you do it today?" Vidocq asked.

"I'm afraid, Monsieur, it will take me this afternoon and most of tomorrow."

"Let me know, at the Sûreté, when you're finished. Whether a single stone is missing."

"Gladly, Monsieur. I'll send you a note by one of our staff."

"If nothing's been taken . . ." Vidocq turned to look at Goury's dazed face, barely visible in the faint reflection from the probing lantern. "Why was Narcisse Tessier murdered? I'm inclined to think at this point that the motive wasn't robbery because of those diamond rings on his fingers."

"They're worth a fortune!" Drumont exclaimed. "I saw when I found his body that none of his rings were missing."

"But if the motive for murder wasn't robbery, what was it?"

CHAPTER 20

Vidocq stood at the open windows of his office, looking down into the street where, because of the unrelenting drizzle, there was not so much as a single sparrow in sight.

Young Revol would be sweltering in that windowless interrogation room in the cellar. He would give him another five minutes there.

The young man had seemed surprised when he was told they were bringing him to Number Six, but in the carriage, on the facing seat beside a Sûreté guard, he had appeared to be at ease and unconcerned.

While he and Goury talked in whispers, Revol had made no attempt to hear what they were saying but looked from side to side through the open windows as they drove here from rue Taitbout.

The carriage brought them to the rear entrance, and either Revol had no fear of the police—which could mean he'd had previous experience with them and thought he could hold his own—or he was innocent.

Vidocq moved away from the windows and went back to stand at his desk, where he had dropped the sketches young Daumier had made. Picked them up and studied each one again. Every sketch was signed "H.D." in the lower right-hand corner. The drawing of Tessier's blood-masked face was particularly fine. Better than Vignon would've done!

Daumier's sketches had greater strength and simplicity. He'd given the youth a gold coin and told Fouché to send him home in a carriage.

As he returned the sheaf of drawings to his desk, he noticed that his perspiring fingers had smudged the pages torn from the artist's sketchbook.

This was another murder case when he wished there existed a

method to preserve fingerprints. There must be many prints in that salon where Tessier died. On the arms of that chair facing his desk and on the edge of the desk. The murderer would have fingered the polished surface of the wood as he leaned forward to threaten the jeweler. They were there certainly, but he couldn't see them, and modern science had as yet found no way to make them visible. One day policemen would somehow be able to take fingerprints from any surface. There had to be a way!

Crossing the antechamber, he motioned for Aubé to follow, handing him the cardboard tube containing the design for the bracelet. "Take this for me. Sit in the next room, as usual, while I question the suspect. His name is Lucien Revol."

Aubé jumped up from his desk, snatching a pencil and pad. "You think he shot Tessier?"

"At this point I don't think anything." He reached the corridor—empty except for a guard in the front—and went toward the rear, aware of Aubé's footsteps following. Down the spiral staircase to the cellar.

He wondered if Fouché and the others had finished questioning everyone at the Tessier mansion. The body should have been taken away, and Doctor Pingard would be removing that bullet.

The cellar corridor was narrow and dim, with many turns and twists. Lighted by metal lanterns suspended from low rafters.

A guard seated beside the unmarked door to the interrogation room heard their footsteps on the stone floor and lurched to his feet. Saluted and swung the door open into a small anteroom, where a lantern was lighted on a wooden table.

"Has the suspect said anything?" Vidocq asked.

"Not a word, Chief. I've been here since they brought him in."

Vidocq entered the square anteroom with closed doors in its three other walls, followed by Aubé with the cardboard tube, as the guard shut the fourth door behind them. "Take down every word he says," he whispered.

Aubé nodded and went toward the door on their right, which he opened into a side room where a lantern was lighted.

"I'll wait a moment. Give you time to get settled."

Aubé nodded again and silently closed the door.

Vidocq glanced around the anteroom, wondering how Revol had acted when they escorted him through here. Instruments of torture displayed on one table, leg irons and a pair of leaded boots on another, leather whips and iron manacles hanging above them. Nothing was ever said about these objects, but they always had their effect on the guilty who passed through here. As did two paintings hanging on either side of the door straight ahead, leading to the interrogation room. These pictures had come from his private collection and had been hung here with a purpose. One was an authentic depiction of a modern guillotine just as its gleaming blade severed a man's head, and the other was a realistic study of a cadaver hanging from an ancient gibbet.

He had seen hardened criminals cringe as they passed between them.

Vidocq crossed to the door and grasped the knob. Opened the door suddenly into what at first appeared to be a dark room.

The air was stale, but the room was not so warm as he had anticipated.

"It's you, Monsieur Vidocq!"

Eyes adjusting to the darkness, he saw that Revol had risen at the far end of the long wooden table.

Only one lantern was lighted. It hung from a beam above the youth and cast light on his face.

"I'm glad, Monsieur, that you're the one who will question me."

Vidocq closed the door and took his place at the end of the table, facing him. "Sit down."

Revol sank down again.

Vidocq glanced toward a small section of wall to his right, which was an oblong of cloth painted to look like plaster. You would only notice it in this light if you knew it was there. Aubé was seated at a table, pencil in hand, on the other side.

This young man was clever. Possibly intelligent. He must ask his questions quickly, or he would not get the truth from him.

"You are Lucien Revol . . ."

"How did you know my name?"

The question was unexpected. "What?"

"I mean earlier. You called me by name when Tessier's staff was gathered for questioning. But I hadn't told you my name, and, far as I know, no one else had told you."

He disregarded the question. "Your age?"

"Twenty-four. Almost twenty-five."

"Place of birth?"

"The city of Rouen in Normandy. Would you care to see my papers?"

"I prefer to hear the facts from you. When did you first come to Paris?"

"Six years ago. When I was nineteen."

"And how long have you been designing jewelry for Tessier?"

"For the past two years. My true métier is sculpture."

"Why did you change to jewelry?"

"Because I like to eat, Monsieur. Didn't earn a centime with my sculpture. Could never afford to have my heroic figures cast in bronze. Tessier saw a miniature group of dancing nymphs I'd modeled in wax. Bought it and persuaded me to try designing jewelry for him."

"You like doing that?"

"Why not! I can afford a small apartment instead of sleeping in a corner of somebody's studio. My designs sell well. Women like them because they're very beautiful."

"You are modest, I see."

"A modest artist is a bad artist."

"Who said that?"

"I did, Monsieur. Just now."

"You prefer jewelry to heroic figures?"

"The only heroic figures that sell these days are dead generals astride their dead horses. But the families of dead generals want you to make them in the image of Napoléon and their horses must look like Bucephalus."

"You enjoy designing jewelry for beautiful women?"

"I like beautiful women."

"One day you hope to marry such a woman?"

"I would only marry a woman if I loved her. Without love, marriage is a counterfeit."

"You designed a diamond bracelet that was sold to the American—Monsieur Penny-packaire?"

"I designed it, and he bought it. But the bracelet was not designed especially for him."

Vidocq shot his next question suddenly. "And do you love his daughter?"

Revol's eyes widened in surprise. "How could you know that?"

106

"You meet late afternoons in the gardens of the Palais-Royal. You were there yesterday—both of you—seated on a bench."

"You've had me followed? Why?"

"I have not had you followed, but I know several things about you."

"You do indeed!"

He snapped another question across the table. "Is Monsieur Penny-packaire involved in the death of your employer, Narcisse Tessier?"

"Involved with murder? That's impossible!"

"Somebody killed your employer, and I must find that person. Was it you?"

"Certainly not!" His answer was immediate.

"Were you aware that the American paid forty thousand francs for that bracelet?"

"We're never told what prices Tessier gets for our designs." He sighed. "Forty thousand francs! For seven diamonds and a filigree of golden leaves . . ."

"Was the bracelet worth that much?"

He shrugged. "The diamonds were said to be perfect stones. Tessier claimed a piece of jewelry was worth as much as he could get for it."

"Did you know this bracelet had disappeared?"

"You mean it's been stolen?" He appeared to be genuinely surprised.

"Didn't Mademoiselle Penny-packaire inform you it was missing?"

"She's never mentioned the bracelet. But then, apparently, she had no idea of its value. She wore it one afternoon when we met, and I questioned her about the stones but discovered, to my amazement, she isn't interested in jewelry. Any jewelry."

"She knew you designed it?"

"I've never told her."

"How did you meet? Did Tessier introduce you?"

"He never permitted any of us to meet his clients."

"Where did you meet her?"

"I saw Mademoiselle Belinda for the first time one afternoon last week, when I was leaving through the side gate from the garden. Staff members are not allowed to use the entrance. I stepped back when I glimpsed the American and his daughter, the majordomo bowing them down the steps, but saw at once that Belinda was wearing my bracelet."

"You knew her name?"

"Not at that moment. I only knew that a rich American had bought the bracelet for his daughter. As they came down the steps, I heard her trying to persuade her father to walk instead of looking for a fiacre. And I followed them along Boulevard des Italiens and down rue de Richelieu to their hotel. Tipped the concierge and learned their names. Also that Mademoiselle Belinda went out alone late afternoons to walk in the Palais-Royal. I was waiting there that afternoon when she appeared. Saw how friendly she was. Smiling and speaking to everyone. I passed her several times, until finally she smiled at me. After that it was a simple matter to walk beside her and talk."

"Did she appear to be shy?"

"Not at all! In fact, I told her she was much too friendly with strangers. She said all Americans are like that. The following afternoon I told her that I was in love with her."

"Was she shocked?"

"She was very pleased. Permitted me to kiss her hand. Of course she was wearing a glove."

"Was she also wearing the diamond bracelet?"

"Yes. That was the only day she wore it in the Palais-Royal."

"Did you ask her the following day where it was?"

"Certainly not! We were supposed to meet this afternoon—if her father didn't take her with him to the country—but when that storm broke over the city, I knew it would be foolish to expect Belinda to keep our rendezvous in the rain. I will go to the Palais-Royal tomorrow at the usual time, in case she didn't go away."

"Did Tessier ever talk about his family? Relatives in Paris—or elsewhere?"

"Only once. He told me last year that he had no living relatives."

"Did he mention a will?"

"Not to me. I believe Monsieur Drumont is in charge of legal matters for Monsieur Tessier."

"Then he should have the will or know where it can be found. I've learned more from you than my associates were able to get from all the other members of Tessier's staff."

"I'm glad, Monsieur. I had hoped to be helpful."

"And you were." He realized that Revol's answers as well as his voice had a ring of truth. This young man was not at all what he had anticipated. He'd been misled by the handsome face, but he was now inclined to believe everything Revol had told him. He appeared to be extremely alert and intelligent.

"Is there anything else I can tell you, Monsieur?"

"What will happen to you now? Do you plan to find another job designing jewelry?"

"I haven't as yet given any thought to the future."

"How would you like to work for me?"

"You, Monsieur?"

"Here at the Sûreté. But you will remain in the Tessier mansion for the present and report to me whatever develops there. Keep me informed each day as to what goes on. Let me know what Drumont does and what you learn from other staff members. You can be my private source of information. And well-paid for your trouble."

"You'll pay me!"

"Later on there might even be a permanent place for you here at Number Six. I'm always looking for ambitious young men."

Revol's eyes brightened. "I would be one of your investigators?"

"Starting immediately."

"I accept!"

"Eventually, of course, you'll be given special training, but for the moment you can report directly to me on what's happening at the Tessier mansion. Also find out anything you can from Mademoiselle Penny-packaire."

"You're not asking me to spy on Belinda?"

"Certainly not! But you could surely question her about the missing bracelet?"

"I suppose I could do that . . ."

"Something else! What can you tell me about the code that's inscribed at the bottom of your design for the bracelet?"

Revol looked puzzled. "Code?"

"There's a row of letters and numbers—very small—printed in ink beneath your drawing."

"Oh, yes! Monsieur Tessier put that under every original design. After the piece of jewelry was sold. Placed it in a cardboard tube for future reference."

"I have the tube with your design for the missing bracelet. Can you tell me what those letters and numerals mean?"

"I'm not certain. I could try."

Vidocq raised his voice without turning toward the wall. "Aubé! Bring me that cardboard tube."

Revol looked around, startled. "Someone else is here?"

Vidocq chuckled. "Aubé is my third arm! And general secretary for the Sûreté. He takes notes whenever I question anyone."

Revol continued to peer into the darkness. "But where is he?"

"He was in the next room, but at this moment he's on his way in here. One more thing I want to ask you."

"Anything!"

"Did you and the other members of Tessier's staff know where he stored his jewels?"

"He never told any of us where he kept them."

"Did you like Monsieur Tessier?"

"I didn't dislike him. Certainly I had no reason to kill him."

"Any idea who might've had such a motive?"

"No. I'm afraid not . . ."

The door opened, and Aubé hurried in, the cardboard tube in his hand.

Vidocq snatched it from him. "This is Monsieur Aubé, Monsieur Revol . . ."

Revol rose from his chair, and both men bowed, facing each other down the length of the table.

"Monsieur Revol will represent Number Six inside the Tessier mansion." Vidocq walked toward Revol as he unscrewed the cap from the tube. "Put him on salary, as of today."

"I've already made a note."

"Order one of our carriages for him. He'll be leaving in a moment." Vidocq slid the rolled sheet of paper from the tube onto the table in the light from the overhead lantern. "I'll come upstairs when I finish here."

Aubé nodded to Revol and turned to go.

"Leave that door open!" Vidocq called after him as he spread the roll of paper flat on the table. "What's this mean? Can you decipher it?"

"I think so . . ." Revol bent closer in order to read the row of printing. "This sort of inscription is on every finished design. The 7-DI means seven diamonds and BRA stands for bracelet."

"So that's what the BRA means on the cap!"

"Next—7-23—the 7 is for the month, and 23 is the year. July 1823! Followed by PE—the first two letters of the purchaser's name."

"Monsieur Penny-packaire! How simple it is once you know the key! Although it isn't a code at all, but a list of abbreviations. Anyone would think it a code and be misled. What about these final two letters? RE ..."

"I don't know what they mean. Never saw them before. The few sketches Tessier showed me—other pieces of jewelry I'd designed—ended with the two letters from the name of the purchaser."

CHAPTER 21

Paris was a strange city tonight. Violet and purple in the rain, with deep black shadows. The street lamps at the corners were faint yellow smudges.

Vidocq sat, suddenly weary, in a corner of his carriage.

The thunderstorm had cooled the air briefly, but now it was even warmer than it had been earlier.

He was perspiring although he had sponged his body at the lavabo in the privacy of his office and splashed himself with eau de cologne before leaving Number Six. He had changed into one of the spare suits he kept in his upstairs dressing room, leaving the new tan suit to dry out from the day's activities, especially that half hour in the interrogation room with Revol. He had sweated, but the young man had remained cool.

Their meeting had worked out in a way he hadn't anticipated. Revol appeared to be an ideal replacement for young Damiot, who would soon be leaving.

After he finished with Revol, he had gone up to his office, where only Goury and Fouché had appeared for the late afternoon staff meeting with Aubé sitting in, making notes and comments.

Today's session had been brief. Each had his own notes on the Tessier murder. They discussed—and he had questioned—every item of information they had turned up in the mansion on rue Taitbout. He had told them what he had learned from Revol and given instructions for the Nun and the Rat to wander through the street tomorrow—looking, listening, and asking questions—talking to Tessier's neighbors as well as every concierge and tradesman.

There had been nothing more they could do this evening, and he had suggested that everyone get a good night's rest.

As his assistants departed, he had pulled Ève's note to Tessier from his pocket and read it again. Changed it to a pocket of the suit he was wearing now and, after dinner, planned a visit to rue de la Chaussée-d'Antin.

He had known Ève since she first surfaced from nowhere into the night life of Paris. Had done her several favors in return for her own very special favors and offered her his protection. Their relationship had been that of friends, not *grande courtisane* and Chief of the Sûreté. However, in the past he'd never gone to her with questions about a murder. His welcome tonight might not be cordial.

Before he left his office, Aubé had hurried in with a small envelope that had just been delivered.

The instant he held it in his hand, he had known from the weight what was inside. As he ripped the envelope open, a bullet had dropped out and rolled across his desk.

He had smiled when he read the enclosed note.

> *Here's your bullet!*
> *Somewhat damaged by skull*
> *of deceased.*
>
> *Pingard*

Had picked up the bullet and seen that its tip was slightly blunted, examined it carefully with his small magnifying glass.

Had destroyed Pingard's note and locked the bullet in a drawer of his desk.

Now his carriage was turning up rue Saint-Florentin, slowing to a stop across from Galerie Marchadier. Like most Paris side streets, this one was dark. The only light was a distant street lamp on the corner of rue Saint-Honoré.

Jumping down from the carriage into an unpleasantly warm drizzle, he saw no evidence of life in any direction. No lighted windows in any of the visible mansions. Nobody walking.

Young Cauler was securing the horse to a hitching post.

An unattended carriage should attract no attention at this hour because most people would be at dinner.

Cauler joined him, his coachman's hat and uniform damp with rain, carrying a small bull's-eye lantern close to his summer greatcoat, where it wouldn't be noticed as they crossed the street.

"You want me to get in through a window?" Cauler asked hopefully.

"That won't be necessary. I always carry a nightingale."

"Why is that thing called a nightingale? In my brief career as a burglar, I was never able to find out how it got the name."

"Apparently, it's been known as a nightingale for centuries. Probably back to the days of François Villon." Vidocq produced his key ring and fingered it to find the small metal device that was more than a key. "I too never found anyone who could tell me how it got the name, but I have a theory." He led the way, as he talked, up the steps to the entrance of the dark gallery and inserted his nightingale into the lock of the door. "Listen to this!" Turning the device slowly and firmly caused a barely audible whirring sound. "I think that is why it's called a nightingale. Because of the song it sings as it turns in a lock. And it usually sings at night."

Cauler laughed quietly. "You know the answer to everything."

"If only I did!" He grasped the knob and pushed the door open. Cauler followed him inside.

"Close this, and lock it." He waited as he heard the door closed, key turned in the lock, returning the key ring to his pocket. "We stand here for a moment and listen, in case anyone's on the premises."

There wasn't a sound, and the darkness was a velvet wall.

"All right," Vidocq whispered. "Shine your lantern." He faced the first gallery as a beam of light moved across the carpet to the far wall, where it revealed the group of peasants still watching those pigeons, before it moved on and was absorbed by the gray velvet covering the walls. "This is the gallery where they display their trash." He moved on toward the next one. "We go this way, my friend . . ."

Cauler followed, aiming his beam of light into the arched passage.

"There are two private galleries where paintings are shown to more privileged customers. We want the second. There's a desk I must see again. Monsieur Marchadier showed it to me yesterday, but I'd like a closer look." He motioned to their right. "Here we are."

The beam of light followed his gesture and revealed the empty easel.

"That desk's just inside. Beyond this archway." He went ahead of Cauler and motioned where he should direct the light.

Cauler sent his beam to the right and found the desk.

113

"Isn't that a beauty!" Vidocq exclaimed. "See how it glows!"

"A red desk?"

"That's a special lacquer. Very rare. May have belonged to La Pompadour."

"The King's whore?"

"If the royal whores owned half the furniture they're supposed to have left behind, the castles of France would've had to be five times larger!" They had come to a stop in front of the desk. "Put your lantern down, and light the nearest hanging lamp." He studied the desk, while Cauler set his bull's-eye on the carpet and lowered a lamp suspended on brass chains from the ceiling. "How much did you learn about antique furniture when you were a burglar?"

"I knew a man who was an expert." Lighting the lamp as he talked. "He taught me how to recognize a genuine antique."

"There's usually some kind of authentication."

"That's right."

"Underneath a drawer or somewhere out of sight."

"If it's genuine there's always something to prove it." Cauler turned up the wick, and the glow from the lamp became brighter.

"Leave that hanging down. Gives us more light."

Cauler joined him to stare at the desk. The scarlet lacquer seemed to give off a rosy light. "Never saw anything like this before."

"Nor I . . ."

"Those mounts are gilded bronze, not gold."

"Are they? You take the left side, I'll examine the right. Check each drawer and every compartment. Look for anything that proves the desk is genuine or tells where it came from."

They went to work, pulling out drawers, hunting for false bottoms and secret panels.

Vidocq found a hidden compartment with a small leather flap and pulled it open with expectation. There was nothing inside.

Cauler was the first to discover anything important. "Look at this!"

Vidocq closed the drawer he'd been examining and knelt beside Cauler to peer under the desk, where a rectangle of yellowed paper was attached to the bottom of the drawer. "Hold your lantern closer . . ."

Cauler picked it up and aimed the beam underneath.

There was writing on the slip of paper.

Vidocq saw that it had been pasted to the wooden surface and its

114

edges were peeling. The writing had faded until only two words were legible. "It's a name. Joubert—Gilles Joubert!"

"He was a famous cabinetmaker. One of the greatest!"

"So it would seem this must be authentic." He squinted beyond the slip of paper and saw something more. A dark spot on the surface of the wood. "Hold your lantern up!"

Cauler raised the beam of light higher.

"It's several numbers. Painted on the wood."

"That's the mark of the cabinetmaker. They numbered each piece, and the numbers were placed in the official records."

"This may have been stolen from one of those châteaux in the Loire valley ..."

"Le Diable Noir?"

"That's my theory." Rising from the floor. "We must leave the desk as we found it. So no one will suspect we've been here."

It required only a few moments to put the desk in order.

Vidocq held the lantern while Cauler blew out the oil lamp and raised it to the ceiling again.

"Now we'll have a look at Marchadier's private office." Handing the lantern back. "It's beyond this gallery. I've been invited there several times for a glass of wine, while I was deciding whether to buy a painting." He led the way, ahead of the bull's-eye, his shadow moving in front of him. "Here we are!" Turning toward an open space where the velvet cloth covering the walls was draped back and held by twisted golden ropes to reveal a pair of closed doors.

They were not locked.

He opened one door into darkness and motioned Cauler ahead.

The lantern revealed a spacious room, richly furnished, two pairs of double windows covered by heavy curtains.

"No need to light a lamp." Vidocq went straight to the flat-topped Louis XV desk. "Hold your lantern over my shoulder." He sat at the desk as Cauler aimed his beam of light at the piles of letters and folders spread across Marchadier's desk.

Working precisely, Vidocq began to go through the stack of folders. Each had a label with a hand-printed inscription. The first and thickest was marked PAINTINGS, the second was SCULPTURE, next ENGRAVINGS. He put them aside, in exact order, as he came to a folder marked FUR-NITURE.

115

This one he opened, beginning to read every bill of sale and letter. Each was concerned with a single piece of furniture. Chairs, tables, and desks. A sheet of paper on which Marchadier had made several notations.

Laqué rouge desk
Gilles Joubert, master cabinetmaker
Authentic Rococo style
Probably belonged to La Pompadour
Donated to Couvent des Carmelites, rue de Vaugirard
From private collection—Baron de Chabrillat
Contact—Sister Agathe

This was followed by several words that made no sense. Written in another private code but unlike the one on Tessier's designs. Probably what Marchadier paid for the desk and the price he wanted from a buyer to make himself a large profit.

Apparently the Baron de Chabrillat, a familiar name in the Parisian social world, had donated the desk to the Carmelite Convent, which had sold it to Marchadier. This was a common practice with gifts from wealthy benefactors. Sister Agathe would have represented the religious order.

He looked up at Cauler. "I've found what I was after."

"Did the desk come from Le Diable?"

"Not according to this. It was donated to a convent here in Paris, and they sold it to Marchadier."

"Who gave it to them?"

"This says it came from Baron de Chabrillat. Of course *he* may have bought it from Le Diable Noir!"

"You think so?"

Vidocq closed the folder, slipped it under the others in the same order he had found them and rose, pushing the chair close to the desk again. "Now you can drive me to the Café Procope, where I'll get some dinner. You're free for the evening. After you take the carriage back to Number Six."

Cauler grinned. "My girl's waiting for me."

"Much too warm for love tonight."

"Never too warm for that, Chief!"

"Perhaps not at your age."

CHAPTER 22

The rain had stopped, but the night sky continued to churn with clouds.

Walking down rue de l'Ancienne Comédie, Vidocq heard Cauler driving up rue Dauphine.

He avoided the puddles left by the storm.

Behind him was the Carrefour de Bucci where, in earlier times, criminals had been chained for weeks. He often wondered if Villon ever sat there in iron chains. Cursing a thunderstorm or shivering in the snow.

As he approached the open windows of Café Procope, he glanced inside and saw that it was half filled. No matter! He would find a quiet corner.

The Procope was one of his favorite restaurants. Legend said it was founded more than a century ago by a Sicilian named Procope who, for the first time in Paris, served an Oriental beverage called coffee. It was supposed to have been the first café in all of France. The Procope, in recent years, had become a meeting place for politicians and writers. Napoléon ate here frequently when he was a young officer, and there was a table, marked with a brass plaque, where Voltaire had dined.

Entering the sweltering café, the air warmed by a hundred candles, he was greeted by the smiling patron who guided him between the crowded tables, complaining that the weather was ruining his business.

Following *le patron* into a half empty side room, he was pleased to see an enormous young man seated alone, stuffing food into his mouth.

Le patron gestured toward him. "Your friend Balzac is here tonight."

"I'll join him. You can add his dinner to my account."

"Very good, Monsieur Vidocq."

He knew from the note of relief in his voice that *le patron* had feared Balzac might once again be unable to pay.

"We have roast goat tonight for our regular customers."

"I'm hungry, but I want a light dinner. Something cold." He moved ahead, leaving *le patron* still bowing, across the small dining room toward the writer.

The first thing one always noticed approaching Balzac, even when he was seated, was that he was like a monument in the midst of average-sized people. One saw his enormous forehead, black hair parted on the left, fleshy face with small eyes, generous mouth, and sparse mustaches, the huge bulk of his body, which tonight was enveloped in a loose blouse of coarse linen. He would be wearing baggy trousers, his feet in worn sandals. At the moment his eyes were on his plate, and there were crumbs in the wisps of hair beneath his lower lip. He was eating a large portion of what looked as though it might be the goat, fingers greasy from sopping gravy with chunks of bread, washing everything down with red wine that, as usual, would be the cheapest.

Balzac sensed he was being observed and raised his leonine head to squint toward the other room before he saw him. "Vidocq! Dear friend!" Reaching his hand out across the table.

Vidocq shook the hand and gestured toward an empty chair. "May I join you?"

"By all means! You know I dislike eating alone."

He removed his hat and placed it on an empty chair as he sat down. "Have you lost weight since we last met?"

"I never lose weight."

"But your blouse appears to be loose."

"Only a police inspector would notice! I had it made loose, in case I put on weight next winter. I always gain, like a bear, in cold weather." Clapping his hands together. "Waiter! Where's my waiter?"

An aged waiter came scuttling out of the shadows. "Monsieur Balzac? More wine?"

"Not yet. My friend wants his dinner."

"Ah, Monsieur Vidocq!" He bowed, smiling. "There's roast goat tonight."

"So I've been told."

"That's what I'm having!" Balzac smacked his lips. "And I can recommend the late son of Capricorn! This is a tender kid. Not last year's ram." He belched.

"Too rich for me in this weather." Looking at the waiter. "I'll have some cold chicken and a small portion of potato salad with your fresh mayonnaise. And a glass of white Burgundy. That should be enough."

"For a hummingbird!" Balzac exclaimed, as the waiter left them. "Or a dyspeptic priest. But insufficient for the busy Chief of Number Six!" His eyes became crafty. "What curious new crimes have we solved today?"

"Don't remember solving anything. Much too hot."

"No appetizing murders?"

"Only one."

"Yes?" He put his fork down.

"But I wouldn't say appetizing, unless you relish a bullet hole in the forehead."

"A bullet!" Wiping his fingers on an already soiled napkin. "Someone important?"

"Every human being is important to the police if they get themselves murdered."

"You are cat-and-mousing me again! Aren't you going to tell me the victim's name? Man or woman?"

"Can I speak in absolute confidence?"

"My lips will be locked!"

"It's a certain Narcisse Tessier . . ."

"The jeweler?"

"He was found this afternoon, seated at his desk."

"Who shot him?"

"Ask me next week, and, hopefully, I might be able to tell you."

"So this is how Tessier's life ends . . ."

"You knew him?"

"Never saw the man, but I've heard stories about him."

"Tell me everything you've ever heard."

"Am I working for the Brigade de la Sûreté now?"

"We can always use help. What do you know about Tessier?" He looked up as the waiter set a wineglass in front of him and filled it from a freshly opened bottle which he left on the table. Tasted the wine before he looked at Balzac again. "Well?"

"There's been talk from time to time about Tessier's private life. I've heard that he frequently has some young woman in residence. Most often a little actress or singer . . ."

"Nothing unusual about that."

"There's a difference in this instance. These are young ladies with absolutely no talent. The latest, some months ago, was a certain Mademoiselle Coralie, who for a brief time sang in the chorus at the Comique."

"Coralie?"

"I heard recently that she'd left him. Or, more likely, was kicked out. Coralie Clodin . . ."

"What about his business?"

"Tessier is—was—a most respected jeweler. His creations—especially those with diamonds—were designed for the wives and mistresses of half the rich men in Paris. He provided crowns for royalty and trinkets for the latest *courtisane* to be set up in a fine apartment by an amorous banker. Was Tessier robbed before he was killed?"

"Nothing appears to be missing from his collection of gems. Have you seen Dumas?"

"I was with the handsome Créole the other night," Balzac said.

"I ran into him at the Gymnase last night. Told me he hadn't seen you."

"This was—two weeks ago. We discussed some of the murders you've solved in the past. We'd both like to observe you at work. Watch you from the start of an investigation. Follow you, step by step, to its conclusion. It would, I think, give us ideas for novels."

"That might be arranged. But not on this Tessier case."

"I'd prefer to see how you handle an investigation with less important people involved in a murder. I would like to study the workings of the mind and heart of a murderer. His reasons for what he does . . ."

"Usually it's revenge or money. And, of course, love and hatred. Rich or poor, those are the most likely motives for one human being to kill another."

"Love and hate are emotions that feed on themselves and on each other. But hate is much more enduring."

"I agree."

Balzac squinted at Vidocq. "Have you ever killed a man?"

"Many times."

"You have!" He looked startled.

"When I was young, I killed several men in duels, others from necessity, or to save my own skin. Times when I was a prisoner or escaping from prison."

"I had no idea!"

"Have you never killed a man?"

"Certainly not! And, if I had, I wouldn't tell the Chief of Number Six."

"Do you think you could?"

"Kill a man? I don't know . . ." His eyes darted around the room briefly before they focused on Vidocq again. "I suppose, in the proper circumstances, I might. Goethe has written that he never heard of a crime he couldn't believe himself capable of performing . . ."

"Any man is capable of murder." Vidocq looked up as the waiter brought a platter of sliced chicken beside an ivory mound of potato salad.

Balzac waited until the old man departed before resuming their conversation. "So even you are capable of hatred . . ."

"Oh, yes!"

"What about the criminals you've known? Did you ever hate one enough to kill him?"

"Enough to send many of them to the guillotine. Without a qualm!" He sliced through a piece of chicken breast as he thought of the falling blade cutting through flesh. "But not enough to murder them. Actually, I've felt pity for many murderers I have known. There've even been a few I've let go free."

"You let a murderer loose to prowl the Paris streets?"

"In most instances I demanded they leave the country. Go to North Africa or the United States. I've even furnished one or two with the price of a ticket to get there." He savored his cool wine as he chewed the chicken and turned his attention to the potato salad.

"Has there been one criminal you've hated more than all the rest? More than any man you ever knew?"

"There is one person I hated. More than any other . . ." He continued to eat as he explained. "I was very young. Only twenty."

"Who was this monster?"

"A completely evil man who betrayed me." He saw that Balzac was leaving several morsels of goat on his plate and realized that, as they talked, the writer had stopped eating. "It was in Lille. I was living with an enchanting young woman . . ."

"A whore?"

"I never found out. Only that she enjoyed making violent love and had several other lovers."

"You didn't object?"

"Of course I objected! Made her promise to get rid of them and thought she had . . ." He ate slowly as he talked, sipping the wine. "Until one night I returned early from an evening of gambling and surprised the lady with an older man, sitting on his knee, drinking champagne."

121

"You killed him."

"No. But I smashed the champagne bottle over his head. Caused such an uproar that the police were summoned. For the first time in my life, I was placed under arrest. Tried and sentenced—also for the first time—to three months in the local jail."

"And this was the man you hated enough to murder?"

"Certainly not! It was while I was serving my sentence in the Lille jail that I met two men I shall never forget. One was a completely honest man. The closest thing to a saint I've ever known. Unfortunately, like most saints, he wasn't very bright . . . The other man was an evil brute who, to this moment, I hate more than any man I've met since."

"Who were they? These two . . ."

"The innocent was Baptiste Lavedan. And the devil was Calamatta. Those are two names I will never forget."

"Why were they in jail?"

"Lavedan was a young farmer who'd been condemned, unjustly, to serve six years behind bars."

"For what crime?"

"He'd stolen some grain so his wife could make bread for their starving children."

"Six years for that! And the other man?"

"Calamatta had assaulted a local merchant. Robbed him, but because of conflicting testimony from witnesses he was given only five months. Young Lavedan had never stolen anything before. Had no previous record. Calamatta, on the other hand, had robbed and murdered. He'd been in prison countless times before, and he ordered the other convicts about like slaves. If they resisted, he and his cronies would beat them. I avoided him, so he didn't get a chance to give me orders. Which naturally made him dislike me even more. He tried to pick quarrels with Lavedan because he knew we were friends, but the youth was so muscular from working on a farm that Calamatta never went too far. I felt sorry for Lavedan and managed to obtain an official form for a pardon. Filled it out and smuggled it outside to a friend who mailed it back to the warden of the prison."

"Good for you!"

"The warden was completely fooled and set Lavedan free. I told him what I'd done. Warned him to return to his farm and go into hiding.

122

Somehow Calamatta found out and reported to the warden that I had forged the pardon. I was ordered to stand a new trial at the end of my three-month term. Knew, of course, that the same stupid judge would give me an even longer sentence. So I picked a fight with Calamatta and caused a riot. During the uproar I managed to escape."

"After you killed Calamatta?"

"Unfortunately I didn't."

"But you escaped!"

"Only briefly. I was captured . . ."

"No!"

"But escaped again. Managed that time to reach Ostend, where I joined a band of smugglers. Was picked up again and again because I had no identity papers. Made repeated escapes from prison and was constantly recaptured and finally brought to trial again for that same forged pardon."

"And acquitted?"

"I was given eight years in the galleys."

"Mon Dieu!"

"They took me to Brest, where convicts did slave labor in the government shipyards. I managed another escape. And everywhere I went I searched for Calamatta. I told you a moment ago that one prime motive for murder is revenge. That was my only motive! I vowed that, when we met, I would kill Calamatta."

"You found him?"

"Never saw him again. Not to this day. But when I do, I swear that I will kill him for what he did to me. All those wretched years I spent in and out of prisons! My only crime a forged pardon for a poor peasant who had stolen food for his family . . ."

"There's an idea for a novel in this . . ." Balzac hesitated, as he considered the possibility. "What would you do today—tonight—now that you're Chief of the Sûreté, if you met Calamatta? Would you have him arrested?"

"I would kill him. Without an instant's hesitation!"

"You carry a weapon on your person?"

"At all times. There's a gun concealed in my cane. When I don't carry a cane, as tonight, I have a small revolver in my belt. Until six years ago, I lived under constant threat of immediate imprisonment. Then the King himself signed my official pardon. After that I was no

123

longer a fugitive from justice. I could have a passport and travel. Could even vote! The irony was that I'd joined the Paris police force as a spy eight years before I was pardoned. I could've been sent to prison at any time for that same forged pardon."

"It's beyond belief!"

"Someday I shall meet Calamatta, and I swear to you, my friend, I will destroy him."

"Have you tried to find him?"

"That's one of the first things I did when I joined the police. Attempted to trace him through official sources, but police records in those days left much to be desired. Even in Paris! I found nothing on Calamatta, except in Lille, but when they released him he had vanished. He must've taken another name. I had many different names in those days."

"Will you recognize him, after so many years?"

"I changed his face so that I will be able to recognize him anywhere."

"What do you mean?"

"He was a squat man. Swarthy, with prominent teeth. They said, in prison, he was a Corsican. When I attacked him, that day I escaped from the Lille jail, I marked him for life. Split his skull with a cleaver from the prison kitchen. Ripped his cheek open and sliced off part of his nose. I fled from the jail in the uproar that followed."

"You realize, of course, he may be dead."

"I most certainly hope not." He put his knife and fork down, lowering his voice as he leaned across the table. "We shall meet again, Calamatta and I."

"Finished, Messieurs?"

Vidocq looked up, startled by the interruption, and laughed when he saw their waiter. "I shall never be finished. Only my dinner."

The puzzled old man began to remove their plates. "Will you have something more?"

"Some black coffee." Vidocq turned to Balzac. "And you?"

Balzac tossed off the last of his wine in one enormous swallow. "I'll have a slice of apple tart. Two slices!"

The waiter smiled. "Coffee, Monsieur Balzac?"

"No coffee. There'll be a pot waiting when I get home. Have to drink coffee all night while I'm writing. With the apple tart, I'll have a marc."

"Certainly, Monsieur." He departed with their dishes.

"You don't eat enough," Balzac observed, sucking bits of food from between his teeth.

"Tonight I ate everything but my plate. Which means I've talked too much."

"No! No! You're always giving me new ideas. Dumas says the same thing."

"What're you writing now?"

"Cheap thrillers." Rolling his eyes. "Using a different name on each. Tell me, have you ever considered writing your autobiography?"

"Briefly. Perhaps I will after I retire from Number Six."

"You're not thinking of retirement?"

"One day. When I'm no longer able to climb at least once a week to the top of Nôtre-Dame. Or if the politicians cut the budget for Number Six and try to interfere with my work."

"I can't imagine you in retirement. Even if you did write about your incredible adventures. All the crimes you've solved. You'd be bored."

"I've made plans for my retirement."

"A trip to the United States? You've talked about that since the first night we met. Your visit to the city of Phil-a-del-phia."

"I'll do that before I die. But the day I retire from Number Six I hope to open an office of my own."

"What sort of office?"

"It will be called a bureau of information."

"You'll be giving information to people?"

"Tracking down information for them. I will take private cases and investigate, for a fee, any crime they bring to my office. Rich and poor alike! No one will be turned away because he can't pay."

"A private investigator? Prowling the streets in search of murderers the regular police are unable to find . . ."

"Even lost wives and husbands!"

"Was there ever such a bureau?"

"Not to my knowledge . . ."

"You already have a reputation as the greatest detector of criminals in France!"

Vidocq shrugged, accepting the compliment.

"As Chief of the Sûreté, you've been a policeman without uniform."

"That was my idea. The better to find the criminal."

"With your own bureau of information, you'll be a private policeman! A private detector ... Private Detector Vidocq!"

Their waiter returned with a tray from which he served a small cup of black coffee to Vidocq, then, smiling, placed a double portion of glazed apple tart before Balzac along with a glass of marc. "Bon appétit, Monsieur Balzac!"

"I always have a good appetite!" He seized a fork and attacked the golden brown tart.

Vidocq tasted his coffee as the waiter withdrew. "And did you always eat so much, my friend? A double portion of apple tart ..."

"Since I was a child! I suppose it's because of the wretched food I was given when my family sent me off to boarding schools. There was never enough! Then, when I came to Paris, my allowance was so small I nearly starved. Bread and coffee was all I could afford for weeks at a time! I'm like a dog. You know dogs gobble everything down because they have an inborn memory of hunger. No matter how well you feed them, they think today's meal is their last. You've observed that?"

"No. I never did."

"Writers, like policemen, learn to observe ... When are you going to let me observe your collection of disguises?"

"Well, I ..."

"You've been promising—for more than a year now—that Dumas and I could see your wigs and costumes."

"What about right now?"

Balzac looked up, surprised, from his destruction of the tart. "Tonight?"

"I must see someone later, but first I have to stop by rue de l'Hirondelle. You can come along and while I'm involved with family matters amuse yourself with the disguises."

"But Dumas ..." Balzac's eyes became crafty. "I shall be the first? The Créole will be furious."

"I'll have the fiacre wait and afterward drop you off wherever you're going."

"Just let me finish this!" He dug into the remainder of his tart as though he hadn't eaten any dinner.

Vidocq smiled as he finished his black coffee.

CHAPTER 23

"Wait for us, and we'll drive on to Boulevard des Italiens."

The coachman of the fiacre touched his hat brim.

Vidocq led Balzac up the entrance steps.

"You live in a mansion!" Balzac was squinting at the stone facade, barely visible through the drizzle, in the light from the lanterns on either side of the massive doors. "I had no idea . . ."

"I've lived in much worse." He brought out his key ring and unlocked one of the doors. "This house was an investment. And a good one." He swung the door open. "Welcome, my dear friend."

Balzac went inside, observing everything in the diffused light from the oil lamp on the console table. "Very handsome!"

Vidocq closed the door and followed him down the long hall. Saw that young Jean hadn't waited up but there was a fold of paper on the table near the lamp. "Here's a note from my mother, which I'd better read . . ."

"By all means!" Balzac moved on, inspecting the paintings, sandals slapping on the polished floor.

Vidocq unfolded the note and smiled as he read it.

> *The mailcoach was an hour late, but*
> *my dear niece—your little cousin—*
> *arrived safely.*
>
> *Doctor Morain brought another man—*
> *I've forgotten his name—to give his*
> *opinion on Jeanne-Victoire. He says*
> *she is seriously ill, but we already*
> *knew that.*
>
> *There was a thunderstorm.*

He folded the note again and thrust it into a pocket as he led Balzac toward the staircase. "Come along upstairs."

"Will I have the pleasure of meeting your family?"

"My mother, unfortunately, has retired."

"And your lovely wife?"

"Jeanne-Victoire rarely meets anyone."

"So I've been told. I've also heard that she is ill."

127

"People gossip."

"That's probably because they haven't seen your wife. So they imagine things, which of course causes talk. I've heard that she is young and beautiful . . ."

"She's very beautiful." They had reached the first floor corridor and were passing the locked gallery. Those canvases in his private collection were not for Balzac's inquisitive eyes. "I must tell you, my friend, I never discuss my family—even with friends. My personal life is something I prefer to keep apart from my public life. This mansion is a haven of privacy and peace. The problems I face at Number Six are never mentioned here. Although my dear mother asks questions when she reads about me in the newspapers. Questions I avoid answering. My wife, on the other hand, has no interest in what I do when I'm away from her. In fact, when the three of us dine out together—and that hasn't been for some time—I protect them from being touched by any part of my other life."

"That's very wise."

Vidocq saw that they were passing his bedroom and lowered his voice, so that Jeanne-Victoire in her suite on the other side of the hall would not be disturbed. "My wife and my mother have never seen my disguises or entered this room where they're kept." He pulled out his keys again and opened the dressing room door into darkness. "Just a moment. I'll bring a light." He picked up the lighted lamp from a table in the corridor and carried it into the room. "You can close that door."

Balzac shut the door and followed him through the foyer. "This is the coolest place I've been in weeks!"

"The heat never penetrates these old walls." He rested the lamp on an elaborate dressing table with a three-paneled mirror placed between a tall pair of curtained windows.

"This is like a dressing room at the theater!" Balzac was inspecting the rows of bottles and jars in front of the mirror. "Only I never saw an actor's dressing table so neat!" He glanced at a pair of armoires placed against opposite walls between closed cupboards, with open shelves beneath holding rows of cardboard boxes.

"Here are some of my costumes." Vidocq flung open the doors of the nearest armoire. "A complete outfit for any character I decide to impersonate. Banker, laborer, ordinary citizen! That's one of the most difficult—ordinary citizen—because he must fade into a crowd. In that other armoire are uniforms and even some women's costumes."

"You've disguised yourself as a woman?"

"I had to slap a man's face last month, when he followed me while I was trailing a suspect. Playing the part of a woman, I always wear gloves because the hands give you away." He motioned toward the closed cupboards. "Those contain hats and shoes, and the boxes underneath hold wigs, beards, and mustaches. They're made for me by the *perroquier* from the Comédie. The man's a genius!" He motioned toward a silver tray on a table, holding a pair of decanters with silver stoppers and several glasses. "One of these is cognac, the other Burgundy." Extending his arms in a sweeping gesture of hospitality. "Enjoy yourself! You're the first visitor ever to enter here.'

"I am indeed honored."

"I'll return in ten minutes." He left the dressing room and hurried back down the corridor to his mother's suite. Listened briefly outside the double doors, but heard nothing. Turned the knob carefully and opened one door.

His mother's voice responded at once. "Is that you again, Fleuride?"

"No, Maman."

"What are you doing home this early? I heard a carriage."

He closed the door as he replied and crossed the foyer into the large bedroom. "I must go out again, but I wanted to know what those doctors told you this afternoon and hear about Fleuride's arrival." He saw that his mother was in bed, propped by a mound of lacy pillows, reading a novel by the light from several shaded candles in a silver candelabra.

She put the book aside and took off her gold-rimmed spectacles. "You found my note?"

"I did." Approaching the bed, he noticed that she was wearing a thin summer nightgown, her nightcap trimmed with violet satin bows. "Tell me . . ." Bending to kiss her lilac-scented cheek. "What did they say about Jeanne-Victoire?"

"Doctor Morain brought a specialist. Very dignified! I may think of his name in a moment. Jeanne-Victoire didn't like him. And neither did I. They asked me to wait downstairs and closed the doors, so I was unable to hear a word that was said. His name is Brindeau! That's it— Doctor Brindeau. You see! I did remember."

"Brindeau has an excellent reputation." He sat facing her on the side of the bed. "What did they tell you?"

"They both used such strange words. I was unable to make sense of half that was said, but they think there's something wrong with the bones of Jeanne-Victoire's spine." She gestured as she talked, jeweled fingers reflecting the candle flames. "And Doctor—what's his name . . ."

"Brindeau?"

". . . thinks Jeanne-Victoire may be suffering from something he called rheumatic fever."

"The bones become swollen."

"So they said. I can't see that Jeanne-Victoire's bones are swollen at all! They also think there's an inflammation of the heart. Which apparently is even more serious."

He frowned, troubled. "Her heart?"

"Doctor Brindeau called it an 'impaired heart.' He says many children suffer from this condition. I told him Jeanne-Victoire is not a child."

"But, Maman, she is a child. In so many ways."

"Doctor Morain privately told me it's sort of an infection. Not contagious."

"Does Jeanne-Victoire know what they said?"

"Of course not! They talked to me downstairs, in the salon."

"You didn't tell her anything?"

"I wanted to speak to you first."

"Good! We shouldn't tell Jeanne-Victoire any of this. It would only disturb her."

"I agree. When I went back into her room, I simply told her they thought she should rest more and eat certain things. Cream and milk and custards. Fresh fruit and fish. But, most of all, she must rest. Where's your new suit? Did you get wet in that storm?"

"A little."

"I wondered if you were out in it. The storm, I mean."

"I was. Several times. Changed my clothes at the office."

"The rain didn't make it any cooler. That mailcoach was an hour late, but Fleuride had a pleasant journey. We arrived home before the storm broke. When that lightning started, I hurried up here and sat on my bed. Told Fleuride it's much safer if you're on a feather bed. Less danger of being struck by lightning. She laughed at me—said that's only superstition—but I stayed here until the storm was over. Fleuride has no fear of lightning. She's a brave little thing."

"Tomorrow night we'll take her out for dinner. Perhaps to the theater."

"Why don't we just have a lovely dinner somewhere? She'll be stay-ing at least a week."

"Whatever you say, Maman."

"Fleuride's a dear child. But much changed since we last saw her. You'll be surprised, I promise you. I'm taking her shopping tomorrow afternoon, to buy her some lovely gowns."

"Spend all the money you wish! Get everything you want for her."

"Cook was asking about dinner the following night."

"What about it?"

"Your birthday!"

"Mon Dieu! I'd forgotten."

"Will you be home? Cook wants to prepare something special . . ."

"You know I dislike birthdays. No! I will not be home. I'll have dinner alone. Some quiet café."

"If that's what you wish. Doesn't seem possible, François! You'll be forty-eight."

"Don't mention that to anyone. Even Jeanne-Victoire! I don't want anybody to know my birthday."

"Very well, *chéri.* Perhaps on your fiftieth anniversary we can have a little celebration."

"Forty-eight! I feel half my age. Some days."

"Twenty-four?"

"On a good day." He laughed and got to his feet. "Sleep well . . ."

"Much too hot. I'll be reading half the night." Reaching for her spectacles. "Fleuride spent most of the evening with Jeanne-Victoire."

"Did she?" He headed toward the corridor.

"They like each other." Pushing the spectacles onto her nose again. "I was hoping they would."

"I'll stop in and see Jeanne-Victoire before I go out again. Good night, Maman." He closed the door and went toward his wife's suite. Annoyed to be reminded that he was facing another birthday. At least no one at Number Six knew his age or date of birth.

The foyer to Jeanne-Victoire's suite was lighted, as usual, by a single candle in a Sèvres holder.

He left the door open and went toward the pair of inner doors standing open into the dimly lighted bedroom. Hesitated in the door-way, his eyes on the gold and ivory bed.

He crossed the room—conscious of his reflection in the tall mirror on his right—to the foot of the bed. His eyes were held by his wife's

131

delicate body, the long blond hair, and the pale oval of her face.

No nightingales singing tonight. Only rain striking against something metallic.

"Who are you, Monsieur?"

He smiled. "I am Vidocq."

She turned, holding out both arms. "And you still love me?"

"Always . . ." Taking her in his arms and kissing her on the forehead. "Did I wake you?"

"I haven't been asleep."

He released her gently onto the pillows. "What did those doctors say this afternoon?" Holding her hand as he talked.

"You'll have to ask your mother about that. I heard them whispering as they examined me—made me stretch out on my stomach while they patted my back up and down—but I couldn't understand their fancy words. Some of it was a foreign language.'

"When doctors get together they like to talk Latin."

"All they said when they finished was that I must rest and eat more. But I can't eat more than I do already."

"Did they prescribe any medicines?"

"Horrible tasting stuff! One of the maids got it from the apothecary."

"And how are you feeling tonight?"

"Weary . . . Except when Fleuride was here earlier.'

"You liked Fleuride?"

"She's a love. Still a child in some ways but, in others, already a young lady. And so beautiful! I've told her to come and see me whenever she wishes. She promised to show me her new wardrobe tomorrow. Imagine! At her age, getting wonderful Paris gowns . . ."

"Wouldn't you like some new gowns?"

"Where would I wear them? You know I don't go out anymore."

"What about tomorrow night? Don't you feel well enough to have dinner with us? We're taking Fleuride to a restaurant."

"I don't even have the strength to arrange my hair, and I wouldn't be able to decide which of my beautiful gowns to wear. No, François, I've no desire to go out." She squeezed his hand gently. "I'm happy, just to be here with you, chéri. Knowing you'll visit me before you leave in the morning and again at night when you return. That is enough, my love . . ."

"Perhaps you might eat more if we dined out."

"But I wouldn't. Remember the last time? You became angry when I barely tasted the delicious food."

"I wasn't angry. I've never been angry with you, my love. Never!"

"No. You haven't."

"Perhaps you'll invite Fleuride up every day to have lunch with you. Then you might eat something."

"What a lovely idea! We have so many things to talk about. Especially you."

"Me?"

"Fleuride asked me about you this evening. Dozens of questions!"

"Did she?"

"She's fascinated by your work. Apparently her parents frequently discuss you. I said you never mention Number Six to me."

"I wouldn't bother you or Maman with that."

"Fleuride's eager to meet you."

"I'll probably see her at breakfast." He raised her fingers to his lips. "Now I must leave you. I'll be out late tonight, so I won't wake you when I return." Resting her hand on the white sheet, he kissed her forehead again as he rose from the bed.

"Will I see you in the morning?"

"Of course!" He went toward the foyer. "I'm pleased that you and Fleuride like each other. I'll tell you what I think of her tomorrow."

"You'll like her, too. I promise . . ."

Her voice faded, blurred by the sound of the rain as he crossed the foyer and started down the corridor.

"You are Vidocq!" The words were whispered.

He turned, startled by the unexpected voice, and looked into the deep shadow cast by a tall cabinet. "Who is it?"

"I am Fleuride." She stepped forward into the light.

He saw that she was, as Jeanne-Victoire had said, a beautiful young woman. She was, in fact, extremely beautiful. He leaned down almost imperceptibly, to kiss her cheek.

Fleuride instantly stood on tiptoe and kissed him on the mouth.

He held her in his arms, supporting her on her toes, and pressed his lips firmly against hers.

She sighed then after a moment, pulled away, and released herself from his grasp. "We are cousins!"

"Yes."

"So I can kiss you."

"Naturally." He smiled, amused by her directness. "This is your first visit to Paris." They were, he realized, speaking in whispers. "I hope it will be a pleasant one."

"I've dreamed of coming here ever since I can remember. My parents talk about Paris every night at dinner. Papa reads the latest news about your work at Number Six! And Maman's proud of the fact that her dear sister is your mother. She says you're the most famous man in all France!"

"Only among criminals."

"There's so much I want to hear about! How you catch them, especially murderers. Do you approve of the guillotine, or are you sorry to see their poor heads chopped off? I wouldn't be! Except for some beautiful lady. Is there much blood?"

He didn't reply to the flood of questions but studied her lovely face. Brown eyes, slightly oval, rimmed by thick black lashes. Red lips, which as she chattered revealed perfect teeth, incredibly white against her olive flesh. Dark from the sun or inherited from her father? Glossy black hair in ringlets which danced as she talked. He saw that she had capable hands with strong fingers. Her body was plump but firm. He had felt her young breasts pressed against him as they kissed. Finally, he noticed that she was wearing a long yellow satin robe over a white nightdress.

" . . . and I've been hiding here in the shadow, waiting for you."

"How'd you know I was home?"

"Heard your voice from Tante's bedroom but couldn't understand a word either of you were saying. I was surprised, because Tante said you would be home after midnight . . ."

"Little Fleuride Maniez . . . Who is not so little anymore."

"I'm in love with you."

"What did you say?"

"I've loved you ever since Maman first told me about you. Years ago! I knew I loved you when I was very young and you came to visit us. I feel I know you from the letters your mother writes. Know all about you . . ."

"*Mon Dieu!* You don't know the meaning of love at your age."

"I'm seventeen."

134

"Sixteen."

"All right. Sixteen . . . I know all about love and marriage and . . ."

"You couldn't!"

"I was eager to come here because I wanted to see you again. Had to know if I was right."

"About what?"

"That I was really in love. Now I know that I am." Her eyes dropped for the first time, the long black lashes quivering on her cheeks. "One day I will be your wife . . ."

"What are you saying?"

"Jeanne-Victoire's been ill ever since you married her." The lids lifted again. "I would never do anything to distress Jeanne-Victoire or make her unhappy. Perhaps, after all, she won't die. In that case, I will come to Paris and be your mistress. And Jeanne-Victoire's best friend. I had to tell you this, my dear cousin, because I truly do love you . . ."

Vidocq reached to take her in his arms again, but she slipped away and ran down the corridor. He saw that her feet were bare, brown against the white marble floor. Smiling and shaking his head, mind whirling, he crossed the corridor to his dressing room. Opened the door and went in, closing it without a sound when he saw Balzac.

The writer, in his blouse and wrinkled trousers, sat at the dressing table facing the mirror. He was wearing a man's curly blond wig with black mustaches covering his own scraggly mustaches and an old-fashioned hat with a high crown perched on top of the wig.

Balzac noticed him in the mirror. "The effect might be better if I could find a blond mustache to match this wig."

"There are several in that lower row of boxes." Vidocq was reminded of Dumas, Marmosetta perched on his shoulder, both of them staring into that other mirror and making faces at their reflections. Balzac, however, recalled not Dumas but the animal. Even his cupped hands with their wiggling fingers looked like simian paws.

"I've always wanted blond hair." Balzac smirked and shrugged. "Instead of this dull black stuff my mother gave me." He pulled off the false mustaches and dropped them into a small cardboard box as he continued to study the effect of the wig with his meager mustaches. "And curls! Why couldn't I have been born with curls like Dumas, instead of these lank strands?"

"If you wanted curls like Dumas, you should've picked a West In-

135

dian for your father!" He saw that one of the wineglasses had been used and emptied. Removing the stopper from the decanter he filled two glasses with Burgundy as Balzac yanked off the hat and wig.

The young writer continued to study his mirrored image with disgust. "Why don't women find me more attractive?"

"You've had complaints?" He picked up the wineglasses and handed one to Balzac.

"No complaints, but they don't pursue me the way they go after Dumas. Or so he says." Raising his glass. "Your health!"

"And yours!" Vidocq tossed off the wine and saw that Balzac was sipping his reflectively.

"One day I will lose some weight." He sighed, studying his chins in the mirror. "Then all the beautiful females will follow me up and down the boulevards!"

"Dumas isn't thin." Vidocq set his empty glass down.

"He gets heavier by the month! I've warned him, in ten years he'll be twice my size." Sipping the wine. "This has been most interesting. Coming here . . . I tried on some kind of uniform jacket but it was too small." Another swallow of wine. "The newspapers say you're a master of disguise. You roam the streets at night, and even the criminals don't recognize you."

"The body and the voice are more important than the disguise."

"What do you mean?" He pushed his massive torso up from the dressing table and faced Vidocq.

"The wigs, makeup, and costumes are of course necessary, but the attitude of the body and tone of voice are what create a living character. Above all, I make myself think like the person I'm impersonating. Put myself inside his brain!"

"Think like him? That's interesting."

"I become this other person. Mind and body."

"How'd you learn to do that?"

"I suppose from observing actors when I was a boy. Several times I was given small parts with the players when they came to Arras. I learned how to observe people, imitate their characteristics. Changed my voice for each role. I watched the actors transform themselves every night. Observed the attention they gave to the smallest detail. Even today, in the street, I study people. Make mental notes, should I ever need to impersonate a similar individual."

"I'm always studying people. Observing them for characters I may one day use in a novel."

"Shall we go?" Vidocq took the lamp from the dressing table. "I'll have the coachman drop you wherever you wish."

"Boulevard des Italiens will be fine. I'll be working all night at another potboiler."

"When will you start putting your own name on these books?" He went ahead toward the door.

"Not until I've learned everything about writing a novel."

"But you've already had several published under various names."

"Three. The first one taught me how to describe backgrounds, and with the second I learned to make people move about against those backgrounds."

"And the third?"

"In that one I made them talk!" He followed Vidocq into the corridor. "Soon I shall know how to write a novel . . ."

CHAPTER 24

As Vidocq walked up rue de la Chaussée-d'Antin, he felt in his pocket and fingered the folded note Ève had sent to Tessier.

Boulevard des Italiens had been deserted, its restaurants and cafés empty. Waiters stood at windows, hoping for customers after the theaters closed.

Only two carriages were waiting in rue de la Chaussée-d'Antin. Most nights by ten o'clock, they were lined up on both sides of the street, wheels crowding together, drivers asleep.

As he passed the first carriage, he saw the coachman hunched down inside, smoking a pipe and staring out at the rain. An old carriage. No Frenchman would use a fine carriage in this weather.

He noticed several whores, their bonnets soggy with rain, huddled in doorways. On a good night they would be strolling the boulevards. How they must envy their prosperous sisters who lived in these fine mansions and never walked the streets anymore.

Distant church bells, faint in the rain, had sounded the half hour as his fiacre crossed the Pont-au-Change. Balzac had sighed at the sound and informed him that he was late starting work tonight but would be writing until dawn.

As the raindrops touched his mouth, he thought of Fleuride's lips. They had been a pleasant surprise. Sixteen years old and talking of marriage!

He was looking forward to her stay in Paris, but he should be wary whenever he was with her. Especially in the presence of his mother. Never tell her what Fleuride had said tonight.

They were cousins, he and Fleuride, and some people thought cousins shouldn't marry. Although there were several areas of France where cousins were actually ordered to marry. In parts of Brittany the custom was common.

Fleuride had said that if Jeanne-Victoire lived she would come to Paris and be his mistress. The idea was amusing . . .

It wasn't possible that Jeanne-Victoire was going to die. Not just yet! Those doctors with their rheumatic fevers and impaired hearts didn't know what they were talking about. She had told him, before their marriage, some doctor had warned her that one day she might become an invalid . . .

No carriages waiting in front of Ève's residence.

He looked up at her windows on the first floor. They were open, but no lights were visible in the front salon.

There had been gossip, which he'd never bothered to investigate, that Ève owned this fine old mansion and rented the ground floor to a family, but he'd never seen anyone going in and out of the downstairs apartment. Another rumor was that a wealthy admirer owned the mansion and had given Ève the first floor for as long as she wished to live here.

He stepped out of the rain under a stone arch and went through an inconspicuous door, down a long sloping passage, which had once been a public alley. Vaulted arches supported lanterns set far apart. There were no windows, and the cobbled passage remained in perpetual twilight.

Only a few of Ève's closest acquaintances knew the passage existed, and he'd never met anyone in the past on those nights he hadn't wished to enter through the front entrance with its uniformed porter. Tonight he was earlier than usual. Ève never received guests before ten o'clock, and supper wasn't served until after midnight.

Another low door at the end of the passage opened into a glass-enclosed greenhouse overflowing with luxuriant plants. Several had exotic blossoms he'd never been able to identify. Lighted lanterns hung among them, and the scented air was unpleasantly humid.

He followed a path between rows of tall plants in porcelain pots to reach another door, which opened into a narrow hall hung with patterned red silk and lighted by more hanging lanterns. A steep wooden staircase carpeted in scarlet led up two flights to the first floor.

These steps brought him to an elaborately carved door, which was left unlocked whenever Ève was free to welcome her intimates.

He grasped the carved ivory knob and turned it, relieved to feel the heavy door swing open under his pressure.

Warm air, heavy with Ève's familiar perfume, enveloped him.

Vidocq smiled in anticipation as he crossed an antechamber where the furniture, to his surprise, was unfamiliar. Ève had refurnished her apartment again! This happened at least twice every year.

He went toward the door straight ahead and opened it cautiously, reaching up to silence the small bell overhead, attached to a coiled spring. Slipping inside, he didn't release the bell until he had closed the door again. It gave only the faintest tinkle.

This was the central corridor of the apartment. He hesitated, listening for voices, while his eyes adjusted to the dim radiance coming from the painted globe of a large oil lamp on a table toward the front. Another hour, and a dozen lamps would be lighted.

Starting down the silent corridor, now that he could make out several unfamiliar pieces of antique furniture, he saw a formidable dark shape emerge from Ève's private suite. As this unexpected female came closer, he saw that she was wearing black satin with a white apron around her waist. The looming figure was imposing. She had elaborately crimped white hair, but he was unable to see her face against the glow of that distant lamp.

"Yes, Monsieur?"

"You're new here?"

"Several weeks now."

Her voice, to his surprise, was not harsh but curiously pleasant.

"I wish to see Mademoiselle Ève."

"Ah, Monsieur Vidocq! She's just out of her bath."

"You know me, do you?"

"I will inform Mademoiselle that you're here."

He followed her down the scarlet-carpeted corridor and saw her black skirt whisk out of sight through the double doors that stood open into the small salon leading to Ève's boudoir. Later tonight this would be thronged with visitors—all masculine—but now it was empty. Crossing the salon he heard a murmur of feminine voices in the boudoir. Ève, as usual, was laughing.

The inner doors were ajar behind a familiar golden screen with carved cherubs framing painted panels that depicted courtiers pursuing nude ladies through a formal garden. One panel that always caught his eye showed a delectable female bottom disappearing through a spraying fountain, which had drenched and delayed her pursuer.

He glanced around the luxurious anteroom furnished with golden chairs and sofas upholstered in white satin—none of which he'd seen before—all very feminine and expensive-looking in the light from the only candelabrum that was lighted. Everything new since his last visit, except for that golden screen.

He suddenly remembered poor Clochette's apartment . . .

Then he noticed one other familiar object, an unlighted oil lamp on one of the white and gold tables. Similar to a dozen other lamps scattered through the apartment. Each globe had a painted scene with a nude nymph and a top-hatted boulevardier shown against familiar Parisian locales. The unusual thing was that all the nymphs unmistakably had Ève's face and golden-red hair.

A marble fireplace that in winter would blaze with burning logs was filled with potted white roses. Some were wilted from the day's heat.

"You may come in, Monsieur Vidocq."

He turned to see that the maid had appeared from behind the golden screen and was motioning for him to enter the boudoir. He swept off his hat as he passed her and glanced at the allegorical painting, more luscious nude bodies, covering the back of an enormous mirror that prevented curious eyes from looking into the boudoir.

Two things, as usual, caught his immediate attention whenever he entered Ève's candlelit boudoir. First the voluptuous figure, plump and enticing, seated at the elaborate dressing table in an alcove, golden-red hair flowing over her bare shoulders and down the back of the chair. She was stroking her lovely hair with golden brushes. And the huge ebony serpent, its scales edged with gold, coiled around the rumpled bed. Its head was poised high above the lacy pillows with an immense gold apple clutched between its black jaws and held by golden fangs.

"Vidocq!" The voice of the eternal enchantress—Lilith, Helen, and Ève—fluted from the alcove. "Is it really you?"

His attention returned to her exquisite figure. "Yes, *chérie.*" He rested his hat on a chair as he crossed the boudoir toward the pink body, which was the most exquisite and expensive object here.

"I didn't expect you tonight." Ève was seated on a tufted white satin chair, pink flesh glowing in the light from a pair of gilt candelabrum on her dressing table. She put down the hairbrushes and held out both hands. "What are you doing here at this early hour?"

He glimpsed the soft golden-red curls of her armpits as he took her hands, the gold-flecked eyes as he bent to kiss her, breathing deeply of her perfume. "I felt a sudden impulse to see you."

"It's been weeks!" She turned to study her exquisite breasts in the large mirror, supporting and stroking one of them enticingly. "I did see you, last evening, in the Bois."

"You recognized me?"

"Recognized your coachman. Didn't tell the others—Maya or Apolline—that it was you. Although they were curious about the faceless man who didn't stop his carriage."

"I'd driven out from the city to escape the heat before dinner. Had no intention of disturbing you." As he talked, he realized that the faint golden pelt, barely visible on her flesh, was arousing him again, as it did all men. "You've done your apartment over since I was here."

"A new admirer. Even richer than the last."

"Congratulations."

"He insisted I have a decorator change everything."

Vidocq smiled, knowing she would have wheedled him into paying a large price for the changes. "At least you kept your famous screen and those lamps with pictures of Ève's tour of Paris."

"I'll never get rid of those!"

A sudden rumble of thunder made her squeal.

Vidocq laughed, glancing toward the open windows in their deep embrasures.

"Another storm?" She shivered. "I'm terrified of lightning."

"It was raining when I came in."

"Then I shouldn't have many guests tonight." She raised her voice toward the bedroom. "Madame Sidoné!"

"Mademoiselle?"

"It's chilly. I think I'll go back to bed . . ."

"I'll have it ready in a moment."

Ève looked up at Vidocq. "I've a surprise for you, *chéri.*"

"I don't enjoy surprises."

"This should amuse you." Rising from the dressing table, her hair falling in a soft curtain below her hips. "I have a new maid."

"Maids do not amuse me. How long have you had this one?"

"Less than a month." She took his hand and led him into the boudoir. "She's a treasure!"

As they entered he saw that the maid had straightened the bed, turned down the white sheet and arranged the pillows.

Ève released his hand and went ahead. "Madame Sidoné! This is my good friend, Monsieur Vidocq . . ." She slipped into the bed and stretched out under the sheet.

The maid glanced at him, bowed, and moved down to the foot of the bed.

"Madame Sidoné?" Vidocq saw her face more clearly in the candle-light. "Haven't we met before, Madame?"

"Many years ago, Monsieur."

"Where was this?" He peered at her face, trying to recall.

"I used to have an—establishment—on rue Blanche . . ."

"Did you?" He moved closer.

"You came there many times. I was blond in those days . . ."

"Is it possible!" He embraced her with undisguised affection. "Sidoné Lurine! You had one of the finest houses in Paris."

"You were very kind to me in those days." She turned to Ève. "He helped me many times when I had trouble with the gendarmes."

"But then you disappeared." He edged around the bed, back toward Ève. "Where did you go?"

"I retired. Bought a place in the country, but rural life eventually became boring. I missed Paris. So here I am!"

"I heard she was back," Ève explained, "and persuaded her to come with me."

"Didn't want to open another place of my own." Sidoné shrugged. "Decided I'd rather work for one person."

"She's my sister and confidante." Ève touched her lips and tossed a kiss toward Madame Sidoné.

"And very happy to be here."

"I hope forever!"

"Now, if you'll excuse me, I'd better see what the chef is doing about supper." She turned and went toward the salon.

"Close those doors!" Ève called after her. "Tell everyone I'm out until eleven."

"Yes, Mademoiselle." She closed the double doors.

Another angry rumble of thunder.

Ève pulled the sheet higher, as though for protection. "You did enjoy your surprise, didn't you?"

"Made me feel years older. Which isn't pleasant, I assure you, because my anniversary is this week."

"Let me give you a party! Lots of new girls and some of your friends from Number Six."

"Certainly not! Nobody knows my birth date, even at Number Six, and that's how I intend to keep it."

"How old will you be?"

He laughed, moving closer to the bed. "I'll tell you that when you tell me your true age."

"Only my mother knew the date of my birth, and I lost track of her years ago."

"Didn't your father know?"

"My mother didn't know who my father was."

"There must be an official record somewhere. I could check."

"Don't you dare! I've never told anyone where I was born. Gave a different city every time I've had to sign any papers or needed a new passport."

"I could arrest you for giving false information."

"You wouldn't do that!"

"No." He smiled. "I never would."

"You are a tease . . ."

Thunder crashed and echoed through the apartment.

Ève let the sheet drop from her shoulders and held out her arms to him. "Hold me! Please . . ."

He pulled off his jacket, tossed it onto a chair, and as he continued to undress, moved around the room blowing out candles.

"What are you doing?"

"I had a wise friend when I was young who claimed that love is always more satisfying in the dark."

"He was absolutely right."

"I thought she was."

"I should've known!"

He blew out the final candle and finished undressing in faint candlelight from the alcove. "A few offstage candles are enough."

"I can still see you." She pushed a long strand of hair away from her face. "You have muscles like an acrobat I saw years ago in the circus. But more hair!"

Vidocq circled the undulating ebony body of the serpent that formed the side of the bed. "I hope, next time you buy furniture, you'll get rid of this damn snake."

"My companion of a thousand nights?"

"Another reason I prefer the dark." He sank onto the bed beside her. "I've never liked snakes."

"Most men feel threatened. That's why I had that sculptor carve this bed for me. The black serpent's my protector."

"I never feel threatened." He glanced up at the monstrous jaws directly above his head, holding the gleaming apple. "I've heard several stories about that apple. Which is the true one?"

"You've asked me that before, *chéri*. But I will never tell you."

"Does it fall if you press a hidden device on your side of the bed?"

"What nonsense!"

"Smash my skull . . ."

There was a tremendous boom of thunder.

Ève screamed and thrust her body against his, squirming with pretended fright.

He laughed and placed an arm around her, stroking her soft flesh with his fingertips, breathing her expensive scent, easing her thighs apart. "They say your precious apple opens and releases a shower of golden louis. What's the truth?"

"You'll never find out," she murmured, into his ear. "There has to be at least one secret in Paris you don't know."

"There are many . . ."

Another cannonade of thunder, followed by torrents of rain.

Their bodies reacted to the surge and sweep of the storm with rhythms of their own.

As he buried his face in the flaming mass of her hair, still damp and perfumed from the bath, he thought of another body beneath him.

Fleuride!

Her body would be smaller, more compact, younger . . .

As his own body performed with pleasure and precision, he kept his eyes closed and continued to imagine that other body. Her fingers would not be as experienced as these. Her flesh would be less knowing, and her tongue not like small darting serpents . . .

"I know all about love and marriage . . ."

He'd done nothing to make her say that. Had intended only to kiss her, with cousinly affection, on her cheek.

"One day I will be your wife . . ."

He didn't want Jeanne-Victoire to die . . .

He'd known several cousins who had enjoyed unusually happy marriages . . .

What about children? They said if cousins had children . . .

He didn't want children! Had never wanted children . . .

"Where are you, *chéri?*"

He opened his eyes slowly and was surprised to see Ève's lovely face. Golden-red hair instead of black curls.

"You were thinking of another woman."

"What makes you say that?"

"I always know when a man does." She laughed. "Hundreds of men must think of me when they're making love to their wives."

"I wouldn't be surprised." Relaxing on his back, extending both legs and looking at his feet in the enormous mirror beyond the foot of the bed. He realized that his chest was beaded with perspiration. He had told Cauler earlier that it was too warm for love tonight. "That damn mirror. Always watching. If it ever talked . . ."

"It wouldn't dare!"

This was the moment, with Ève beside him, to ask several questions. "Tell me, *chérie,* do you know a man named Tessier? Narcisse Tessier . . ."

"So that's why you're here tonight!"

"I never need a reason to visit you. Other than my need to enjoy your exquisite body again."

"Have you found out who shot him?"

Her question surprised him. "When did you hear he'd been killed?"

"Late this afternoon. You're looking for his murderer?"

"Not at the moment."

"I should hope not!" She laughed, shaking the bed. "Although there'll be several gentlemen arriving for supper who will be delighted to hear that Tessier is dead."

"He was disliked?"

"All men have enemies, rich men more than others."

"Was Tessier rich?"

"He was called the King of Diamonds."

"You knew him?"

"Casually."

"Intimately?"

"He was never in this bed, if that's what you're suggesting. One snake's quite enough."

"You didn't like him?"

"I don't like his kind."

"He was here frequently?"

"Perhaps once a month. He admired young girls who could sing. Usually had one living with him but all they did was eat together. After she sang for her supper. Which must get terribly boring for a girl. Since he ate very little."

He pushed himself up from the bed as they talked and circled the boudoir, retrieving his clothes. "He was your neighbor. Only two or three streets away. Did you ever visit him on rue Taitbout?"

"Several times."

"Why?"

"Are these questions official? Or social?"

"Social. For the moment." He pulled on his trousers.

"Warn me when they become something else."

"Why did you visit Tessier if you didn't like him?"

"I liked his diamonds. I was always taken there by an—admirer . . ."

"Ah!"

". . . who arranged for Tessier to design a piece of jewelry especially for me. His creations were the finest in Paris. Some say in all of Europe!"

"Were these creations he designed for you, by any chance, made with diamonds?"

"Lovely big stones!"

"You still have them?" He sank onto a *bergère* to pull on his socks and boots.

"Of course I have them. All of them." Her voice hardened. "I never return any presents to a lover. Even if I return the lover! Send him back to his wife."

"Who were Tessier's close friends?"

"I've no idea."

A bell sounded, far away in the apartment.

He asked his next question abruptly. "What do you know about the Midnight Club?"

"Very little."

"But you've heard of it?" Rising from the *bergère*.

"I lost interest in the place when I learned that women wouldn't be allowed to dine there. Imagine! Not even respectable women . . ."

He picked up his ruffled shirt. "Did you ever hear Tessier mention that he was a member?"

"Never. He didn't talk much at the table. Can't you stay for supper tonight?"

"Another time."

"I must warn you . . ."

"Yes?"

"Move cautiously, if you plan to investigate the Midnight Club."

"Why do you say that?"

"I've always had a feeling—there's danger there."

"I enjoy danger." He finished tying his cravat and reached for his jacket.

"Important men are involved. Rich and powerful men . . ."

"What are you telling me?"

"Nothing. I simply have a feeling. Any place that doesn't permit female guests . . ."

"I am grateful for your warning." He shrugged his arms into the jacket and felt in his pocket for the folded note. "Tomorrow morning I'll return to rue Taitbout and continue my investigation of Tessier's murder."

"I heard he was found with a bullet in his head."

"Your information is accurate. He was seated at his desk when an unknown intruder fired a single shot."

"Couldn't it have been suicide?"

"The pistol was missing. Without that it can't be suicide."

"Oh . . ."

"You wrote a note to Monsieur Tessier. Earlier this week . . ."

"I?" She sat up in the bed. "Are you trying to involve me in murder?"

The bell rang again in the distance.

147

"You complained that he hadn't dined here recently." He pulled the note from his pocket.

Her eyes were held by the fold of notepaper. "Where'd you get that?"

"From Tessier's desk." He handed it to her. "I found this with several other letters."

There was a discreet series of light knocks.

"Enter!" Ève called, without looking up from the note.

Vidocq snatched up his hat and set it on his head as Madame Sidoné came in with a tray of food.

"Forgive me, Madame. Thought I should warn you on my way back from the kitchen. Your guests are arriving. I've told them you won't be home until after eleven."

"Let them wait in the front salon." She raised her eyes from the note and looked at Vidocq. "Why did you bring this to me?"

"So that nobody else would find it."

"Oh . . ."

He moved toward the door, pausing to inspect the food on the silver tray. "What do we have here?"

Madame Sidoné held the tray up for him to see. "Young larks the chef stuffed for supper. They're cool enough to eat."

"Are they?" He picked up a bird by one tiny leg and popped it into his mouth. The flesh was tender, the stuffing fragrant with tarragon. "My compliments to your chef." He turned to see Ève leaning forward in the serpent bed, still holding the note. "I suggest you burn that."

She smiled. "Thank you, *chéri.*"

As he followed Madame Sidoné out of the boudoir, he crunched the delicate bones between his strong teeth.

"Vidocq!" Ève called after him. "Be careful . . ."

"Always." He licked his fingers.

CHAPTER 25

Vidocq strode across the dim dining room, past the polished oak table his mother had brought to Paris from Arras—it had survived a dozen moves since the death of his father—and saw that the gardens beyond

148

the shadow of the mansion were shimmering in bright sunshine.

His mother, seated with her back to the windows, was already eating breakfast on the shaded terrace. Her gray curls bobbing, the satin ribbons on her nightcap fluttering like small violet butterflies, as she poured herself more coffee and hot milk.

The rain had stopped as he drove home from rue de la Chaussée-d'Antin, last night, leaving the air fresh and cool, but this morning it seemed as uncomfortably warm as yesterday. The glare of sunlight on the distant flowers gave promise of still another hot day.

He leaned down and kissed the top of his mother's lace nightcap. "Good morning, Maman."

"Ah, François!" She continued pouring twin streams of coffee and milk into the Limoges bowl. "You slept well?"

He shrugged as he sat in his customary place, on her right.

"I went to sleep immediately, after you left my room." Setting the porcelain pot down. "Were you out late?"

"Didn't notice what time I came in." Unfolding his napkin as he glanced at the empty place across the table, set for Fleuride.

"I'll ring for your coffee." She picked up the silver bell and shook it briskly. "Before I fell asleep, I heard voices in the upstairs hall. Was it you?"

She had heard him talking to Fleuride! "Tried to keep my voice low, so we wouldn't disturb you. I'd brought Balzac home with me."

"That young writer you've told me about?"

"Been promising, for months, to show him my disguises."

"How nice!"

"I suppose Fleuride's sleeping late ..."

"She was up ahead of me! Telling the gardener how they plant things in Arras."

"Didn't she want any breakfast?"

"She waited to eat with you. She's making a special omelette for the two of you."

"Hope she doesn't annoy cook."

"Cook adores her." She looked around as the two maids appeared.

Vidocq smiled, as always, at sight of their fresh young faces. "Good morning, Prudence! Rosine!"

They responded together. "Good morning, Monsieur!"

He watched as Prudence set a brioche in front of him and Rosine placed the coffeepot to his right.

"Where's my niece?" Madame Vidocq asked.

"She's coming," Rosine answered.

He looked toward the open windows as Fleuride hurried out from the dining room in the same yellow robe she had worn last night, bearing a silver-lidded platter as the maids returned inside.

"Here it is, Tante! You're certain you won't have some?"

"None for me, dear child. Eggs tend to colic me in the summer."

Fleuride smiled at Vidocq as she set the platter in front of him and removed the silver lid. "Voilà! Omelette Fleuride!"

He saw that it was a magnificent specimen, plump and crusty. "You made this?"

"I always make one at home, Sunday mornings."

Madame Vidocq peered at the omelette as though it might explode. "How many eggs?"

"Only four." She kissed Vidocq suddenly, on the cheek. "Good morning, cousin!"

"Good morning, cousine!" He saw that his mother was beaming.

"Permit me to divide it." Fleuride picked up a silver serving fork and sliced the omelette in half.

He leaned forward, inhaling the aroma escaping from its center. "Ah! If I were a gourmet, I would name each of your ingredients from this combination of scents."

"What's in it?" Madame Vidocq asked.

"See if he can tell when he eats it." Fleuride placed the omelette halves on two plates, handed one to Vidocq then carried the other to her place and sat down as the maids brought her a warm brioche, hot milk, and fresh coffee. Opened her napkin, then broke off the top of her brioche and ate it greedily.

He reached for his fork. "Maman says you were up early."

"Not so early as at home. Before breakfast I have to feed the chickens and milk our goat."

"Do you!" He cut into the omelette. Found it crisp outside and melting in the center. He took a first and sizeable bite.

"Well?" His mother was watching him.

"Best omelette I've ever tasted . . ."

"I prefer a plain one-egg omelette with a bit of grated cheese."

"This has cheese. Taste it, Maman." He held the second forkful toward her. "I've never eaten better in the finest Paris restaurant!"

Madame Vidocq took it, delicately, as though it might scorch her tongue.

They waited for her reaction, as she chewed vigorously.

She smiled and swallowed. "You are my dear sister's daughter! She was always a better cook than I."

Fleuride squirmed with pleasure. "You really mean that, Tante?"

"Before you leave, you must give this recipe to cook. I can see François likes it."

He only grunted, his mouth full of omelette and brioche.

"What do you think is in it?" Fleuride asked.

"I suspect duck liver," Vidocq began, "along with the cheese but something else . . ."

"There are many other things!" She laughed. "I will tell cook all but one. That I'll leave out so you'll have a true Omelette Fleuride only when I'm here to fix it for you myself."

Madame Vidocq turned to her son. "She's going to make someone a good wife. Aren't there any healthy young men at Number Six who are ready for marriage?"

He looked at Fleuride across the table and saw that she was amused by his mother's questions. Eating with appetite but watching him with twin devils in her eyes. "Fleuride wouldn't want to marry a policeman."

"But I would!" she announced, tearing her brioche apart. "I would certainly like to live in Paris. And I'd be happy to marry a policeman if he were like you, Cousin François."

"Why would you want a policeman for a husband?" he asked. "What possible reason?"

"Because it would be such an exciting life!"

"Never home! Always bad tempered . . ."

"That's not true!" Madame Vidocq exclaimed. "You're like your dear father. Never bad tempered!" Turning to her niece. "You should marry the owner of a nice dry goods shop. They always make a good living. Provide a comfortable home and . . ."

"Not the owner of a dry goods shop!" Fleuride set her fork down.

"Why not?" Her aunt looked displeased. "It's a steady job, and you meet the best people if it's a smart shop in the center of town. I managed several such establishments after I left Arras and eventually had one of my own. François worked in all of them."

"I enjoyed working in a shop." Vidocq wiped his mouth with the napkin and put it aside. "Liked to observe the people. Realized, even then, that many of them were criminals. While others were only fools." He raised his voice, imitating a snobbish woman. "Tell me, Madame Vidocq! Is this material really crépe de Chine?" Then giving an uncanny re-creation of his mother's voice. "Absolutely, Madame. Handmade by the finest Chinese virgins."

Fleuride and his mother laughed together.

And suddenly Vidocq was reminded of how his mother had laughed when his father made jokes.

She looked at him, aware of his sudden silence. "What is it?"

"The way you laugh, Maman. I remember how it was when Papa was alive. How we all laughed. The three of us."

Madame Vidocq sighed. "Ours was a happy home. Except you were always leaving us, running away, even then . . ."

"Why did you run away?" Fleuride asked. "If you were happy."

"Because I was always being pursued by the gendarmes!"

"Unjustly." Madame Vidocq explained. "I still don't like gendarmes."

"There was another reason. Why I was always leaving home . . ."

"What other reason?" Fleuride leaned forward, fascinated. "There've been many times I wanted to run away but, if you're a girl, it's more difficult."

"I wanted to travel," Vidocq explained. "See all the foreign countries I'd read about in books. I dreamed of sailing off to the United States of America."

"So do I!"

"I'd read everything I could find about its great cities. Especially one city—Phil-a-del-phia!"

Fleuride giggled. "That's a funny name!"

"I've always dreamed of going to Phil-a-del-phia and making my fortune. I still want to go there. Someday . . ."

"I would be afraid of the Indians. I read about them when I was in school." Her eyes sparkled as she talked. "The nuns found the book I was reading and burned it."

"I studied with the Franciscans." He glanced at his mother. "They gave me a fine education."

"They certainly did." Madame nodded her head vigorously.

"Tutored me in Greek and Latin. Encouraged me to recite scenes from classic plays." Using a dramatic voice as he declaimed. " ...'and it's no more a passion hidden in my veins! 'Tis the goddess—Venus, herself—fastened on her prey' ... How's that?"

Fleuride applauded.

"The fathers taught me to enjoy books, and to this day reading gives me great pleasure."

"I wanted him to have a good education," Madame Vidocq murmured, "hoping he would become a priest."

"Papa thought I should be a baker, but I didn't want to be a priest or a baker."

"Did you want to be a policeman?" Fleuride asked.

"Like one of those stupid gendarmes who were always pursuing me? The idea never entered my head. At one point I did think I might like to be an actor, but that didn't last."

"I should hope not!" His mother sniffed. "Actors ..."

"That was also because I wanted to travel. Actors are always going from city to city, and I suppose even then I liked to play different roles. Imitate people ..." He realized that Fleuride had been watching him intently.

"Could I come to Number Six while I'm in Paris?" she asked, rising from the table and standing with one hand on her aunt's shoulder. "Observe you at work?"

"Someday perhaps, when you're a little older."

"Oh."

Madame Vidocq shrugged. "He never lets anyone visit Number Six. Even his mother! Not that I would ever ask to go there."

He glanced from face to face, his mother and her young niece. "It's amazing! How much you're alike. The two of you."

Madame Vidocq studied her niece's features. "I was aware of a family resemblance, yesterday, when she stepped down from the diligence. Fleuride looks exactly like her dear mother, except for the black hair, and her mother and I were always thought to resemble each other."

"I'm glad that I do." Fleuride kissed her on the cheek. "Now I must see if Jeanne-Victoire's breakfast is ready. I promised to bring it to her." She turned, moving quickly toward the open windows.

"We'll be dining out tonight!" Vidocq called after her.

"I plan to eat an enormous dinner!"

He laughed as he watched her go inside.

"Where will we dine?" his mother asked.

"I thought she might enjoy the Café de Paris."

"And how do you like your little cousin?"

"Very much."

"The child's certainly not shy. Always managing things. Just like her mother!"

"Also like you, Maman."

"I suppose . . . She's a dear girl! Seems very wise for her years. Perhaps a little too wise. When I was her age, I wasn't quite that knowing. Young people these days are so different."

He pushed his chair back and rose from the table. "The Revolution freed people, I think, in ways they don't yet begin to realize or understand. It's certainly affected the youth of France. And for the better."

"I wonder . . ." She frowned, puzzled by the thought.

He bent to kiss her forehead. "Spend all the money you want when you take her shopping. There's plenty more." He headed for the open windows. "I'll see Jeanne-Victoire before I leave."

"What time will you get home this evening?"

"I'll do my best to be early. Tell cook I'll want a hot bath. Let's dine at eight-thirty." He smiled, anticipating a pleasant evening, as he went inside, circling the dining room table and hurrying upstairs to his wife's suite.

Jeanne-Victoire was waiting for him, sitting up in the white and gold bed. She held out both arms, the sleeves of her négligée falling in a froth of lace.

"Good morning, *chérie* . . ." He kissed her pale forehead.

"Good morning, *mon amour* . . ." She hugged him.

He straightened to look down at her radiant face. "How are you today?"

"Much rested. I slept better last night. I think having Fleuride in the house has helped. How do you like her?"

Vidocq sat on the side of the bed, facing her. "Very much. I've just told her she reminds me of Maman."

"I know! The way she gives orders . . ."

"It will be pleasant having her here." He chose his words with care. "A young—child—in our home."

"I love children!"

"You've never said that before."

"I suppose because I'll never be able to have one of my own."

"Why not?"

"Doctor Morain warned me last year that I should never try. Because of my heart . . ."

He saw tears in her eyes. "You never told me."

"I was afraid you would be disappointed. That one day you might want me to give you a son."

"*Mon Dieu!* A small Vidocq? Never."

"A small Vidocq . . ." She laughed.

It was the first time he'd heard her laugh in many weeks. "What a horrible thought! One Vidocq is quite enough. I'm going to be late." Rising and starting toward the foyer. "We're dining out with Fleuride this evening. Wish you could be with us. I'll see you when I come home to dress . . ."

"Breakfast's served, Madame Vidocq!" Fleuride swept in, a fresh white apron over her yellow robe, carrying a breakfast tray. She smiled as she passed him. "And Madame's going to eat her breakfast this morning! That's an order."

Striding down the corridor toward the front staircase, he heard their laughter. Like happy children.

CHAPTER 26

Vidocq sat, his back to the open windows, staring at the large map spread across the morning dossiers and reports that covered his desk. Checking each red circle Aubé had drawn. He had been studying them since the end of a brief and unproductive staff meeting, hoping to discover the secret he suspected they might hold. He had examined the map from every angle but learned nothing.

Blue arrows indicated the directions Le Diable Noir and his band of cutthroats took on those nights when they were observed by some farmer or villager who had been roused by the thunder of horses' hooves and their rumbling carts. A parallel blue arrow always returned toward the north, the direction from which they had come. So they must have a hideaway near Paris where they brought their booty.

Aubé had inscribed a date at the site of each robbery and listed the time under every arrow when the horsemen and their procession of carts had been seen or heard.

Monsieur Pennypacker would have an unlimited letter of credit on a Paris bank and would pay Le Diable Noir with gold that could never be traced. Those stolen objects could be carried aboard ships in the night and never be seen again. Impossible to locate them once they reached the United States.

He got to his feet and, eyes on the map, paced around the desk once more. From this angle, looking down, the circles drawn around each château were like red-rimmed coins scattered across the map.

He'd seen only one of those great châteaux—Chambord—and that was years ago when he'd been making his way to Paris by begging rides. The farmer who was carting a load of cabbages to the city had waved his whip toward the stone turrets poking up from the morning mist . . .

A knock interrupted his thoughts.

"Enter!" He didn't turn his head as he heard one of the doors open, then familiar footsteps approaching. "You did an excellent job with this map." Without looking around, he sensed Aubé standing behind him. "But you shouldn't have worked last night."

"I did it this morning. Couldn't sleep, so I came in before dawn and checked through those reports. Marked every village where Le Diable has been seen . . ."

"I know this map has something to tell me—a secret to reveal—but as yet I've not discovered what it may be." He moved around the desk to sit in his leather armchair facing Aubé. "Any word from Ronquetti about Penny-packaire or his daughter?"

"This early?"

"If there's a message from him later, I'll be at the Tessier mansion. Have it brought to me there."

"How long will you be at rue Taitbout?"

"Most of the morning. After that I may stop by the Hôtel Belvedere myself, if there's been no word from Ronquetti."

"I came to tell you, there's someone waiting—an old man—with a note from Monsieur Tessier's administrator."

"Is that what Drumont calls himself? Administrator ..." He

shrugged. "He's certainly the keeper of the jewels. Send the old man in." Folding the map and slipping it into a drawer as Aubé went toward the antechamber.

His morning staff meeting had turned up nothing new on the Tessier murder. The Rat and the Nun learned less than usual from their inquiries on rue Taitbout. Tessier's neighbors knew little about him. They had never seen him, except from a distance, driving past in his carriage.

A small figure appeared in the open doorway and bowed.

"Come in, my friend." He saw, as the old man—hat in hand—stepped into the light from the windows, that his appearance was ghostly. Thin gray hair and pale face, worn gray clothes, even the ruffles of his white shirt had turned gray from many washings. He bowed with an air of old-fashioned elegance. It was Tessier's majordomo, who had worn a powdered wig and gray satin livery yesterday.

"Monsieur Vidocq . . ." His hand, holding a white envelope across the desk, wore a gray cotton glove that had been carefully darned. "This is from Monsieur Drumont who instructed me to give it to no one but you."

"Sit down. There may be an answer." He ripped open the envelope and slid out a folded sheet of paper. Revolved in his chair toward the light in order to read what was written.

> Monsieur Vidocq . . .
> I have completed an inventory of all the jewels,
> uncut stones as well as completed pieces of jewelry.
> Everything is accounted for, nothing missing.
> If I can be of further service to you, please command me.
> Your servant,
> Alcidor Drumont

The signature brought Drumont's face to mind. Pockmarked sallow skin and darting, furtive eyes. The image was unpleasant.

He turned to see that his visitor had remained standing. The hat held in his hand seemed to be trembling, and the old man's face was ashen. "Sit down! Sit down!"

"Oh, no, Monsieur." Even his voice was quivering. "I am not permitted to do that."

"This is my private office, and I order you to sit down. At once!" The command seemed to intimidate the old man, and the frail body began to sway. Vidocq tossed the note onto his desk and sprang to his feet. Hurried to grasp the old man's arm, felt the delicate bone through the thin sleeves. "What is it, Monsieur? What's wrong?" Easing him into an armchair as he called toward the antechamber. "Aubé! A bottle of cognac. Quickly!" He heard Aubé calling to the guard as he left the old man in the chair, hat resting upon his knee, and sat on the edge of his desk, facing him. "You didn't walk here in this heat?"

"I always walk. Monsieur Tessier never allowed me to use his carriage. Even Monsieur Drumont doesn't ride in it. Only Monsieur Tessier. When he went out to dine at some private residence or visit the Midnight Club ..."

"Did he frequently go to the Midnight Club?"

"Several times each week I would hear him direct the coachman to take him there."

"And would he remain out for the entire evening?"

"I would wait up for him to return home. Which was never before two in the morning, frequently not before dawn ..."

"Keeping you up all night?"

"I was able to nap on a sofa in the downstairs salon. The sound of his carriage wheels always roused me. He never discovered I slept there." Breathing more easily now, the color returning to his face. "Monsieur Tessier wasn't a bad master ..."

"Chief?"

Vidocq rose as a guard hurried in with a tray holding an open bottle of cognac and two glasses. "Leave that on my desk." He was aware that the old man's eyes were drawn to the bottle as the guard carried it past him. "Thank you, my friend."

The guard touched his cap and departed.

Vidocq filled both glasses. "A cognac will revive you, and in a moment I'll take you back to rue Taitbout in my carriage."

"Oh no, Monsieur!" He attempted to rise from the armchair. "I must walk back."

"Nonsense! Sit down." Handing a glass of cognac to him as the old man sank into the chair. "I'd planned to pay another visit there this morning. You'll ride with me." Raising his own glass. "Your health!"

"And yours, Monsieur Vidocq!" Raising the glass to his lips and taking a swallow of the cognac.

Vidocq downed his glass. "You haven't told me your name."

"Ah!" He smacked his lips. "This is indeed a fine cognac. My name is Marpon—Auguste Marpon—but most people, even Monsieur Tessier, call me Marpon. Been years since anyone's called me Auguste . . ."

"I shall call you Monsieur Marpon."

The old man smiled for the first time, displaying a complete absence of teeth.

"How long had you worked for Tessier?"

"Five years, I believe . . . I'd been with Comte Guyon until his death. He was a friend of Monsieur Tessier's, and when Monsieur moved into the mansion on rue Taitbout he asked me to become his majordomo . . ."

"He moved there five years ago?"

"Before that he had a shop on rue Saint-Honoré, where he lived upstairs. I understand he bought the rue Taitbout property when he inherited a fortune from some relative . . ."

"Did he?" He realized that Marpon was growing more talkative with each sip of cognac. "Will you stay on there, now Tessier is dead?"

"Oh no, Monsieur. The staff's to be discharged. Monsieur Drumont informed me privately this morning. He will continue to work on the premises for the moment, but unfortunately he will require only the chef and one maid. All the rest of us are to go."

"What are your plans?"

"I have no plans, Monsieur. Everything's happened so quickly. It will be difficult, at my age, to find another employer . . ."

"You've probably saved some money."

"A little."

"You might live more cheaply in the country."

"I could never leave Paris. I was born here. Paris is like a wife one has loved for many years . . ."

"Does Monsieur Drumont live in the rue Taitbout mansion?"

"He only used an office there. I'm told he has an apartment of his own. I've never known where."

"Were they old friends—Drumont and Tessier?"

"From what Drumont has said at various times, I gathered he had known Monsieur Tessier for many years. In his youth, Drumont was in Africa. He still has contacts there, and I believe he was in charge of importing diamonds for Monsieur Tessier."

"Then he was a partner?"

"I suppose you might say that. He always paid the staff, and he's discharging them this morning. Even the goldsmiths and craftsmen. All those people you saw yesterday will be out of work."

"Including young Revol?"

"Oh, yes! He's the youngest designer, but Monsieur Tessier told me recently he's the most talented."

"What do you, personally, think of him?"

"Monsieur Revol? A fine young man. From an old family. All three of the designers are supposed to be among the best in Paris!"

Vidocq saw that Marpon had finished his cognac. "Let me have your glass." He took it from the gloved fingers and set it on his desk. "What personal things can you tell me about Tessier?"

"Personal? I don't understand . . ."

"You must've observed him during the five years you've been in his service. Peculiarities only you might have noticed. Seemingly unimportant things, perhaps, which appeared strange to you. Something odd he said one day or something unusual about the way he acted. Not only recently but at any time in the past."

"Nothing unusual." Marpon frowned. "No . . ."

"Who were his friends?"

"If he had any, I never saw them. They certainly didn't come to rue Taitbout. Only the rich people who bought his jewelry. And of course those young women who lived in the small suite next to Monsieur Tessier's private suite on the second floor."

"Young women?"

"They lasted, at most, a few months. Then there would be a scene, and he would order them to leave. A few actresses, but mostly singers. Always sopranos! They would be thin when they arrived, but before they left they all got fat from the food they ate. Mademoiselle Coralie was the last."

"Tell me about her."

"Coralie Clodin . . ."

"How long ago did she leave?"

"A matter of seven or eight months. Mademoiselle Coralie ate more than her sisters. She grew to be enormous, while Tessier remained thin. I served their dinner each night. Monsieur was a gourmet and ate very little, but he liked to see his young ladies enjoy themselves. Mademoiselle Coralie had been in the chorus at the Comique but had given up

160

singing professionally. She was the most pleasant of all the young ladies but the most demanding."

"You mean money?"

"And everything else! I heard her frequently pleading with Monsieur for one of his fine pieces of jewelry."

"What would he do?"

"Some evenings he would let her wear a few of the jewels while they dined. I've seen her fondle a string of pearls as though she was about to devour them."

"He never gave her the jewels to keep?"

"Not to my knowledge. I heard him tell her one night that he couldn't give her any because they didn't belong to him."

"What did he mean?"

"He didn't explain. Only that it was impossible to give so much as a single pearl to her or anyone else."

"They didn't belong to him . . ."

"I never felt he had real affection for any of these young ladies. He needed companionship. Someone to enjoy dinner with him. When he was alone, he scarcely ate anything."

"These dinners were elaborate?"

"The chef prepared at least six courses each night. Mademoiselle Coralie always ate two servings of dessert!"

"Delicious, I suppose . . ."

"The staff never tasted them. We had a good cassoulet or a *fricandeau* with, perhaps, a small slice of cheese. The fancy food was for Monsieur and his young ladies. Music was his other passion. But I suspect he liked diamonds best!"

"You've been helpful, my friend. Told me things I couldn't have learned from anyone else." Vidocq went to the table near the door, snatched up his hat and cane. "We'll go downstairs and get a carriage."

"This is very kind, Monsieur Vidocq." He got to his feet shakily and put on his ancient gray hat. "I never thought Number Six would be like this. A glass of cognac and a pleasant conversation."

"Number Six is never the same to any two people. It changes in relation to the innocence or guilt of each visitor. Come along . . ."

As they went toward the open doors, Vidocq made a mental note. Mademoiselle Coralie must be found and questioned . . .

CHAPTER 27

" . . . and Monsieur Tessier enjoyed going to the Opéra every week before it was closed, following the assassination of the Duc de Berry . . ."

Vidocq was barely listening to Marpon's rambling, his senses dulled by the heat and the swaying of the carriage. He peered from side to side as the old man chattered, observing the people crowding the streets in hot sunlight that had dried all the puddles. Haggard faces, as though nobody slept last night.

This heat would wither his rosebud before noon!

Glancing down, he was surprised to see that his lapel was empty. He'd forgotten to take one of the fresh yellow buds from his desk. No matter! It would have died.

Where was Calamatta today? Had he returned to his native Corsica and long ago been killed in some local vendetta? God forbid! That would prevent his ever achieving revenge . . .

What was the old man saying?

". . . and I believe, Monsieur, you mentioned earlier you wished to find Mademoiselle Coralie . . ."

"I'll put one of my assistants on that."

"Mademoiselle lives in rue de la Lune."

Vidocq came alert. "What did you say?"

"Number three. I've taken messages there many times. Always left them with the concierge if Mademoiselle wasn't home."

"Once again, Monsieur, you've been a help."

"I should've told you at Number Six, but you didn't ask me, and at the moment I was thinking of other matters."

"Were you?" He was amused to see that Marpon was seated like an aristocrat, leaning back against the cushions, his gloved hands folded. "At this moment, I'm thinking how many years it's been since I rode in a fine carriage. Not since before my wife and I fled to London . . ."

"You've been abroad?"

"We escaped to England before they seized the Queen and brought her from Versailles to Paris. That was a bad time."

"You were a Royalist?"

"By circumstance, not from conviction." The old man sighed. "I suppose one shouldn't admit that. Even today."

"It doesn't matter anymore, except with a few fanatics. So you were one of those who fled to England? You were fortunate."

"The Queen had warned us for months, my wife and I, that we should escape, but we stayed with her until a few weeks before the end."

"You and your wife knew Marie Antoinette?"

"My wife was one of her maids, and I was a personal valet to the King." He fumbled in a pocket of his waistcoat and brought out a small brooch, which he handed to Vidocq.

Holding it in his palm, Vidocq saw that it was a miniature of the Queen, mounted in gold and encrusted with jewels. "Where did you get this?"

"The Queen herself gave it to my dear wife before we fled. A token of her affection. You see, Monsieur, my wife was very like the Queen. She took her place many times in the royal coach when a double was required. My wife was much younger than I . . ."

Vidocq handed the brooch back. "This is precious, my friend. An heirloom."

"I will have no heirs." Marpon stared at the portrait. "It never leaves my person. Day or night."

"Your wife must be very beautiful."

"She was as beautiful as the Queen. And full of life! Both of them." He slipped the brooch into his waistcoat pocket again. "Both dead . . . The British climate killed my dear wife. We worked as maid and valet for an English milord and his wife, but the winters were too severe. My wife didn't survive. I was lost without her and returned to France. But it isn't the same. Paris has changed . . ."

"Paris is always changing." Vidocq saw tears in Marpon's eyes. Tears for a way of life that would never return. He looked away and realized that the carriage was turning up rue Taitbout. "We're nearly there!"

The old man straightened. "I think, Monsieur, I should leave you. It would not be wise for anyone to see me in your carriage."

Vidocq tapped on the overhead window with the head of his cane. "Stop here!"

The horses were reined in, and the carriage slowed to a halt.

"Give me a few moments before you ring the bell." Marpon struggled to his feet. "I will go through the alley to the rear entrance, and the servants will think I walked back."

"Tell no one of our conversation."

"Certainly not!" Opening the carriage door and stepping down to the pavement. "You can count on my discretion, Monsieur." He bowed formally and disappeared down a tree-shaded alley.

Vidocq sat for a moment, considering what he had to do inside the Tessier mansion. First of all he would question Drumont about his importing diamonds from Africa. Find out whether Tessier left a will and who were his heirs. He tapped on the overhead window again. "Drive on! But slowly."

The coachman's whip cracked, and the carriage moved up the street at a more leisurely pace.

When they reached their destination, Vidocq restrained himself for once, until the carriage came to a complete stop, before jumping down. Instructed the coachman to wait and, as he walked toward the entrance, inspected the facade of the mansion once more. It must have cost Tessier a fortune! The ground floor windows were open again, their golden curtains drawn back now. The upper windows also stood open, inner shutters folded out of sight.

He went up the marble steps, taking his time, and gave the bell pull a sharp jerk. Turned, leaning on his cane, to peer at the other mansions behind their walled gardens. No windows visible through the trees from which neighbors might observe who went in and out of the Tessier establishment. The sound of the door opening behind him made him turn to face Marpon, still in his shabby gray suit, bowing for him to enter.

"Monsieur Drumont's upstairs in his office," the old man whispered. "Shall I tell him you're here?"

Vidocq's eyes probed the entrance hall as Marpon closed the door. "No. Tell him you delivered his note to me, but there was no answer. That should puzzle him briefly." He walked toward the marble staircase, through a spill of light from the overhead skylight. "Wait fifteen minutes. Then inform him that I wish to speak to him in the salon."

"Fifteen minutes." Marpon walked beside him. "The chef informed me just now that Monsieur Drumont paid the staff in full to the end of next week and ordered them off the premises by noon."

"Including young Revol?"

"Everyone, except the chef and a maid. He left my money in an envelope."

"Don't leave, however. You may be of further help to me."

"My pleasure, Monsieur Vidocq."

"You will be paid to remain here. I'd hoped to see Revol ..."

"He's in the kitchen. Having a farewell glass of wine."

"Tell him not to go until I've talked to him." As Vidocq climbed the marble steps, he watched the old man heading for the central passage under the staircase.

The upstairs corridors were silent except for the sound of his heels on the marble floors.

He swung open one of the double doors to the salon where sunlight came through the open windows overlooking the gardens. Goury and Fouché were engaged in another systematic search of the room. Both heads turned when they heard the door open.

"We've about finished here," Goury announced.

"Examined every corner but found nothing." Fouché placed the books he was holding back on the shelves.

"All the papers in Tessier's desk appear to be unimportant." Goury closed the drawer he'd been examining.

"Shall we go over the other rooms again?" Fouché asked.

"Even more thoroughly than yesterday. Except Drumont's office. I'll do that one." Vidocq rested his hat and cane on the desk. "Did the ladies turn up anything more on this street?"

"Don't know yet. They're going from house to house separately, asking for work," Goury answered. "Talking to the servants, telling them they worked for Tessier. I told them to wait in the carriage when they finish until we're ready to leave."

"I want to sit here quietly for a moment. Visualize this room as it was at the moment Tessier was killed." He noticed that the massive armchair in which the jeweler died had been pushed to one side, against the wall, its tapestry seat stained with dried blood. A smaller *fauteuil* had replaced it at the elegant antique desk.

Which reminded him unexpectedly of that other desk at Galerie Marchadier.

As Vidocq sat at the desk, he was aware of the others leaving and closing the door.

Leaning back in the small *fauteuil*, he shut his eyes and imagined how it must have been here at the time of the murder.

He heard birds singing in the gardens ...

Were they singing yesterday? Had the pistol shot silenced them? Did they resume their singing as Tessier died?

He had a curious feeling that something was missing.

Vidocq opened his eyes and looked around. What was it that he missed?

That humming sound yesterday!

Now there was only silence.

Tessier must have had an appointment with his killer. Did that mean he knew him? Not necessarily. The bell hadn't rung while the staff ate lunch, so Tessier must have been downstairs watching for his visitor and brought him up here to discuss their business.

The murderer had sat facing him. Demanded that he be given diamonds . . .

But Drumont said no jewels were missing. What about money?

Had Tessier told the intruder there were no jewels here? And no money! Was that when he pulled out his revolver? Aimed it across the desk and fired . . .

"Monsieur Vidocq!"

He turned and saw Drumont coming through the panel in the *boiserie.*

"Marpon said you wished to see me."

"I'd like to ask several questions that have come to mind since our previous meeting."

"Of course! Anything I can tell you."

"Please . . ." Vidocq motioned to the other *fauteuil.* "I received your note reporting that none of the jewels are missing."

"Not a single stone." Drumont sat down, clutching both arms of the chair but smiling.

Vidocq sensed that the smile was contrived, the eyes evasive, the man ill at ease. His pockmarked face, which seemed sallow before, had a decided yellow cast in the reflected sunlight. Even the whites of his eyes were yellowish.

Mustn't allow his distaste for Drumont to affect his questioning. Start slowly. "First of all, did Monsieur Tessier keep money here?"

"In this room? Never."

"Nothing of value in this desk?"

"He kept all money and valuables in his private suite upstairs."

"A few personal jewels and some money were found there yesterday.

166

So the murderer apparently took nothing. Only Monsieur Tessier's life! Did Tessier leave a will?"

"He never mentioned any will. I'm certain if there'd been one, he would've told me."

Vidocq realized that his questions as yet hadn't troubled Drumont. His hands were no longer clasping the arms of his chair. "What about his family? Are they in Paris?"

"He's told me many times he had no living relatives."

"Where did he keep his personal papers? When we searched his suite, none were discovered. Nor here in his desk."

"He didn't have any."

"Every wealthy man has important letters, statements from banks. As well as countless documents concerned with business matters."

"I keep those in my office. All documents relating to his business, but among them you'll find nothing of a personal nature."

He was aware that Drumont, for the first time, was showing some discomfort. "Perhaps we can look through those documents . . ."

"Certainly! I'll be happy to show you everything."

"I suppose there are papers concerning the purchase of this property. I'm told Tessier bought it after he inherited money from a relative."

"But he didn't own this property."

"No?"

"He leased it. Monsieur Tessier, to my knowledge, never inherited anything from anyone!"

"Do you have a copy of that lease?"

"In my office."

"Excellent. What about those jewels you showed me yesterday? Did Tessier own them or only have them on credit?"

"He owned every stone! Imported them himself."

"I'm told that you were in charge of importing the diamonds."

Drumont's eyes became wary. "I have certain connections, from my visits to Africa, and arranged for Monsieur Tessier to meet several people, but I had nothing to do with importing diamonds into France."

"So I was misinformed." He shrugged. "I presume you have records, for the past five years at the very least, of all dealers who sold diamonds to Tessier? Names of importers . . ."

"Oh, yes!"

"I will come to your office and have a look at those documents. After that I'd like to see the jewels again."

"I'll be pleased to show you everything." Drumont rose. "Give me half an hour to get everything in order."

"Meanwhile I'll pay another visit to the atelier. I want to look at those designs again."

"I'll be waiting when you've finished." Going toward the open panel in the *boiserie*.

Vidocq waited until Drumont had disappeared, closing the panel behind him, before rising and walking to one of the open windows. Looked down at the sunny gardens through waves of mist rising from the moisture left by last night's rain. Turned to stand, his back to the windows, studying the salon again.

He thought of young Honoré's sketch. The dead man's faced blurred by the dried blood that had flowed from the hole in his forehead.

Leaving his hat and cane on the desk, he went to the panel in the *boiserie* and pushed it open. Stepped out into the corridor and headed toward the atelier.

He opened the atelier door cautiously and saw that the empty room was bright with sunlight. The tables where the designers had worked were bare. He went straight to the carved wooden cabinet and swung the doors back. The cardboard tubes rested as before in their initialed cubicles. Removing one at random from the compartment marked S, he carried it to the nearest table. Unscrewed the metal top and slid out the rolled sheet of paper. Spread it flat and studied the sketch, a design for an elaborate brooch. Leaned closer to read the inscription near the bottom: 20-DI-BRO-5-21-SA-RE-DE.

Glancing at the drawing, he saw that there were diamonds of graduated size, the largest in the center, surrounded by a setting of flying birds. The 20-DI meant twenty diamonds. He counted the stones and found that there were exactly twenty. BRO of course meant brooch and 5-21 was May 1821 . . .

SA, according to Revol, would be the first letters of the buyer's name. Confirmed by the fact that he had removed this tube from the S compartment. RE were the last two letters on the Pennypacker design. Revol hadn't known what they meant. And now RE-DE!

He returned the brooch design to the cabinet. Withdrew another tube and quickly opened it. This design showed an elaborate tiara with many stones. The inscription near the bottom was somewhat different: 100-DI-30-EM-80-PE-TIA-10-19-CO.

He studied the sketch more carefully and saw that the tiara was made of pearls and diamonds as well as other gems. Counting them carefully, he found there were indeed one hundred diamonds, eighty pearls, and thirty of the other stones. EM? Emeralds! The TIA was for tiara and 10-19 meant October 1819. CO must be the first letters of the purchaser's name.

But why didn't this inscription finish with RE or RE-DE?

He inserted the sketch into the tube and returned it to the cabinet.

"Am I disturbing you, Chief?"

He turned to face Revol. "Ah, my friend! I was coming in a moment to look for you."

"Monsieur Marpon told me you were in the upstairs salon, and when I didn't find you there, I knew you must be here."

"Good judgment." Smiling as he crossed the atelier to meet him. "You're starting to think like an investigator."

"Monsieur Aubé said yesterday that since I'm now working for Number Six I should call you 'Chief'."

"On formal public occasions. 'My friend' is sufficient at other times. I like to think every man at Number Six is my friend. From Aubé to the youngest stableboy. Now that you've explained how to read the inscriptions on these designs, I was able to decipher several more, all but those final pairs of letters—RE-DE—and, of course, the name of the purchasers. I found that some of these inscriptions don't have RE-DE at the end. And the Penny-packaire bracelet has only RE! Does that mean something?"

"I've no idea. Some of these designs were created before my time."

"I want you to take all these cardboard tubes to Number Six."

"All of them?"

"Tell Aubé to give you one of our empty offices. You can spend the afternoon deciphering the inscriptions as far as you're able. Find out, if you can, what RE-DE means. I suspect those four letters may be significant. Tell Goury you're to take them in one of the carriages, but send it back here immediately. I suppose you were paid this morning by Monsieur Drumont, with the other staff members."

"Paid to the end of next week. All of us were saddened at losing our jobs so unexpectedly. I feel especially sorry for the old man. Marpon . . ."

"I'm going to arrange for him to remain here for a while. With the chef and one of the maids. They're to be kept on temporarily. Monsieur Drumont will continue to manage everything while Tessier's estate is being settled. He calls himself 'administrator,' and of course he must be available until Tessier's murderer is found."

"Then I don't understand . . ."

"What?"

"I went to Monsieur Drumont's office just now, but he wasn't there. The door was open. Everything in disorder . . ."

"Drumont wasn't there?"

"No sign of him."

"Mon Dieu!" Vidocq rushed toward the open door. "I've been a fool!"

Revol followed him through the corridor.

Vidocq was running now, heels pounding on marble floors.

He paused in the open doorway, staring at the bare desk and empty shelves. All the leather boxes were gone, and the armoire doors stood open. He sprang into the armoire, the wooden boards cracking under his weight. At the back was the yawning black mouth of the empty vault. "The jewels are gone! With the gold and silver ingots! He's taken everything!"

CHAPTER 28

"Vidocq, you are an idiot," Vidocq murmured. "I've told you so before. A stupid fool!" He was hunched in a corner of his carriage, clutching his cane with both hands.

They had found no trace of the missing "administrator."

Drumont must have removed everything of importance in the night. The jewels, Tessier's private papers and documents, as well as his own personal belongings.

He had questioned Marpon, along with the chef and the remaining maid—all the others had departed—but nobody had heard any unusual sounds from their attic quarters.

The two guards from Number Six assigned by Goury to night duty had slept. They acknowledged that Drumont brought each of them a bottle of wine early last evening. One man had been stationed in that small salon near the front entrance, the other in the kitchen, and they had been ordered to patrol the corridors at hourly intervals. Those wine bottles, of course, were drugged.

Drumont emptied his office undisturbed. Probably, with someone's help, carried everything through the garden where a rear gate opened into the alley. In Paris there was always a convenient alley for escape.

Fouché had returned to Number Six and dispatched orders to local police headquarters in all twenty-four districts of Paris to be on the lookout for Alcidor Drumont, who was to be held for robbery and suspicion of murder. His description had been sent to every barrier leading out of the city.

Drumont had been smart to stay and face him this morning, knowing the jewels were already removed from the premises. Then, after talking to him, he must have fled through the gardens to that rear alley where a carriage would be waiting. He could have escaped through one of the barriers and be on his way to refuge in some distant city or country. He would certainly have a false passport and the means to change his appearance.

This would seem to confirm that Drumont was involved with Tessier's death. Or had he taken advantage of the murder to get away with all those jewels? The gold and silver . . .

Goury would be checking on him later through all the records at Number Six and the few files kept at the Préfecture.

He should've ordered that yesterday—an investigation of Drumont's past—but he had been involved with more immediate matters.

His instinct, from their first meeting, had been correct about Drumont, but he hadn't trusted it. That sallow pockmarked face and those constantly shifting amber eyes had made him appear too guilty . . .

Aubé would send Drumont's description to every Préfecture in France.

When the carriage returned after taking Fouché to Number Six, the coachman had helped Revol secure all those cardboard tubes into the luggage rack. More than a hundred of them. Goury had ridden with Revol, leaving Cauler on duty at the Tessier mansion with a new pair of guards for the night.

He had ordered the old man, Marpon, to remain in residence, although the chef and the maid had departed. There was enough food in the kitchen to last him several days.

The Nun and the Rat had returned to Number Six with Fouché, after learning nothing of importance from the neighbors in rue Taitbout.

Before leaving, he had once again gone through Tessier's private suite. The only interesting objects—he had noticed them yesterday—were the huge antique bed surrounded by piles of rare volumes on precious stones, some scattered across the Aubusson carpet, and an ornate gilded piano in the center of the salon. Spread across its top were copies of songs by Mozart, Lully, and Cherubini. Everything in the adjoining smaller suite indicated a female occupant, including the cloying perfume lingering in the air. All the windows stood open, but the scent was overpowering although Mademoiselle Coralie, according to Marpon, had been gone for months.

He wondered briefly if his mother was shopping on rue Saint-Honoré, at this moment with Fleuride . . .

He was looking forward to dinner tonight with Fleuride in her new gown. Would it be white satin? Young girls looked even younger dressed in white. He would be proud of them—his mother and his lovely cousin.

He'd come to enjoy quiet dinners with his mother since Jeanne-Victoire refused to go out. Always at the best restaurants.

His personal friends, writers and theater people, couldn't afford the sort of restaurant where he and his mother dined and *les grandes courtisanes* rarely appeared in public places. Sometimes they dined with a wealthy admirer, but they would arrive through a side entrance and reach their private dining room by a hidden staircase.

He had dined like that several times, alone with his wife, in the early months after their marriage. She hadn't realized why he did it but had enjoyed the privacy, away from curious eyes, with an aged waiter who treated her like royalty.

Jeanne-Victoire! He hoped she was resting today while his mother and Fleuride were shopping.

"Chief?"

He looked up to see his coachman squinting down at him from the small window overhead. "Yes, my friend?"

"Hôtel Belvedere."

"Ah!" He saw that his carriage had come to a stop in the hotel court-yard. "Wait for me. From here we'll go to rue de la Lune." He jumped down, cane in hand, and hurried through the sunlight toward the bronze and marble entrance to the hotel.

The interior again appeared to be suspended in twilight. As he went toward the desk, he glimpsed himself like some unfamiliar fish swim-ming in the distant mirrors and noticed pairs of people sitting on sofas or slowly promenading between the marble columns.

The concierge put a newspaper aside as he got to his feet. "Ah, Monsieur Vidocq! I see that the jeweler, Tessier, has been murdered and you're in charge of the investigation."

"In the paper, is it? I'd hoped to have a few more days before they found out." He shrugged. "I've come to see . . ."

"Monsieur Penny-packaire has gone to the country."

"Not the American. Today it's the Duc de Modena."

The old man glanced toward the key rack. "Haven't seen Monsieur le Duc this morning. His key isn't here, so he must be in his suite. I'll send one of the pages to say you're here."

"I'll go up myself. What number?"

"Seventeen, Monsieur."

He crossed the lobby and climbed the marble staircase to the first floor, where he found number seventeen in a side corridor. Tapped on the door with the silver head of his cane.

"Who is it?" Ronquetti's voice, faint and faraway.

"I am Vidocq."

"The door isn't locked."

He entered the customary foyer and continued on into a handsomely furnished salon with tall windows shuttered against the sun.

"I'm still in bed!"

Reaching the open inner doorway, he saw Ronquetti's muscular body stretched out on the bed, partially wrapped in a large towel, breakfast tray resting on a pillow beside him.

"Are all young American women so exhausting?" The brown-skinned satyr laughed, revealing his white teeth.

"I've never had the pleasure of an American woman."

"For your information, this one was no virgin."

"You've done a good night's work, Monsieur le Duc. I was right,

173

and her father was wrong. I'll not tell him. He might suspect I had personally conducted the investigation." He set his hat and cane on a table. "I see you've had breakfast."

"Just finished. The young lady didn't leave until an hour ago."

Vidocq sat on a *fauteuil* facing the bed. "You brought her to your suite last night?"

"Certainly not! I planned to wait another night. When we returned from dinner, after eleven, she retired to her own suite while I remained downstairs to finish my cigar. Ten minutes later I came up alone. Was sound asleep when a faint knocking wakened me. For a moment I feared it was a little maid I'd noticed several times, but then a voice called my name and I recognized an American accent. I admitted her, of course, at once . . ."

"What did you learn about her father?"

"He told her he might be gone for several days, but she thinks he may return tomorrow."

"She didn't tell you where he'd gone?"

"He apparently was rather mysterious about his destination. Even with her."

"Was he?"

"She says he never tells her anything about his personal affairs, and she suspects he's gone to arrange a business deal of some sort . . ."

Vidocq smiled. Pennypacker was meeting someone to purchase furniture and paintings stolen from those châteaux . . .

" . . . a private estate in the country. He mentioned that he'd be visiting a certain—what was the name?"

"Yes?"

"Motier! That's it—Monsieur Motier."

"Motier? Sounds familiar." He stared at a finger of sunlight reaching between the closed curtains. "Motier?" Facing Ronquetti. "I've heard that name somewhere. But I think not recently . . ."

Ronquetti shrugged, his muscles rippling. "I avoid estates in the country. Too many country people."

"Perhaps Mademoiselle Belinda will think of something more that her father said. Will you be seeing her today?"

"She won't be free until evening—because of some previous engagement this afternoon—but we'll be dining together tonight."

"Excellent! Has she said anything about her missing bracelet?"

"Not a word. She acts as though it never existed."

"It hasn't turned up at any of the usual places that deal in stolen gems."

"The bracelet may have been taken apart, the diamonds smuggled out of the country."

"We may never trace it. One thing more, my friend. What can you tell me about the Midnight Club? Any recent gossip?"

"I seldom hear anyone mention the place and rarely go there. They have a magnificent chef, but who wants to dine where no women are allowed? Not I!"

"I would imagine, since women are not present, the principal topic of conversation would be women." Vidocq laughed and rose from the chair, snatching up his hat and cane.

"I'm told they have a private conference room where important business matters are discussed. Deals are planned and ordered to be carried out or brought to a halt. Fortunes can be made or destroyed and neither the politicians nor the public ever suspect their fate was decided at the Midnight Club. They only learn the results when their lives are affected."

"So it's not political?"

"I heard a banker in Rome say the Midnight Club of Paris was beyond politics."

Vidocq shrugged and turned to leave. "Perhaps one night I should pay a visit to the Midnight Club."

"You won't get through the front door unless you have one of their golden coins. Slightly larger than a louis d'or but not so heavy. I suspect there's very little gold in them." Ronquetti pushed himself up against the pillows. "There was one other thing I learned from Mademoiselle Belinda . . ."

Vidocq turned at the open door. "What was that?"

"Her father owns a fleet of merchant ships. They came to France on one of them. Penny-packaire takes cargoes from all over the world back to his emporium in New Orléans."

"That's interesting. A fleet of ships . . . You'd better rest here this afternoon where it's cool, in preparation for another evening on the boulevards with Mademoiselle Belinda."

"The duties I am required to perform for Number Six!"

Vidocq smiled as he put on his hat and crossed the salon toward the corridor, but his mind was occupied with what he had learned.

Pennypacker could ship the treasures he bought from Le Diable Noir in his own merchant ships to New Orléans. Take them aboard unnoticed in the middle of the night . . .

Was that why he was visiting this Monsieur Motier? Arranging for another shipment of treasures . . .

Motier! Where had he heard that name in the past?

CHAPTER 29

Motier . . .

The name circled through his head as the carriage carried him up the hill through the twisting streets of Montmartre to rue de la Lune.

Number three was an old stone building that had been turned into cheap apartments, most of which would be occupied by people who owned shops nearby.

The concierge was one of that inquisitive sisterhood of dragons who inhabited lairs at the entrance to most such buildings, where they belabored tenants for their rent and protected them from bill collectors or inquisitive policemen. This one had a river quail hanging in a cage outside her door, and there was a growling mongrel at her feet.

"What is it now?" she demanded, as the dog barked.

Vidocq raised his hat. "Where will I find Mademoiselle Clodin?"

"No one lives here with that name."

"But I was told . . ."

"Police, aren't you?"

"I'm from the Sûreté . . ."

"One of Vidocq's men? I always like to help the law." Holding out a filthy hand.

He dropped some coins into her palm, and the dog stopped barking.

"You're looking for Madame Blanc. But she's never home at this hour. You'll find her in that *pâtisserie* on the corner."

"Works there, does she?"

"You could say that, I suppose. Although I would think she eats more than she works."

"How long has she lived here?"

"Several months now. Fortunately I had a ground floor apartment vacant in the rear. She's too fat to climb steps. Why all these questions, Monsieur? What's Coralie done?"

"She hasn't, to my knowledge, done anything. I happen to be an inquisitive man and enjoy asking people questions."

"They're good tenants. Always bring me fresh pastries."

"They?"

"Madame and Monsieur Blanc. He's the baker at the *pâtisserie*. Though I've heard it's Madame herself who owns it. If she does, she's eating up her own profits." She cackled, and the dog barked again.

"Thank you, Madame." He escaped to the street and walked toward the corner, pausing at the *pâtisserie* window. Housewives from the neighborhood lined a counter in the shop, where a young girl was filling orders from shelves lined with trays of baked goods. There was a buzz of female voices and as he entered the familiar smell of freshly baked bread. The appetizing odors reminded him that he hadn't eaten since early morning.

Several of the women stopped chattering as they saw him enter, in a long mirror behind the counter. All the others looked around to see what had silenced them. The girl who was dropping croissants into a twist of paper stood frozen, mouth open, as she saw the visitor.

"Where will I find Madame Blanc?" he asked.

She looked toward the kitchen and shouted. "Madame! Someone wants to see you!"

The women resumed their chatter.

His eyes remained on the kitchen, where he glimpsed a heavyset young man in white opening and closing the oven doors. His hair was black but, like his face and arms, covered with a dusting of flour.

The view of the baker was obscured by an enormous female who was chewing vigorously as she came into the shop.

He observed that she had blond hair. Curls like plump sausages held back with pink ribbons, and the vast expanse of her white dress was sprinkled with tiny pink bows. Her small blue eyes and rosy lips were barely visible in the pink flesh of her face.

She smiled. "Monsieur?"

"Madame Blanc?" He was aware that the women were silent again, so he lowered his voice. "You are also known as Coralie Clodin?"

177

"Yes, Monsieur." Dropping her voice. "I am. Although my neighbors think I am Madame Blanc, and I never tell them otherwise." Her next words were barely audible. "You are Vidocq . . ."

"I must ask you a few questions."

"I've done nothing wrong!"

He saw that her blue eyes were troubled. "My questions are in regard to a certain Narcisse Tessier."

"Tessier!" The eyes brightened. "That sly devil! What's he done? Come, sit down. What do you want to know about Tessier?" She led him to a row of small café tables, none occupied at the moment, along the wall opposite the counter. "Perhaps you'll have a fresh pastry with me? Silvestre makes the best fruit tarts in Paris!"

"That's very kind, Madame. I didn't have any lunch."

"Sit here." Plump pink fingers fluttered toward a chair, as she sank slowly onto another and the wooden seat creaked beneath her massive buttocks. "Coffee?"

"Black."

She squirmed around toward the kitchen and shouted. "Two peach tarts and two coffees. Quickly!" Turning around to Vidocq. "The peaches are sweet this summer. They say it's the hot weather." Leaning closer. "You don't remember me, do you?"

"We've met before?"

"Of course I didn't look like this. I was only sixteen. I'd come to Paris hoping to make my way as a singer. You spoke to me one night on Boulevard de Bonne-Nouvelle. Not far from here! You took me to a hotel. I never knew which one . . ."

He searched her face, trying to recall that first meeting.

"My name in those days was Delphine . . . I was much thinner then. Matter of fact, that night we met, I hadn't eaten for two days. We went to a café, and you gave me dinner. I still remember what I ate . . ."

He continued to study her features, trying—with no success—to see the other face hidden behind the mask of flesh.

". . . didn't get fat until much later. After I'd given up trying for a singing career . . ."

Another young girl came from the kitchen and rested a metal tray on the table. Set a plate holding a pastry in front of each with a thick white china cup of steaming black coffee.

Each tart held half a glazed peach.

"Sugar, Monsieur?" Coralie held out the china bowl.

"None for me." He picked up his fork and cut into the pastry as Coralie spooned sugar into her coffee.

"Like all girls who come to Paris hoping to be singers, I dreamed of singing at the Comique. Studied with a woman who'd sung there years ago . . ."

He grunted in response, enjoying his tart, still warm from the oven, washing it down with hot coffee.

". . . who eventually told me I might one day get into the chorus, but I'd never sing a leading role unless I found myself a wealthy lover. I did sing in the chorus, and I had many lovers, but unfortunately none of them were rich or interested in my voice. I decided I liked to eat more than I wanted to sing. So I gave up singing!"

"This tart is excellent!"

"Silvestre's a fine baker. I put up the money for him to open this shop."

"Did you? My father was a baker. Famous for his bread."

"The great Vidocq, son of a baker? I had no idea! Silvestre can cook anything. Our shop's making money, and next year we plan to open a little restaurant."

"I wish you well." He drank the last of his coffee and asked his next question abruptly, as he set the cup down. "Did you know that Tessier had been murdered?"

Her face paled. "So that's why you're here." She stared at him as she dropped her fork on the plate, tart unfinished. "Poor Narcisse . . . Who killed him?"

"I don't know yet." He saw, to his surprise, that tears were trickling down her cheeks. "Somebody put a bullet into his forehead."

"*Mon Dieu!* Where did this happen?"

"The mansion on rue Taitbout. They found him yesterday at his desk."

She wiped the tears away with the back of her hand. "Why would anyone want to kill him?"

"That's why I've come to you. Hoping you could tell me."

"It's been months since I've seen Narcisse."

"You loved him?"

"I didn't dislike him." She shrugged, breasts heaving under the thin dress. "Although he was a mean man. Wouldn't give me the price of a

179

fiacre when I wanted to go out, much less the cost of a new bonnet! And yet, when he kicked me out, he gave me enough to pay for this *pâtisserie!* I suppose the reason I didn't dislike him more was because he loved music. He would have me sing for him, every night before dinner. And what dinners! He never ate much, but he liked to watch me."

"Did you know your present husband, Monsieur Blanc, at the time you were living with Tessier?"

"We didn't meet, Silvestre and I, until after I'd left rue Taitbout. And we're not married—not yet—but we're thinking about it. Silvestre wants to get married more than I . . ."

"Who do you think might have killed Tessier?"

"How would I know! He never introduced me to his friends. The only time I was allowed out of my room, not that I minded, was when he sent Auguste to escort me to his private suite before dinner."

"Monsieur Marpon?"

"He was my dear friend. But I never saw who came to visit Narcisse or any of the customers who bought his jewelry." She sighed. "And now he's dead . . ."

"Did he have enemies?"

"I wouldn't know . . . What will happen to his beautiful jewels?"

"You saw the jewels?"

"Many times."

He realized that she had hesitated, obviously considering how much to tell him. "Where did you see them? In the vault?"

"No harm in telling you, I suppose. Auguste knew I wore them. You can ask him."

"Tessier allowed you to wear his jewelry?"

"Sometimes when a necklace or bracelet had been returned. Before they were put away."

"Why were they returned?"

"I suppose the owner wanted to have them repaired. Although I never saw anything wrong with any of them. They were so beautiful!"

"How long would Tessier let you wear them?"

"Only for one evening. He would have them in his suite when Auguste took me there before dinner. I could always tell something was up because Narcisse would be so excited. Then he would bring out a velvet tray. I would gasp when I saw the diamonds glittering. If it was a necklace, he would hang it around my neck. Then he would ask me to sit at the piano and sing for him. One night it was a tiara. Other times several rings or strings of pearls. Auguste would see me wearing them when Tessier and I went down to dinner. Such happy evenings! Narcisse was always in a good mood when I wore his jewels. As though he was pleased they'd been returned to him. I never understood why . . ."

"He was pleased when the jewels had to be repaired?"

"He never said they were being repaired. I guessed it must be something like that."

"And those were the only times he allowed you to see the jewelry?"

"Well, no . . ."

"He showed you the vault where they were kept?"

"I had no idea where he hid them. And Auguste swore he didn't know. He thought the only person who might know was that creature—Drumont . . ."

"You disliked Drumont?"

"Everyone did! All the servants. Even Auguste."

"For what reason?"

"He treated them as though they worked for him. Ordered the staff about and reprimanded them. Tried the same thing with me, but I told Narcisse and it never happened again."

"You say there were other times you wore the jewels?"

She glanced around to be certain no one was near them. "You're a man of experience, Monsieur. Chief of the Sûreté. You know that some men enjoy strange pleasures when they make love to a woman . . ."

"And what did Tessier enjoy when he invited you into his bed?"

"That's just it! He never did." She giggled. "Most nights after dinner we went to our separate suites. But at least once a month he would tell me to wait in my suite and he would join me. 'Prepare your lovely body,' he would say. 'I will be with you in a moment.' I would undress and get into bed, and he would come dancing in like a young man. A large red velvet bag in each hand. He would pull the sheet off my body, open his velvet bags, and, very carefully, sprinkle diamonds all over me! I would scream, because they bit my flesh like bits of glass." She laughed. "Tessier would hop up and down. Laughing and shouting . . ."

"And that was all?"

"Oh, no! He would reach down with both hands, like a naughty

181

child, and scramble the diamonds over my breasts, while all the time I kept shrieking. When they rolled across my stomach, it gave me the strangest feelings."

"Always diamonds? Never emeralds or . . ."

"Only diamonds. He would fondle them, pick up a handful and let them trickle through his fingers onto my body until he was gasping for breath. Then he would collapse onto the sofa. Tell me he wanted to look at me covered with diamonds. He said no woman in the world—empress or queen—ever wore so many! After a while he would stumble to his feet and tell me not to move. Always had to count them—every diamond—as he put them back in his velvet bags."

"Counted them?"

"I remember one night a diamond was missing. He counted them a second time, but the diamond had vanished. I don't remember how many there were supposed to be, but it must've been several hundred. He made me get out of bed while he searched between the sheets. Without finding it! Then I had to jump up and down. You won't believe what happened!"

"The diamond dropped to the floor."

"From under my armpit." She laughed, her breasts swaying.

"Did Tessier give you any of his diamonds to keep?"

"Oh, no! He said he couldn't."

"Why not?"

"He told me many times none of the jewels belonged to him. He handled them for someone else. His designers made the jewelry, which he sold to rich customers, but he never owned the jewels."

"Did he tell who those owners were?"

"Never."

"You said a moment ago Tessier gave you money when you left rue Taitbout?"

"Not money . . ."

"What then?"

"One beautiful perfect diamond!"

"How could he? If all those jewels belonged to someone else?"

"He said it was one that had been lost. One of the servants had been accused of stealing it years ago and was dismissed by Monsieur Drumont, but Narcisse didn't report the theft to the police . . ."

"Why not?"

"He said he knew it would turn up one day. And it did! In a drawer of his desk. He thought it must've rolled there when he was showing diamonds to a customer. Rolled to the back and got stuck under some letters. He told me it had long ago been written off and forgotten. So he gave it to me. Said I was his favorite of all the singers who'd lived with him. Told me he thought I could've had a career, if only I hadn't gotten so fat. That's the nicest thing anyone ever said. That I might've had a career as a singer . . ."

"What became of that diamond?"

"I sold it." She picked up her fork and attacked the remainder of her pastry.

"To whom?"

"I never really knew. A friend of Silvestre's arranged everything. That's where I got the money to buy this *pâtisserie* for Silvestre."

"Did Tessier have visitors late at night?"

"Not to my knowledge . . ."

"Did he frequently go out for dinner?"

"Once or twice a week. Then I would eat alone. He told me he used to go to the Opéra, but of course the opera house had been closed . . ."

He realized, as they talked, that the heat from the kitchen was becoming intolerable and saw that there was a film of perspiration on her upper lip. "Did Monsieur Tessier have a family?"

"He never mentioned relatives to me."

"What about Drumont?"

"I never knew anything about him. Such a strange man! Nobody had any idea where he lived."

"My assistants are going over the premises at this moment. Room by room."

"Only three of the staff slept there. The chef, one maid, and of course my friend Auguste. The others had families and lived at home. I never saw Monsieur Drumont at night. In fact, I didn't like to leave my room after dark. Of course, when I went down to dinner, Narcisse was with me and Auguste went ahead of us with a lighted candelabra."

Vidocq reached for his hat and cane as he got to his feet. "The pastry was excellent."

"Is this all you wanted to ask me?"

"For the moment, Mademoiselle." He bowed and set his hat on his head as he went toward the street, past the women lining the counter, aware of Coralie calling toward the kitchen again.

"Another peach tart! Quickly!"

CHAPTER 30

Vidocq sat at his desk enjoying a cool glass of Burgundy, which Madame Babelay had just brought up from the cellars.

When he returned to Number Six, after a brief visit with Doctor Morain, he had told Aubé that he would see no one for the next hour.

Aubé was accustomed to that, aware that Vidocq needed to consider whatever information he'd turned up this morning.

Doctor Morain, like most physicians, had been extremely vague about his patient. Impossible to get the truth from him. Only that Jeanne-Victoire's condition was slowly worsening. He had repeated the nonsense about an "impaired heart" but offered no additional information.

Unfortunately, he couldn't shout at Morain, the way he did at doctors who worked with Number Six. The only thing he'd learned was that the specialist, Doctor Brindeau, had suggested a new treatment developed in London that might at least make Jeanne-Victoire more comfortable. Meanwhile she must continue to have complete rest with brief intervals of exercise. One of the maids could help her out to the balcony, where she could walk back and forth in the fresh air.

Who was this mysterious Monsieur Motier that Pennypacker was visiting in the country? Was he the link to Le Diable Noir?

Motier! Where had he heard that name before? Not recently but in the past . . .

He wondered if Monsieur Pennypacker was the only American businessman who bought jewels from Tessier? Did the missing diamond bracelet have some connection with Tessier's death, or was that only coincidence? There were many such improbable coincidences in every investigation . . .

Motier? Motier . . .

The Marquis de Lafayette! That's where he'd heard the name. The old man had called himself Monsieur Motier when he settled down in the country as a private citizen. It was a family name—du Motier. So Pennypacker had gone to visit Lafayette! For what possible reason?

Lafayette had helped the Americans win their Revolution against the British and was known, even in France, as America's friend. Could he be involved with a scheme to sell Pennypacker the treasures Le Diable had been stealing? There had been rumors that his fortune had diminished during the years of political upheaval in France . . .

He finished the wine and, setting the glass on a tray, reached for the stack of sketches young Honoré had made at the Tessier mansion. Examined each, then returned to the one of Tessier slumped at his desk, face masked by blood . . .

He put the drawings aside and glanced at the newspapers Aubé had waiting for him when he returned.

The morning papers reported little more than the simple fact that the well-known jeweler Narcisse Tessier had been found in his residence on rue Taitbout with a bullet in his head. There was a list of famous personages who had been his customers—royal ladies as well as queens of the Paris and London theatrical worlds—the bankers and politicians who had ordered special items for their wives and daughters. No mention of their mistresses!

He set the papers down and glanced at the map spread open under young Honoré's drawings. Noticed the red circles drawn around each plundered château, the blue arrows marking directions and routes taken by Le Diable and his followers. All of them south of Paris. They had to be selling their loot somewhere, and the most likely buyers would be in Paris. But how did Le Diable manage to get his treasures into the city?

The blue arrows seemed to quiver before his eyes.

They would have to pass through one of the southern barriers to enter Paris. Probably bringing their stolen treasures in farm carts. The drivers would be familiar to the inspectors on duty, their passports in order . . .

"That's how they do it!" he shouted.

"What, Chief?" Aubé responded.

"Come in here!"

"Yes, Chief. Goury and Fouché are waiting to see you."

"Come in! All of you!"

Aubé hurried in, ahead of the others.

"Sit down!" Gesturing toward the armchairs. "I've only this moment thought of a plan to find those treasures Le Diable Noir has stolen. Put an end to the thefts and capture Le Diable!" He hesitated as they sank into chairs, facing him, Aubé beside his desk. "They have to bring their loot to Paris! Here's where they'll get the highest prices!

Furniture and paintings that belonged to kings! There are many rich men in Paris who will pay for such treasures. Wealthy men in England and the United States who will buy works of art and no questions asked. So Le Diable Noir brings his plunder here. And I know how he does it!" As he explained, Vidocq became even more certain that he was right. "They are brought, one at a time, in carts belonging to members of his gang disguised as farmers, or farmers who are members of the band and deliver fresh produce to the central markets every night. They will have only one painting or piece of furniture in each cart. Buried under a load of chickens from Houdan or sacks of flour from Corbel . . ."

"Of course!" Goury exclaimed. "That's the only possible way they could manage it without being noticed! The roads are busy every night with farmers bringing their produce to market."

"A perfect way to smuggle them into Paris!" Aubé nodded. "But he would need an army of farmers transporting this many stolen objects."

"Not at all!" Vidocq responded. "They wouldn't attempt to pass more than one or two items through the barriers each night. But this has been going on for months! If two come through in one night—say three times a week—that's six every week!" He got up from his desk as he talked and strode up and down in front of the open windows, organizing the operation as a general would plan to attack an army. "Starting tonight, I want men from Number Six assigned to every barrier leading into Paris from the south. The Saint-Jacques barrier is the most likely one for them to use."

Aubé made a note.

"Put two of our men on each southern barrier. One in the uniform of a customs inspector. The other should appear to be an innocent citizen who's been stopped for questioning. Take every driver into the office, while our other man searches each cart. If a farmer has anything hidden under his vegetables, he's to be told there's something wrong with his passport. Have him drive over to one side, out of the way, and hold him there. Then while he's arguing, as he's certain to do, let him notice one of the regular inspectors release our man, who will appear to have been questioned and found innocent. He will get on his horse and gallop straight here."

"You'll be waiting?" Fouché asked.

"I'll leave word at the end of each day where I can be found that night. Early or late. I must be informed at once if a farmer's being held.

I will return here for a horse, and within minutes I shall be at that barrier. I will not, however, question the farmer. We're after a more important prize—Le Diable himself! When I reach the barrier, the farmer will be allowed to proceed on his way, and he will lead us to the rendezvous where those stolen articles are being taken for disposal."

Goury grinned in anticipation. "We'll seize him as he enters!"

"Certainly not! We'll ride past and let him drive inside. Unaware that he's being followed. I suspect it will be near the markets. The following night we'll surround the place. Observe it from the streets and the rooftops. Wait until another cart arrives with a hidden cargo. Before their suspicions are aroused, we will storm the place."

"And seize Le Diable!" Fouché growled.

"Or someone who can tell us where to find him."

Aubé continued to nod as he made more notes. "This should certainly do it!"

"Warn our men to be cautious when they stop these farm carts. Anyone involved with Le Diable is certain to be armed. If he thinks he's cornered, he'll kill in order to get away with whatever's hidden in his cart. Take no chances! I want none of our men injured. All of you must be armed. But use your pistols only if the suspect attempts to escape or produces a weapon of his own. However! I do not want him killed. We'll question him until he tells us where we can find Le Diable." He continued to pace as he talked. "I want all available men from Number Six on duty every night. Starting tonight. See that they're supplied with fast horses, and keep one available here at all times for me. The grooms and stableboys must be on twenty-four-hour duty. They'll bed down in the stables. The others can sleep upstairs. Tell Madame Babelay to have cold food and hot coffee available through the night." He smiled, rubbing his hands together, anticipating success. "This should bring an end to the reign of Le Diable Noir! Something those rural Préfectures have been unable to achieve. Another victory for Number Six!"

"And another kick in the rump for our neighbors across the street!" Fouché muttered.

Vidocq sat at his desk again. "Have our records produced any information on Tessier or Drumont?"

"Nothing," Goury responded.

"I suspected we didn't have anything or I'd have remembered their names. However, I've a strong feeling Drumont must have a record somewhere. He spent some time in Africa. Check the local Préfectures in all major seaports, especially Marseille. Find out if they know him. Send a detailed description. His shifty eyes and pockmarked face . . ."

Aubé made another note. "Right away."

He turned to Fouché. "No word as to where he may have gone?"

"Not a clue."

"What about the missing jewels?"

"Nothing's turned up, and nobody's come forward—relative or lawyer—with a will or any other document."

"I've never known a murder with so many things unaccounted for! No one seems to know where Drumont lived. He's managed to hide his present as well as his past. As though he never existed!" Turning back to Aubé. "Tonight I'm dining with my family. A young cousin's visiting us from Arras. We're taking her, my mother and I, to the Café de Paris. We'll be there for at least two hours—I should think from eight to ten—and afterward we'll drive straight home. Send word immediately, no matter the hour, if a farmer is detained at one of those barriers. I'll leave my family, even if we're in the middle of dinner, and come straight here. Tomorrow evening, by the way, I plan to visit the Midnight Club. I've learned that Tessier frequently dined there. Which means he was probably a member."

Fouché grunted. "They say you have to be a millionaire to belong."

"It's possible Tessier was a millionaire. Certainly the jewels I saw in his vault—especially those loose diamonds—were worth a fortune."

"I checked several banks today," Goury added, "but nobody seems to know anything about Tessier or his finances."

"And Drumont removed all evidence of Tessier's wealth when he emptied his office. Took all the records. Only hope he hasn't destroyed them." Vidocq glanced at Aubé. "Where's young Revol?"

"He's using Damiot's office."

"And Damiot?"

"Went up to Montmartre with the Nun and the Rat. They're still searching for that young woman who was kidnapped."

"The Pirelli woman?" He rose from his desk. "We have to look, of course, but my guess is we'll never find any trace of her."

"That's what Damiot thinks."

"The husband disposed of her body so cleverly that he felt confident enough to report his wife missing. They hunted for her without success—the gendarmes in Montmartre—for more than a month before

188

turning the case over to us. This is one of those hundreds of young women who disappear in Paris every year and are never heard from again. Let Damiot and the ladies pursue their investigation today, for the record, then we'll report back to Montmartre that we can't waste any more time on it."

Aubé scribbled another brief note.

"I'll see if Revol's discovered anything from those jewelry designs. I hope they may reveal something about Tessier's clients. Any small piece of information would be useful!" He strode toward the doors as they stood up. "I'll be with Revol if I'm needed." He crossed the silent antechamber aware of the others behind him, Aubé returning to his desk as Goury and Fouché headed for their own offices.

Vidocq turned down the corridor toward the rear and swung open the door of Damiot's small office to see Revol seated at a large table facing the windows, his back to the door. "Any luck?"

Revol looked around. "I think I may have found something!"

"That's what I hoped to hear." He crossed the office, past Damiot's neat desk, as Revol rose from the leather-topped work table covered with the cardboard tubes.

"There's something here I don't understand . . ."

Vidocq saw, as he reached the table, that several sheets of paper, each with a jewelry design, had been removed from their tubes and flattened in two groups with an empty tube set above each. "What have you discovered?"

"I'm not certain. Except for these designs I created myself." He indicated a row of five sketches.

Vidocq leaned forward to study them more carefully. "You have real talent, my friend."

"Here's the design for Mademoiselle Belinda's bracelet." He stroked the sketch with his fingertips. "Which you've already seen. Next to that is a diamond necklace I created for Baron Sabatier."

"The banker?"

"I believe so. Monsieur Tessier never told us who any of the designs were for. In this case he said that a wealthy gentleman had ordered the necklace for a lady. Frequently the maids would gossip about who had bought a certain piece. That's how I knew about this necklace. Baron Sabatier ordered it for his mistress. Whoever she might be! The maids repeated what they heard Monsieur Tessier saying to Monsieur Drumont at lunch."

"Do you know where Drumont lived?"

"I never heard him say. The other designers and I seldom talked to him. We ate our lunch in the kitchen with the goldsmiths. The maids would gossip as they served us."

"You still haven't told me. What you've found here . . ."

Revol tapped one of the drawings with a forefinger. "These four sketches, but not the Penny-packaire bracelet, have the same pairs of letters—RE-DE—at the end of each inscription at the bottom. The seven sketches in this next group were created by the two other designers, Jean Ponsard and Marcel Jaune. They too have a row of letters and numerals ending with RE-DE."

"So I see. But not the Penny-packaire bracelet? Most curious . . ."

"And there are many more!"

"You still don't know their meaning? RE-DE?"

"I've no idea what they could mean."

"Is there anyone who might? Some person who worked with Tessier longer than you?"

"Jean Ponsard might. He's the oldest designer. Or Pierre Thanot, chief of the goldsmiths. Both of them have been with Tessier since he had his shop on rue Saint-Honoré."

"Could you bring them here?"

"I suppose so. I know where they live."

"This afternoon?"

"Well . . . Unfortunately, I've an engagement. I was going to tell Monsieur Aubé I'd be leaving early because of something I had arranged earlier in the week."

"Then tomorrow? Around eleven."

"Eleven o'clock."

"Tell them it's an official matter concerning Tessier's murder. Perhaps you'd better say you're working with me."

Revol's eyes brightened. "May I?"

"See you in the morning." He strode toward the door. "We'll talk to them in the interrogation room downstairs, where I questioned you." Glancing back as he reached the door, Vidocq saw that Revol was watching him. "You remember that room?"

"I'll never forget it."

He swung the door open and hurried back to his own office.

So Revol was meeting the American girl this afternoon. Mademoiselle Belinda had told Ronquetti she had an engagement. That's why

Revol was wearing what was obviously his best suit. Short black coat with a high black satin collar, blue silk cravat, white shirt and blue waistcoat, pale blue trousers and polished black boots.

Aubé looked up from a stack of reports on his desk. "There's a parcel from the morgue. I left it on your desk."

"That will be the contents of Monsieur Tessier's pockets. They should have sent them over this morning." He saw the small parcel as he reached his desk and snatched it up. Broke the cord and pulled apart the heavy butcher's paper.

The first thing to drop onto his desk was a gold coin, followed by three rings encrusted with diamonds and an assortment of the usual small articles men keep in their pockets. The rings had come from Tessier's fingers and would be placed in the office safe.

The only object of interest was the coin.

He picked it up and found that it was slightly larger but thinner than a louis d'or. Ronquetti was right!

The golden surface was bare except for the hands of a clock, straight up, at the hour of midnight.

With this he would have no difficulty getting into the Midnight Club.

CHAPTER 31

Madame Vidocq, her skirts and petticoats rustling, led Fleuride across the sidewalk into the Café de Paris.

Vidocq followed, aware of young Jean in his summer dress livery driving their open landau up Boulevard des Italiens. He would hitch the matched team of bays and observe the constant parade of strollers.

He glanced at the chattering people dining on the terrace in a glow of candlelight. They called this a terrace, but it was only a few rows of small tables on the sidewalk, parallel to the curb, with potted plants set at intervals. The early theater crowd had departed, and the garçons were flying about, resetting tables. No one was waiting for a table in the entrance foyer as he followed his family inside.

Le patron was bowing to Madame Vidocq, waving the headwaiter out of his way. "A great pleasure, Madame Vidocq!"

"Ah, Monsieur! This is my sister's daughter, Mademoiselle Maniez."

"Mademoiselle!" He bowed again. "Welcome . . ."

"You have a cool table for us?" Vidocq asked.

"We haven't had a cool table, inside or out, for weeks. There's not a cool table in all of Paris!"

"Then give us your most secluded table so that our dinner won't be disturbed by intruders."

"I have just the spot. This way . . ." He bowed once more and led them into the high-ceilinged room. "I have a table away from the open windows so that the voices from the terrace can't disturb you."

As Vidocq followed he saw that half the tables were unoccupied. Black-coated waiters standing in a line at the back, looking bored as only waiters can look when they realize their tips will not be large. All the gas globes overhead and on the side walls were dark, and only the occupied tables had lighted candles under lacy pink shades.

"Vidocq! I must speak with you . . ."

He looked around, annoyed by the intrusion, to see a familiar and unpleasantly arrogant face approaching through the dimness. "Monsieur Pradier?"

"Meant to send you a note this past week." Motioning for the two middle-aged gentlemen who were following him from the dining room to continue on into the foyer as he lowered his voice. "Regret I've been unable to pay the interest I owe you on that loan."

"I've heard recently your company is having more trouble."

"A slight delay in certain matters, from which, I assure you, we shall recover. But, for the moment, I find myself unable to . . ."

"The interest was due last month."

"I'm quite aware of that, but I . . ."

"Your loan was for one hundred thousand francs."

"I wonder if you could let me have another ten thousand? At the same interest . . ."

"I'm sorry, Monsieur . . ."

" . . . to keep me solvent until these matters I've just been discussing at dinner reach a profitable conclusion . . ."

"I never permit business matters to intrude, Monsieur Pradier, when I'm dining with my family." He bowed. "Forgive me . . ."

Pradier paled as he watched Vidocq continue on.

Vidocq was seething. So the fool wasn't going to pay that interest on

192

his debt. And he'd presumed to borrow another ten thousand! He would put an end to Monsieur Pradier tomorrow.

Hurrying after the others, he was aware of his reflection moving against the lighted candles in the gilt-framed mirrors lining the walls. As he removed his broad-brimmed black hat, the curls of his reddish-brown hair caught glints of light from the candle flames. The ruffles of his silk shirt were ghostly white from this distance, and it was impossible to glimpse the sparkle of his diamond studs. It had been much too warm to wear his black cape with the scarlet satin lining, but his lightweight gray evening suit looked elegant.

His mother was waving her white-gloved hands for Fleuride to sit opposite her at the damask-covered table.

Two waiters held their chairs, and *le patron* pulled out a third chair for Vidocq to occupy between them facing the distant entrance.

He handed his hat and gold-headed evening cane to a garçon, sank into the chair, and began to peel off his own white gloves. Saw that their table was in the center of the room, but the surrounding tables were empty. Observed that the nearest diners were barely visible in the candlelight. So his face should not be recognized again.

Le patron bowed to Madame Vidocq. "Everyone's eating cold food tonight."

"And so, I suspect, shall I!" she exclaimed.

"Champagne with our dinner." Vidocq turned to the sommelier. "A magnum of your finest."

The old man bowed and headed for the cellars, passing a waiter who presented menus to *le patron*.

"I'll order dinner for the ladies." Vidocq slipped his gloves into a pocket. "And, instead of consulting your menu, I prefer to discuss what you would suggest. We're celebrating my young cousin's first visit to Paris."

"Ah, Mademoiselle!" *Le patron* rolled his eyes. "To see Paris for the first time! Such an experience . . ."

Fleuride stared at him as though he were a minor character in a Molière comedy.

"We want a very special dinner," Vidocq continued. "Something she will never forget."

"I am honored, Mademoiselle. And my chef, I assure you, will surpass himself for your pleasure."

"What shall we have to start?" Vidocq asked.

"Perhaps one of our famous pâtés . . ."

"What's the meat in them?" Madame Vidocq asked.

"I would suggest the special pâté our chef makes with rabbit. Very light and delicate. It contains diamonds of truffles and is served on a bed of chopped golden aspic."

Vidocq saw that Fleuride's eyes were dancing with anticipation. "And following that?"

"Perhaps cold pheasant? Cooked with fresh herbs and cognac . . ."

"I've never tasted pheasant!" Fleuride exclaimed.

"I promise you'll never forget eating pheasant for the first time, Mademoiselle!"

"And what vegetables?" Madame Vidocq was removing her white lace gloves.

"I would suggest cold asparagus vinaigrette . . ."

Madame nodded. "I adore asparagus!"

Vidocq turned to Fleuride. "How does that sound, cousine?"

"Fit for a king!"

Le patron bowed again. "If I may say so, Mademoiselle looks more like a princess, and we shall see that she dines like one."

"I'm as hungry as a pig."

Le patron, still smiling, departed for the kitchen.

"Mon Dieu!" Madame Vidocq exclaimed. "What a thing to say. A pig? Young ladies do not use such a word at the dinner table."

"I have a lovely pig at home."

Vidocq chuckled, amused at her independence.

"Nothing wrong with pigs," Fleuride added.

"They're filthy creatures!" Madame protested.

"Not mine! He's pure white. I feed him every morning. Did you know, Tante, pigs eat nothing but vegetables?"

"I am aware of what the greedy creatures devour, but they are not a topic one discusses at dinner." She glanced around the room, dismissing the subject. "I do believe it's slightly cooler here than it was driving across the city." Turning to her son. "Do you suppose this weather is finally changing?"

"I never predict Paris weather for more than an hour."

"Who was that gentleman you spoke to as we came in?"

"A stupid fool."

His mother gave him a brief seriocomic look and turned back to Fleuride. "Be sure to remove your gloves, *chérie*, before you eat."

"I was going to in a moment. Maman always told me to take them off unobtrusively."

"Where did my dear sister get that idea? I take off my gloves when I please. Usually, in a restaurant, I remove them the moment I sit down."

Vidocq observed them with affection as they discussed the preferred time to remove gloves.

His mother was wearing violet tonight, which with her silver-gray curls was most becoming. A gown of some soft violet material with ruffles trimmed in purple and a white bonnet decorated with artificial violets. Encircling her plump neck was the diamond necklace he'd given her many years ago.

Compared to the designs from Tessier's atelier, this necklace was little more than a thin gold chain strung with small stones.

He saw, as they talked, that Fleuride was taking off her white lace gloves. She was not dressed in white, as he'd anticipated, but was wearing pale green with a strand of pearls around her throat and some delicate white blossoms tucked into her blue-black hair. She looked slightly older tonight, firm young breasts accentuated by the low neck and simple lines of her first Paris gown.

"You like my new dress, Cousin François?"

He smiled. She had noticed he was studying her. "It's beautiful. And so are you."

"As I told you earlier I'm very grateful for all the lovely things Tante bought for me this afternoon. This is my favorite, but wait 'til you see the others!"

Madame Vidocq smiled. "I wanted her to have a white dress for this evening. Young girls look so lovely in white . . ."

"White's for little girls!" Fleuride turned to Vidocq, her eyes flashing coquettishly. "I prefer green. This is so exciting! My first dinner in a famous Paris restaurant. Is this an old one?"

"Oh, no!" He glanced around the dining room. "Café de Paris was opened last year."

"And quickly became very popular," Madame Vidocq added.

"In the winter, during the social season," Vidocq continued, "this room is brightly lighted, crowded, and noisy. I prefer it like this. The chef can take all the time he needs to prepare each dish. That's how it was when I first came to Paris. Nobody seemed to be hurried. Today everything moves more quickly. People even eat too fast." He looked up as the sommelier returned with their wine. "Here we are! This heat has made me thirsty."

The old man rested his silver wine bucket on the serving table and, as they watched, removed the cork with the faintest of plupps then circled the table filling their glasses.

Vidocq glanced at his niece. "You've drunk champagne before?"

"We always have champagne to celebrate Maman's and Papa's wedding anniversary, the date of my birth, and of course the eve of Noël . . ."

"But the champagne we used to have in Arras," Madame observed, "was never as good as this."

"Papa orders all his wines from Paris."

"Does he?" Madame Vidocq picked up her glass and peered at the golden bubbles.

"Things have changed, Maman." Vidocq smiled. "Since you and I lived there." He raised his glass as the sommelier bowed and departed. "To Fleuride's stay in Paris! May it be the first of many."

Fleuride smiled, lifting her glass. "I can drink to that, can't I?"

"Of course!" Madame responded. "But not too fast, or you'll have hiccups."

As they drank their wine, Vidocq was startled to feel something lightly nudge his foot.

Fleuride winked over the edge of her glass.

He smiled and moved his leg carefully, returning the pressure of her slippered foot. And, as he did so, he wondered about Jeanne-Victoire. Was she asleep or wide awake and thinking about them—he and Fleuride—dining in some restaurant. His wife had stopped going out before this café opened, so there were no memories of her here . . .

"What are you thinking?" Fleuride asked.

"Thinking?" He faced her.

"You seemed far away. I could tell from your eyes. Looking at me, and yet you weren't . . ."

"I was considering some of the things which happened today at Number Six. Planning other things I must do tomorrow."

Madame Vidocq sighed dramatically. "He always does this when we

196

dine out." Frowning at him. "You promised you'd forget about Number Six tonight."

"Yes, Maman."

"And no murders, if you please! Murders are even worse at the dinner table than pigs."

"Much worse." He chuckled as he watched a trio of waiters approaching. The first bore a silver-lidded tray, which he held for their inspection after the second whipped off the lid.

"How beautiful!" Fleuride exclaimed.

The first waiter set his tray down and proceeded to slice the pâté.

Vidocq saw the oblong pâté resting in a circle of chopped aspic and watched the second waiter present the first slice to Madame Vidocq. The third waiter at the same time served fresh bread with individual silver crocks of butter.

Madame Vidocq quickly buttered a morsel of bread and spread it with pâté. She was the first to eat and, rolling her eyes with pleasure, the first to speak. "Much better than we ever have at home!"

As he ate, aware of Fleuride's chattering, Vidocq's thoughts moved up the street—the Café de Paris was on the corner of Boulevard des Italiens and rue Taitbout—to the Tessier mansion. Only Marpon and two men from Number Six remained on the premises. The old man would be asleep in his attic room, the other two prowling those marble corridors on the lookout for intruders.

He wondered where Alcidor Drumont was tonight. Still in Paris? Every man had at least one friend who would take him in and give him shelter. In his own youth he had learned that the perfect place to hide was in the bed of a prostitute.

As he finished his pâté, he felt eyes observing him and looked up to see a middle-aged man hesitate before passing their table. Stocky body, big head with curly black hair. The face came into focus through the candlelight. Flashing black eyes. "My dear friend!" Vidocq sprang, hand outstretched. "I had no idea you were in Paris." Shaking hands.

"I noticed you arrive with your party as I was finishing dinner."

"May I present Monsieur Beyle," Vidocq gestured. "My mother . . ."

Beyle bowed. "Madame! A great honor . . ."

Vidocq saw that Fleuride was staring at his friend. "And this is . . ."

"Your charming wife! I'd heard she was beautiful but was not prepared for such beauty as this . . ."

"No, no! This is my cousin—Mademoiselle Maniez . . ."

"Mademoiselle!" Beyle bowed again.

" . . . who's visiting Paris for the first time."

"Pardon my intrusion, Madame. Mademoiselle . . ." His eyes were held by Fleuride's enchanting face. "Forgive me, disturbing you at dinner. I'm on my way to a concert where, unfortunately, they are playing Beethoven. German din! I prefer the wit and subtlety of Mozart. He composed like a Frenchman." Turning to Vidocq. "I was at a dinner party last night where the Marquis de Luynes said he'd met you recently."

"Did he?" Vidocq moved back a few steps away from the table, causing his friend to follow.

"You've become the most romantic figure in Paris. Men are curious about you, and women adore you. Or your legend! I continue to read about your successes in the newspapers."

Vidocq shrugged.

"I'm sure your most fascinating investigations are never reported to the public."

"It would be indiscreet for all concerned to publicize them. What about you? Still writing?"

"A few pieces for some of the more obscure journals. Mostly about music. We must have dinner one evening. I would enjoy hearing about your latest adventures. I'm still hoping to start a novel. One day soon!" He bowed toward the ladies. "Good evening, Madame. Mademoiselle . . ."

Vidocq sank into his chair as Beyle continued on toward the entrance.

"Who was that?" Madame Vidocq whispered.

"Henri Beyle . . . He served with Napoléon in Russia. I've known him for several years."

"Most distinguished looking." Madame Vidocq's inquisitive eyes followed him out of the restaurant. "Is he married?"

"Not to my knowledge. He's reputed to be something of a Don Juan."

"I know what that means." Fleuride giggled. "Is he a writer?"

"A journalist but he's always talking about the novels he plans to write. Balzac calls him an amateur."

"Balzac? Who's he?"

"A young friend who claims to have published several novels, but he writes under names that he refuses to disclose to anyone."

Two garçons removed their empty plates as the trio of waiters returned with their next course.

Vidocq observed Fleuride as she watched them serve the plates of cold pheasant with plump stalks of white asparagus. So Beyle had thought she was his wife . . .

Fleuride looked up, aware that his eyes were on her again. "You know some important people, cousin."

"That's part of my work. Meeting people from every level of Parisian life."

"This pheasant looks like chicken," she observed, picking up her fork. "I must tell Maman I ate pheasant in Paris."

Madame Vidocq hiccuped. "Oh, dear!"

Fleuride laughed. "Tante! You have hiccups."

"My own fault. Eating at the same time I was talking. One should never attempt conversation, except between courses. Something's certain to go down one's gullet the wrong way." She hiccuped again, covering her mouth with the damask napkin.

"Hold your nose!" Fleuride directed. "At the same time, drink a little wine. But not too much!"

Madame Vidocq reluctantly followed directions, as Fleuride laughed.

"I think the hiccups have stopped," Madame whispered. She breathed deeply and waited with apprehension, but nothing happened.

"Years ago," Vidocq observed, "I saw a man choke to death with hiccups. He was eating and a lump of meat stuck in his throat."

"François, I do not find that amusing." Madame sliced through an asparagus stalk.

He glanced at Fleuride and winked.

They ate without further conversation, although the two women from time to time discussed their afternoon shopping.

Vidocq retreated into his personal thoughts and wondered briefly if the American would be returning from his visit to Lafayette tomorrow . . .

Was Ronquetti dining tonight with Mademoiselle Belinda? They might even be here, invisible in some distant corner.

Fleuride and his mother finished their wine with elaborate pastries while he had black coffee.

He drank it slowly, his mind darting and turning, seeking answers.

Much to be done tomorrow. Revol was bringing those two men—the senior designer and one of the goldsmiths—to Number Six . . .

He glimpsed a familiar plump figure in the foyer. Talking to *le patron*. His plan to catch Le Diable was working more quickly than he had dared to hope.

"What is it?" Fleuride asked. "Who do you see?"

"I'm afraid, my dear, I'm about to be summoned to Number Six."

Madame Vidocq set her wineglass down. "This happens every time we dine out!" Peering toward the foyer. "It's Aubé!"

"You and Fleuride will return home in the landau. I'll ride with Aubé." He pushed his chair back and rose from the table as the urgent figure hurried closer. Aubé was wearing a neat gray suit, carrying his hat in one hand, looking out of place in this elegant restaurant. His sparse hair was in disarray, and his eyes behind the spectacles were troubled. "What is it, my friend?"

"Forgive me, Chief!" Aubé hesitated, bowing to the ladies. "Madame! Mademoiselle . . ."

Madame Vidocq nodded. "Monsieur Aubé, as usual . . ."

"I regret having to interrupt your dinner, Madame."

She sniffed. "You did the same thing last time I dined out with my son. Tonight, at least, I managed to finish my dessert."

"I left my schedule for the evening at Number Six," Vidocq explained to Fleuride, "in case I should be needed." Turning back to Aubé and dropping his voice. "They've detained a cart at one of the barriers?"

"Oh no!" Aubé moved closer. "It's a murder . . ."

"Murder?"

"In rue de Provence. One of *les grandes courtisanes*. The Spanish whore . . ."

"Maya!"

CHAPTER 32

Maya's body with its olive flesh and lustrous long black hair was stretched out, full length, in her sumptuous black and silver bed.

There was a small circle in the center of her forehead and a dark veil

200

of blood similar to the one that had covered Tessier's face. Only this veil had parted and flowed down both cheeks instead of over the nose and mouth.

Two people shot in the head. Tessier at his desk yesterday and Maya in her antique Spanish bed.

Rue de Provence crossed rue Taitbout and the Tessier mansion was only a few streets south of here.

The faint sound of a guitar, mournful and despairing, came from a distant room.

Vidocq was aware of the others gathered behind him, watching as he studied the body of this incredibly beautiful woman, heard them whispering together.

He wondered if Maya had known Tessier. Perhaps visited him on rue Taitbout, along with one of her wealthy protectors, to inspect his collection of diamonds. Or had Tessier come here after Coralie's departure, to this room and this bed, to enjoy the pleasure of Maya's living body? Those pleasures had been the talk of Paris a few years ago when she was younger.

From what he had now learned about Tessier, the jeweler would more likely have visited Maya to enjoy a supper of exotic Spanish food. And nothing more!

Maya, like Ève, had been one of the most famous *courtisanes* for many years.

He remembered when she first appeared, like all her sisters, from nowhere. Her sultry beauty had caused much talk and a wealthy admirer had almost immediately established her in this apartment.

That first admirer lasted only a few months before he was replaced by an endless series of other wealthy men. Each of whom became her lover and protector.

He had no idea who the most recent favorite might have been.

Her long fingers, clutching the black lace coverlet, displayed no rings, and there were no bracelets around her arms. He remembered that she had always worn heavy barbaric jewelry. Her plump body, visible beneath the black lace, was invitingly mysterious in spite of the weight she had recently gained.

Vidocq paused near the head of the bed to study her face. How many times had he kissed those sensuous lips . . .

He heard the entrance bell far away as the lonely guitar continued softly, like a faint echo of Maya's presence.

In another moment he would have to start asking questions. He dreaded that. It was as though, as long as he stared at her remembered flesh, she was alive. The moment he turned away she would die.

Also, at the scene of any murder, his first impressions were the most important.

Maya had welcomed him to this enormous bed the first night he came to her apartment. The bed remained the same, although he had noticed as he came through the apartment that the other rooms had been redecorated again. More ornate than he remembered in the past, but as always in the Spanish style.

She had told him the bed had belong to her family in Spain, but he suspected that might be a lie.

This bed, like Ève's, was notorious. Ève's black-scaled serpent with its golden apple. Maya's bed of carved wood, lacquered black, its foot and headboard carved with obscene figures of hammered silver.

Both were the envy of less successful harlots, who hoped one day to have such an impressive bed of their own. Rich men who patronized the world of vice joked about the two beds and their exquisite occupants. Boasted of the nights they had occupied both.

He was aware of Aubé behind him, his footsteps muffled by the thick black carpet.

Fouché stood beside an unfamiliar doctor from Montmartre police headquarters who had examined Maya's body and was waiting to sign the death certificate. Other local officials had been shepherded out when he arrived to take over the investigation. The death of a famous *courtisane* was potentially too scandalous for the Préfecture to handle.

Vidocq frowned. Little Clochette had once been famous . . .

Behind him, near the double doors open onto the antechamber, a single gendarme was stationed to keep everyone out.

The only other person in the room was young Daumier. Fouché had gone to his home and roused him from sleep. Now the youth was perched on a tufted black velvet pouf at the foot of the bed, perspiring as he worked. The sketch of the body had to be done quickly before it was removed.

Vidocq glanced at the youth and saw that his eyes were red-rimmed from lack of sleep, but his hand, holding a stick of crayon, was moving like a thing possessed across a page of his large sketchbook.

There would be a dossier on Maya at Number Six. One was kept on every known *putain*. He would go through that tomorrow. Learn whatever facts—or lies—it contained.

He didn't know her name—only Maya—or remember anything of her past. Was she really Spanish? He'd never been aware of a foreign accent when she spoke French. Did she have a criminal record? He couldn't recall ever glancing through her dossier.

Most of the ambitious young women who became famous *courtisanes* were careful not to become involved with the police. Perhaps a few small thefts from their customers when they first showed up in the city, but those were seldom reported. Most of them from the start planned to keep out of trouble and devote every effort toward becoming rich and having a fine apartment, with eventually a small property in the country. That was because most of them came to Paris from some distant village.

Many of them had invisible small children being raised by a friend or relative. He knew that Ève had two children hidden away somewhere.

Les grandes courtisanes! He respected them for the way they kept out of trouble and were frequently—especially Ève—of great help when he needed information. They knew all the Paris gossip, past and present. He admired their finesse in business matters and was amused at the way they managed to obtain endless amounts of money from rich men, which they invested in property, stocks, and bonds.

Studying Maya's face, he wondered how much she'd been able to squirrel away in gold and property? What would happen to that now? If she had children, the female who was raising them would undoubtedly get her claws into everything. And the unfortunate progeny would be turned out into the streets. That frequently happened.

He didn't glance at the others behind him just yet but, turning slowly, let his eyes circle the luxurious room.

Maya's boudoir was as large and as extraordinary as Ève's. Only, where Ève's was scarlet except for that ebony serpent, this room was black and silver and more black. Two pairs of double windows draped with striped black and silver curtains, a row of silver tassels across the top. Silver cords with more tassels, held the curtains back from the windows. All of them stood open, but the moon was not yet visible, and the trees in the garden were black silhouettes against the purple night sky.

The walls of the room were covered with black leather, doors leather paneled, spiked with silver. All the leather was embossed in intricate designs. Whenever he'd been here in the past, he was aware of the strong scent of leather that dominated the perfumes floating out from the adjoining dressing room, where rows of bottles and pots were arranged in front of a silver-framed mirror on Maya's dressing table. Candelabra were lighted, but their small flames seemed to be absorbed into the black leather walls.

Her body appeared to float in a haze of light from twin oil lamps with ornate glass globes painted in a design of peacock feathers and placed on carved tables at each side of the bed. The local police would have lighted those when they arrived. He'd never seen them illuminated before.

All the furniture was made of heavily carved dark wood. He supposed it was Spanish, probably old, and could have come from some convent or monastery. The religious effect was accentuated tonight by a large oil painting hanging on a side wall, depicting the Virgin in elaborate Spanish robes with votive candles flickering on a shelf underneath. The painting had been hidden when he was here in the past behind a tapestry, which tonight was pushed aside.

Maya, like most prostitutes, had been religious.

He moved away reluctantly from the bed and permitted her to die.

His voice, when he spoke, was low but incisive. "Doctor, I want that bullet removed from her skull."

"Impossible!" The aging, weary face quivered with shock at such a request. "You know the Code Napoléon forbids an autopsy."

"One day there must be a law that will allow the medical profession to dissect human bodies, as they cut up cadavers today in medical schools."

"The public will never permit that!"

"They'll have to when it becomes law. I want that bullet." He saw that the old man's forehead was covered with perspiration. "And I must have it tomorrow."

"But, Chief, I—I . . ."

"Removing one bullet is not an autopsy. Dig it out, or I'll report you to the Préfecture for lack of cooperation."

"I'll have it for you." He shrugged, accepting defeat. "First thing in the morning."

"Send it to my office." Vidocq turned to Honoré. "Aren't you nearly finished there, my friend?"

"It's done." Daumier rose awkwardy from the pouf, holding out his sketchbook.

Vidocq was surprised once again by the crude power of the youth's work. Maya stretched out in the bed, her body suggested under the lace, mouth open—as Tessier's had been—the drying blood like two ends of a scarf down the sides of her face. "Excellent. Now make several more, just as good, of this room."

"Yes, Chief." He turned a page of his sketchbook and pulled the velvet pouf to another position.

"You can have the cadaver, Doctor."

The doctor hurried out of the boudoir, muttering to himself.

Vidocq glanced at Fouché. "Go over everything, Charles."

Fouché nodded. "As always."

"And the dressing room." He crossed the boudoir, toward the antechamber, Aubé trotting beside him. "Why don't you take one of our carriages and go home?"

"You won't need me?"

The gendarme on duty at the open doors saluted as they passed.

"I'll question the servants briefly, then head home myself. Goury can station gendarmes at all the doors and return in the morning to go over everything by daylight. So get some sleep. If you can manage it in this heat."

"I'll try." Aubé followed the doctor toward the foyer past a group of local gendarmes.

Vidocq strode after them down the corridor, turning into the salon where Goury, his back to the open doors, was questioning the servants.

There were four of them, three women and a man. An attractive maid, a cook wearing a white apron over her uniform, one kitchen-maid, and a manservant he recognized from the Bois as Maya's footman. All four were young, dark-skinned, raven-haired. Their black eyes, apprehensive and mistrustful, turned to him at once.

Goury, aware of this, looked around. "It's you." He came to meet him. "I've learned nothing here, Chief."

"Let me try a few questions." He stood in the center of the pleasant salon, glancing from face to face. Noticing as he had in the past that this salon was not so dark as the boudoir. Instead of black leather walls, these were hung with brocade which had a pattern of purple flowers against white and gray stripes. The general effect was more cheerful. Even the furniture was lighter.

205

He saw that the young man held a guitar in one hand and realized that he hadn't heard the plaintive music for several minutes.

"Which of you found the body?"

"I did." The maid stepped forward. "Señora Maya sleeps for an hour every evening after her bath. I went in, as usual, to wake her."

"What time?"

"Always at eight o'clock. It takes the Señora two hours to dress in the evening, and she likes to receive her first guest at ten."

"Your name?"

"Carlotta."

"I remember you, Carlotta, from other evenings I've been here."

"The Señora used to say you were the only gentleman who was welcome at any time."

"Did she? I suppose you are Spanish . . ."

"Oh, yes!"

"Was Madame Maya also Spanish?"

"Her father was from Madrid, but her mother was French. The Señora told me she was born in Marseille where her parents owned a tavern. She spoke only a few words of Spanish, but she liked everyone to think she came from Castille. Josefina, the cook, is my sister. The housemaid, Viktoria, is her daughter, and Ernesto is my brother."

As she named them, each made a small bow of acknowledgment.

"You were all living in Paris when she hired you?"

"I was the only one." Carlotta smiled for the first time. "I was the first. Later, when the Señora had problems finding servants, I told her about my relatives in Spain, and she gave me the money for their journey to Paris."

"We have been so happy working for the Señora!" Josefina exclaimed, eyes brimming with tears. "But we wonder what will happen to us now . . ."

"You should have no trouble finding employment." He looked at Carlotta again. "What happened when you went into the boudoir?"

"I called the Señora, but she did not answer. That was usual. We sometimes played a little game. When I tried to wake her. So, as always, I grasped her arm and shook her."

"And then?"

"Her flesh was so cold that I screamed. I knew at once the Señora was dead."

"You didn't see the blood as you touched her?"

"None of the candles were lighted."

"And, when you screamed, the others came running?"

"They didn't hear me."

"Why not?"

"I was preparing our dinner," Josefina explained. "The walls are so thick. No sounds are ever heard in the kitchen."

"Carlotta came to tell us." Ernesto continued the story. "The Señora was dead. I ran to the boudoir ahead of the others and saw the bullet hole in her forehead when I lighted a lamp." Making a sign of the cross. "Knew, without touching her, that she was dead."

His relatives crossed themselves.

"I went," he added, "to tell the police."

"What time did they get here?"

"I returned with them at once, and when I led them into the boudoir, I looked at my watch." He pulled a heavy gold watch out proudly from a pocket of his white vest. "It was half past eight." Slipping the watch back into his pocket.

"And I arrived here after ten-thirty. So, it would seem Madame Maya was shot sometime between seven o'clock, when she finished her bath . . ." Turning to Carlotta. " . . . and eight o'clock when you went to wake her. Had there been anyone, during that hour, ringing your bell?"

"Nobody." The maid glanced toward her relatives for confirmation. They shook their heads in unison.

Carlotta faced Vidocq again. "Her friends knew the Señora did not receive anyone before ten."

"No strangers at your door this afternoon? Perhaps leaving a message for Madame? Delivering something she'd ordered from a shop?"

"The doorbell didn't ring, Señor," Ernesto answered. "I'm the one always answers the bell. It rings in the kitchen."

"Nothing missing from the apartment?"

"I haven't looked." Carlotta glanced at Ernesto. "Have you?"

"There's been no time. When I returned with the gendarmes, they were only interested in who had shot the Señora."

"I didn't think about anything being missing." Carlotta's face was troubled. "We were much too upset."

"I understand, Señorita."

"Poor Señora!" The cook was weeping now. "We will never have such a good mistress again."

"I noticed," Vidocq continued, over their sobs, "there were no rings on Madame's fingers. No bracelets around her arms. She always wore many rings and bracelets . . ."

"She removed them before her bath," Carlotta explained. "The Señora always did that. Wouldn't select her jewelry for the evening until after she had dressed."

"Where are those jewels?"

"She kept them in her dressing room."

"We'd better see if anything's missing."

"Certainly, Señor."

"The rest of you wait here." As he followed Carlotta through the corridor, he remembered the last time he was here. Remembered Maya's strident laugh. Loud and harsh. She had tossed her sleek black mane of hair as he told her an amusing story he'd heard in some Montmartre cabaret. Her laughter had echoed from the leather walls.

Crossing the bedroom, he saw that the body had not been removed but the black lace coverlet was pulled up over her face. Fouché looked up from the drawer of a chest he'd been examining, and Honoré, squatting in a corner, was making a sketch of the room.

The maid led him into the small dressing room and went straight to a section of the paneled wall. "This was her hiding place. Even my family doesn't know it's here." Running a finger down the edge of a wooden panel. "There are some things about the Señora I will never tell anyone. Except you, Señor."

"I understand your loyalty." He heard a click as she swung the panel out from the wall. Saw shelves holding a large collection of jewels arranged on black velvet trays.

Carlotta gasped. "It's gone!"

"What?"

"Her beautiful necklace." Pointing to an oblong tray in the center of a shelf. The tray was empty. "I saw it here earlier, when I put the Señora's rings and bracelets away. When she was preparing for her bath."

"What sort of necklace?"

"Diamonds! The prize of her collection."

"What is it, Chief?" Fouché's voice, growling behind them.

"A diamond necklace seems to be missing," Vidocq replied without turning.

"So it's robbery," Fouché muttered, "as well as murder."

"Is that the only piece of jewelry missing?" Vidocq asked.

"All the others are here." Carlotta moved closer to the shelves. "I'm the only one ever touched them. Always brought out the jewels for the Señora and returned them at the end of the evening. I know which belong on each tray. See for yourself! Only this tray is empty."

"Were the diamonds real?"

"The Señora said they were worth a fortune. That the necklace was a gift from an admirer before I came to work for her. It was the most valuable thing she owned, and she only wore it half a dozen times each year."

"You have any idea who gave her the necklace?"

"She never told me. Only that it was made by one of the best jewelers in Paris."

"Was it Tessier?"

"That's the name! Tessier . . ."

"Please, Señor! Let me go . . ." A girl's voice behind them. "I must talk to my aunt . . ."

They turned to see that Fouché had stopped the housemaid from entering the boudoir.

"Let her come in." Vidocq ordered.

Fouché released her arm, and she stepped forward, eyes blazing.

"What is it, Viktoria?" Carlotta asked.

"I have remembered. There was someone this afternoon."

Vidocq moved toward her. "Somebody came here?"

"No. Across the street. While the Señora has her bath, I always set the table for supper. She and her guests usually eat around midnight. It was so warm that, after I'd finished, I went to the windows for a breath of air. That's when I saw her."

"Who?"

"The nun. Standing across the street . . ."

"You saw a nun?"

"It was twilight, but I could see her under the big archway."

"What was she doing there?"

"Just standing. Looking up at our windows."

"You saw her face?"

"No, Señor. Her face was in shadow."

"You're certain it was a nun?"

"Oh, yes! I am Catholic, and I know a nun when I see one. She wasn't there ten minutes later when I looked again."

"What color was her habit?"

"Black. With a black veil. At first I only saw her black skirts, but then she leaned forward and I could see white around her face under the black veil. It was too dark for me to see her features."

Vidocq frowned. "A nun . . ."

"I realized she must've been waiting for a carriage to take her back to some convent. She'd probably been in the neighborhood on an errand of charity. Visiting the sick . . ."

"Or the dead."

CHAPTER 33

Vidocq found his key and unlocked the carved entrance door as the carriage from Number Six rolled on through rue de l'Hirondelle.

The street of swallows! Tonight he would like to be a swallow and soar high above the city until he reached cool air.

He closed the heavy door and snapped the bolt.

Striding toward the steps, he saw that his mother hadn't left a note on the console table after she and Fleuride returned home.

As he went up the staircase, more slowly than usual, he continued to wonder why a nun would be waiting under an archway on rue de Provence? Standing there in the twilight, like some black-robed figure of ill omen.

Hesitating at the top of the marble steps, he listened for any sound from his mother's suite or Fleuride's bedroom in the front.

Not a whisper.

He smiled. The champagne at dinner, along with this heat, would have worked like a sleeping potion for both of them.

Continuing down the long corridor past the doors to his own suite, he hoped that Jeanne-Victoire would also be asleep. He was much too exhausted for more than a brief conversation.

He grasped the porcelain knob of her door, and, to his surprise, it felt cool under his hand. Pushed the door open, careful to make no sound, leaving it ajar as he crossed the foyer toward the candlelight beyond the open bedroom doors.

As he went toward the bed, he heard the nightingale singing outside.

Jeanne-Victoire was uncovered again, her slim body visible under a thin summer nightdress. Long blond hair spread across her breasts. Face turned away from the shaded candle on the bedside table.

He was distracted as he glimpsed himself, reflected in the tall mirror. "Who are you?"

He saw that she was watching him in the mirror. "I am Vidocq . . ."

"In this heat even Vidocq must be tired . . ."

"I am weary." He sank onto the edge of the bed, took her hand in his and kissed it. Her flesh felt feverish.

"Maman said you were called away from the restaurant . . ."

"Aubé came for me as we were having our coffee. There was a murder tonight." He seldom told her about his investigations but knew this would interest her. "Someone has killed Maya."

"Poor Maya . . ."

He felt her fingers tighten in his hand. "You knew her?"

"I've seen her in her shiny black carriage, driving with some gentleman. She was so beautiful! Why would anyone kill Maya? Did she suffer?"

"The police doctor said she died instantly. How are you feeling?"

"Always the same . . . Maman brought Fleuride to see me after they came home. Fleuride said it was the best dinner she's ever eaten."

"It probably was. I wished you were there."

"They were tired, both of them, so they went straight to bed."

"And so must I." He kissed her on the cheek and got to his feet.

"She's in love with you."

"What?"

"Fleuride . . . Talked about you constantly today and again tonight. She loves you."

"But I'm in love with you, *chérie.*"

"Nobody else?"

"Only you." He turned to leave. "See you in the morning . . ."

"Good night, my love . . ."

He glanced back from the doorway and saw that she had turned her face away from the light again. "Good night . . ."

The house was silent, except for the sound of his heels on the marble floor of the corridor.

Reaching his own suite, where one lamp had been lighted in the bedroom, he stripped and sponged himself with water from a china pitcher in the alcove beyond his bed.

One of the maids had turned down his bed, but he yanked the sheet still farther and let it hang over the carved footboard.

Noticed a volume of Ovid on the bed table. Much too warm for erotic poetry tonight. Blew out the flame of the oil lamp and went toward the open windows. Stepped outside, onto the shallow balcony. Stood there, the moonlight covering his flesh, and looked down into the side garden.

He could smell the perfume rising from invisible rosebushes.

The surrounding streets were quiet. No clopping of horses.

He turned from the windows and went toward his bed reluctantly, doubtful that he could sleep. Even the linen sheet under his body had none of its usual freshness when he stretched out. As his head sank into the pillows, he saw that the room was bright with moonlight reflected from the balcony.

He had noticed, as his carriage crossed the Pont Neuf, that the moon was nearly full. There was always an increase of crime when a full moon floated over Paris. Happened every month but especially during the summer. Aubé would have extra men on night duty at Number Six, in addition to the pairs of men stationed at those southern barriers.

Le Diable Noir! What a feather that would be in his cap if he could track him down. A crown of feathers for Number Six if they could unmask Le Diable and put him in a solitary cell at La Force!

He closed his eyes, shutting out the moonlight.

And immediately saw Maya's face again.

Paris would have another sensation when news got out that one of *les grandes courtisanes* had been murdered in her bed. The Spanish whore. Although it seemed she was only half Spanish . . .

This murder, on top of Tessier's, must be solved quickly or he would be getting complaints from the Minister who welcomed any opportunity to goad him when he didn't find a murderer in twenty-four hours.

And little Clochette? Was there a connection between her death and Maya's? Not likely . . .

He turned over, away from the windows, to escape the moonlight that penetrated his closed eyelids.

Before leaving Maya's apartment, he had instructed Goury and Fouché to order everyone from Number Six, as well as those from Montmartre police headquarters, not to talk about Maya's death.

Unfortunately, someone would. News of her murder would seep like drops of poison into the dark streets. One of Maya's household staff would whisper it to a neighbor's servant, or a talkative gendarme would mention it to his mistress later tonight, in bed. The news would trickle through the gutters of Montmartre until by morning it would flow down the hills and flood half of Paris.

He must find her murderer immediately! Tomorrow . . .

Tomorrow, on his own, he would look into the matter of that diamond necklace missing from Maya's dressing room.

Tessier again! First the bracelet sold to Monsieur Pennypacker and now a necklace someone had given to Maya . . .

Was it possible that Tessier's murder somehow could be involved with the death of Maya? Life was full of such accidents of proximity, time and space, which appeared to be involved with each other but actually were not.

That nun across the street could have been nursing some sick person in another mansion on rue de Provence.

All convents were closed during the Revolution, but many had been reopened and resumed their charitable activities. Sending nuns out to nurse the aged or give help to the poor.

Tomorrow he would have his own Nun question other residents of rue de Provence. Find out if anyone else had seen a nun in that archway.

A whisper of sound, barely more than a rustle of movement, came across the bedroom.

His eyes opened instantly.

Fleuride stood beside his bed in her yellow satin robe.

"What the devil are you doing here?" he whispered.

"Couldn't sleep. Heard you come up the steps and knew you'd see Jeanne-Victoire. Listened until you returned down the corridor. Gave you time to undress . . ."

"That was good of you. Did Maman hear you coming to my room?"

"She's been snoring for hours!"

"You shouldn't be here."

213

Fleuride let her robe drop to the floor.

He saw that her body was like unblemished ivory in the reflected moonlight. The small breasts were round and firm.

She kicked off her yellow satin slippers and came toward the bed.

He held out his arms.

Fleuride sighed and collapsed into his embrace.

Vidocq kissed her lightly on the cheek.

Her lips brushed across his throat as she stretched out beside him. "You aren't angry? That I'm here . . ."

"I am pleased."

"It was such a lovely evening. That restaurant . . ." She snuggled down, resting her face on his chest, pushing her body against his side.

He felt one firm nipple pressing into his flesh. "Aren't you sleepy?"

"Yes . . . But I had to see you before I slept. Talk to you . . ."

Slowly, casually, he slipped an arm under her.

"I told Tante. I've never had such an exciting evening. Eating pheasant and drinking champagne . . ."

"I'm glad you enjoyed it." He felt her arm resting on his belly, delicate fingers moving across his chest like inquisitive small animals.

"That man tonight . . ."

"Which man?"

"The handsome one. Although not so handsome as you." Her fingers had come to a stop on his shoulder. "He came to our table . . ."

"Monsieur Beyle?"

"He thought I was your wife . . ."

"Yes . . ."

He realized that she was still feeling the champagne. Probably the most wine she'd ever drunk. He remembered his first champagne. When he went to Calais with that actress. She had ordered champagne with dinner, and he didn't realize, until next morning, that he had drunk most of the bottle. The actress had taken all his money. And all these years he'd wondered if she used it to sail off to Phil-a-del-phia . . .

He glanced down at Fleuride beside him, her lovely face. Eyes closed. Smiling. Looked closer and saw that she was asleep.

CHAPTER 34

A yellow rosebud from the vase on his desk was in his lapel, releasing its fragrance as the morning air became warmer.

The first thing to catch his eye as he sat down had been a small brown envelope, which he knew would be from the doctor who worked with Montmartre police headquarters.

Inside the envelope was the bullet from Maya's skull.

He rested it on the leather surface of his desk, then reached down to bring out the Tessier bullet from a drawer and placed it beside the other one. Picked up his magnifying glass and studied both. They appeared to be identical. Precisely the same size, both slightly crushed at the tip. Any judge would probably agree that they appeared to have been discharged from the same pistol, but there was no way to prove that.

Had one person shot both of them using one gun? If so their deaths would be connected in other ways. Or had two people with similar pistols fired those shots? He would, until he found evidence to the contrary, hold to the theory that there was one murderer and one gun.

Pushing the two bullets carefully to an open space between piles of documents, he picked up a dossier marked MAYA, which Aubé had left for him to examine. Opened it and glanced through the papers inside.

Maya had indeed used many names, none of which were believed to be the one she was given at birth. One report said that she was born in Seville, her mother Greek, father French. Another that she had been born in Bayonne, mother French, father Spanish. She had been in a Marseille prison years ago for fighting in cafés and using a knife indiscriminately on both men and women.

Vidocq shook his head.

She had also been in several Paris hospitals for the usual complaints suffered by prostitutes but also from time to time, for problems with her lungs. Had given birth to several children, but there was no record of what had happened to them.

He closed the dossier and set it aside for Aubé to return to the locked files. Glanced through yesterday's reports from his staff but found nothing to require his attention. Set them on top of Maya's dossier and picked up young Honoré's sketches of Maya and her boudoir. There

215

must be something in her apartment—one small fact— that could lead to the identity of her murderer and hopefully the murderer of Tessier. If so, it wasn't apparent in these drawings. He sighed as he put them aside. Amused that Daumier had signed his initials—"H.D."—on each sketch.

"Isn't this your natal day, Chief?"

He looked up to see Aubé with his pencil and notebook. "Certainly not! Where'd you get that idea?"

"You've changed the date of your birth many times, but I saw some official document that said you were born on this date."

"Did you! Somebody gave them the wrong date. Are you trying to ruin my morning?"

Aubé chuckled. "Will you be staying in today?"

"I'll be out most of this morning. Sit down, my friend, and I'll give you my approximate itinerary."

Aubé took his usual chair on Vidocq's right, resting his notebook on the leather arm and holding his pencil in readiness.

"First of all, I plan another visit to the Tessier residence to see if we've turned up anything more there or found any trace of the missing Drumont. And I want to have another talk with Marpon."

"Such a pathetic old man . . ."

"Confided to me he was on the King's staff at Versailles. Which means he had to develop the high art of eavesdropping. Marpon knows much more about Tessier, I suspect, than he's divulged. When I finish on rue Taitbout, I intend to have another look at Maya's apartment. Any word on what happened last night at those southern barriers?"

"There was nothing of a suspicious nature at any of them."

"Put other men on duty tonight. Change them each night, so no one will become suspicious of the additional inspectors. When's the full moon?"

"Tomorrow night, I think . . ."

"Later this morning I plan to visit Baron de Chabrillat to question him about a certain desk . . . I'll return here, hopefully before noon, but tell Madame Babelay I won't require any lunch. Have you seen young Revol?"

"Not today. He told me yesterday he'd be late. You instructed him to bring in two of Tessier's former employees for questioning."

"Let me know when they arrive."

Aubé pushed himself to his feet. "I was certain this was your anniversary . . ."

"Not this year, my friend. Anything more from the Préfecture about Le Diable Noir?"

"Nothing in today's official report." He headed for the anteroom. "The young ladies are waiting to see you."

"Send them in."

Vidocq revolved his chair and faced the open windows, squinting at the glare of sunlight in Petite rue Sainte-Anne.

His birthday! The thought depressed him. Fortunately nobody else at Number Six suspected the truth.

He had left rue de l'Hirondelle earlier than usual, before his mother or Fleuride were awake. The servants—including Jean, his driver—were asleep so he walked to Place du Pont Saint-Michel and found a fiacre to bring him here and had gone upstairs for Madame Babelay's croissants and coffee.

Forty-eight years old! Age didn't interest him, only annoyed him—once a year. Even his wife had no idea that this was his natal day. She too had been asleep this morning.

He was aware of the Rat's clumping steps behind him and the light sound of the Nun's slippers on the bare floor. "Good morning, ladies!" Turning his chair to inspect them across his desk and smiling. This unlikely pair always amused him.

"Good morning, Chief!" The Rat responded, her gutter voice harsh, but the Nun only smiled sweetly. They stood side by side waiting for instructions.

"I've jobs for you. Have one of our carriages take you and bring you back to report to me before noon." As he talked, he saw that both young women were dressed for another hot day. The Rat was in a coarse brown blouse and skirt, but the Nun wore faded gray, with scarves of the same colors around their heads, hiding their hair and making them even more anonymous. He spoke first to the Nun. "I want you to question the neighbors on rue de Provence where the Spanish whore, Maya, was murdered last night."

The Nun crossed herself.

"Goury just told us." The Rat's eyes glittered with curiosity.

"The killer, I suspect, could be the same person who shot Narcisse Tessier." He pointed to the bullets. "These appear to be identical. One

217

of Maya's servants observed a nun standing under an archway across the street shortly before Maya's murder, apparently watching their windows. I want that nun found."

"What color habit was she wearing?" the Nun asked.

"Black. With white around her face and a black veil."

"Sounds like an Ursuline. They wear white wimples."

"Tell people you're searching for a missing nun. Find out if anyone else noticed her last evening. Get her description. The maid who glimpsed her in the twilight was unable to see her face." He turned to the Rat. "I want you to find out everything you can about Maya. What the neighbors say about her and what they've observed. But don't—either of you—tell anyone she's been murdered. We don't want the newspapers to know, just yet. They'll find out soon enough!"

The Rat nodded.

"Say you're looking for a maid's job. That you've recently worked for Maya but didn't like her. That should make people talk." He made a gesture of dismissal. "I should return here myself before noon and will await your reports."

The two young women left single file, the Rat hurrying ahead, passing Aubé who entered with Goury, Fouché, and Allard behind him.

Vidocq waited to speak until all were seated and the young women had reached the distant corridor. His first question was to Goury. "Find anything more last night in Maya's apartment?"

"Nothing."

"Take two men this morning and have them strip that boudoir and dressing room. Tear out the wall compartment where her jewels were kept. Rip all the leather from the walls. There must be something hidden there."

"I've been thinking." Goury frowned. "Could there be some link between these two murders—Maya and Tessier?"

"I'm wondering the same thing." Pointing toward the bullets on his desk. "The two bullets seem identical."

They all leaned forward to peer at them.

"We now have a diamond necklace missing, as well as a diamond bracelet. Both bought from Tessier. The bracelet purchased by Monsieur Penny-packaire for his daughter and the necklace ordered by some unknown admirer as a present for the Spanish whore. You can get an exact description of the necklace from Revol. The design will be in one of those cardboard tubes we removed from the Tessier mansion."

"Revol, by the way, just came in." Aubé's spectacles caught reflections of sunlight from outside the windows. "He's waiting for you, downstairs, with another man."

"Only one man? I'll join them in a moment." Facing the others. "And what about all those diamonds that vanished with Drumont?"

"No trace of them," Fouché muttered. "Diamonds or man."

"Has anything turned up about Drumont's past?"

"Not a single fact. He's disappeared as though he never existed. The police at rue Taitbout headquarters have no record on him."

He glanced at Aubé. "You notified Marseille?"

"Yesterday. But it will be at least a week before we hear from those southerners."

Vidocq shook his head, puzzled. "This Tessier murder seems to have so few facts. Except that Tessier is dead! Nobody's turned up to claim his money or the missing diamonds and his lawyers haven't appeared with a will!" He frowned. "Perhaps there's an important fact contained in this lack of facts." He turned, abruptly, to Allard. "Any strange couples staying at the Hôtel Belvedere?"

"One middle-aged couple from London. They're strange, but they're not criminal types. I saw Ronquetti in the lobby. He gave me a signal not to approach him."

"Ronquetti's staying there, observing the American and his daughter. I thought it would be better for you to check on the other guests. Might look suspicious if the Duc de Modena asked questions about them." He remembered something suddenly and turned back to Fouché. "I want you to send three of our best men—former burglars— to the home of Monsieur Pradier tonight. I ran into the gentleman at the Café de Paris, last evening, where I'd gone to dine with my family. The fool presumed to approach me as we entered the restaurant and say he was unable to pay the interest on some money he borrowed last year. A matter of one hundred thousand francs."

Allard whistled softly.

Fouché laughed. "I know what you want done, Chief."

"Three men should be able to handle it. Tell them to remove articles from Pradier's residence—preferably paintings and fine silver—to the precise value of one hundred thousand francs. You know where to dispose of them."

"I'll tend to it."

"When Pradier storms in here to report the robbery I won't see him." Facing Aubé. "If I'm in, warn the guards not to permit him upstairs until you've closed these doors. You will send Pradier across to the Préfecture. Inform him the matter isn't important enough for the Sûreté to investigate. That should infuriate him. If the Préfecture wants us to look into the matter we will of course agree to do so, but after a week we'll say we've found no trace of the missing articles or the robbers. This should teach Monsieur Pradier a lesson. And he'll still owe me one hundred thousand francs! Which, of course, he'll never repay."

His assistants were laughing as they got to their feet.

"I'll be leaving in half an hour." Rising from his desk and striding toward the open door trailed by the others. "After I see Revol."

CHAPTER 35

Revol was waiting in the dim anteroom, studying the painting of a guillotine hanging above the lighted oil lamp. He looked around as Vidocq entered. "Good morning, Chief."

"Good morning, my friend. You brought only one man?"

"Ponsard. The other man, Thanot, wasn't home. Nobody answered his door."

"Oh?"

"Monsieur Ponsard's waiting inside and, to my surprise, looking very guilty."

Vidocq chuckled. "Even the innocent appear guilty when they visit our interrogation room. Tell me again, who is he?"

"Jean Ponsard—eldest of the three designers."

"What's he like?"

"Constantly grumbling and threatening to leave. For my taste, his designs are old-fashioned, but he's taught me a great deal about the technical side of designing jewelry."

Vidocq moved toward the inner door, reaching for the knob. "How was Mademoiselle Penny-packaire yesterday afternoon?" Glancing back, he saw Revol's face crimson. "You did meet the young American lady?"

"You do know everything."

He was smiling as he opened the door into the dark interrogation room and saw a gray-haired man seated at the far end of the long table, in a circle of light from the overhead lantern. "Good morning, Monsieur ..."

Ponsard jerked erect, startled by the voice.

"We have met before." He stood at the end of the table, facing Ponsard, as Revol closed the door.

"Monsieur Ponsard ..." Vidocq hesitated, noticing the rows of cardboard tubes arranged in groups down the table. "I requested your associate, Monsieur Revol, to bring you here for questioning. Not as a suspect but as someone who, I hope, may be able to assist us with important information concerning the murder of your employer, Narcisse Tessier."

Ponsard appeared to relax slightly, folding his hands in front of him on the table.

Vidocq noticed that they were thin and pale. "First, what can you tell me about a diamond necklace that was designed for the Spanish whore—Maya? Do you know who purchased it?"

"That was ordered four years ago by the Baron de Chabrillat."

"Baron de Chabrillat?"

"The Baron has in the past purchased several pieces of jewelry. None recently, to my knowledge."

"Diamonds?"

"Always diamonds."

"Could you identify those items from the sketches in these tubes?"

"I can show you which pieces we designed for the Baron, but I may not be able to tell you who got them. We rarely knew what became of our creations. From time to time, Monsieur Tessier—if he was in a pleasant mood—would mention that a certain item had been purchased for some gentleman's wife or daughter. He was much too discreet to say it was intended for a mistress. One day, when he was unusually friendly, he said the Baron had given that particular necklace to Maya."

"You didn't like your employer?"

"No, Monsieur, but I didn't dislike him enough to kill him."

"Why did you dislike him?"

221

Ponsard shrugged. "There was something about the man that offended me. Something furtive and, I suspect, dishonorable. I was never able to discover what it was. I've discussed this with my wife, many times, without finding the answer."

"Could you pick out the designs created for the Baron and let me see them?"

"Certainly. The letters CH will be on each one."

"Revol will assist you."

Ponsard rose and joined Revol at the side of the table, where another lantern had been lighted above the cardboard tubes.

Revol picked up several tubes from one group and examined the labels pasted across the metal lids. "Here's one that was sold to the Baron." He unscrewed the lid and slid out the rolled sketch.

Vidocq moved closer as Revol spread the sheet of paper on the table, resting the empty tube across the top of the drawing to hold it flat. He saw that it was a sketch for an exquisite diamond necklace.

"This isn't the one the Baron gave to Maya," Ponsard explained. "That necklace was less elaborate. And less expensive."

"To whom did the Baron give this one?" Vidocq asked.

"I've no idea. Tessier never told me."

Revol picked up several more of the tubes and checked the names.

"Here are two more designs made for Baron de Chabrillat." Revol was spreading them flat on the table. "Another necklace and a small cross. His name's on the tube and his initials are under both sketches."

"A cross?" Vidocq moved closer as Ponsard inspected them. He saw that this necklace was not so elaborate as the first, and the cross was small but covered with diamonds. And suddenly he was certain that he was looking at Clochette's cross.

"I designed this necklace!" Ponsard tapped the drawing with a forefinger. "It's the one the Baron gave to that Spanish woman."

"And the cross?"

"I've no idea who got that."

"Which of you designed it?"

"That's Marcel's design," Revol responded.

"Marcel Jaune," Ponsard continued. "There's nothing on any of these drawings to indicate who received them. Only who bought them. See here?" Tapping the letters CH on both sheets. "This means sold to Baron de Chabrillat. And his name is on the lids."

"Can you tell me," Vidocq asked, "what these pairs of letters mean at the end of both these inscriptions? RE and DE . . . Why aren't they on this other, more elaborate, necklace design?"

Ponsard faced Vidocq. "I suppose there's no reason for me not to tell you, Monsieur. The matter is confidential, but since Tessier is dead. Murdered . . ."

"There's been another murder. Maya was shot last night. Like Tessier, a bullet in her forehead. And her necklace is missing."

"*Mon Dieu!*" Ponsard murmured.

"Tell him, Monsieur Jean, if you know," Revol urged. "The meaning of these letters."

"It's very simple," Ponsard explained. "The RE means returned."

"So Maya's necklace had been returned to Tessier!" Vidocq stepped back, out of the light from the lantern. "But not this other necklace. Why not? Why wasn't it returned?"

"I've no idea."

"And DE?"

"DE means that item was destroyed after it was returned."

"Destroyed? For what reason?"

"I couldn't say, Monsieur. Many designs have those two pairs of initials at the bottom. Thanot, the goldsmith, told me their meaning years ago. He sometimes informed me when something was returned to him with an order from Tessier to destroy it."

"I never knew that!" Revol exclaimed.

"And what, exactly, do you mean—destroyed?" Vidocq asked.

"The jewels would be removed from their setting, and the metals— gold and silver—would be melted down," Ponsard explained.

"What happened to the jewels?"

"They would be used in other designs. Thanot always recognized them. He knows more about precious gems than I, and he would inform me when they became part of a new piece of jewelry."

"How often did this happen? Jewels would be used again . . ."

"Constantly, Monsieur. I didn't attempt to keep track. Of course a copy was always made of each original design with imitation stones."

"What became of them?"

"I never knew."

"Could those have been copies I saw in Tessier's vault? Necklaces, tiaras and the rest . . ."

"Who showed them to you?"

"Drumont."

"We never, any of us, knew where the jewels were kept. I always suspected there had to be a vault somewhere. Monsieur Drumont, by the way, could answer your questions better than I."

"Drumont has disappeared, along with all the jewels. The gold and silver. That vault is empty."

The door opened and Aubé hurried in. "Excuse me, Chief."

"What is it, my friend?"

"There's a journalist upstairs, asking about the Tessier murder. I've told him you're not in the building, but he demands to know when he can see you."

"Send him over to the Préfecture with his questions."

"They'll only send him back to us."

"By that time I won't be here. When he returns, say I'm working on the Tessier investigation and there should be information for him in a few days."

"I'll tell him."

"He didn't ask about Maya?"

"Not a word."

"So the newspapers haven't heard! Order me a carriage and have one of the guards bring my hat and cane down to the stables."

"Right away!" Aubé hurried off, leaving the door open.

Vidocq turned back to Ponsard. "You've been very helpful, Monsieur. I may need to see you again."

"Certainly, Monsieur Vidocq."

"Revol will take you home in a carriage." Glancing at Revol as he went toward the door. "I'm going back to rue Taitbout."

CHAPTER 36

Vidocq sat facing Tessier's desk, in the same comfortable *fauteuil* the murderer must have occupied, eyes darting about the sunny salon.

Birds were singing in the trees beyond the open windows, and the panel in the *boiserie* stood open.

He'd come in here after observing what his assistants were doing. Goury had been supervising one group of men as they ripped Drumont's office apart, and Fouché, with another group, was digging up that stone floor in the empty vault.

There had to be something hidden somewhere.

He had headed for the salon because he wanted a moment of quiet to consider what he'd learned from Ponsard at Number Six.

The most important fact was that many pieces of jewelry were returned to Tessier and destroyed. Including that necklace Baron de Chabrillat had given to Maya. So the necklace stolen by her killer had to be a duplicate. And Clochette's cross . . .

Now he must find out who had received that other diamond necklace from the Baron. The one that had not been returned and destroyed . . .

He looked around, hearing footsteps, and saw Goury come through the open panel. "Found something, my friend?"

"Not so much as a lost centime. We're still tearing the paneling from the walls. I wanted to tell you . . ."

"Have you seen Marpon this morning?"

"I asked about the old man when I arrived, but nobody had seen him since last night."

"Mon Dieu!" Vidocq sprang to his feet and strode toward the open panel. "Didn't that suggest something might be wrong?"

Goury followed, out of the salon, down the long corridor.

Vidocq was running, heading for the remembered inner staircase. Taking the steps two at a time. Not talking in order to conserve his breath. Down an upstairs hall to another flight of steps—narrow, twisting, and wooden—to the attic where he'd seen the servants' rooms on his previous tour of the mansion.

Goury followed.

Past open doors, which revealed cubicles where members of the staff had slept. All empty, except for a single plain chair, crude wooden table and narrow bed, its straw mattress exposed. Under each high circular window was a small armoire.

Only one door was closed.

Vidocq slowed to a stop and waited until Goury, panting for breath, caught up with him. Only then did he knock gently on the cracked wood.

No sound came from inside.

He grasped the knob reluctantly, turned it, and pushed the door open.

The old man's diminutive figure, in a white nightshirt, was on the small wooden bed.

Vidocq hesitated in the doorway. "Monsieur Marpon?" For a brief moment he thought the thin legs moved slightly, but he knew they hadn't.

The attic was sweltering in the rays of sunlight slanting from the round window overhead as he approached the bed.

He reached down to touch the old man's bony shoulder. "He's dead." Leaning closer, he saw dark bruises on the emaciated neck and the protruding tongue. "Strangled." He straightened and turned to Goury. "Send a man to rue Taitbout police headquarters. Tell them there's been another murder here. They'd better bring the same doctor who examined Tessier."

"I'm sorry, Chief." Goury's face was troubled. "I should've warned the guards to watch the old man last night. I didn't realize he might be in danger . . ."

"I'm the one should've ordered them to look out for him." Shaking his head. "We can't think of everything, my friend."

"I'll be right back."

Left alone, Vidocq made a quick search of the bare room. Not a picture on the soiled gray walls or a rug on the splintered floor.

The only chair held the clothes Marpon would have worn this morning. A pair of thin gray trousers and a patched shirt. Gray socks, darned many times, one draped over each cracked shoe.

On the bedside table, resting on a wooden block, was the powdered wig the old man had worn when they first met. Beside it were the stub of a candle in an iron holder with an empty wineglass.

Vidocq picked up the glass and held it to his nose. There was a faint scent of wine. Marpon must've had a glass of wine to make him sleep.

He set the glass down and pulled out the drawer under the table. Inside was a pile of white silk handkerchiefs, carefully mended, relics of the past. Three pairs of gray socks, two neatly folded white waistcoats.

Opening the armoire, he recognized the gray satin livery, embroidered waistcoat, and ruffled white shirt—the uniform of the major-domo—polished black shoes with silver buckles. Two threadbare gray suits on the other side, a pair of scuffed shoes beneath them.

He turned away from these pathetic relics and went back to the small figure on the bed. Leaned down for a closer examination. He could see that the dark bruises on the old man's throat were finger marks.

Someone must have entered the mansion last night while those guards napped and made their way up here. Someone who knew where to find Marpon.

Drumont had come back because he feared Marpon would talk to the police! Returned to silence him ...

So Drumont was in Paris last night!

He would have Aubé send out word that Alcidor Drumont was now wanted for questioning about the murder of Auguste Marpon.

Something was clutched in the old man's right hand.

He reached down and tried to remove the object from the icy fingers, but they were rigid.

Leaned closer and, using both hands, pulled the fingers away from a round object which fell onto the bed.

The brooch!

Vidocq snatched it up and examined it more carefully than he'd been able to do in the carriage.

The delicate face of the dead Queen, smiling happily, forever young.

CHAPTER 37

The maid, Carlotta, opened the door. "Ah, Señor!"

He entered without a word and saw tall wax candles, thick and white, burning in the black and silver foyer as he was engulfed by a heavy pall of incense.

The only sound was the mournful cadence of that distant guitar. Today it sounded like a dirge.

Vidocq turned as he heard the door close behind him. "Are my assistants here, Señorita?"

"Three men arrived this morning. They have upset everything again in the Señora's boudoir."

"That unfortunately is necessary." He didn't bother to remove his hat as, flourishing his cane, he strode down the corridor.

She followed, petticoats rustling. "But, Señor ..."

"And the two men on guard duty? Why didn't one of them answer my ring?"

"They're in the kitchen, drinking coffee while they listen to Ernesto's guitar. Today his music is very sad . . ."

"When they finish their coffee, inform them that I'm here."

"There's a gentleman . . ."

"Today I want to have another look at . . . Gentleman?"

". . . in the salon."

"What gentleman?"

"The Vicomte de Manceau."

"What's a Vicomte doing here?"

"He's been the Señora's friend—her *cavalier ardente*—for the past year."

Vidocq turned to face her. "The Señora's lover?"

"Oh, yes! He loved her very much."

"Have my assistants questioned him?"

"He only arrived a moment ago."

"Does he know she was murdered?"

"I was following him toward the salon when you rang the bell. Didn't have a chance to talk to him." There was a wail of anguish from the kitchen, accompanied by dark chords from the guitar. "My brother is part gypsy. He's playing music for the dead."

Vidocq continued on toward the double doors of the salon, which, as usual, stood open. "I will speak to the Vicomte."

"He is a good man. He, truly, loved the Señora . . ."

An elegantly dressed man sat on a black divan piled with rose velvet cushions, his high-crowned gray hat beside him. He seemed an illusion in the haze of incense. Wearing a tan summer suit, yellow waistcoat over a ruffled white silk shirt with a flowered cravat. Both yellow-gloved hands clutched a cane as he leaned forward, staring at the full-length portrait of Maya hanging in the center of one wall. Curtains were closed across the windows, but lighted candles in silver candelabra were arranged on a table beneath the painting, around a large black pottery bowl in which the incense was burning.

The air was suffocating, heated by the candle flames, the odor of incense unpleasant.

Realizing that the Vicomte was unaware of his presence, Vidocq moved forward to get a better view of his face and was surprised to see tears on the one visible cheek. He appeared to be in his early forties. Strikingly handsome, with a prominent jaw and the long French nose that is seen in old portraits. His curly hair was pale brown, the jaw softened by a neatly trimmed beard.

Vidocq realized that he had seen him many times, dining in fine restaurants and riding in his carriage. "Monsieur le Vicomte . . ."

"Who is it?" He turned to peer through the veil of incense.

Vidocq saw that his eyes were blue. "Forgive my intrusion, Monsieur. I am . . ."

"Vidocq."

"You know me . . ."

"You've been pointed out to me many times on the boulevards." He rested his cane on the divan, pulled a silk handkerchief from his cuff, and wiped his eyes. "So! Your presence confirms the rumor I heard earlier. She has been murdered . . ."

"Yes."

"I was about to question the maid, Carlotta, when you rang the bell and she hurried away. Which gave me a moment alone with my beloved's portrait. I am grieving, you see . . ." He tucked the handkerchief into his cuff again. "I loved her. As I've never loved another woman. Including my dear wife."

"Where did you hear that Madame Maya had been murdered?"

"At my bank. Some friends were talking and laughing. When I asked what amused them they told me the Spanish whore was dead. Murdered . . . I didn't realize at first whom they were discussing. Then one of them said that every whore in Paris would wear black to Maya's funeral. And another man said that she would make a beautiful corpse. I turned, hiding my shock, and left the bank without tending to my business. Tell me, Monsieur, who did this horrible thing? Who killed my beloved?"

"I've no idea, as yet."

"But you will find her murderer? You must!"

"That's my intention. May I ask you several questions?"

"Of course."

"Some may seem indiscreet."

"Most questions are indiscreet, Monsieur."

"How long had Maya been your mistress?"

He shrugged. "Perhaps a year . . ."

229

"Where did you meet her?"

"Here. In this apartment. I'd seen her, of course, in her box at the theater. Usually I would be with my wife, but I was able many times to admire Maya's beauty from a distance. Then, one spring evening, I was having dinner at my club with some male acquaintances . . ."

"Which club?"

"The Midnight Club. After dinner they insisted I come here and finish the evening with Maya. I did so with reluctance but was entranced by the lady, from the moment our eyes met."

"You were aware that she'd had other wealthy lovers?"

"She confessed to me that she'd been the mistress of many men, but there had been no one man for more than a year. Also that she hadn't actually loved any of them."

"You believed her?"

"I wanted to believe her. You see, from the start, I was completely enthralled. I left here with my friends but returned within the hour. Maya promised to send everyone away, and she had done so. I stayed until dawn. I've never known such a glorious night. Even with my wife, in the early years of our marriage . . ."

"I can understand that."

"I've never before been involved in the world of *les grandes courtisanes*. I had heard gossip about them and observed them in public, but my marriage was a happy one. Until two years ago when my wife, after bearing three children, informed me that she had no further interest in her duties as wife and mother. She told me that love was for young people, not middle-aged married couples. I soon discovered what she meant. She had taken a young lover. I suppose, in the following months, I began to look for a mistress without realizing what I was doing. When I met Maya, I was aware that I was in love as I'd never been before."

"Did your wife find out?"

"She has never suspected anything. We have separate suites, so she is never aware of the hour I come home at night or whether I return at all. What's more, she doesn't care. I warned Maya, from the start, that I would not permit a scandal. We must never be seen together in public. I would dine here only when there were no other guests. And, most important, she must have no other lovers."

"She agreed to this?"

"Without a moment's hesitation. I of course have paid all her expenses. This has been the happiest year of my life. But now my life is finished."

"Have you any idea, Monsieur, who had a motive to kill her?"

"There could be no motive for anyone to kill Maya. She was an angel!"

"But someone did kill her, and there can be no murder without motive. Did she have enemies?"

"She never mentioned any to me."

"Some person she feared? Perhaps from her past . . ."

"None!"

"A previous lover? One with whom she had quarreled . . ."

"Her quarrels were like summer storms. Sudden and violent, because of her Spanish blood, but gone without a trace."

"Did she ever mention the Baron de Chabrillat?"

"Several times. Told me she hadn't seen him in more than two years. I believed her."

"Did she tell you the Baron had given her an expensive diamond necklace?"

"Yes, she did."

"Did she say he bought it from the jeweler Tessier?"

"She never mentioned where the Baron had purchased it, and I wasn't interested."

"You knew Tessier?"

"I'd heard of him, but to my knowledge we've never met."

"Tessier was also a member of the Midnight Club."

"Most prominent Parisian businessmen are."

"You never saw him there?"

"I wouldn't recognize him if I did. Why are you questioning me about Tessier? I don't understand . . ."

"He too has been murdered."

"What?"

"Both of them with a bullet in the forehead."

"There can be no connection between their deaths!"

"I suspect there may be. That diamond necklace was missing when Maya's body was found."

"Stolen?"

"By the murderer. That's the only thing he took . . ."

"You think it was a common thief?"

"I only know that Maya is dead and the necklace is gone." He bowed slightly. "Thank you for answering my questions."

The Vicomte rose from the divan. "Is it possible that my name can be kept out of your investigation?"

"I will make every effort to do so."

"The de Manceau name has been unblemished for centuries. If it were linked with Maya's murder—and I swear to you I had nothing to do with her death . . ."

"I believe you, Monsieur le Vicomte."

" . . . my children's lives would be damaged, my political career finished . . ."

"Your name need not be mentioned in any of my official reports. Unless, of course, I discover you are involved with Maya's murder."

"I loved her, Monsieur. I could never have harmed her." He walked toward the portrait. "The thought that she's—gone—is inconceivable. I will not, of course, attend her funeral, because I would be unable to control my grief." Looking up at her painted face. "But I will arrange for a requiem mass with clouds of white roses around your bier. You loved white roses . . ."

Vidocq retreated silently, aware that the Vicomte was talking to the portrait.

"I will arrange for your loyal servants, Carlotta and her family, to have a fine new home. They too loved you . . ."

The sound of the guitar became distinct again as Vidocq continued down the corridor toward Maya's boudoir. Crossing the anteroom, his footsteps silent on the thick black carpet, he saw young Damiot with two other men from Number Six tearing strips of black leather from the boudoir walls.

This morning none of the candles were lighted, including the votive lights beneath the painting of the Virgin. Curtains had been pulled back, and harsh daylight came through all the open windows. The room had been destroyed. Bed torn apart, the feather mattress dumped to the floor and ripped apart, some of the silver figures pried from the headboard. Drawers pulled out, upholstery slashed from chairs.

Damiot sensed eyes watching him and turned from his work of destruction with a knife in his hand.

"Found anything?" Vidocq asked.

Damiot came to meet him. "The metal figures on the bed are made of nickel, not silver, and most of the leather's so thin it tears like paper. All those silver tassels and cords at the windows are painted. Everything is false!"

"That doesn't surprise me. Whoever decorates a whore's apartment always cheats her. I want another look at that dressing room."

"Where's Goury?"

"He and Fouché are busy at rue Taitbout." Vidocq saw that Carlotta had followed him into the boudoir. "Señorita, you can open that panel again. I wish to see the other jewels."

"But your men sealed it yesterday."

"I'll break the seals." Continuing on into the dressing room, he noticed that a window he'd never seen before had been opened and none of the candelabra were lighted. He approached the paneled wall and saw two scarlet seals with the official imprint of the Sûreté. Shattered them with sharp blows from the silver head of his cane. "Now you can open it."

She moved past him, ran her fingers along the wooden edge and pulled the panel back.

He propped his cane against a chair. "I'll have a look at the jewels by daylight." Lifting one of the black velvet trays and carrying it to the open window.

Carlotta followed.

This tray held a pair of diamond earrings, a large gold bracelet encrusted with emeralds, and several heavy Spanish-looking necklaces.

He picked up an earring and examined it as Carlotta watched. "You thought that necklace—the one that was stolen—was genuine? The diamonds real?"

"Well, Señor, I . . ."

Vidocq glanced at her as she hesitated, searching her eyes for the truth. "Didn't Madame Maya ever tell you they were false? The necklace was only a copy? That she had sold the original necklace . . ."

"Yes, Señor. She told me."

He held the diamond earring toward the light. The stones were lifeless, without sparkle. "These too are false. She had sold everything."

"Yes, Señor. All the Señora's jewels are false . . ."

"To whom did she sell them?"

"The Señora never told me."

CHAPTER 38

Vidocq leaned forward as his carriage slowed on the Avenue des Champs-Élysées past what appeared to be a walled garden. He'd driven along here countless times but had never known who lived here. The horses turned in through open wrought-iron gates, one of which was rusted and hanging from a single hinge. On either side of the broad drive were desolate stretches of lawn, which hadn't been watered in months. Flower beds were overgrown and withered. Marble statues stained and cracked. The carriage stopped in front of a mansion with a handsomely proportioned facade that had crumbled into ruin. Tiles missing from the roof and rust stains running down the walls like opened veins.

He stepped down into a filthy courtyard where weeds flourished between the cobbles and the broad marble steps leading to the entrance were covered with dead leaves, which his boots crushed to dust.

There was no bell pull, only a bronze knocker formed by the leering face of a horned satyr.

He grasped one of the horns and banged the knocker.

Moving away from the tall doors, he gazed down at the lawn scorched by the summer sun and realized that the Champs-Élysées was invisible beyond the trees. No sound of passing carriages or horses' hooves reached in here.

"Monsieur?"

He whirled to face a smiling servant woman. "I am Vidocq."

"Yes, Monsieur?"

His name obviously meant nothing. "I wish to see Baron de Chabrillat."

"Monsieur le Baron doesn't see anyone, these days . . ."

"It is urgent that I talk to him." He studied her pleasant face as she attempted to make a decision. A thin woman, white-haired and pink-cheeked, wearing a clean white apron over her faded blue dress.

"Come in, Monsieur." Pushing the door for him to enter. "I will speak to Monsieur le Baron."

He stepped into an immense entrance hall with a curving marble staircase larger than the one in the Tessier mansion.

The woman closed the door. "If you will wait here, Monsieur . . ."

As he watched her scurry away silently into the shadows, he realized that the only illumination came from tall windows on either side of the entrance doors, but their panes were so dirty that a minimum of light managed to penetrate. He saw that the entrance hall was bare, the parquet floor dusty. Double doors, on both sides, were closed.

He went to the nearest pair of doors, grasped a silver knob and pushed one door open. Stepped into a dim room that must have been a library. The windows were curtained, but he could make out paneled walls and many bookshelves. There was no furniture, and the shelves were empty. He closed the door and, crossing to the doors directly opposite, swung one open. A small salon was revealed, curtained and unfurnished.

Vidocq shut the door and returned to stand where the servant had left him. Removing his hat, he fanned himself because the air was oppressive.

The old woman appeared out of the shadows, her feet making no sound in their felt slippers. "Come, Monsieur. You can see Monsieur le Baron." She motioned for him to follow. "Although he didn't seem to know what I said to him just now, and I doubt you'll be able to make him understand."

He followed her past the staircase, into the silent depths of the mansion. "Is the Baron ill?"

"The poor man hasn't been himself for more than a year. Some mornings he recognizes me, but today he seems in another world. You can talk to him and I think he will hear you, but he may not answer. Did you know the Baron in the past?"

"We've never met."

"Then you won't notice the change in him. I've worked for the family since he was a boy."

"There are other servants here?"

"Not anymore. I'm Madame Bette. Used to be the housekeeper, but now I'm cook and everything else!"

"Are any members of the family in residence?"

"Nobody. Madame de Chabrillat died some years ago and his daughter became a nun."

"A nun?"

"Mademoiselle Constance did that, in my opinion, to escape from her father. And I don't blame her! When her dear mother was alive, things were different . . ."

"She's his only child?"

235

"There used to be a son. He was a lieutenant in a regiment of the Royal Guards ..."

"He was killed?"

"The Baron disowned Flavian—his only son—when he was expelled from the Guards because of gambling debts. That's two years ago! The Baron ordered him never to come here again. Refused to see him the one time he returned ..."

"Where is he now?"

"Some place in America. His mother's people live there. He told me they would help him make his fortune ..."

"He and his father quarreled?"

"Constantly, Monsieur. Even when Flavian was a boy ..."

"What's wrong with the Baron?"

She paused before still another pair of closed doors. "The doctor hasn't told me, and I never ask questions."

He was prepared for another empty room, but as Madame Bette opened one of the doors he saw a handsomely furnished salon, bright with sunlight from a row of windows open onto a balustraded terrace.

She went in, motioning for him to follow, and bowed to the invisible Baron. "This is the gentleman who asked to see you ..."

Vidocq stepped forward, glancing from side to side. There was no sign of the Baron. Large framed paintings on the walls, fine Aubusson rugs, bric-a-brac, and objets d'art on every table. Some of the paintings, he realized, must be family portraits. He peered in every direction without seeing anyone. "Monsieur le Baron?"

There was a faint gurgle of sound.

Vidocq turned to stare at the tapestry-upholstered back of a large chair he had noticed upon entering because it was taller than the other chairs and was placed facing the open windows. He saw now that it had small wooden wheels instead of legs. Moving closer, circling a table, he perceived the slight figure of a man seated in the chair, his hands resting on the arms. He was dressed in a dark-gray silk suit, no waistcoat or cravat, white shirt open at the throat. "Baron de Chabrillat?"

Another gurgle.

He realized as the Baron's face came into view that the sound was coming from his open mouth.

"I am Vidocq."

The head turned slightly, and his strangely opaque eyes rolled, but the body remained rigid. His mouth apparently was trying to repeat

236

Vidocq's name, but only another choked bubble of sound came from the throat.

Vidocq rested his hat on a table and took a few more steps until he was facing the unpleasant figure in the chair.

The thin hands appeared to be covered with brownish scabs, and there were more of them on his pale forehead. This man, who was reported to be in his early fifties, appeared to be many years older. Gray hair, barely hiding a bony skull, fell in lank strands to his shoulders, but the eyebrows were thick and black, as though they had retained some of the life lost by his hair. The eyes, under hooded lids, appeared to be covered by a gray film. Arrogant beak of nose—the same nose that was in those family portraits—above sensual lips that had the only color in the pallid flesh of the face. His lips, however, were not a healthy pink but purplish.

"Tell me, Monsieur le Baron. Can you hear me? Do you understand what I'm saying?"

The head nodded, jerking like an automaton.

"But you can't speak?"

A negative motion of the head.

"Can you see me?"

The Baron shook his head again, slowly, from side to side.

"You are blind?"

A firm nod.

"Can't you move your body? Legs or hands?"

Another shake of the head.

"But you can answer my questions by nodding your head?"

A more affirmative nod.

"You know who I am? Vidocq, Chief of the Sûreté . . ."

An unintelligible gurgle, followed by a nod.

"I believe you have two children. A daughter and a son?"

Two nods.

"Do you know anything about a desk that was sold recently to Galerie Marchadier? A *laqué rouge* desk from your private collection . . ."

The head shook, several times, as though he didn't remember such a piece of furniture.

"Your son, Flavian, is in America?"

The mention of the name brought an angry rumble from the open mouth.

"I believe at one time you knew the Spanish whore, Maya . . ."

237

At first there was no reaction, then the purplish lips tried to form the name but failed. The eyes rolled desperately with the effort, and the head finally nodded again.

"She is dead—this unfortunate woman—murdered."

A harsh gurgle.

"Can you tell me anyone, man or woman, who might have had a motive to kill her?"

His head shook, negatively, long strands of gray hair swaying.

"You gave Maya a necklace? A diamond necklace . . ."

Another nod, and for the first time the lips attempted a smile.

"Did Maya tell you she had sold it? Had a duplicate made with false diamonds?"

The lizard head shook, angrily.

"The murderer took that necklace after he killed her. The copy with the worthless stones. You bought that diamond necklace from Narcisse Tessier?"

A nod.

"And you had a second diamond necklace and a diamond-studded cross designed by Tessier . . ."

He nodded.

"You gave the cross to little Clochette . . ."

Another nod.

"To whom did you give that other necklace? The more expensive one . . ."

The response to this was a gurgle.

"One of *les grandes courtisanes?*"

A nod.

"Which?"

The Baron tried desperately to speak, but the effort caused a spasm, which shook his frail body. A thin string of spittle slipped from one corner of his mouth.

"Tessier and Clochette have also been murdered. You must tell me the name of the *courtisane* to whom you gave that other necklace. Her life could be in danger . . ."

The old man continued to choke, his head jerking back and forth as though controlled by invisible cords. He appeared to be strangling, mouth wide, gasping for breath.

Vidocq looked around as he heard the door open and saw the servant

238

woman hurrying toward them. She paused to snatch a china pitcher from a table and poured water into a crystal goblet.

"The poor man! I could hear him in the hall. Always does this when he tries to talk." She held the glass to the Baron's mouth, supporting the back of his head with her other hand. "He doesn't like water, but he can't have brandy anymore. The doctor says it would kill him."

Water was dripping from the Baron's chin onto his shirt.

"You've upset him, Monsieur!" She patted the Baron's shoulder as she placed the glass on a table beside him.

His head was tipped back, mouth open, eyes closed.

"I don't think he'll be of any more help to you, Monsieur. He can't answer your questions."

"Perhaps another time . . ." He followed her across the salon, glancing back as he retrieved his hat but was unable to see the Baron in his chair. Only one motionless hand resting on an arm.

Madame Bette didn't speak until they reached the entrance hall. "You shouldn't have disturbed him, Monsieur."

"What can you tell me, Madame, about a desk that was sold?"

"Desk? I know nothing about any desk."

"You must've known when it was taken away from here."

She sighed. "All the good pieces have been sold."

"For what reason?"

"The money's for the Baron. To feed him and, for the moment, keep his creditors away."

"You've seen the furniture removed?"

"Men come and take things. Only that one salon where you talked to the Baron is furnished and the kitchen, where I live. All the other rooms are empty. The Baron doesn't know."

"His son never writes him?"

"Never. They were like wild animals the last time Flavian came here before he left France. The doctor feared, if they had another quarrel, it would kill the Baron. It was the doctor who ordered the son to stay away. Told him never to write his father."

"Does Mademoiselle Constance visit him frequently?"

"Oh no!" Opening the door. "She isn't allowed to leave the convent."

"I will go there. Talk to her."

239

"They won't let anyone see her because she's taken a vow of silence. Her name's Sister Agathe now."

"Sister Agathe? Good day, Madame." He stepped out of the dark mansion into bright sunlight.

CHAPTER 39

He watched the barefooted young nun in the coarse brown bombazine habit disappear under a low archway into shadow before glancing around the small chapel.

Her eyes were wary when she answered the summons of the bell, hanging inside the entrance gate and had appeared to be shocked when he asked to see Sister Agathe. As he told her his name, there had been a flash of recognition in her eyes. She had quickly unlocked and swung open the heavy wooden gate. Motioned for him to follow her through a garden where doves fluttered above the white roses edging graveled paths that brought them to this chapel. Only after they were inside did she speak. "I will tell Mother Superior. Wait . . ."

Somewhere out of sight an organ was being played softly when they entered, and the music continued as Vidocq walked toward a handsome Gothic reredos, which extended from floor to ceiling. A tapestry hung behind it to hide the nuns who would sit there, probably on hard benches, when they sang the mass. He realized that the music was coming from pipes on a balcony above the entrance at the rear. Now the organist was playing what sounded like a Magnificat. The notes tremulous, barely audible.

The air was fragrant with a delicate scent of incense, nothing like the incense that had been burning under Maya's portrait. He never before realized that there was sacred and profane incense.

As he inspected the dim chapel, he remembered that the Vicomte had said he would arrange a requiem mass for Maya and wondered if anybody would order one for poor Marpon. Not likely. He would have Aubé send someone across Place du Parvis to Nôtre-Dame with money to pay for a mass. The old man would have a final moment of glory in the great cathedral where his beloved Queen had knelt in prayer.

His thoughts were interrupted by a faint rustling sound, and he turned to face the Mother Superior. As she approached from under the archway, he was aware of an aristocratic face with black eyebrows above intelligent gray eyes. Her skin was without a wrinkle, although as she spoke he knew from her voice that she was older than she appeared.

"I am Mother Thérèse. I was informed that you are Monsieur Vidocq . . ."

"Yes, Mother."

"And you wish to speak with Sister Agathe . . ."

"If I may."

"It is forbidden for anyone to visit or talk with a member of our order. No man may enter our convent unless he is a priest and has obtained permission from the archbishop."

"I understand."

"No nun is allowed to see strangers, unless there is serious illness in her family or some unusual emergency. Even then she would need special permission."

"This is a matter that concerns her father, Baron de Chabrillat . . ."

"I suppose you have some sort of identification?"

"Certainly." Producing his identity card.

She glanced at the signatures and the official seal. "Very well, Monsieur. I have already arranged for Sister Agathe to join us."

He returned the card to his waistcoat pocket.

"If you will stand over here," motioning toward the reredos, "I will bring Sister Agathe from the anteroom where she is waiting. I must remain with her, of course, while she talks to you."

"But I would like to see her face!"

"I will have the tapestry drawn back, Monsieur. I've been told the police prefer to face anyone they question." She turned and went through a dim passage, her brown habit melting into the darkness.

It was comfortably cool here. Only a few rays of sunlight penetrated the narrow stained glass windows.

The organ had been silenced.

Moving closer to the reredos, he glimpsed strangely costumed figures woven into the tapestry with a field of curious flowers where small animals and birds were hiding.

The folds of the tapestry began to move slowly and silently.

After a moment he managed to see that the dark space behind the

241

carved screen held two long wooden benches facing the chapel. A young nun was pulling a heavy cord with both hands, and when the tapestry had completely opened she withdrew into the shadows.

There was a moment of silence before he realized that two robed figures were seated on chairs close to the screen. He hadn't noticed them, at first, and it was impossible to see their faces.

"Monsieur Vidocq . . ."

He recognized the gentle voice. "Yes, Mother Thérèse?"

"Sister Agathe is here, beside me. I have told her that she is permitted to answer your questions. If she wishes."

"I am grateful."

"If any of your questions seem improper, I shall of course forbid her to reply."

"I understand."

"I've told her that you are Inspector Vidocq, Chief of the Brigade de la Sûreté. She understands why you are here. You may proceed, Monsieur."

"Thank you." He looked toward the other figure but, even moving close to the reredos, was unable to see her face. "Mademoiselle Constance . . ."

"I am Sister Agathe."

"Certainly. Forgive me . . . You knew that your father, the Baron, is very ill?"

"No, Monsieur. I did not."

"When was the last time you saw him?" Moving closer to the carved reredos as he began his questions.

"I never returned to my former home after I entered this convent as a novitiate. I have rejected my former life and the world outside these walls. This is my home now."

He was conscious of the calm tone of her young voice. "How long have you been here?"

"I'm not aware of time anymore, Monsieur. I suppose it has been several years."

"Two years and four months," the Mother Superior whispered. "Sister Agathe has never asked for permission to leave the convent."

"During this time were you ever visited by your father?"

"He has never come here. And, if he had, I would not have seen him."

"I can confirm that, Monsieur," the Mother Superior murmured. "He would have had to obtain my permission to visit his daughter."

He could see her face more clearly now. "You've had no communication of any sort from your father?"

"None. I was never close to my father. Even when I was a child. I was always closer to my mother. She too was religious. My father is not. Maman had no interest in the social life my father enjoyed. For many years before her death, she refused to venture beyond the gardens surrounding our home. She wouldn't drive out in her carriage and seldom received visitors. Soon after she died, I decided to become a nun. I began to receive instruction and eventually was accepted into the Carmelite order."

"Are you happy here?"

"I have never known such peace . . ."

"You have not personally, or through any other person, arranged for the sale of furniture or any other valuable objects from your former home?"

"Never."

"Do you think the housekeeper may have sold such things without your father's knowledge?"

"Oh no! Madame Bette has been with our family for many years."

"There were other servants?"

"At least a dozen when I lived at home."

"You knew that there are none today? Only the housekeeper who is now the cook and, as she told me this morning, everything else."

"Madame Bette's the only servant? I had no idea. Has my father lost his money?"

"So it would seem."

"Poor Maman! She, at least, will never know. He was wasting her fortune even when she was alive. Has much of the furniture been sold?"

"Everything. Except for the salon where your father lives. All the other rooms are empty."

"How sad! All those beautiful things Maman loved . . ."

"Where is your brother?"

"Flavian? I have no idea, Monsieur."

"The housekeeper says he went to the United States in search of his fortune."

"He was always talking about that. Maman had relatives in New York. Flavian dreamed of going there. I hope he too has found peace."

"Your father is unable to walk. He cannot talk, and he is blind."

"I will pray for his immortal soul. But I never wish to see him again." Her voice held a tinge of hysteria now. "He is an evil man and he must pay for the way he treated my dear mother . . ."

"Silence, Sister Agathe." Mother Thérèse's voice was sharper. "You must go, Monsieur. This interview is finished."

CHAPTER 40

Vidocq took the brooch from his pocket and examined the miniature portrait on the lid. The Queen's young face forever smiling. Nobody in authority had ever been able to tell him what became of her head. Pieces of hair were hawked in the streets after her execution, but they had without doubt come from the heads of female relatives or mistresses of the vendors.

As he turned the brooch over, examining the enamel back and the tiny jewels in the gold rim encircling the portrait, he heard the Rat's voice and, looking up, saw her standing with the Nun at Aubé's desk. Studying the brooch again, he found a gold catch cleverly hidden under the clasp. He lifted it with his thumbnail, released the lid, and raised it with a forefinger.

A folded scrap of paper fell onto his desk.

He set the brooch down and snatched up the slip of paper. Unfolded it and saw several lines scrawled in ink.

> *Tessier was a scoundrel.*
> *Everything ends at midnight.*
> *Drumont says I will die if I tell what I know.*
> *May the Lord Christ have mercy on my soul . . .*

So Marpon knew something about Tessier, and Drumont had threatened to kill him if he told anyone.

Everything ends at midnight. What did he mean by that?

The Midnight Club?

This brooch must have been hidden under Marpon's pillow. He'd reached for it as he was dying. This precious relic from his former life ...

Marpon must have written this yesterday, after his visit to Number Six, and hidden it inside the brooch. Clutched it as he died, hoping someone would find his message. Hoping he, Vidocq, would find it?

"Excuse me, Chief ..."

He looked up to see Aubé. "There's something I want you to do for me." He brought out a louis d'or from a pocket. "Send one of our guards to Nôtre-Dame. Tell him to arrange a requiem mass for one Auguste Marpon."

"The old man who was here yesterday?"

"We have another murder on rue Taitbout. This will pay for a first-class mass with a choir." He dropped the coin into Aubé's hand.

"I will see to it."

"Also pay any other expenses for his funeral. Take the money from our weekly budget."

"How shall I list it in the records?"

"Payment to Auguste Marpon for information received. The ladies can come in."

"Ah yes! That's what I was going to tell you. I believe they have some information." Aubé turned back toward his office.

Vidocq folded the slip of paper carefully and placed it in the desk drawer under the brooch. As he did so, he noticed the golden coin from the Midnight Club. Picked it up and studied it for a moment.

Everything ends at midnight?

He scowled, dropping the coin into a pocket of his waistcoat and closing the drawer, as the young women hurried in. "What did you learn in rue de Provence?"

The Rat hurried ahead, pulling the leather chairs closer to the desk.

"More than we learned yesterday," the Nun answered. "Again I told people I was looking for a nun who had recently been in the neighborhood seeking alms." They sat down, the Nun erect, delicate hands folded in her laps. "Some people refused to talk. Strong feelings still exist against all nuns and priests."

"For two hours we had no luck at all!" The Rat sat forward in her chair. "Then I stopped a little maid who was bringing fresh bread from a bakery. Works in that house with the arched passage across from

Maya's apartment. She saw that nun yesterday. Not once but twice!"

"When?" Vidocq straightened in his chair. "What time?"

"First was late in the afternoon. She'd come out to do some shopping for dinner and passed a nun in the street. Didn't give it a thought until last evening when she was taking out a pail of slops. As she carried it through that passage, she saw a nun standing under the archway. After she emptied her pail in the gutter, she turned back and saw the nun was watching her. That's when she realized it was the same nun she'd seen earlier."

"Did the nun speak to her?"

"Not a word."

"Could the maid describe her?"

"Only that she had a pale face."

Vidocq grunted. "Most nuns do."

"They don't get enough sunlight," the Nun explained.

"This nun had dark eyebrows," the Rat continued. "She wore a black habit with some sort of white headdress under a black veil."

"The black robe could be Ursuline," the Nun interrupted. "Though they have a starched headdress like wings. It might be an order of mendicants. There are several of those. They wear any kind of habit. Mostly castoffs."

"Or a woman wearing the habit as a disguise." Vidocq turned back to the Rat. "Why did this maid recall seeing her? Was there something unusual about this nun?"

"She said it was the first nun she'd seen in a long time," the Rat went on, "that it was odd seeing her in the afternoon, then again a few hours later. She thought it strange a nun would be looking up at Maya's windows . . ."

"So she was watching Maya's apartment. You've done a fine morning's work."

"Excuse me, Chief . . ."

Vidocq saw Aubé in the open doorway. "What now, my friend?"

"The Duc de Modena has arrived."

The Rat squealed and the Nun giggled as they rose from their chairs. Vidocq chuckled. "That will be all, Mesdemoiselles."

"Did you have lunch, Chief?" Aubé asked.

"No time."

"I'll have Madame Babelay bring you something."

"A glass of wine. Nothing more." He saw Ronquetti in the doorway, coolly elegant in a white linen suit and wide-brimmed straw hat. "Monsieur le Duc?"

"My dear friends!" Ronquetti flashed a dazzling smile at the young women as they departed, leaning toward the Nun to whisper something, at the same time pinching the Rat on a buttock.

The Nun laughed, and the Rat slapped him on the shoulder affectionately, as they followed Aubé out.

"Women!" Ronquetti sighed appreciatively, as he approached the desk. "Life would be empty without them."

"Sit down, my friend."

"I've some news for you."

"Everybody has news for me today."

Ronquetti swept off his straw hat, as he sank into the chair vacated by the Nun, and dropped it on the Rat's chair. "The American—Signore Penny-packaire—has returned."

"When?"

"Late last night."

"You've seen him?"

"In the lobby of the hotel. He was coming from the dining room as I went in for breakfast."

"You talked?"

"Briefly. I asked if he'd had a successful trip."

"What did he say?"

"That the weather was much cooler in the country. But not a word about where he'd been or why he'd gone there."

"Nothing more about his host? Motier . . ."

"Not a word."

"Crafty fellow!"

"Told me he wouldn't be free today because he had to write several letters . . ."

"Oh?"

"To be carried back to the United States by diplomatic courier. So they must be of some importance . . ."

"I suspect they are. And did you see Mademoiselle Belinda today?"

"The Signorina was rushing downstairs as I returned to my suite after breakfast. Informed me she was late for a rendezvous with an English lady to select new bonnets. Yesterday it was slippers! American girls are always hurrying off to spend money or look at ruins." He pulled a fresh handkerchief from his cuff and patted his forehead. "This weather reminds me of Naples. How much longer do I remain at the Belvedere, now that Penny-packaire has returned?"

"At least to the end of this week." As Ronquetti talked, Vidocq fingered the golden coin in his waistcoat pocket. "There are two things you can do for me . . ."

"Consider them accomplished!"

"Is Penny-packaire a member of the Midnight Club?"

"I don't know. He's mentioned the place, several times . . ."

"They probably give guest cards to rich Americans. Tell him you've never been there."

"But I have! When it first opened."

"He doesn't know that. Tonight would be too soon I suppose, since he's only just returned to Paris. Arrange for him to take you there for dinner tomorrow night. Perhaps, after several glasses of wine, he will divulge the purpose of his trip to the country. At the same time observe what goes on at the Midnight Club. Especially the guests. Who is dining with whom? Have a look at the staff, from the commissionnaire at the entrance to the waiters. Find out who's in charge. Let me know if you notice anything suspicious . . ."

"Is something going on at the Midnight Club I haven't been told? Have they installed gambling tables?"

"That's what I want to find out. I plan to go there myself this evening to ask certain questions about Tessier—I've learned he was a member—but you can look it over tomorrow night. You'll observe much more if you're there as a guest." He was aware of Madame Babelay hurrying through the anteroom with a tray. "Find out who Penny-packaire knows at the Midnight Club. See who his friends are . . . Ah, Madame! Thank you."

"A glass of wine's not enough for the middle of the day." She rested her silver tray on the desk in front of him. "I've a cold chicken that I roasted this morning . . ."

"I have no appetite in this heat." He reached for the wine bottle. "A glass of Burgundy for you, Ronquetti?"

"I've only just had breakfast."

Madame Babelay laughed. "The Duc's up early today! Never saw him before at this hour."

Vidocq poured half a glass of wine as she left them.

"What was the other thing you wanted me to do?" Ronquetti asked.

"Ah yes . . ." He tasted the wine as he considered how to word his second request. "This afternoon, while Penny-packaire is writing his letters, I'd like you to make a tour of the more popular boulevard cafés. Listen to the gossip about the Spanish whore . . ."

"You're investigating Maya?"

"Her murder."

"Maya! I hadn't heard."

"You've been absent from your usual haunts for several days."

"And nights! Poor Maya . . . That beautiful tawny body. Like a great cat . . ."

"She was found last night in her famous black and silver bed—which we discovered is not silver—with a bullet in her lovely forehead. Find out, if you can, what people are saying about her death."

"You know who killed her?"

"No suspicion as yet. But I'm beginning to think the murderer may be the same person who shot Tessier. I also want to know certain facts about Baron de Chabrillat . . ."

"Maya used to be his mistress."

"Whoever killed Maya took a diamond necklace from her apartment. The necklace had been purchased from Tessier by the Baron."

"So their murders are connected!"

"There's no evidence as yet to prove that. Except for the two bullets, which I suspect were fired from the same pistol." He was distracted as he talked to see that the bullets he'd left on his desk were no longer there. "I want to trace another diamond necklace Tessier sold to Baron de Chabrillat . . ."

"Another one?"

"More expensive than the one he gave Maya."

"Why not ask the Baron?"

"I questioned him this morning, but unfortunately he has no memory of the past and, more important, he's unable to speak. I suspect he may have given the necklace to one of the other *grandes courtisanes*. Find out, if you can, which one. Meanwhile, I'll be asking questions of my own. The Baron was always discreet in his amatory escapades, so we never kept a dossier on him."

"Ah! To be rich and lavish jewels on beautiful women . . ."

"Baron de Chabrillat at this moment hasn't a centime! Because of his fondness for diamonds and other expensive pleasures. Including women!"

"Women are becoming too complicated. And Signorina Belinda is one of the most complicated. I suspect she has a lover in Paris."

"What makes you say that?"

"She disappears every afternoon and doesn't return to the hotel until time to dress for dinner. I think she meets a young man."

Vidocq smiled.

"Of course, that's what makes women fascinating." Ronquetti picked up his hat and got to his feet. "They wouldn't be half so intriguing if they were less complicated."

"Pardon me, Gentlemen . . ."

Vidocq looked toward the doorway as Aubé entered again. "What became of those bullets I left here on my desk?"

"I knew they were important, so I locked them away for safekeeping."

"But I won't know which bullet is which!" Vidocq felt a sudden surge of anger. "As long as they remained on my desk, I could tell the Maya bullet from the Tessier bullet by their positions near the lamp."

"But I put them in separate envelopes."

"I still won't know them apart!" He laughed, his anger fading as quickly as it had been aroused. "No matter. There's no way to prove they came from the same pistol. I will say in court, with great conviction, that they did and no man can disprove me. At least we have the bullets. Write Maya on one envelope and Tessier on the other. At least that will look official."

Aubé was beaming now. "Yes, Chief. I'll do that."

Ronquetti placed his hat on his head, pulling the brim down. "I'll report what gossip I pick up in the cafés this afternoon."

Vidocq rose from his desk. "Meanwhile there are several questions I must ask Monsieur Penny-packaire . . ."

CHAPTER 41

Vidocq had learned from the concierge of the Hôtel Belvedere that both the Pennypackers, father and daughter, were in. The upstairs corridor was empty as he knocked on the door to their suite.

"Come in! Come in!"

He swung the door open into a large foyer.

"You can put those in the bedroom, if you will . . ."

Vidocq closed the door silently. Crossed the foyer to the open doors of a pleasant salon and paused to study the American seated near a row of open windows at a small desk. Pennypacker was writing with a quill pen, and several completed letters in sealed envelopes were stacked in front of him.

The American looked around, sensing an intruder. "Ah, Vidocq!"

"Monsieur Zeb . . ."

"Pull up a chair! While I finish this sentence . . ."

Vidocq crossed the salon as the quill resumed its scratching. Picked up a gilt chair and moved it closer, facing the desk, as Pennypacker set his quill aside. "I was told you'd returned from the country."

"Last night."

"A successful trip, I trust?"

"Eminently!" He pushed his armchair back from the desk and dried his perspiring hands on a large handkerchief. "When you knocked, I thought it was the valet. Gave him two suits to be brushed and pressed. I returned to Paris covered with dust!"

In spite of his journey, the American appeared to be rested.

"Could I offer you a glass of wine? Coffee?"

"Nothing. Thank you." He must edge into a discussion of that missing bracelet carefully and not go into all the facts as yet . . .

"I suppose you've come to tell me that Monsieur Tessier is dead. Murdered . . ."

"So you've heard?"

"There was an item in the newspaper this morning, which barely gave the essential facts. Apparently the poor man was shot."

"Seated at his desk in the mansion on rue Taitbout."

"But nothing was said about his murderer."

"We don't as yet have any idea who killed him. The murderer left no clue."

"That was clever of him."

"Murderers are never clever. Only lucky. For a time . . ."

"You have no suspects?"

"None. To make matters worse, one of our most famous *courtisanes* has been killed in precisely the same way as Tessier. Probably with the same pistol."

"Which *courtisane?*"

"The Spanish whore. Maya . . ."

"I've heard of her. Some of my Parisian business acquaintances are constantly talking about *les grandes courtisanes.* When their wives aren't within earshot, of course. Why would anyone murder a *courtisane? Grande,* or otherwise?"

"Murder unfortunately is one of the hazards of their trade."

"You've found a connection to join these two murders?"

"Not as yet."

"What about my daughter's missing bracelet? Any trace of that?"

"I'd hoped that the thief would attempt to sell it, but none of the Paris fences have reported being offered any diamonds. Either a bracelet or loose stones."

"Then you think it was a thief?"

"Without evidence, Monsieur, I cannot say."

"And have you learned anything about young Revol? I suspect my dear daughter continues to see him every afternoon. Although I realized this morning at breakfast that she appears to be greatly attracted to your friend, the Duc de Modena. Constantly talking about him. Such a fine gentleman! There's nothing like an upper-class Italian."

Vidocq smiled. He would never tell Ronquetti any of this.

"We, my daughter and I, can learn much from observing him. I try to bring more culture to New Orleans by taking back European treasures from each of my visits."

"I suppose you found some treasures on your trip to the country."

"I was much too busy carrying out an important commission for someone else. You were about to tell me about Revol . . ."

"He has no criminal record."

"I'm glad to hear that!"

"I've learned that he worked for Narcisse Tessier."

"Did he? I never saw him there. Belinda told me she met him in the gardens of the Palais-Royal. What did he do at Tessier's?"

"He was one of the designers. In fact, he designed that bracelet you bought."

"My daughter thinks she's in love with him. I could use a good designer in my New Orleans emporium . . ."

"I doubt if he'd want to leave Paris."

"He would for the money I'd offer him. His ability to design fine jewelry could be of great value to our store. Later on, he might even become an executive. He would certainly be useful with our shipping company . . ."

"Shipping?"

"We own a fleet of merchant ships that bring cargoes to New Orleans from all over the world. Many of our crews are French."

"Tell me, Monsieur, do you happen to know an American city called Phil-a-del-phia?"

"We're considering opening a branch there!"

"I've always wanted to go to Phil-a-del-phia . . ."

"Have you? By the way! Do you know—does the Duc de Modena have a wife?"

"Not to my knowledge."

"Never been married?"

"I don't think so . . ."

"Like to know the facts, in case Belinda's seriously considering marriage. I realize one day she's going to find herself a husband, but he'll have to answer some questions from me. Except a gentleman like your friend. I wouldn't mind having the Duc de Modena for a son-in-law . . ."

Vidocq smiled. Ronquetti for a son-in-law! This American was more virginal than his daughter. *Le vierge Americain . . .*

"Am I interrupting something important, daddy?"

They looked around to see Belinda coming from the adjoining bedroom, parasol in hand and dressed for the street.

"Ah, Mademoiselle!" Vidocq rose and bowed.

"Monsieur Vidocq! How nice to see you again. I'm going out, Papa. That English lady, this morning, gave me the address of a shop where she buys her gloves. Claims they're better quality than in London . . ."

"I'll make a buyer out of you while you're in Paris." Pennypacker beamed as he turned to Vidocq. "She's got her mother's good taste, and I'm teaching her how to bargain."

"I'll be having tea with the English lady and her daughter." She looked at Vidocq. "Your friend, the Duc de Modena, is such a dear! We're dining with him tonight." Heading for the foyer. *"Au revoir, Monsieur Vidocq!"*

"Mademoiselle . . ." He watched her leave, then turned to her father. "I must ask you, Monsieur . . ."

"Yes?"

"The reason for your visit to La Grange?"

"So you know where I went!"

"The countryseat of a certain Monsieur du Motier. Better known as the Marquis de Lafayette."

"Back in the States, we still call him General Lafayette. So! You do know everything."

"Not quite everything, Monsieur." Vidocq stood, eyes unwavering, looking down at the seated American. "I would like to know the purpose of your meeting with the Marquis."

"Officially?"

Vidocq shrugged. "The Brigade de la Sûreté is only concerned with the security of Paris, but if your conference at La Grange was political I would be forced to inform the political branch of the police."

"This was not a political matter."

Vidocq glanced at the letters. "You are, I suspect, sending reports back to the United States concerning your meeting with the Marquis."

"They will be taken by diplomatic courier to Washington. One letter goes directly to the President."

"Then it is political?"

"Permit me to explain."

Vidocq sat down again, facing Pennypacker.

"General Lafayette was, as you know, a hero of our Revolutionary War. Wounded in the battle of Brandywine. He's the only surviving major general of our war for independence. A living legend to all Americans, even though he hasn't stepped foot in our country for more than forty years. He's a moderate like myself, but—unlike me—he took sides in the French government. A dangerous thing to do when France swings like a pendulum from Royalist to Republican and back to Royalist. He lost most of his fortune because of that and until recently was out of favor. I shall always admire him for the way he fought to protect the freedom of the individual in France. I brought him a letter from our President which I was instructed to deliver in person. President Monroe wanted it given to the General by a private citizen. Not a government official. Someone in Washington was aware of my annual visits to France and suggested I undertake the assignment. Talk to the General and, hopefully, persuade him."

"Is the United States planning another war with the British?"

"God forbid! We never want war again. With anybody! My mission was to persuade General Lafayette to pay another visit to the United States. When I arrived in Paris, I immediately sent a note to the General and asked his permission to deliver it by hand at La Grange. When he didn't reply within a few days, I thought my mission was doomed to failure, but finally a message arrived. An invitation to visit the General at once. When I reached La Grange, I learned that he hadn't responded sooner because of illness. At first, after he read the President's letter, he refused to consider such a trip because of his health. I spent hours convincing him that he should."

"Then he's agreed?"

"Not yet. He's considering the matter and will let me know his answer within the week."

"Would this American visit be political?"

"Absolutely not! There will of course be an official reception to welcome the General and a national celebration for the American populace. He would be the nation's honored guest."

"For how long?"

"President Monroe has invited him to stay for, at the very least, a year. He will travel from city to city. Fêted wherever he goes! A tour of as many states as possible! There will be fireworks, parades, and banquets. Balls will be given in all the major cities."

"What does the old man look like?"

"He appears to be in his eighties, but actually he's only sixty-six. In his prime! The United States should restore his vigor. As well as his fortune."

"There's money involved?"

"My country will most certainly show its gratitude to the only surviving major general of the American Revolution. In countless ways! Honors, awards, and gifts."

"You think he'll accept your President's invitation?"

"I don't know. At first I was aware that he feared such a long voyage;

255

I promised he would make the trip in less than a month and the entire population of New York City will be waiting to welcome him. Once he accepts, an official invitation will be voted by the American Congress and extended to the General through proper diplomatic channels by President Monroe. He's a charming gentleman, Lafayette! Great dignity and intelligence. In the event that he agrees to take the trip, he made one proviso. He must be accompanied by his son and his secretary. I assured him both gentlemen would be welcomed like heroes. I had no idea his son is named for our first President. George Washington Lafayette!"

"I agree, Monsieur Zeb." Vidocq rose from the gilt chair. "Your mission was not political. Lafayette will bring great honor to France by this visit to your country."

Pennypacker jumped up from the desk and shook hands. "If you'll forgive me, I won't see you to the door. More letters I must write. Then I've several business matters of my own which have been neglected. I'm here, as you know, on a purchasing expedition for my New Orleans emporium. This afternoon I must spend some time at the Galerie Marchadier . . ."

"Marchadier?"

"I've purchased many works of art and pieces of antique furniture from Marchadier in the past."

"An excellent gallery. I've bought paintings there for my private collection."

"Found a note, when I returned, Marchadier has a *laqué rouge* desk and several other items he wishes me to see."

"*Laqué rouge?*"

"That's a particularly rare scarlet lacquer. Difficult to find these days."

"I wish you well with your official mission to the Marquis de Lafayette."

"You won't report what I've told you? For the moment at least the President hopes to avoid anything in your newspapers. Until the matter is settled."

"There's no reason for me to report your visit to Monsieur du Motier, private citizen." He went toward the foyer without glancing back.

CHAPTER 42

Vidocq knocked on the polished mahogany door of the apartment on the first floor and, suddenly weary, leaned on his cane as he studied the great marble staircase with its bronze balustrade spiraling up through the building. His life seemed to be spent riding back and forth across the city, climbing stairs and knocking on doors.

He'd gone up and down thousands of steps since he became a member of the Paris police, probably more steps than any other man in the entire city.

The door was opened cautiously by a scowling Madame Sidoné, her hair in paper twists, wearing an apron over a plain gray dress. "What do you ... Ah, Monsieur Vidocq!"

"I'm disturbing you ..."

"Certainly not. Come in."

He entered the dark foyer as she explained.

"This is our domestic hour. We're like housewives! I've been sewing, and Madame's checking over last week's bills. I've no idea where all the maids are. Little sluts! Probably asleep." She closed the door and walked beside him through the long central hall. "No one ever comes here in the afternoon. Madame will be happy to see you. She's hard at work in the dining room."

He rested his hat, cane, and gloves on a console table.

"I wouldn't have heard your knock if I hadn't been crossing the hall with a pile of sheets to be darned. You should have pulled the bell."

"Thought you might all be asleep at this hour, and in this heat."

"Your visit isn't ... official ..."

"Nothing like that. I was in the neighborhood, visiting an American gentleman at the Hôtel Belvedere."

"I'm working in the linen room. The quality of sheets these days is a scandal! Always wearing out. Could I bring you a glass of champagne?"

"That might help my parched throat."

"This weather reminds me of Marseille when I was a girl." She turned down a side corridor. "You know your way ..."

Continuing on, he saw that every door stood open. The spacious rooms looked unfamiliar by daylight. Windows had been opened, curtains pulled back, to empty the apartment of last night's cigar smoke.

257

The new furniture, which had seemed attractive by candlelight, looked tawdry today. Statues on carved pedestals, nude marble figures, were vulgar. Everything expensive, but lacking in taste.

He paused in the open doorway to the dining room. Again all the curtains were drawn apart, the windows wide open. Beyond wrought-iron balconies he glimpsed green trees in a haze of sunlight, so there must be a garden on this side of the building. The long dining table was so highly polished that a glare of sunlight was reflected from its empty surface. A small table stood in an open space near the windows.

Ève sat there, on a comfortable *fauteuil,* studying a sheet of paper. She put it aside as he watched, placing it on a stack of similar sheets then picked up another from a second pile. He saw that her golden red curls were gathered on top of her head and she was wearing a pink négligée, through which he glimpsed one lovely breast against the sunlight. She was also wearing gold spectacles.

Walking the length of the room, careful not to make a sound on the bare floor with his leather heels, he realized that the heavily carved dining room chairs had been placed in rows against the walls on either side of enormous sideboards, which at night held elaborate displays of food and wines for midnight supper.

Ève apparently heard a whisper of movement because she turned and, lifting her spectacles from her nose, squinted toward the hall. "Who was it, Sidoné?" She peered more carefully when she saw it was a man. "Vidocq?"

"Yes, *chérie.*" He smiled as she whisked off the spectacles and thrust them out of sight.

"What brings you here at this unlikely hour?"

"I was driving past and wondered if I might find you alone."

"Which means you're after information again." Dropping the sheet of paper onto the table. "Don't look at me! My hair's a disgrace, and I left my face on the dressing table." Clutching the folds of her robe. "Wearing my oldest négligée . . ."

"But looking beautiful!" He kissed her on the cheek. "And smelling delicious!"

"Find yourself a chair."

He lifted the nearest chair away from the wall and placed it close to the table, facing her.

"I only finished breakfast a moment ago."

As he sat down, he noticed a silver tray with the remnants of a sizeable repast.

"Can I have Sidoné fix you fresh coffee?"

"She mentioned champagne."

"I hope she brings two glasses." Glancing at the piles of papers on the table. "I've been going over the week's expenses. This new chef will use nothing but the best ingredients and everything's so expensive! I don't complain, however, because my suppers are becoming famous. You must dine here one night."

"My first free evening."

"Unfortunately, they're so lavish I'm gaining weight."

"You've never looked more desirable."

"You've come to question me about Maya . . ."

"Whatever you can tell me."

"They say she was murdered."

"Yes."

"I've heard every sort of rumor. She was stabbed by a jealous Spaniard, strangled by a burglar, and shot by an unknown admirer. You're the only one who can tell me the truth."

"She was shot, and a piece of jewelry appears to be missing."

"You know who killed her?"

"I haven't as yet so much as a suspicion."

"But it was a thief? A prowler . . ."

"I didn't say that. Whoever killed her took a diamond necklace from a hiding place in her dressing room."

"Diamond necklace! Maya?"

"Which her maid says was made with imitation stones."

"Oh . . . That one! It was false."

"You're certain?"

"Positive. Maya's told me about it. In fact, all her jewels were imitation. Tessier would make a copy for her and take back the original."

"Then you may also know that the original was a gift from . . ."

"Baron de Chabrillat, who bought it from Tessier."

"Maya was shot in the forehead. Exactly like Tessier."

"You think the same person killed both of them?"

"I have two bullets, and I suspect they were fired from the same pistol. How well did you know Maya?"

"Who can say how well one knows any person? Even a relative!

259

Maya and I had been—friendly—since she first turned up in Paris. Must be seven or eight years ago ..."

"Pardon, Madame."

They looked around as Madame Sidoné brought an open bottle of champagne with two glasses on a tray.

"Madame Sidoné ..." Vidocq watched her face as he asked his question. "Did you know Maya?" He saw no change in her expression.

"No, Monsieur. I never met the lady. I hear she's been murdered." Pouring the wine as she talked. "She came along after I left Paris. I've seen her of course, in her fine black and silver landau." Serving a glass of wine to each. "If you're questioning Madame about her, I can tell you Maya's never been here since I came to work."

"I simply wondered what you could tell me about Maya."

"Nothing, Monsieur. I never repeat gossip." She bowed and departed.

He held up his glass and studied the golden wine against the sunlight before facing Ève again. "You were with Maya the other evening in the Bois ..."

"That was the last time I saw her." She raised her glass. "Shall we drink to Maya?"

"I prefer to toast the living. Let's drink to us. *A nous, toujours à nous!*"

"Toujours à nous!"

They drank, their throats grateful for the cool wine.

Vidocq watched Madame Sidoné turn left through the hall. "Did Maya ever mention Narcisse Tessier to you?"

"Many times. But casually ... We always talked about our new jewels or gowns or how we planned to redecorate our apartments. Never discussed our lovers. Past or present! That would be too vulgar. Like common whores ..."

"Baron de Chabrillat bought another diamond necklace from Tessier and a diamond-studded cross. Probably for two different women. I've found Tessier's designs for each piece of jewelry he sold—with the name of the purchaser—but unfortunately nothing to show who received them as gifts."

"Won't the Baron tell you who they were?"

"He can't. Baron de Chabrillat is gravely ill."

"So I've heard."

"We must trace that other necklace." He finished his wine and set the glass down.

"Whoever has it won't know anything about Tessier's murder. Or Maya's . . ."

"Perhaps. But I must find the owner and warn her. We know the Baron gave the cross to Clochette. She too has been murdered."

"I know." She hesitated, frowning.

"Whoever has that other diamond necklace may be in mortal danger. The murderer may kill again. At any moment. I've no idea what his motive may be. Only that he's killed three people."

"But Maya's necklace was a copy! She had a duplicate made because she was afraid to wear real diamonds in public."

"I suspect the killer didn't know those diamonds were false. Or the diamonds in Clochette's cross." He rose and placed the chair against the wall. "My thanks for the wine."

"Another glass?"

"I must get back to Number Six." He kissed the top of her head and started toward the hall.

"You said, the other night, you planned to visit the Midnight Club . . ."

"I'm going there this evening."

"I do wish you wouldn't, chéri."

Glancing back, he saw that she was watching him. "Why not?"

"There's evil there."

"Evil is everywhere."

She shrugged. "Happy anniversary!"

"What?"

"Your birthday . . ."

"Damn all birthdays!" He continued on, his leather heels striking angry blows on the parquet floor.

CHAPTER 43

Vidocq sat facing the open windows, aware that the late afternoon sun was moving west and had left the street below in shadow, as he considered the few facts he had learned today.

He had been sitting here, his back to the desk, for several hours.

Much too warm for him to think of climbing to the top of Nôtre-Dame this evening. There would be no fresh air, even up there, and Paris would be covered with a pall of gray smoke from thousands of chimneys as dinner was prepared in every kitchen, small or large, from slum to palace.

Now he could hear some of the staff filing in behind him for the last meeting of the day. Recognized the individual footsteps. Visualized each face. Smiled when he heard the clumsy tread of the Rat. Strained to hear the light slippers of the Nun but only caught a whisper of her skirts. Last of all Aubé's brisk footsteps, as precise as the ticking of a clock. Waited until he heard him grunt as he sank into his customary armchair before turning to face them.

His office was dim in the light reflected from the windows, but he could see that the row of chairs Aubé had arranged earlier was occupied. Each familiar face appeared to float in the air without a body. They were waiting for him to speak.

He cleared his throat. "We must be prepared for every sort of emergency tonight." Turning to Aubé who sat, pencil in hand, small pad on his knee. "I want two men stationed at those southern barriers again. Like last night. If a farmer's cart shows up with anything hidden under its load of fruit or vegetables, the driver's to be detained until one of our men comes for me. I shall be available all night. I'll remain here in my office until eight o'clock. Then I plan to visit the Midnight Club and talk to whoever's in charge. I intend to ask certain questions about the jeweler Tessier, who was a member. Find out what they know about him. They must keep a record on each member. All private clubs do. From there I'll go to the Café Procope for dinner. After that I plan to drive straight to rue de l'Hirondelle."

"That's early for you to go home," Fouché muttered.

"Much too warm for prowling the boulevards or thrashing about in some lady's bed."

"The ladies suffer in this weather," Goury observed. "Business is always better in the winter."

Vidocq laughed. "In cold weather every man seeks a warm bed." Turning to Aubé. "I want to be summoned, no matter the hour, if anything happens at one of those barriers."

"Yes, Chief."

His eyes darted from face to face. "I plan to spend the remainder of this afternoon looking through some of these." He motioned toward a fresh stack of reports waiting on his desk. "I pray there'll be at least a faint breeze by evening and a complete change of weather before morning."

"Not likely," Fouché rumbled. "This heat will continue for at least another week."

"Charles . . . Did you learn anything about that mansion on rue Taitbout? Was Tessier the owner of record?"

"He was not."

"Oh?"

"I learned from an inquisitive neighbor that the property is owned by a real estate company. When I visited their office I was informed that the mansion is leased."

"To Tessier?"

"To Alcidor Drumont."

"Drumont!"

"They showed me his signature on the lease."

"Any further information about Monsieur Drumont?"

"Nothing," Goury responded.

"There's been no response as yet from Marseille," Aubé added.

"Prod them and keep prodding. Those southerners are always slow in replying to any request from Paris."

"I attended the requiem mass this morning for Clochette," Allard announced.

"Was it this morning?" Vidocq frowned. "I had no idea."

"Saint-Pierre in Montmartre was crowded. Rows of whores dressed in black and looking like nuns."

"What an insulting thing to say," the Nun whispered.

"I stood at the rear, searching every face, but nobody looked or acted suspicious."

"There's to be a requiem next Monday for Maya." The Nun's voice was clearer now. "We went back to her apartment this afternoon—the Rat and I—talked to the servants again."

"Maya's last lover was a Vicomte!" The Rat took up their report. "The maid told us he's arranged a mass at Saint-Severin . . ."

Vidocq nodded. "I met the Vicomte de Manceau this morning."

"You want us to be there?" the Nun asked. "This mass for Maya . . ."

"That might be a good idea."

"The evening papers have only brief reports of Maya's murder."

Aubé held up a folded newspaper. "Saying the murderer remains unknown but Monsieur Vidocq, Chief of the Brigade de la Sûreté, is in charge of the investigation."

"They must've gotten their lack of information, as usual, from someone at the Préfecture."

"Speaking of requiem masses," Aubé glanced at his pad. "I've arranged one, as you suggested, for Monsieur Auguste Marpon. Tuesday morning, at Nôtre-Dame."

"I'm afraid there will be no mourners . . . We can take care of that! I want all the younger members of our staff to attend. Make that an order."

"Yes, Chief." Aubé made the notation.

"And anyone else who has no urgent assignment for Tuesday morning. Marpon, before his death, furnished us with valuable information. I shall be there myself." He glanced from face to face. "Anything more?"

No one responded.

Aubé got to his feet—pencil, pad, and newspaper in hand—as everyone rose.

"One thing, ladies . . ."

The Nun and the Rat turned as the others left.

"I want you to check all fences for Maya's necklace and Clochette's cross. Has anyone tried to see them? Perhaps a nun . . ." He picked up a report from the nearest pile. "What do we have here?"

"Routine. Nothing important," Aubé answered.

He watched Aubé hurry after the others as he returned the report to the day's stack of documents.

Must consider what questions he would ask the manager of the Midnight Club this evening . . .

He pulled out the golden coin from his waistcoat pocket. No point in taking that with him. They would admit him when he gave his name. As he returned it to the drawer, he noticed the brooch he'd taken from Marpon's hand. Picked it up and, as he slipped it into a pocket of his waistcoat, noticed the fold of paper underneath. Reached down and held it up to read the written words again.

Tessier was a scoundrel.
Everything ends at midnight.

264

Drumont says I will die if I tell what I know.
May the Lord Christ have mercy on my soul ...

Marpon had died without telling what he knew, but he had written this as a message for him to find.

Everything ends at midnight. The Midnight Club?

CHAPTER 44

Vidocq stepped down from his dark gray carriage on rue Royale at some distance from his destination, instructing the driver from Number Six to wait, and strolled toward the glow of lanterns in the distance.

This tree-lined street extended from Place Louis XVI to the still un-finished Église Sainte Marie-Madeleine where open fires were flickering among the piles of new marble and bricks. No one seemed to know when the church would be finished.

In another hour there would be a stream of vehicles as people left their homes for dinner parties or, in elaborate evening dress, to attend a ball. The rich gave balls even in July!

At this hour only two pairs of wrought-iron lanterns cast light on the entrance to the Midnight Club. The cobbled courtyard, soon to be filled with carriages, was empty except for a stableboy slumped against a wall in the shadow, sound asleep.

Vidocq twirled his gold-headed cane as he crossed to the marble steps, with their graceful gilded balustrades, leading to the carved en-trance doors.

There was nothing to indicate that this was a private club.

All the windows stood open, and he glimpsed lighted candles in dim rooms that appeared to be small salons. The first floor, overhead, was more brightly lighted. All the dining rooms, public or private, would be up there.

He went up the steps and grasped a silver bell pull. Yanked it twice.

Glancing back, toward the open windows of a mansion partially hid-den behind trees directly across the street, he glimpsed a lighted salon where elderly people sat listening to a young woman perform on a spinet. From this distance it was impossible to see her face or hear the music.

Turning as one of the doors opened, he saw an impressive white-haired man wearing a dark-gray uniform braided with gold, his hands in white cotton gloves.

"Monsieur?"

"I wish to see whoever's in charge."

"I'm afraid that would be impossible at the moment. May I ask the purpose of your visit?"

"I am—Vidocq." He was aware as he gave his name of a subtle change in the *commissionnaire's* face.

"Ah, Monsieur Vidocq!" Bowing and stepping back. "I'm sure that Monsieur de Plessis will be free to see you."

He removed his hat as he went inside. "Would that be the banker, Monsieur Louis de Plessis?"

"He's the director of the club as well as chairman of the board, but he's always busy at this hour, preparing for the evening ahead. If you'll wait for a moment, I'll inform him that you're here."

"Certainly."

"Could I have one of our waiters bring you a glass of champagne?" Gesturing toward a pair of young men, also in gold-braided uniforms, chatting quietly near the open doors to an empty salon.

"Nothing."

"Make yourself comfortable, Monsieur." Indicating a pair of *fauteuils* placed near a small table.

"I prefer to stand." Vidocq glanced around the enormous lobby, as the *commissionnaire* went toward one of a pair of identical curving marble staircases carpeted in dark green and leading to a broad marble balcony. Below the balcony was an antique chest holding an enormous bouquet of fresh flowers in a porcelain urn. At the rear of the balcony half a dozen marble steps led to the first floor. Smaller staircases on either side of the balcony would lead to side wings of the mansion. Walls were hung with fine paintings, and console tables holding lighted candelabra were placed between comfortable sofas with groups of *fauteuils* and small tables in the center of the lobby. In spite of the many lighted candles, the air was surprisingly cool. Perhaps because of the height of the ceiling. Looking up, peering into the shadows, he saw that this lobby was at least three floors high.

"If Monsieur will follow me . . ."

Vidocq looked around, surprised that the man had returned so quickly.

The white-haired *commissionnaire* bowed and went toward the steps.

Vidocq followed, up one of the curving staircases to the balcony, then up the second flight of steps to the first floor, where the dark-green carpet continued down a broad corridor that led toward the marble-columned entrance of an elegant dining room as large as a restaurant.

One of a pair of doors on his right opened to permit a hum of conversation to escape into the corridor.

Vidocq glanced at the man who came out and saw that it was a waiter, carrying a tray of empty wineglasses. He was like a shadow figure until he turned to close the door and the candlelight from inside the room revealed half of his face. Balding head, sparse gray hair. Solemn face with sunken eyes and hollow cheeks. He had seen that face before.

In the brief moment before the door closed, he glimpsed some men seated around a long table, their faces obscured by cigar smoke.

"Our conference room," the *commissionnaire* explained. "The club's business affairs are discussed there. And this is our director's office." He motioned toward the next pair of closed doors before he knocked on one.

"Enter!" A man's voice, sharp and irritable, responded.

As the *commissionnaire* pushed the door open, Vidocq glanced toward the dining room. Each table held shaded candles, and garçons were darting about, arranging napkins and silver before the first customers of the evening arrived. He was aware of the *commissionnaire*'s voice as he continued to wonder where he'd seen that waiter in the past.

"You may go in. Monsieur de Plessis will see you."

He entered a paneled office that reminded him of the elegant salon where Tessier was murdered. Another antique desk stood in front of another *boiserie* wall, and a man was seated at the desk. Only Monsieur de Plessis was very much alive.

"Vidocq!" He rose, hand extended. "This is indeed a surprise. We're not accustomed to visits from the Sûreté."

"My visit is not official, Monsieur." He shook the outstretched hand.

"Sit down." Motioning toward an armchair. "May I offer you a cigar?"

"Nothing, at the moment." Resting his hat and cane on a table before sinking into the comfortable chair. "We have never met in the past," Vidocq began, easing into the important questions he must presently ask with conversation intended to disarm. "I had one of my staff inspect your club when it first opened, but since there was no gambling on the premises the Sûreté had no further interest."

"Any of our members who care to gamble can visit the gambling clubs on the Palais-Royal or on the boulevards. Those of us who, like myself, are bankers have no interest in games of chance. Gambling attracts an inferior element, which would be out of place here."

As Monsieur de Plessis talked, Vidocq studied his physical appearance and personality. At first glance he seemed to be arrogant and pompous. The banker had the florid complexion of one who enjoyed rich food and rare wines. He appeared to be in his fifties, with thinning black hair, slightly overweight. Holding his body erect, as though he might be wearing a corset. Glittering black eyes above a prominent nose, narrow lips, which became even thinner as he talked. Wearing a plum-colored coat made by an expensive tailor. High black velvet collar that seemed to support his head. Ruffled white silk shirt with a black satin cravat. His hands, for a moment, clasped each other. Then the fingers seemed to move independently, stroking the air to emphasize a word.

". . . surprised that you've never become a member. We have a superb chef and pleasant dining rooms where our members complete business transactions in an atmosphere of luxury. Including several intimate rooms where more personal matters may be discussed."

"I've never joined a private club, Monsieur."

"Why not, may I ask?"

"I've found that such clubs have too many rules."

"But a few rules are absolutely necessary."

"I object to any rule which forbids me the pleasure of female companions at dinner."

"That was, I believe, the first rule we agreed on. In fact, it was one of the reasons for the founding of our club. The company of women, after all, may be enjoyed in every other Parisian club and restaurant. Some of us have visited London and discovered clubs where business can be discussed without hearing female chatter. We decided to try such a club in Paris where our wives and daughters would never set foot. The Midnight Club proved to be a success from the night it opened."

"It has no attraction for me, I'm afraid, because I don't talk business matters—police business—with anyone except my staff at Number Six. And when I dine out, I enjoy seeing beautiful women."

"So do I, Monsieur. But not in the Midnight Club."

Vidocq realized that the banker had hesitated, obviously still wondering the purpose of his visit. "I wish to ask you several questions about Monsieur Narcisse Tessier . . ."

"Ah, Tessier! So that's what brings you here. I've just come from a meeting of our board where his name was mentioned. That he had been murdered. I had no idea!"

"It was, I believe, in the newspapers."

"I read only the financial news."

"I've been informed by several persons that Monsieur Tessier was a member of your club."

"He was among the first to join."

"I'm told he dined here frequently."

"That's quite right. He was a man of taste and a prominent jeweler. Most successful Parisian businessmen are among our members."

"Can you tell me the names of his dining companions?"

"We keep no lists of who dines with whom. Most of us bankers prefer to dine with our fellow bankers. I suppose Tessier enjoyed the company of other gentlemen who deal in precious jewels . . ."

"Did you know a Monsieur Auguste Marpon?"

"The name is not familiar . . ."

"He was employed by Tessier as his majordomo."

"I've never visited Monsieur Tessier's establishment. I believe it's on rue Taitbout . . ."

"Monsieur Marpon has also been murdered."

"Indeed?"

"Strangled. In an attic room of the rue Taitbout mansion."

"How shocking!"

"Do you know of a man named Drumont—Alcidor Drumont?"

"Never heard of him."

"He was Tessier's administrator—at least that's what he called himself. Drumont has disappeared. Taking with him every jewel, as well as gold and silver ingots, Tessier kept in a vault."

"How was he able to remove them?" The cold eyes became crafty. "Surely you had the place guarded?"

"Two men from the Sûreté are on the premises day and night. Can you tell me anything of Tessier's financial standing?"

"I've always supposed him to be a man of some wealth. Actually I have no personal knowledge of his fortune. He never dealt with my bank, and we don't question future members, when they join, about their financial worth. Tessier, of course, was one of the founders. Each of us made an initial investment to get it started. I suggest you contact the bank that handled Tessier's money. They should be able to answer your questions."

"Who are his bankers?"

"I've no idea."

"We've found no documents of any sort, business or personal, in the Tessier mansion. Drumont, apparently, removed or destroyed every scrap of paper relating to Tessier's fortune, his private life, and his business affairs."

"You are a master of surprise, Monsieur Vidocq." The banker smiled, but his eyes showed no hint of amusement.

"I have sent orders to every local police headquarters in France to be on the lookout for Drumont. I wish to question him in regard to several matters. Including two murders—Tessier and Marpon. He may also be involved with the murder of a prostitute—Maya . . ."

"Three murders?" His eyes widened as Vidocq got to his feet.

"I came to you, Monsieur, hoping you might be able to tell me something about Tessier. His past and his friends . . ."

"I know absolutely nothing about his personal life. Our members' private affairs are of no interest to me."

Vidocq snatched up his hat and cane. "If you recall anything more about Tessier, no matter how unimportant it may seem to you, I would like to hear what it is."

Monsieur de Plessis pushed himself back in his chair, fingers clutching the edge of the desk. "I doubt very much I would know anything that could be of the slightest interest to the Sûreté."

"Permit me to be the judge of that." He put on his hat and, cane in hand, went toward the door. Glanced back, as he swung it open, and saw that the banker hadn't moved. "Good evening, Monsieur."

Striding down the corridor, toward the staircase, Vidocq was aware that he'd learned very little from Monsieur de Plessis. The banker had shown no glimmer of recognition at the names of Marpon or Drumont.

270

He heard voices muffled by the closed doors as he passed the conference room. Would de Plessis return to his interrupted meeting?

As he started down the first shallow flight of carpeted steps, he wondered again about that waiter. Where had he encountered that face in the past? He was certain it was the face of a criminal.

Crossing the marble balcony, he saw that two middle-aged gentlemen had just entered below in the lobby and were leaving their hats and canes with one of the attendants, talking to the *commissionnaire* as the other attendant closed the entrance door.

Descending the curving staircase, he had a sudden flash of memory and the waiter's face began to take shape in his mind's eye. A much younger face. It was . . .

Goron! Goron who had been missing from his Montmartre haunts. The gray man who never came out from his lair before dusk. The Twilight Owl! He had found Crépuscule! Master thief! Pickpocket and cutthroat. How could Goron have obtained employment in an exclusive private club? Had he given up his life of crime and left the Paris underworld to take an honest job? Not likely . . .

The *commissionnaire* opened the entrance door and bowed. "Good evening, Monsieur Vidocq . . ."

Vidocq nodded and stepped outside. Descending the steps to the courtyard, he saw that several expensive carriages were now waiting, their uniformed coachmen huddled together. They looked up when they heard his heels on the marble steps but resumed their conversations when they saw a stranger.

Hesitating before crossing the courtyard, as another smart carriage pulled in from rue Royale. He glimpsed a man seated inside. A ray of light from one of the lanterns above the entrance revealed his face briefly.

Marchadier!

The proprietor of Galerie Marchadier was leaning forward, peering at the upstairs windows of the club and hadn't noticed him.

Vidocq smiled. His visit here had not, after all, been a total loss. He had found the missing Goron and observed the arrival of Marchadier. The expression on the art dealer's face revealed a man anticipating trouble. Had he been summoned to that meeting upstairs?

Striding up rue Royale toward his carriage, he decided that, for the first time this week, he had an appetite for dinner.

CHAPTER 45

Café Procope was crowded, in spite of the heat.

Vidocq was aware, as *le patron* led him through the main dining room, that several people had recognized him. He straightened, swaggering slightly, but kept his eyes straight ahead to avoid any conversation with strangers.

"Two of your friends are here tonight." *Le patron* motioned toward a side room where windows stood open onto a garden. "Monsieur Dumas arrived first. He hadn't started to order when Monsieur Balzac appeared. Now they argue about what to eat for dinner."

He saw them, Dumas laughing as Balzac glowered at the bill of fare.

"Put whatever they want on my account. When they see me, they will stop arguing and order your most expensive dishes. With my approval."

Le patron bowed. "Yes, Monsieur. My pleasure."

Dumas had seen him. "My dear friend!" He jumped up, arms outstretched. "Come dine with us!"

"Who is it?" Balzac looked up, his small eyes squinting. "Vidocq!" He put the bill of fare aside. "I'm trying to persuade Alexandre to order chicken with a bottle of wine so that we can celebrate, but he claims he can only afford sausage and a beer."

Vidocq embraced Dumas.

"I don't get paid my miserable salary until Saturday," Dumas explained. "It's beer and sausage or nothing."

Vidocq shook Balzac's plump hand and sat across from him as Dumas subsided into the chair between them. "And what are you two celebrating?"

Balzac's eyes gleamed mischievously. "It's Alexandre's birthday!"

Vidocq looked at Dumas. "But that's impossible!"

"Monsieur Vidocq . . ."

He turned to see the aged waiter who always served him. "Bring a magnum of your best champagne."

The waiter bowed and disappeared.

Balzac licked his lips. "Birthdays should always be drowned with champagne."

"Why do you say it's impossible for this to be my birthday?" Dumas asked. "I can show you an official document to prove it."

"Why?" Vidocq laughed. "Because this is *my* anniversary."

"Both of you?" Balzac's eyes were round with wonder. "On the same day! I don't believe it."

Vidocq disregarded him as he continued to face Dumas. "You never told me this was your natal day."

Dumas shrugged. "I'm not in the habit of disclosing my age to anyone. I prefer people to think I'm older."

"If I put this into a novel, nobody would believe it!" Balzac smiled at the idea. "Two friends learning for the first time they were born on the same day of the month. It's like a scene from Shakespeare. This makes you both Leos. I'm sitting here in a den of lions!"

Dumas smiled. "We are rather like lions. Always roaring . . ."

"I never roar." Vidocq laughed. "You believe in astrology?"

"Of course I do!"

Vidocq turned to Balzac. "And you, my friend?"

"Let me say I have no reason to disbelieve . . ."

"Astrology is older than most religions," Dumas continued. "I've always been interested in the heavens. I suppose because of my father's ancestors in San Domingo who practiced a primitive sort of astrology. I find it romantic to think our lives are influenced by the stars. And especially the moon!"

"I think there's a full moon tonight," Balzac interrupted. "Which always affects my writing. I most certainly do believe in my own star!"

"You have a personal star?" Vidocq asked.

"A star of destiny! Everybody has one, but most people don't realize it. What about you? Don't you believe in astrology?"

Vidocq shrugged. "I believe in any philosophy—religion or astrology—that helps a man to survive from day to day . . ."

"You never told me this was your birthday!" Balzac pouted. "Either of you."

"We've never been together before on this date." Dumas glanced at Vidocq. "I was sitting here alone, preparing to have a solitary birthday dinner when Honoré joined me . . ."

"Pardon, Messieurs . . ."

Vidocq looked up to see the waiter bearing a tray with a magnum of champagne and three glasses. "We must drink a toast!"

Balzac applauded.

The waiter uncorked the bottle and filled their glasses.

Vidocq was smiling again. "We shall have a birthday dinner, Alexandre, we'll never forget. In spite of the heat."

"What heat?" Dumas asked. "I find this weather as pleasant as a beautiful woman's warm embrace."

"I saw Henri Beyle last night. Looking cool and dignified, as usual. He's planning to write a novel."

"Everyone thinks he can write a novel!" Balzac complained.

Vidocq reached for his wineglass as the waiter departed. "Here's to our birthday!"

"Two birthdays!" Dumas lifted his glass.

"Everybody but me," Balzac muttered.

"When's yours?" Vidocq asked.

"The twentieth of May . . ."

"He's a Taurus!" Dumas threw back his head and laughed. "I should've guessed. Bellowing and snorting!"

"To both our birthdays, my friend." Vidocq held his glass toward Dumas.

Dumas touched it with his. "My twin!"

Vidocq smiled. "My brother . . ."

"To the two of you!" Balzac exclaimed.

They drank in unison, draining their glasses.

"Ah!" Vidocq sighed happily. "This makes an unpleasant day seem better."

"A bad day at Number Six?" Dumas asked, his interest aroused.

"Most of the day I was away from Number Six."

"Pursuing criminals?"

"Pursuing facts that proved to be as elusive as criminals." He reached for the bottle and refilled their glasses. "Now I will order us a fine birthday dinner. That includes you, Honoré, even though it's two months late."

"I accept." His greedy eyes sparkled with anticipation.

"My only suggestion is that we should have a cold dinner, start to finish."

Balzac frowned. "I was thinking about roast chicken . . ."

"Cold roast chicken? Excellent!"

Balzac beamed.

Vidocq raised his glass again. "To us! All three of us."

"To us!" they exclaimed, lifting their glasses.

"And nobody else!" Balzac added.

Their waiter returned as they drank and placed a menu in front of Vidocq. "There's rabbit stew tonight."

"Stew!" All three repeated the word in horror.

Vidocq chuckled. "We've decided to have cold roast chicken."

"Certainly, Monsieur . . ."

"And I," Vidocq continued, "as host as well as celebrant, will order." The old waiter smiled.

"To start," he studied the bill of fare, "perhaps the eel in aspic . . ." Balzac smiled his approval.

"After that the roast chicken. Bring a whole one. I'll carve it. With potato salad and a platter of cold asparagus, leeks, and whatever else the chef is hoarding in his kitchen. A special sauce for each!" He glanced from Dumas to Balzac. "How's that?"

Balzac sighed in anticipation.

"Another bottle of champagne with our dinner," Vidocq added. "Later we'll have a selection of cheeses, and after that we can decide about pastries."

"Very good, Monsieur." The waiter bowed and removed the menu.

Vidocq glanced at his two friends. They had only one thing in common, their delicate small hands. Although Dumas's fingers were thin and tapering while Balzac's were short and plump. Dumas always managed to look neat and fashionably dressed, while Balzac, as usual, was rumpled and shabby. Dumas was more a man of the boulevards than Balzac, although younger and just as insolvent.

Dumas was the first to speak. "I hear that two of the great whores have been murdered . . ."

Balzac peered at him. "Which whores?"

"Clochette and Maya," Dumas answered.

"What curious names they take!" Balzac shook his head. "A small bellflower and a whole civilization."

"Maya was also a Hindu goddess," Dumas continued. "I prefer to think that's where Maya found her name. Although she couldn't remember when I asked."

"You knew her?"

"Intimately. Both of them." Dumas smiled smugly. "Clochette was the younger but no less experienced. She was a pink and gold toy!

275

With blue eyes. And Maya was like a dark mythic figure glimpsed in the depths of a jungle."

"You've never seen a jungle!" Balzac exclaimed.

"Jungles surge through my veins! One day I hope to explore the vast jungles of Africa."

"You slept with these famous whores?"

"Many times. Although I haven't seen Clochette lately. I heard she had fallen in love."

"How could you afford them?"

Dumas shrugged. "They knew I had no money."

"*Les grandes courtisanes* demand enormous sums from their rich patrons," Vidocq explained, "but offer themselves freely to younger men whom they find more attractive than their wealthy protectors."

"You, too, have had these women?" Balzac asked.

"Both of them," Vidocq answered.

"What do they charge you?"

"I never pay. Sometimes I leave them a small bottle of perfume or a piece of inexpensive jewelry . . ."

"That's all?"

"One doesn't pay money to a friend for a pleasant hour's work at their profession."

Dumas laughed. "I agree!"

"I've never seen one of *les grandes courtisanes!* Even from a distance." Balzac glanced at each of them in turn. "Where do you go to see them?"

"Don't tell him!" Dumas ordered. "He's much too young."

"I'm three years older than you!" Balzac exploded. "You're only twenty-one. Today!"

"My grandmother was a Haitian whore. That makes me wiser for my years than any Frenchman." Turning to Vidocq again. "Do you know who killed them? Clochette and Maya . . ."

"I've no idea. As yet."

"They say every pimp and prostitute in Paris showed up for Clochette's funeral."

"I'd like to have seen that!" Balzac exclaimed.

"You can go to Maya's, if you wish," Dumas replied. "Monday morning at Saint-Séverin."

"I might do that! Although I shouldn't take the time from my writing."

"Still finishing a novel a month?" Dumas asked.

"I've slowed down a little. Although I'm still working as hard as Henri the Fourth's horse! Before it was cast in bronze."

"What name are you using on these new books?" Vidocq asked.

"I've finished with Lord R'honne and taken another. Horace de Saint Aubin."

"Very impressive!" Dumas winked at Vidocq, his blue eyes twinkling.

"Trash, all of them!" Balzac scowled. "They vanish as fast as they're printed, and they've brought me neither love, gold, nor fame! One day very soon I will write a good one and put my own name on it." Tucking his napkin under his chin. "Here's our food!"

They watched their waiter, assisted by a garçon, serve the first course.

Vidocq inspected the ivory strips of eel in a ring of amber aspic which was placed in front of him. "I am hungry!"

Dumas tore a piece of bread from a fresh loaf as Balzac dug into the aspic with his fork and lifted a coil of eel to his mouth. Closed his eyes as he chewed, a smile of gluttonous joy lighting his face.

Vidocq had another swallow of champagne before tasting the eel. The first strip rested like cool silk on his tongue as its subtle flavor spread to all his senses. He chewed, swallowed with regret, and immediately ate more.

They remained silent until the eel had vanished.

Balzac was the first to finish.

Vidocq put his fork down, slipped his fingers into a pocket of his waistcoat and brought out the jeweled brooch. "This might interest both of you. I found it in the hand of a dead man."

Balzac's eyes glittered with curiosity. "Murdered?"

"Strangled." He held out the brooch and saw Balzac pull back.

"Take it in your hand, my friend. Examine it for yourself."

He took the brooch cautiously and studied the painted miniature. "The dead Queen!"

"This brooch belonged to her. The old man who clutched it as he died had been in the Queen's service. She gave this to him before he fled to England."

"She was indeed very beautiful." Balzac handed the brooch to Dumas who stared at the portrait.

"The old man must've been a Royalist fool!" Dumas exclaimed. "To keep such an incriminating bauble."

Vidocq shrugged. "A sentimental fool, perhaps. I don't believe he was interested in politics. Working for the Queen was only a job. He was a human being, and he apparently worshipped her."

"Who do you think killed this old man?" Balzac asked.

"I've no idea as yet. At the moment I have three murders to solve. The murderers are walking free tonight in the dark streets of Paris."

"More likely," Dumas suggested, handing the brooch back to Vidocq, who slipped it into his waistcoat pocket, "they're in bed with a beautiful woman, forgetting their crimes!"

"Or enjoying a good dinner!" Balzac said, laughing.

Vidocq observed his two friends. They both had shiny black hair. Crisp curls rising to a peak on Dumas' handsome head, made him appear taller. As usual, Balzac's long hair was untidy, brushed back in a greasy mane, his mustaches drooping, a sparse tuft of hair beneath his lower lip. Dumas at the moment was clean shaven. Oddly Balzac's lips were thick and somewhat Negroid, although it was Dumas whose father had been mulatto. Dumas had blue eyes, a small mouth and perfect white teeth, while Balzac's eyes were brown, his teeth crumbling. Dumas was slim, Balzac's bull-like neck and thick torso made him appear much heavier.

" . . . and, to this day, she's a monster!" Balzac exclaimed.

"Who?" Vidocq asked.

"My dear mother. Alexandre inquired about her health. Which continues to be excellent. Because of her, I had a miserable childhood. I escaped finally to Paris, but she's driving my sister into her grave. Even though she got married and moved away."

"I adore my mother!" Dumas murmured.

"And I," Vidocq nodded. "I also liked my father."

"You both had the intelligence," Balzac complained, "to select better parents than I."

They were laughing as the garçon removed their empty plates.

Their waiter brought a large roast chicken on a silver platter which he set before Vidocq. A second garçon arranged dishes of cold vegetables around the table, a sauce boat beside each, while the first garçon placed a pile of three dinner plates in front of Vidocq who seized the carving utensils and held them ready. "What do you prefer, my friends?"

"A little of the white meat for me," Dumas requested.

Balzac studied the chicken. "I'll have a leg. A whole leg! With a slice of breast and perhaps a wing. I'm fond of wings."

Vidocq carved quickly and expertly.

"You use that knife like a rapier," Dumas observed.

"My father taught me to carve, when I was a boy."

"Do you think," Balzac asked, "that the old man who had that brooch in his hand was killed by the same person who murdered those whores?"

"No. I don't." Vidocq set an entire leg on the first plate.

"When you're looking for a murderer, don't you fear for your own life?" Dumas asked. "He must be aware you're on his trail."

"All criminals know I'm after them." Slicing the breast. "Especially murderers."

"Surely they would kill you to save their own necks!"

"A few have tried. With no success, as you can see." He had arranged two slices of breast on the plate, including the first slice with its herb-crusted skin, along with a wing and handed it to Balzac.

"Aren't you afraid of some desperate criminals attacking you in a dark street?" Balzac reached for the bowl of potato salad and began to pile it on his plate.

"Such a thought never enters my mind."

"But you must fear death! Every man does."

"Not I." He cut thin slices of breast for Dumas as he talked and handed him the plate. "Death is only another adventure. Like life! My life has been an endless series of adventures. Birth was a surprise, and death will certainly be another. I didn't anticipate life, but I look forward, with curiosity, to death. The final surprise!"

"You're a brave man." Dumas was serving himself small portions of the vegetables.

Vidocq shrugged, cutting two slices of breast for himself. "Bravery is a matter of circumstance. Or, more often, stupidity."

"You told me the other night," Balzac was helping himself to large portions of the cold vegetables, "there's only one man, in all the world, you really hate . . ."

"Calamatta!" He spat the word like a curse.

"One day you intend to kill him . . ."

"And I shall! For the injustice he did to me in my youth. Those long years of fleeing from the police. The pain he caused my parents! One day I will meet Calamatta and destroy him. With bullet or sword. Or my two bare hands!" He sat down, his plate in front of him, and reached for the potato salad. "One day I shall have my revenge."

"Is he your 'dearest foe'?" Dumas asked.

"I suppose you might call him that. Dearest foe? Where did you find that expression? Sounds like an author's turn of phrase."

"The greatest! It's from Shakespeare's *Hamlet.*"

"I've heard of the play but have never read or seen it." Serving himself a few vegetables.

"When I was younger," Dumas explained, "I found a French copy and within three days learned all of Hamlet's speeches."

"I've read several of Shakespeare's plays," Balzac said, spooning sauce on his asparagus. "I suspect they read much better in English."

"Someday I must read Shakespeare." Vidocq accepted a boat of sauce from Dumas. "When I was in school the priests insisted I read only Latin. Even Voltaire and Rabelais were forbidden. Of course later I read both."

"This chicken is excellent!" Balzac smacked his lips.

"What other investigations concern you at the moment?" Dumas asked. "In addition to murder."

"There was an apparent attempt at blackmail, last week, which turned out to be something more complicated." He ate slowly as he talked, enjoying the chicken and the young asparagus. "I managed to unmask the supposed blackmailer."

"Someday I must write a novel about blackmail." Balzac chewed rapidly, gulping his food. "The hatred that causes a person to attempt such an evil thing."

"There is one current investigation I might tell you about . . ."

"Splendid!" Dumas exclaimed, eyes alert with interest. "What sort of investigation?"

"Tell us!" Balzac urged, helping himself to another sauce, which he dribbled across the plump leeks reposing on his plate.

"You may have read in the newspapers. Many châteaux in the Loire Valley have been pillaged during the past year."

"I didn't know that!"

Dumas laughed. "You don't read the papers, my friend."

"I have no time."

"I've read several accounts," Dumas continued, "but none of them gave much information. Only that some of the great castles had been plundered. Without any hint as to the culprits or what they've stolen."

"They take everything that can be moved!" Vidocq continued, "I believe it's a large band of thieves. They have a leader, but I don't as yet know his identity. Only that he's called Le Diable Noir . . ."

"The Black Devil?" Dumas dropped his fork on the plate with a sharp clink. "That's what his soldiers called my father, the General—because of his dark skin—when he led them in the march on Bolzano. Only they said it in German. *Der Schwarze Teufel!*"

"Could it be your father?" Balzac asked.

"It would have to be his ghost!"

"The local authorities have been unable to catch Le Diable or any of his gang." Vidocq ate slowly, aware that Balzac was gobbling food like a starving child. "The local people have seen these brigands at night, a procession of them riding across the field, but they fear to venture out, and the local gendarmes never stir from their headquartes after dark."

"Tell us more," Balzac pleaded, chewing vigorously.

"We obtained a large map of the Loire Valley and circled each plundered château with red. Marked every farm and village where the gang was seen passing through in the night with blue arrows indicating the direction they took. Back and forth!" He saw that Balzac had finished his chicken. "I studied the map for several days until I made a discovery."

"What did you find?"

"In every instance, the procession of horses and carts came from the north and returned north, with their loot, after each robbery!"

"What does this prove?" Dumas asked.

"That their headquarters has to be north of the Loire Valley. Probably halfway to Paris. I think an entire village may be involved! Unfortunately, an investigation would take several weeks, and the government is demanding the gang be stopped at once, Le Diable Noir caught and unmasked!"

"So what can be done?" Balzac asked, serving himself more potato salad.

"I finally came to what I hope is the solution. I realized those stolen treasures would have to be sold in Paris!"

Dumas nodded.

"So the gang brings their loot here. But how? The simplest way would be for them to hide each piece of antique furniture and painting under a load of vegetables. Nobody searches a farmer's cart as it passes through a barrier."

"But which barrier?" Balzac asked.

"One of the southern barriers. Last night I put two men from Number Six on each of them."

"What did they find?" Balzac's eyes glinted with excitement.

"Nothing. But I have other men there tonight."

"Doesn't one of you want more of this chicken?" Balzac asked.

Dumas shook his head. "None for me."

Vidocq smiled. "I've had enough. Help yourself."

"Then, perhaps, I'll finish it." Balzac grasped his fork and stabbed the chicken, lifting it from the platter to his plate. Held it firmly, with the fork, while he pulled off the remaining leg. Drops of grease spattered his napkin as he bit into the flesh and tore it from the bone.

Vidocq glanced from Balzac to Dumas. He wondered what they would look like in ten years. Balzac would surely be enormous!

Dumas winked.

Vidocq refilled their glasses as Balzac ate. Raised his glass to Dumas and, as they drank, became aware of a man hurrying toward their table, wearing faded blue work clothes and a workman's cloth cap. He set his wineglass down as the approaching face was revealed by the candlelight. "Damiot?"

"Aubé said you'd be here." He hesitated beside Vidocq, glancing at the others.

"It's all right to talk in front of these gentlemen. What's happened?"

"We've found something in a farmer's cart at the Saint-Jacques barrier."

"The old Roman road!" Dumas exclaimed.

"The road to Orléans!" Balzac added.

"What did you find?" Vidocq asked.

"A piece of antique furniture. Looks like a small sofa, under a load of carrots," Damiot answered.

"They're holding the driver?"

"Until you come."

"At once." Vidocq rose, pushing his chair back.

"Can't we come with you?" Balzac pulled the napkin from around his neck and began to clean his greasy fingers.

"This is official business, my friends."

"But you've promised many times," Balzac insisted, "that one day you'd allow us to observe you at work."

"I would also like to come with you," Dumas added quietly. "See the great Vidocq actually catch a criminal. Especially Le Diable Noir! In case it's my father returned to his beloved Paris from—wherever he's been . . ."

Vidocq laughed. "I'll be stopping at Number Six to change my clothes and pick up a horse. That's the quickest way to reach the barrier. You would both have to ride a horse."

"I'm an expert horseman," Dumas announced proudly. "My father, the General, taught me to ride."

Vidocq turned to Balzac. "And you, my friend?"

"I once rode a horse all the way from Villers-Cotterets to Paris!"

Vidocq turned to Damiot. "Do you suppose we could find two obedient mounts for these gentlemen?"

"All our horses are obedient, Chief, or they wouldn't be working for Number Six."

"You see!" Balzac exclaimed.

"Very well! Come along. Both of you." Vidocq picked up his hat and cane from the chair.

Dumas sprang to his feet, but Balzac dipped his napkin into the wine and proceeded to wipe his mouth and chin.

"We should finish our champagne!" Vidocq set his hat upon his head then snatched up his glass and raised it toward his friends.

Dumas picked up his glass and clinked it against Vidocq's, then they both held their glasses toward Balzac.

He pushed himself to his feet and belched. "Pardon!" Grabbed his almost empty glass and raised it. "One for all and all for one!"

They repeated the toast together. "One for all and all for one!" Set their empty glasses down and, reaching for their hats from a row of wall hooks, followed young Damiot through the dining room.

As Balzac trailed after the others, he glanced regretfully at the display of cheeses and pastries on a marble-topped table near the entrance. "We didn't finish our dinner!"

CHAPTER 46

The three horses galloped south through the dark and silent streets, Vidocq leading on the same dark gray stallion he always rode.

Dumas and Balzac were close behind on a pair of chestnut mares the night stableman had assured Vidocq were the best behaved of all the horses owned by the Sûreté.

He glanced back and saw they were having no trouble, although Balzac appeared to be bouncing more than Dumas, who sat in the saddle like a professional. His father, the General, had taught him well.

This long street, stretching south, was dark except for a single street lamp at each crossing, but the moon was rising, illuminating the rooftops and upper stories of the houses on their right.

Vidocq had changed into the worn clothes of a laborer, a bandanna tied around his neck, the visor of a cloth cap pulled down over his eyes.

At the same time Aubé had escorted Dumas and Balzac into the big room at Number Six where disguises and wardrobe were kept for the staff. It had been easy to select faded work clothes for Dumas but difficult to find any large enough to fit Balzac. They had finally settled on patched trousers and a loose-fitting farmer's blouse. Both had visored caps covering their hair.

They had ridden across the Pont Saint-Michel and avoided the boulevards as they headed south.

Not a breath of air ruffled the trees or cooled their faces.

Paris was silent, as though the oppressive heat had sent everyone to bed. No sign of life in any of the dark side streets or alleys.

The only sound was their horses' hooves on the cobbles.

Vidocq glimpsed the lights of the barrier ahead, two crossings away, and reined his horse until Balzac and Dumas joined him. "Remember my instructions and follow them precisely."

"We ride straight to a clump of trees on the left when we reach the barrier," Dumas repeated.

"Remain there in shadow," Balzac added, "while you talk to the officer."

"We will follow this farmer to his destination. Discover where he's taking whatever's hidden under his carrots."

"One for all and all for one!" Balzac exclaimed, his voice hushed.

"Where did you get that, my friend?" Dumas asked.

"This also comes from Shakespeare."

Vidocq chuckled. "I'll ride ahead. Give me a few seconds before you follow."

Balzac saluted awkwardly.

Vidocq jerked the bridle and dug in his heels. The stallion tossed his mane and galloped toward the barrier.

His friends followed at a slow canter.

Approaching the barrier, Vidocq saw a clumsy charrette, filled with baskets of carrots, standing in a circle of light from an overhead lantern with a sturdy farm horse tied to a hitching post. The old-fashioned cart had enormous wooden wheels built to withstand rough country roads.

Another lantern was suspended from a tree at the far side of the barrier where a uniformed officer stood guard. Probably asleep on his feet, because he didn't look around at the sound of the approaching horse.

The office was lighted, door and windows open.

Vidocq glanced back but was unable to see anything of Dumas or Balzac in the dark street. They, however, would be able to see him against the lights of the barrier.

A man appeared from the office without haste and came toward him.

Vidocq saw that it was young Damiot. He pulled the stallion to a halt.

Damiot reached up and grasped the bridle. "Where are the others?"

"Following close behind. What's happened?"

"They're still questioning that farmer. Telling him his passport should've been renewed. The old man fortunately can't read."

"They can release him now. Let him drive into the city. I'll wait in the shadow with my friends. We will follow him." He heard two horses approaching and saw Balzac and Dumas turn their mounts off the road and slow to a halt in the darkness. "You saw the sofa yourself, under those carrots?"

"When one of the inspectors pulled back a corner of the cloth."

"Did the farmer get excited?"

"No. He said it was an old sofa that belonged to his wife and he's taking it to her mother in Paris. But I looked at his eyes and saw that he was frightened. You taught me that, Chief. Never believe what suspects say but look at their eyes. The eyes give them away."

"Good work. I'll be waiting when you bring him out." He turned the stallion's head and joined the others.

"What's happening?" Balzac whispered.

"The farmer's coming out in a moment. They're letting him continue on his way. We'll follow."

"You think he's one of Le Diable Noir's band?" Dumas asked.

"I'm positive he is. Do nothing to attract attention. And no talking while we wait." He turned the stallion to face the street as Balzac and Dumas moved into position behind him.

They waited, their eyes on the charrette.

Vidocq was conscious of the silence. If there were any birds in these trees, they must be asleep.

Waiting always made him impatient.

This farmer had to be one of Le Diable's cutthroats. Once he had him in the interrogation room at Number Six, he would learn the identity of Le Diable Noir. But first he must find out where he was taking this sofa and arrest whoever was waiting to receive it. Damiot would ride after them into Paris with the other man from Number Six, but he would ride ahead and track the farmer to his destination.

He reached under his workman's blouse and felt the revolver tucked into the waist of his trousers.

The moonlight seemed to be getting brighter, but that was because his eyes had grown accustomed to the darkness under these trees. Glancing behind him, he saw that Dumas appeared to be relaxed but Balzac was leaning forward, eyes focused on the charrette.

Young Damiot had come out from the office and was standing in the moonlight.

Vidocq clutched his reins and stroked the neck of the stallion, which gave a faint snort of pleasure. "Quiet!" he whispered.

A group of men appeared, and Damiot joined them as they walked across to the charrette.

Vidocq saw that the farmer wore a faded smock and a wide-brimmed straw hat. Watched him climb onto the driver's seat and take up his whip. Observed the customs officers surround the cart as he reached for his reins and Damiot untied the horse.

The farmer cracked his whip, and the charrette lumbered out onto the road and turned into the long street leading into Paris.

Vidocq watched Damiot and the others going back to the office as the sound of the clumsy wooden wheels faded.

"Another five seconds," he whispered over his shoulder, "and we follow. Stay well behind me. No matter what happens. Two of my men from Number Six will follow you. In case of trouble they'll ride ahead to join me, but in that event rein your horses at once and wait for me to come back. Understand?"

"Yes, Chief."

Vidocq smiled. It was Dumas who had answered, accepting orders.

"You're expecting trouble?" Balzac asked, timorously.

"I always expect trouble and am prepared." Easing the stallion out of the shadow and into bright moonlight. The horse trotted slowly, and after a few moments Vidocq heard the others following. He could see a lighted lantern swinging behind the charrette, two streets ahead, and kept his eyes on that swaying pinpoint of light. At the same time he was aware of the other horses behind him. Their sound would be covered by the creaking wooden cart.

Vidocq peered at the sky and saw that it was shimmering with stars.

The champagne he had drunk, combined with the heat, had made him slightly light-headed. Usually he didn't have that much wine at dinner. He felt as though he was galloping headlong through a strange city, but actually the stallion was moving at an easy pace.

These dark side streets were unfamiliar, but he knew the charrette was heading toward the Seine.

He realized, to his surprise, that the pinpoint of lantern light was no longer moving. The charrette had stopped!

Glancing behind as he urged the stallion forward, he was unable to see the others in the dark. Approaching the charrette, he saw that the farmer had gotten down and was securing ropes around the rear of his load.

The farmer looked up as he heard the horse slowing to a stop.

Vidocq reined in the stallion. "Pardon, my friend . . ."

"Monsieur?" He touched his hat.

"I seem to be lost. I'm looking for rue du Bac . . ."

"I'm a stranger here. Bring fresh vegetables into the city nearly every week, but only know the same streets I've been following for years. Get lost myself, many times. Taking a wrong turn."

"Having trouble with your cart?"

"Always stop before I reach the bridge and check these ropes. If they're not secure, I can lose half my vegetables. Paris is a city of thieves!" Climbing onto the cart again. "Hope you find your street, Monsieur." Picking up the reins. "Good luck!"

Vidocq pulled the stallion around, as the charrette rolled on, its wheels clattering. Heading back the way he had come, he goaded the stallion so he could quickly tell the others what had happened and return before the farmer traveled too far.

As he glimpsed his waiting friends, he saw Damiot and the other man from Number Six come riding out of the night. All three reached the two halted horses at the same instant.

In the confusion, Balzac unfortunately jerked his reins and the mare arched back on her haunches.

"Careful!" Vidocq shouted as he watched Balzac's enormous bulk slide slowly back on the horse's rump and drop with a thud onto the cobbles.

Balzac gave a gargantuan belch, and the startled mare released an enormous fart.

The two eruptions of sound combined with roars of laughter from Vidocq and Dumas—joined by the others—reverberated through the silent street.

Balzac, seated on the cobbles, was cursing.

Dumas jumped off his horse with a flash of long legs, bending to assist his fallen friend. "Honoré! Are you hurt?"

"It was the wine and this full moon. A dangerous combination . . ."

Vidocq jumped down and helped Dumas pull him to his feet. "No bones broken?"

"I think not." Balzac fingered his buttocks gingerly.

Vidocq looked up at Damiot, who was still laughing, seated on his horse. "Go after that farmer and don't lose him. I'll catch up with you."

"Yes, Chief." He motioned for his companion to follow, and they raced off up the long street, the sound of their horses' hooves fading.

Vidocq restrained a smile, observing Balzac's pained expression as he continued to prod his bones. "You pulled those reins too suddenly. Caused your horse to rear."

"You appeared so unexpectedly, I thought you were Le Diable Noir!"

"I'm the one who usually falls!" Dumas announced. "I've had a fear of height all my life, the instant I'm off the ground. Even on a horse."

Seeing Balzac standing beside Dumas, Vidocq became aware for the first time of his short legs. They were what made him appear squat, along with the thickness of his torso and massive shoulders. Dumas seemed taller, but actually he wasn't.

"Come!" Dumas urged. "We'll help you mount again."

Balzac scowled. "Must I?"

"I'll give you a hand." Vidocq smiled as they grasped both his arms. "Put your foot in the stirrup."

Balzac obeyed reluctantly.

They heaved him onto the saddle.

Balzac clutched the reins as Vidocq and Dumas mounted their horses.

"We'll keep together for a few moments." Vidocq turned in the saddle to explain. "Then I'll ride ahead and join the others. Here we go!" He nudged the stallion with his knee and rode ahead of them.

"All for one and one for all!" Balzac exclaimed.

Dumas laughed. "Sounds like a battle cry!"

The three horses trotted up the dark street between the silent houses—Vidocq slightly ahead—in and out of the moonlight, which grew brighter as the moon rose on their right. After a few moments of silence, except for the even clopping of their own steeds, they heard hoofbeats approaching, clattering on the cobbles, coming fast.

Vidocq raised his hand for the others to halt as he reined his stallion.

Damiot materialized alone, pulling his horse to a stop.

"What happened?" Vidocq asked.

"We lost him! Before we reached the river. He must've turned into a side street and crossed one of the bridges. No chance of finding him."

Vidocq whispered a single word under his breath.

CHAPTER 47

The carriage from Number Six drove on as Vidocq closed the door of the mansion on rue de l'Hirondelle. He knew that all his coachmen had orders from Aubé not to leave until they saw him safely inside, in case anyone was lurking in the darkness, hoping to attack him. That had happened, many times, in the past.

He bolted the door then headed for the console table with its lighted oil lamp.

A fold of notepaper waited beside the lamp.

He picked it up and read his mother's writing.

> *You were unable to honor us with your presence but we enjoyed a delicious dinner to celebrate your anniversary.*
> *Even Jeanne-Victoire ate a small piece of birthday cake.*
> *I took Fleuride shopping again, in spite of this wretched heat.*
> *My love to you on this, your natal day, as on every other day ...*

Vidocq slipped the note into a pocket as he went toward the staircase.

Climbing the carpeted steps, he cursed his wasted evening. If Balzac hadn't slid off his horse, he'd have tracked that charrette to its destination. By now he'd have been interrogating the farmer and getting information that would have led to Le Diable! Should never have consented to take Balzac and Dumas with him tonight. Wouldn't make that mistake again.

Pausing briefly at the top of the staircase, he heard no sound from his mother's suite or from Fleuride's adjoining bedroom. Following their afternoon of shopping, they should be sleeping soundly.

Or would Fleuride be waiting in his bed? Lying naked on the fresh white sheet ...

He started down the hall, quickening his steps in anticipation.

They had returned to Number Six—he, Balzac, and Dumas—where they climbed to the second floor and changed to their own clothes again. Balzac was limping, and Dumas was visibly tired. He had sent them home in a carriage.

Opening the door to his own suite, he could see, beyond the dark foyer, the lamp lighted on his bedside table. The bed had been turned down but was unoccupied.

He left the door ajar, in case Fleuride heard him come upstairs. The open door would show he was expecting her.

Crossing the hall, he pushed the door of his wife's suite open and saw a dim glow of candlelight in her bedroom. He left the door open and, careful not to make a sound, went toward the bed.

Jeanne-Victoire was lying on her side, turned away from the shaded candle on the bed table.

The only sound was the faint rasping of *cigales* in the garden.

He saw his wife's face in the tall mirror on the far side of the room but was unable to tell whether her eyes were open, could only make out the delicate oval of her face.

Perhaps it was just as well she wasn't awake. He would sponge his body with cold water and get to bed. Relax and rest between fresh sheets, even if he couldn't sleep. Lie awake and consider the events of his day. It had been a long one . . .

"Who are you, Monsieur?"

As he heard the whispered question, he saw that her eyes were open. His own voice, as he answered, was gentle. "I am Vidocq . . ."

She pushed herself over onto her back and held out both arms.

He sank onto the bed and embraced her, breathing her familiar perfume, as he kissed the tip of her nose. "My little wife . . ."

"My dearest. You're home early."

"It was a day of many problems, most of which I was unable to solve. So I must face them again in the morning. Along with tomorrow's problems."

"Everyone brings you their problems! From the King himself to me."

"Louis hasn't sought my assistance lately, and you, my love, have no problems. Except to recover your health. Was the doctor here again?"

"He won't be back until next week. The maids helped me out to the balcony this evening."

"Did they!"

"Where I dined with your dear mother and cousin. We had a celebration in your honor. I didn't know this was the date of your birth. You never told me! July twenty-fourth . . ."

"Maman shouldn't have told you today."

"She didn't. It was Fleuride."

"My little cousin talks too much."

"She adores you! Talks about you all the time. Was sorry you weren't here to join us. Your mother told her it was also a dinner to celebrate her visit to Paris. I had no idea she'd be leaving next week."

"Will she?"

"Perhaps you could persuade her to stay another week . . ."

"Would that please you?"

"Oh, yes!"

"Then I shall most certainly try."

"Your mother's planning a drive into the country for a picnic. She wants me to go."

"The fresh air would be excellent for you!"

"I've never been on a picnic . . ."

"We'll find a pleasant spot near a river. Hang a hammock between the trees so that you can rest. Spread a cloth on the grass when we eat with a nest of pillows for you . . ."

"Sounds like a dream! If you go, so will I."

"Nothing could prevent my going. I'll take the day off from Number Six, no matter how busy we are. We used to have picnics every summer when I was a boy. Papa baked special cakes, and Maman packed everything in baskets. Patés and sausages! My job was to tie cords around the wine bottles and drop them in the river to cool."

"Cook baked a lovely cake for your birthday."

"Not as good as Papa used to make!"

"Dinner looked delicious."

"Didn't you eat anything?"

"A slice of cake. With a glass of champagne. Fleuride ate everything and, as a matter of fact, drank a little too much wine. Maman had to take her off to bed."

"Did she behave at dinner? Not chatter too much?"

"I like to hear her chatter. And laugh! Makes me feel young to be with her. I'm glad she told me it's your birthday. I wouldn't have known, if she hadn't. We drank several toasts to you. Such a lovely evening!" She looked into his eyes, smiling. "You're going to marry her one day . . ."

"What are you saying?"

"Fleuride. You'll marry her, after I leave you."

"You will never leave me, _chérie!_"

"We both know that I will. We've always known. From the first . . . It won't be difficult for me now. Knowing that Fleuride loves you."

"But I love you!"

"You will marry her. With my blessing . . ."

"No, no!" Her words had startled him. Did she have a premonition of death? "I won't listen to such talk. I'll always love you! Always . . ." Embracing her again, kissing her gently. "Now you must sleep." He released her onto the pillow and got to his feet. Circled the bed but looked back as he reached the open doors and saw that she was watching him. "Good night, my love."

"Good night . . ."

He frowned as he closed the door. Jeanne-Victoire's words had disturbed him.

Returning down the corridor, he paused at the open door to his own suite. His bed remained empty.

He continued on past the staircase. Paused at the closed doors to his mother's suite but could hear no sound inside. Moved on more quickly to Fleuride's door. Swung it open and went inside.

Hesitated in the dark foyer, peering into her bedroom. The only light was a faint reflection of moonlight coming through the open windows.

He could see Fleuride in the bed. Black curls on white pillows.

Moving closer, he saw that she was wearing a négligée but had left it open because of the heat. Heard her regular breathing. Saw her breasts moving up and down as she slept.

He slipped the brooch from his waistcoat pocket and, leaning closer, pinned it onto a pillow where she would find it when she wakened.

Felt an urge to touch one of her breasts with his lips but resisted the impulse.

CHAPTER 48

Crossing the dining room toward the open windows, he saw that the breakfast table on the shaded terrace was set for three, but unless Fleuride was in the kitchen he was the first to come downstairs.

Sitting at his place, facing the garden, he reached for the silver bell and shook it several times. Unfolded his napkin and draped it across his knees as he looked at the sunlight on a rose tree covered with white blossoms. This weather had caused everything to bloom.

He was perspiring already, even though he wore another light summer suit.

Footsteps hurrying from the dining room.

"Good morning, Rosine!" he called. "Good morning, Prudence!"

Only one voice responded. "Good morning, Monsieur!"

He looked around to see Prudence bearing a porcelain coffeepot and napkin-covered brioche on a silver tray. "Where's Rosine?"

"Madame gave her permission to sleep late."

"Did she?" He watched Prudence set the tray down and pour black coffee into his usual Sèvres bowl.

"There was a late dinner last night to celebrate Monsieur's anniversary."

He grunted. "So I've heard."

"Madame told me to open a bottle of champagne for ourselves in the kitchen—Jean and the rest of us—but Rosine isn't used to drinking two glasses of wine."

"Where's my mother this morning?"

"I served her breakfast in bed. She only wanted black coffee."

"And Mademoiselle Fleuride?"

"She'll be down in a moment. I saw her when I was in Madame's room, but she said she'd have breakfast with you."

"Good!"

"Would you like some fruit?" Lifting her empty tray from the table. "Cook brought some peaches back from market this morning."

"None for me at the moment, but you can bring them in. My cousin may enjoy them."

"Yes, Monsieur." She gave a tentative curtsy and disappeared through the dining room with her tray.

He tasted the coffee then broke the brioche apart. Dug his knife into the butter and spread it on the warm brioche. Took a large bite, chewing vigorously, as he wondered what this new day would bring . . .

"Good morning, cousin!"

"Ah! Good morning!" He looked around to see Fleuride in a new white satin robe, hurrying out from the dining room. "You're late today."

"I overslept." She kissed him delicately on the back of his neck, then sat at his right. "I planned to come down early and cook you another omelette."

"Not this morning. Much too warm." He smiled, noticing the brooch pinned to the lapel of her robe. "Where did you buy that charming piece of jewelry? I suppose you found it yesterday, while you were shopping with Maman."

"It was pinned to my pillow this morning when I wakened. I turned over and bumped my nose against it."

"Did you!"

"Of course I knew who had left it there."

"You've questioned all suspects, weighed the evidence, and caught the culprit?"

"It had to be you! I showed it to Tante, and she agreed."

"A most intelligent woman."

"It was all right for me to let her see it?"

"Of course."

"A miniature of Marie Antoinette, isn't it?"

"It belonged to her."

"The Queen actually wore this?" Touching the brooch delicately with her fingertips.

"She presented it to a loyal friend before her death."

"A young man? Her lover!"

"He wasn't young, even then, and he was never her lover."

"Oh . . ."

"But she must have been fond of him, respected him, to reward him with such a treasure. He had it in his hand when he died."

"You knew him?"

"Yes."

"Such a sad story! I'll think of them—the Queen and her loyal friend—whenever I wear the brooch."

"I would suggest, for the moment, you shouldn't wear it in public. Unless you wish people to think you're a Royalist."

"Perhaps I am. I've always admired kings and queens. Especially Marie Antoinette . . ."

"But people might think your father is a Royalist."

"He isn't! And he wouldn't want anyone to think so."

"Then put the little brooch away for a few years. Until no one cares any longer whether you're a Royalist or not."

"Perhaps I'd better not even show it to Papa! I will do as you suggest when I return home and hide it in my room. I've a special secret place." She looked up as Prudence set a bowl of peaches on the table. "Coffee for me, please. No omelette this morning and only one brioche. I ate too much last night."

"Yes, Mademoiselle." The maid headed toward the kitchen.

295

"Jeanne-Victoire tells me you're leaving next week." He drank his coffee and finished the brioche as they talked.

"I was only invited for a week."

"Why not write your parents? Tell them you're staying a second week."

Her eyes danced with excitement. "Your mother won't object?"

"Maman will be delighted. And so will Jeanne-Victoire."

"I adore her. Last night she seemed to come alive as we had dinner on her balcony. Tante and I ate everything while Jeanne-Victoire barely tasted a slice of cake. But she seemed so happy! Tante thought so too. Laughing and talking. It was as though she wasn't going to die, after all!"

"I refuse to accept the idea that Jeanne-Victoire is dying."

"But you know she is. The doctors give no hope."

"Doctors are fools!"

"That's what Papa says."

"So, will you write your parents at once and tell them we want you to remain in Paris at least another week? If they can spare you. I'll speak to Maman. Tell her you're staying."

"I do love you." She reached out and clutched his hand on the table.

"Monsieur . . ."

Vidocq turned to see Prudence with Aubé, hat in hand, behind her. "What brings you at this hour, my friend?"

"I thought you'd want to know . . ."

He saw the maid returning inside as Aubé approached the breakfast table.

Aubé bowed, formally. "Mademoiselle . . ."

"You can speak freely in front of my cousin. What's happened?"

"Alcidor Drumont has been found."

Vidocq was on his feet. "When? Where?"

"Last night. But I didn't learn about it until the morning reports came over from the Préfecture. He's dead."

Fleuride's eyes widened.

Vidocq dropped his napkin on the table. "Cause of death?"

"A knife through the throat. His body was found in an attic on rue de la Lune."

"I should have guessed!" Motioning for Aubé to follow him inside.

"Return to Number Six. I'll take my own carriage and come to the office later. No staff meeting this morning . . ."

CHAPTER 49

Vidocq sprang up the final steep flight of steps and found himself in a narrow hall where the air was stifling and motes of dust floated in the sunlight coming through an open skylight.

"Monsieur?"

He whirled to face a young gendarme seated beside a closed door. "I am Vidocq." He saw the youth's eyes open with astonishment as he struggled to his feet. "Is this where they found the body?"

"Yes, Chief." He saluted suddenly, realizing he'd forgotten to do so.

"Open that door."

The gendarme seized the knob and pushed the door back.

Vidocq strode into the cramped box of a room and saw the bed at once, the dark stain which had soaked into a pillow and spread across a torn mattress that was leaking straw. No sheets or covers. The only other furniture was a small wooden table and a crude chair. On the table was a wine bottle covered with drippings of wax from a stub of dead candle stuck into its mouth. A circular window stood open onto an endless expanse of chimneys and rooftops, but the air was suffocating and there was a sickeningly unpleasant odor. "When did they take the body away?"

"In the night, I think . . ."

"Was there no luggage? Clothing?"

"They must've taken everything."

"Who found the body?"

He shrugged. "I couldn't say."

"Don't know much, do you?"

"I got here when the others were leaving. Was ordered to stay until someone else takes over."

"Too bad you don't have a book to pass the time."

"I can't read."

"You'll go far."

He grinned. "Thanks, Chief."

Vidocq turned on his heels and hurried back toward the stairs. Clattered down the twisting steps to the ground floor. Passed the concierge's closed door, where the mongrel was barking, followed the passage to the street and headed for the corner. Reaching the *pâtisserie* window, he peered inside and saw neighborhood women crowding the counter, making their morning purchases.

The smell of freshly baked bread, as always, recalled his father.

As he entered into a wave of heat from the kitchen, he saw Coralie where he'd known he would find her, seated at the same table and drinking coffee. Today her white dress was sprigged with blue flowers.

She watched him apprehensively as he came toward her.

Vidocq laid his cane on the marble-topped table and sat facing her. Removed his hat without a word and placed it on a chair.

Coralie smiled timidly. "I've been expecting you."

"Did those gendarmes ask you any questions?" He kept his voice low.

"They didn't come near me. I was in bed, but I heard them clomping up and down the stairs. Silvestre slept beside me, but he didn't hear anything. I'm so upset I couldn't eat my breakfast."

He glanced toward the counter and saw that none of the women were watching them. "Who found the body?"

"The concierge."

"What was she doing in the attic?"

"She heard people coming downstairs and, at that late hour, thought they were prowlers."

"She must have heard the killers." He noticed her husband—face and arms white with flour again—busy at his ovens.

"The old woman took the mutt upstairs with her, but he's no good for anything. Barks a lot, then runs and hides if I shake my fist at him. When they got to the attic, there was a door standing open. Candle burning in the room. She saw the blood and came running downstairs. I heard her screaming but didn't get out of bed. She sent her husband for the police."

"I suppose none of the tenants bothered to see what was happening."

"Nobody wants to get involved with other people's troubles."

"Who rents those attic rooms?"

"Tenants who hide their poor relations up there. Mostly old people. Some of the rooms are used for storage."

"This room, where Drumont's body was found, was rented to you?"

"No. I never had anything to store up there."

"You knew the room was vacant. There was a bed."

She sighed. "Yes. I told him."

"Was Drumont up there two days ago? When I was here?"

"He came to see me that night while my husband was out drinking with his friends, and said he needed a place to stay. I told him we don't have a spare room, but I could arrange with the concierge for him to sleep in the attic. He moved in during the night."

"Why didn't you report this to me at Number Six?"

"I'm not a spy for the police. And I promised him I wouldn't tell anyone he was here. You never said you were looking for him."

"But you knew I was after Tessier's murderer."

She looked startled. "You think Drumont killed Tessier?"

"It's possible. You were foolish to let him hide here."

"He didn't say he was hiding."

"You knew he was."

"I was afraid not to take him in. Drumont was an evil man. He's always frightened me . . ."

"How long did he plan to stay?"

"He said for a few days. There were people he had to see. Who could help him get to Marseille where he would find a ship."

"How much money did he pay the old woman?"

"I don't know."

"I suppose he went in and out, yesterday, as he pleased."

"I saw him once, going past here . . ."

"He would have contacted persons to arrange his escape to Marseille. Someone else for a forged passport. One of those people told the killers where Drumont could be found. That's how the murderer located him. Did you see what baggage he brought when he moved in?"

"I'd gone to bed, but the concierge told me he arrived after dark with several leather bags. Some of them seemed heavy. There was a man helping him. She watched them, from her window, carry the bags through the passage."

"Those heavy bags held the jewels and ingots he removed from rue Taitbout."

"He took the diamonds?"

"Everything! He was the only one, it seems, who knew where they were hidden."

"I suppose I can tell you now . . ."

"What?"

"Now that Drumont's dead, I can talk. There's nothing he can do to me anymore . . ."

"Tell me everything you know, or you could be in trouble. A whisper from me and the local gendarmes will take you in for questioning. You don't want that, do you? Involving your husband with murder!"

"Drumont said he needed a place to sleep because he'd killed a man."

"He confessed to you he'd shot Tessier?"

"Not Tessier! He told me he'd strangled poor Marpon." Tears appeared in her eyes. "That dear little man . . ."

"Why would he kill Marpon?"

"The old man knew everything." She sobbed, her breasts heaving.

"Everything?"

"About the house on rue Taitbout."

"So Drumont killed Marpon, and now someone's murdered Drumont!"

"I was furious when he said he'd strangled Marpon." Tears rolled down her plump cheeks. "Auguste was my friend. He used to tell me such lovely stories about the Queen. How kind she was . . ." Dabbing her eyes with a scrap of handkerchief. "Alcidor Drumont was evil! I'm glad he's dead." She peered toward the kitchen. "Would you like a cup of fresh coffee?"

"Nothing. You were afraid of Drumont?"

"Everyone feared him. It was his yellow eyes. Like a cat!"

"Opium addicts frequently have such eyes."

"You know about that?"

"I suspected the moment I saw him, and just now, upstairs, there was a disgusting smell of opium in that hole where he died."

"He smoked a pipe carved from jade and ivory. The police must've found it. I caught him many times smoking in his office on rue Taitbout."

"Your husband knows you were hiding Drumont upstairs?"

"I've told Silvestre everything! He already knew about my past. My life with Tessier and all the others. None of that matters to Silvestre." She looked toward the kitchen where her husband was singing at his work. "Silvestre had nothing to do with Drumont coming here. He didn't even see him!"

Vidocq glanced toward the counter where more customers were buying their morning loaves of fresh bread. Something stirred in his mind. Some fact he'd learned from Coralie on his previous visit? "That diamond!" he exclaimed, facing her again.

She looked uneasy. "What diamond?"

"The one you told me Tessier gave you." He saw perspiration drops on her forehead as she pulled at the blond curls around her face with plump fingers. "Tessier didn't give it to you!"

"What are you saying?" Her face was suffused with guilt.

"Drumont gave you that diamond. Not Tessier!"

"How could you know that?"

"Because Drumont was Tessier's administrator and in charge of all those jewels, apparently for the real owner. Why would Drumont give you a valuable diamond? What was he paying for? Your silence? Or did he make love to you behind Tessier's back?"

"Drumont never touched me! But he liked to look at me. That's all! No harm in that. He would sneak back into the house after Tessier went to bed and come up to my suite."

"Climb into your bed?"

"Never! He sat on the sofa, smoking his jade pipe. He only wanted to watch me."

"Watch you?"

"He taught me to dance—the way women dance in Africa—called me his blond odalisque. Whatever that is!"

"Odalisque? And that's all he wanted? To see you dancing?"

"I swear it!"

"Tessier fed you, and Drumont watched you dance! Tessier covered you with diamonds, and Drumont gave you a diamond to keep!"

She shrugged and leaned toward him, lowering her voice. "You aren't going to question Silvestre, are you? About any of this?"

"I see no reason to involve him. Unless, of course, I find Drumont was killed with some kind of knife that's used only by bakers."

"No! The concierge said it was a small knife. Like a poniard. She saw it stuck through his throat."

"A poniard, eh?" He reached for his hat and cane. "If you hear anything more about Drumont, come and see me at Number Six or send me a message."

"There's one thing I don't understand . . ."

"Yes?"

"Why Drumont would want to hide here, when he had a suite of rooms nobody knew about. Even the staff at rue Taitbout didn't know! Except Tessier. He's the one told me . . ."

"Suite of rooms? Where?"

"Narcisse mentioned several times that Drumont lived in a small suite at the Midnight Club."

"Did he?"

"Lived there ever since the club was opened."

"And that, *chérie,* may be the most important piece of information you've given me."

"Is it?" She looked up, puzzled, as he rose to leave. "There's something I'd like to ask you . . ."

"Information you want in return?"

"You might say that, I suppose . . ." She giggled nervously, but her face remained solemn. "Have you found out who killed Clochette?"

"How does Clochette's death concern you?"

"She befriended me years ago when I first arrived in Paris."

"Told you which were the best street corners?"

"She gave me a place to sleep and fed me. Taught me the ropes. We kept in touch until I moved in with Tessier. He wouldn't let me go anywhere. Later, after I met Silvestre, I didn't want to see anybody from my old life. What's been worrying me . . . I've wondered what happened to her baby. A girl. I heard she looked just like Clochette. A little beauty! She must be six months old now. I'd like to know what's become of her . . ."

"Why should you care?"

"Well . . ." She hesitated, dropping her eyes. "Silvestre and I want a child, but I'll never be able to have one."

"My wife's like that."

"Is she?" Raising her eyes to his face again. "I've been thinking, if such a thing's possible, I would like to adopt Clochette's baby. Otherwise she might be put in one of those horrible places they keep orphans. Like prisons! The poor children don't have a chance . . ."

"Who was the father?"

"I don't know. Doesn't matter . . ."

"I'll find out what's become of the child. If possible, I'll arrange for you to have her. You'd make a good mother." He turned and, putting

302

on his hat, crossed the shop toward the street. Before he reached the open door, he heard Coralie's voice behind him, calling toward the kitchen.

"Another cup of coffee! And two of those raspberry tarts!"

CHAPTER 50

Vidocq jumped down from his carriage on rue Bréda, telling Jean to wait, and entered the scabrous building. Hurried across the dark entrance foyer and went upstairs.

The door to Clochette's apartment was wide open.

He strode through the hall to the small salon and saw that all the furniture had been removed.

The air was dead and smelled of dust.

He continued on, past the empty boudoir, to a door standing open into a dark hole of a kitchen where the only light came from a window facing a stone wall.

The old woman was seated at a bare table, eating from a bowl she clutched in one hand. She looked around and saw him. "It's you again?" Setting the bowl down. "They took all her furniture this morning. Everything she had owned. Did you go to her funeral?"

"Didn't know about it until too late."

"Couldn't go, myself. Knew Madame would want me to stay with the baby."

"Has somebody taken her child?"

"She's right here. Next to my cot." Looking toward a dark corner. "Hasn't been crying. So she must be asleep."

Vidocq saw the narrow cot and moved closer.

"Don't wake her! She'll only scream again. Like she did all day yesterday."

There was a tiny wicker basket beside the cot.

"Nobody wants her, and I don't know what to do with her."

He looked down at the sleeping baby in the basket.

"Poor little thing! No mother, and any moment they'll throw both of us into the street."

303

The small face did indeed look like Clochette's. Same features and pale flesh, surrounded by blond curls. "What's her name?"

"Angèle."

"How old?"

"Almost six months but small for her age."

He saw that the baby's eyes had opened. The woman's voice had wakened her. Her eyes were the color of bluebells. "She's awake, and she's smiling."

"That's more than she did yesterday. I had to give her a few swallows of wine to keep her quiet."

"You could make her a drunkard."

She shrugged. "Does it matter, Monsieur?"

"Are there any relatives to take the child? Didn't Clochette have any family?"

"Madame always said she had nobody. And that worthless young poet she's been feeding for the past year or more, paying his rent, wants no part of the baby. Says it isn't his! Told me himself, after Madame was killed. Took off for the country so he wouldn't be questioned, but I can tell you he had nothing to do with Madame's death. His sort wouldn't kill a mouse!"

"Does the child have clothes?"

"Oh, yes! Madame had lovely dresses for her. I have them hidden away."

"They'll be picked up later." He reached down and lifted the basket with both hands. "I'm taking the baby with me."

"But, Monsieur . . ."

"There's someone—a friend of Clochette's—who wants to adopt her. Madame Blanc! You may have heard Clochette mention her. She knew her as Coralie . . ."

"Coralie Clodin? She used to visit Madame when I first came here. We heard she was married. Madame would be pleased if she knew Coralie was taking little Angèle . . ."

He headed for the hall, the woman at his heels and the baby making happy sounds in her basket.

"Can you manage to carry her, Monsieur?"

"I have a carriage waiting."

She followed him through the silent hall.

"If anyone asks about the baby, tell them she's being adopted by a friend. Nothing more."

"I understand, Monsieur."

He paused at the open door. "Was there, by chance, a nun in this neighborhood shortly before Clochette's death?"

"I'd forgotten until this moment—a nun came to our door the day before. Asking for alms, as usual, but I had no coins to give her."

"What sort of habit did she wear?"

"I don't know one religious order from another. This nun was in black—like a bad omen—only I didn't realize it at the time. With a black veil over some kind of white thing around her face."

"Did you tell the gendarmes a nun was here the day before Clochette was murdered?"

"Nobody asked me. You're the first."

Vidocq set the basket on the floor, and the baby at once began to whimper. "Be quiet, little one." He straightened and found some coins in his pocket which he dropped into the woman's hand. "Get food for yourself."

"Madame always said you were a kind man . . ."

He picked up the basket and continued on toward the stairs. "They'll probably send for her clothes tomorrow."

"I'll still be here."

As he hurried down the steps, balancing the basket carefully, he realized that the whimpering had stopped and the blue eyes were watching him.

His coachman, Jean, showed no surprise at seeing him with a baby in a basket as he ordered him to return to rue de la Lune.

Inside the carriage, he rested the basket on the leather seat beside him and studied the baby's face. So like Clochette's!

He wondered what would happen to Angèle. Another prostitute?

As the carriage rolled over the cobbles, he hoped its rocking motion would make her sleep, but instead she reached out a hand toward him. He touched it with a forefinger, and the tiny fingers clasped it firmly.

Vidocq smiled.

He wondered suddenly if Fleuride wanted to bear children. Did he, for that matter, want a child? A son! He wasn't at all certain that he did.

The baby clutched his finger until they reached rue de la Lune, whimpering again when he pulled free and lifted the basket down to the street. He carried it into the *pâtisserie* where Coralie was sitting at the same table, an empty plate in front of her.

She struggled to her feet, body bulging under the thin dress, eyes bright with anticipation. "You're back, are you?"

He rested the basket on the table. "This is Clochette's child. Her name's Angèle."

"Angèle! The little angel . . ."

"You can adopt her. I'll help you get the papers. Have someone pick up her clothes at the apartment on rue Bréda. Good luck!" He turned and strode back toward the street.

"Silvestre!" she shrieked. "Quickly! We have a baby . . ."

Reaching his carriage, Vidocq ordered Jean to take him to Number Six.

He was going to be late this morning.

CHAPTER 51

Vidocq stared at the piles of reports and dossiers Aubé had left on his desk without seeing them.

The unrelenting heat had made him sluggish. His mind was in a turmoil, considering the bits of information he'd turned up in the past twenty-four hours.

He knew now that Drumont had strangled Marpon but had no idea who had stabbed Drumont or shot Clochette, Tessier, and Maya. It seemed likely that one man had killed Clochette and Maya, but another person must have shot Tessier, even though the bullets taken from Maya and Tessier appeared to have been fired from the same pistol. Unfortunately, he couldn't prove they had, and the bullet that killed Clochette hadn't been recovered.

"Aubé!" he shouted.

"Yes, Chief?" Aubé leaned forward at his desk in the outer office until he could see Vidocq through the open doors.

"Did we get anything from Montmartre headquarters this morning on the Drumont murder?"

"A brief report. It's on your desk."

He reached for the pile of police reports and flipped through them until he found the one he sought. Slipped the single sheet from between the others and read the scribbled words as Aubé came through the antechamber.

Alcidor Drumont had bled to death from a dagger wound in the throat. The examining doctor reported that Drumont was killed with a single thrust and had, very likely, been unconscious when attacked. An opium pipe was found beside him, along with a teak box containing opium.

He looked up to see Aubé standing on the other side of his desk. "Montmartre still needs to make their daily reports more complete." He rested the sheet of paper on top of the other reports. "I want every available man on duty tonight. Two men at each of those southern barriers again. We nearly caught a farmer last night. Unfortunately he managed to elude us. They may try again tonight. With a different farmer. I want all my assistants here this afternoon at five. Promptly! Unless they have good cause to be absent. By then I will have a plan of operation for tonight. We're going to raid the Midnight Club."

"Are we?"

"I'll spend this afternoon working on the details. Leave all these doors open but I don't wish to be disturbed unless it's a matter of importance."

"Yes, Chief."

"And I'd like some black coffee."

"I'll send upstairs for a fresh pot."

"Anything urgent in these other reports?" He indicated the documents spread across his desk.

"Dozens of petty crimes last night. Nothing that would require your attention."

"Then I won't bother to read them."

"I'll order your coffee." Aubé trotted toward the corridor where he would pass the order on to one of the guards.

Vidocq pushed everything out of his way and picked up a pad of paper, which he set directly in front of him. Raised the lid of his silver inkwell, then selected a fresh quill.

He made a list of brief notes on the Midnight Club raid. That done he listed every piece of information he had discovered about those three murders. Tessier, Maya, and Drumont. As well as Clochette and Marpon. He worked silently, except for the scratching of his quill, until he

307

heard Aubé's voice and looked up to see one of the guards bringing his coffee. "Leave that. I'll pour it myself."

The guard set the silver tray within easy reach on the desk. "Madame Babelay told me to ask if you want any lunch?"

"Tell her I'm too busy."

The guard saluted and departed.

Vidocq stared at what he had written, but his chain of thought had been shattered by the interruption. His own fault, ordering coffee. He set his quill on the silver pen rack and reached for the coffeepot. Black coffee should clear his head. As he poured the steaming brew into a Sèvres bowl the air was perfumed with its rich aroma.

Bowl in hand, he swiveled his armchair to face the open windows and took a tentative swallow.

Three murders—Tessier, Maya, and Drumont—must be resolved quickly or inquiries would start coming from the Minister of Interior, and there would be taunts from the Préfecture.

Fortunately, as yet the newspapers were not demanding action. The murders had been committed in such a brief period of time—a few days apart—that the papers hadn't given them much attention. This gave him a little time . . .

He gulped the last of his coffee and turned back to stare at what he had written.

His scrawled words must contain several clues. But which words?

Why had a piece of worthless jewelry been stolen from both Maya and Clochette? And why had that nun come to Clochette's door, then a few days later watched Maya's windows? Or was that only a coincidence? Two different nuns . . .

This was the familiar moment—it happened with every important investigation—when he felt like a spider sitting at his desk. Weaving a web to catch not one criminal this time, but several.

At least he knew where to find Goron. He would arrest him tonight when he returned to the Midnight Club and bring him here for questioning.

"Excuse me, Chief . . ."

He looked up and saw young Revol, hat in hand, in the open doorway. "Yes?"

"Monsieur Aubé said I could interrupt you . . ."

"Then it must be important, my friend! Come in."

308

Revol approached the desk. "I've just been to see Madame Thanot."

"Thanot?"

"Pierre's wife. He was Tessier's oldest employee. Chief goldsmith and master craftsman."

"Ah, yes!"

"She says he'll be home tomorrow. He's visiting their married daughter in Belleville. With Tessier dead, he's taking the first vacation he's had in years according to his wife, spending a few days with his grandchildren. I told her I would come for him tomorrow and bring him to Number Six."

"Did that frighten her?"

"Madame Thanot had never heard of Number Six."

"There's an honest woman!" He laughed. "Tell Aubé to arrange for you to have a carriage when you go to get Monsieur Thanot."

"I heard, as I came in, that every staff member is to be on duty this evening."

"News spreads quickly! Yes. There may be two important investigations in progress tonight."

"Oh . . ." Revol hesitated, revolving his hat between his hands. "I had planned to take Mademoiselle Penny-packaire to dinner."

"Did you?"

"Her father's dining out, so for the first time she's free to spend an evening with me."

"Take the evening off! With my blessing."

"Thanks, Chief."

"Monsieur Penny-packaire, I believe, will be dining at the Midnight Club tonight."

"That's what Belinda told me. He invited the Duc de Modena to have dinner with him. He's an Italian, staying at the Hôtel Belvedere. Belinda likes him, but in my opinion he's a rather suspicious type . . ."

"You think so?" Vidocq smiled, amused. "Tell Aubé I said to give you enough money to cover your expenses. Dinner and the rest!" He saw Revol's eyes brighten. "Tell him you're on a special assignment for me. I'll want a complete report on everything you learn about her father. Enjoy your evening!" He waved Revol out of his office and, as he settled down to work, watched the young man stop at Aubé's desk.

So Ronquetti had arranged to dine at the Midnight Club with the American. It might be useful, having them on the scene tonight.

He began to go over each step of his visit to the Midnight Club, the questions he would ask the arrogant Monsieur de Plessis. Tonight he would require more definite answers.

"Forgive me, Chief . . ."

He didn't look up as Aubé came toward him, but finished what he was writing. "Who is it now?"

"A letter from the Minister. Delivered by hand."

Vidocq put his quill aside. "I've been expecting to hear from the old man." He reached for the envelope and ripped it open. "Complaining we haven't found Tessier's killer, and what are we doing about the murder of Maya?" Pulling the folded sheet of paper from the envelope. He read the note quickly, surprised to see only a few brief lines. "It's not what I anticipated. Seems the old man has had a visit from his dear friend, Monsieur de Plessis, who was shocked by my intrusion last evening into the sacred domain of his precious Midnight Club to ask questions about one of their members, a certain Monsieur Tessier who, unfortunately, has been murdered. The Midnight Club is not responsible for its members, except when they are on the club premises. The Minister writes that Monsieur de Plessis is a respected banker, as well as his personal friend and suggests I refrain from involving the Midnight Club any further with my investigation of the Tessier murder. Monsieur de Plessis is an arrogant fool and a snob! His attempt to keep me away only makes me more suspicious of his motives." He handed the note back to Aubé. "This needs no reply. File it with the Minister's other communications."

"Yes, Chief." Folding the note, without glancing at the writing. "Young Daumier would like a word with you. He's been waiting half an hour. I told him you were busy, but I would tell you he was here."

Vidocq looked toward the outer office. "Honoré! Come in . . ."

The stocky youth, wearing his same patched work clothes, passed Aubé as he entered.

Vidocq studied Daumier as he came closer, the black curly hair and inquisitive eyes. "What brings you here, my young friend?"

"I was sketching in one of the courtrooms, but they've adjourned for lunch." He hesitated. "I wondered if there were any more murders you'd like me to record for you."

"There was one this morning—a knife in the throat—unfortunately the local police removed the cadaver before I was called. Nothing to see

310

but a bare attic room." As he explained, he wondered if the youth needed money. "Not worth sketching."

"Actually, I stopped by to tell you I'll be working in the Palais de Justice every day. Sketching the judges. Such crafty faces! Like ancient vultures with sharp beaks waiting to tear the flesh from those poor souls they're judging. They watch them as though they're going to pounce."

"Some of them do!" He chuckled. "You should have no trouble selling your sketches."

"I've already sold a few. To the judges themselves. Such vain old birds. Always preening and posing . . ."

"I've been using your sketches today." Motioning toward the drawings on his desk. "They're very helpful. Keeping both those murders fresh in my mind."

"I'm glad."

Vidocq felt in a waistcoat pocket for some coins. "I want to pay you something more." He held out his hand.

"That's not necessary, Monsieur. My sketches aren't worth much yet."

"You're the best artist ever worked for me. Here! Take these."

Daumier reached out, palm up.

Vidocq dropped two louis d'or into the youth's dirty hand.

His eyes danced when he saw them. "I'm cheating you!"

"Nobody ever cheats Vidocq! I'll have other corpses for you to sketch."

"Now I can have a glass of wine before I go back to that hot court-room."

As Daumier turned to leave, Vidocq saw that one of his trouser legs was ripped. He frowned, remembering when he escaped from the galleys, clothes in shreds, and made his way across the winter fields.

He glanced at his notes for tonight's visit to the Midnight Club, adding a reminder to deploy half a dozen of his men up and down rue Royale. He would take a small silver whistle in one of his pockets, which he would use as a signal for them to join him inside . . .

"Pardon, Chief . . ."

He looked up to see Aubé again. "Yes?"

"A lady asking to see you . . ."

"Her name?"

"Madame Serciers."

"Never heard of her." He looked past Aubé and saw a woman standing in the outer office. Middle-aged, black hair, spectacles. Smartly dressed in pale gray lace, with a wide-brimmed hat shadowing her face, carrying a gray lace parasol.

"She says it's an urgent matter . . ."

"All these women think their petty problems are urgent. And sometimes they are!" Glancing at the waiting woman again. "This one has a better figure than most. I suppose I'd better see her, but warn her I can only spare a few moments."

"I've already told her." Aubé turned, hiding a smile, and went toward his office.

Vidocq dried his perspiring hands on a silk handkerchief and rose as the stranger crossed the antechamber. Saw that her straw hat was trimmed with yellow flowers and she wore no jewelry except a strand of pearls. Rings, if any, were hidden by white lace gloves. Her walk was graceful, and without the spectacles, he suspected she might be attractive. He bowed. "Madame Serciers?"

"Monsieur?"

He motioned toward an armchair.

"I'm grateful to you for sparing me a few minutes. Your assistant informed me you are extremely busy." She sank into the chair, holding the ivory handle of her parasol with both gloved hands.

"Well, Madame?"

She smiled. "You don't recognize me?"

"Should I?" He sat, facing her across the desk.

"Mon Dieu!" Lowering her voice. "I thought I might fool everyone else, but I didn't hope to deceive the great Vidocq!"

"Who are you, Madame?"

"Years ago when I worked briefly as an actress, I learned many tricks of makeup. Discovered that none at all is the best disguise."

"I've learned that myself."

"So today I used only a light dusting of powder, darkened my eyebrows, and wore a brunette wig. The spectacles you saw yesterday."

"Yesterday?" He peered at her face.

She laughed, making the flowers tremble on her hat.

The laughter was familiar. "Ève!"

"I really fooled you?"

"Completely."

"Vidocq, the master of disguises!"

He held his voice down with difficulty. "What the devil are you doing here? This is most indiscreet . . ."

"For one thing, I've always wanted to see your famous office . . ." Glancing around as she talked. "It's quite elegant. I had to see you but couldn't ask you to come to me, because I feared you might be observed." Facing him again. "But I didn't wish anyone to see me come here either! So I changed my appearance, wore my most inconspicuous summer frock, and walked down to Boulevard des Italiens where I found a fiacre. Didn't dare use my scarlet landau. Too many gentlemen might recognize it."

"And what urgent matter brings you here?"

"You told me yesterday you planned to visit the Midnight Club."

He straightened, suddenly alert. "I went there last evening."

"I warned you of danger."

"You did."

"But I didn't tell you what I know about the place. I couldn't sleep, last night—partly, of course, because of the heat—but most of all because I feared you might be entering a nest of serpents, and I was fearful for your life."

"What are you saying, *chérie?*"

"I've decided to tell you everything I know about the Midnight Club—what I've heard and, beyond that, what I suspect."

He leaned forward. "I am listening."

"First the few facts I've learned over the years. The Midnight Club was the idea of one man—the banker, de Plessis."

"I met the gentleman, and did not like him."

"Nor do I. He has from time to time been one of my—clients. It was he who had the idea to start a private club for men only. Where wealthy businessmen can dine together, discuss important deals, and arrange the most private sort of personal as well as business affairs. Involving companies with branches all over the world. Monsieur de Plessis heads a board of five men who are known as The Five. Each member of the club knows that de Plessis is the chairman, but the other four have never been revealed. These men—The Five— have tremendous power. They must approve a new member before he can join. Leaders from every major business belong to the club. Bankers, real estate and stock brokers, jewelers, restaurant owners, caterers, and florists. Even carriage manufacturers! They all belong to the Midnight Club! Rich men who own the finest hotels, the most elegant art galleries, and the best shops! They are the men who run Paris!"

"Are you telling me that all these men are contolled by the Midnight Club? Take orders from this group who call themselves The Five?"

"I'm saying that members of the Midnight Club may be the single most powerful group in France today. And The Five are the most powerful of all!"

"I had no idea . . ."

"They even control some of the politicians!"

"This explains why nobody talks about the Midnight Club. I've never heard any rumors or gossip."

"Each member, under oath, agrees to obey certain rules. One of which is that nothing concerning the club is ever repeated to any person who is not a member. That, of course, includes their wives! But men like to boast. Especially when they're relaxing in bed. Several have been indiscreet while they were with me."

"I'm sure they have!"

"Until this moment, I have never repeated anything they've said to me. But I can tell you, from personal experience, that The Five control all *les grandes courtisanes.*"

"Control the prostitutes of Paris?"

"Certainly not! They wouldn't be bothered with common tarts. Only the most celebrated and expensive. At last count there were two dozen of us. Long ago, The Five informed me through one of their brutes—before the club opened—that they would provide me with every luxury I required. In return for certain small favors. When I took a new lover I must convince him that my apartment needed to be redecorated. All new paintings and furniture! He would receive the bills. Whenever I take another lover, this is repeated. Everything is returned to the dealers and sold again. To another of *les grandes courtisanes.* Whenever we give a large party—which is at least once a week—all foods and wines are catered by firms controlled by The Five! And the bills go to our current lover . . ."

"This is done no matter what you buy?"

"Everything! Gowns, hairdresser, new carriage. Enormous prices are charged."

"Even your jewelry?"

"All our jewelry!"

"Tessier was a member of the Midnight Club. What other jewelers are involved?"

"I can't give you their names."

"Why not?"

"If I tell you too much, my life could be in jeopardy . . ."

"From whom?"

"Those brutes employed by the Midnight Club. I've been told most of their staff is made up of criminal types they find in Montmartre."

"Indeed?" He was reminded of Goron. Crépuscule . . .

"They work at the club as waiters and attendants. Even sleep there. Never venture out, except to perform some job for The Five."

"Why haven't you told me any of this before?"

"I will be killed if they learn I've talked to you now!"

"You think they killed Maya?"

"I've thought about that, constantly. And wondered . . ."

"You said earlier in the week you never returned jewelry that's been given to you."

"I refused."

"And some of it came from Tessier?"

"Yes."

"Who gave it to you?"

"Don't ask me that, because I shall never tell you. I told them, when they ordered me to return my jewels, that I preferred to keep the real diamonds and pearls. I have never worn imitations."

"What did they say to that?"

"They sent one of their brutes to frighten me."

"Did he harm you?"

"He tried. Beat me with his fists to make me tell where the jewels were hidden, but he didn't succeed."

"You recognized him?"

"I never saw his face. He appeared in the middle of the night, wearing a mask."

"Why didn't you call for help?"

"Because he threatened to kill me, and I knew he would. Remember, three years ago, when I told everyone I'd been in the country for several weeks? I was hiding in my apartment. Waiting for the bruises on my face to disappear."

"Have you known the names of anyone they sent to threaten you?"

315

"Only one. The first man. He tried to persuade me to return a string of pearls. These pearls I'm wearing now. He's the one who comes and suggests you should convince your lover to buy a new wardrobe for you or refurnish your apartment. Tells you to which restaurants you should have your lover take you to dine. I called him Yellow Eyes . . ."

"You learned his name?"

"Maya told me. He is called Drumont. Alcidor Drumont . . ."

"Drumont's dead."

"Mon Dieu!" She straightened in the armchair, startled by this news. "How did he die?"

"A knife in his throat."

She rose, clutching her parasol. "I've talked too much."

Vidocq jumped up.

"Nobody liked Drumont. Maya said he made her flesh shiver when he touched her."

Vidocq circled the desk and followed her toward the open doors.

"I only came here to warn you," she whispered. "Be careful if you go to the Midnight Club again. And do nothing to involve me!"

"Naturally." He took her gloved hand and bent to kiss it.

"Don't come out with me. The fiacre is waiting on Quai des Orfèvres." She paused, looking into his eyes. "You've been a good friend, *chéri,* for so many years. This was a small thing for me to do in return." She suddenly kissed him on the cheek. "Take care of yourself . . ."

Vidocq watched her, parasol in one gloved hand, hurry through the antechamber before he returned to his desk and sat down. Stared at the notes he'd made earlier. Snatched up a fresh quill and began to make several changes in his plan of operation for tonight. The siege of the Midnight Club and his confrontation with The Five . . .

CHAPTER 52

A smart tan landau with gleaming brass fixtures and a crest painted on the door, drawn by a chestnut mare, rolled up the dimly lighted rue Royale from Place Louis XVI. The coachman and footman wore summer liveries of pale brown, their hats and gloves a darker shade of the same color.

This was the dinner hour, and the facade of the Midnight Club was illuminated by flambeaux in ornamental bronze holders.

The landau turned into the courtyard, where several other vehicles waited, and slowed to a stop in front of the entrance as the footman jumped down.

He opened the door and touched the brim of his hat as an elegant young man rose from the silk-cushioned seat and slowly descended to the marble strip of pavement.

The waiting coachmen observed this latest arrival with curiosity.

The young man paused briefly, glancing around the courtyard with the arrogantly bored look of the very rich.

His observers remained silent.

The young man, in his early thirties, wore an evening suit of light tan that matched the color of his hair, mustaches, and neatly trimmed beard. His yellow brocade waistcoat was worn over a ruffled ivory silk shirt, and his cravat was a rich dark yellow. Reflections of light from the flambeaux revealed diamond studs. A high-crowned hat matched the color of his highly polished brown boots. In his left hand he held a pair of pale yellow gloves. He walked without haste up the marble steps to the entrance and gave the silver bell pull a single brief yank.

One of the narrow entrance doors was opened by a white-haired *commissionnaire* in a dark-gray uniform wearing white gloves. "Monsieur?"

The man in the tan suit produced a golden coin from a pocket of his waistcoat and held it out briefly toward the attendant.

"Welcome to the Midnight Club, Monsieur." Bowing the visitor into the lobby.

The young man returned the coin to his pocket as he entered.

"Your first visit, Monsieur?"

"Matter of fact, it is. Yes . . ."

The *commissionnaire* closed the door and followed him across the high-ceilinged lobby where several small sofas were occupied by pairs of distinguished gentlemen talking intently. "One moment, Monsieur . . ."

The young man, inspecting the elegant scene, aware of distant music played by a string orchestra, paused but did not turn.

"Forgive me, Monsieur. I must ask. Are you a member?"

"Certainly not! I am not even a resident of Paris." His voice was high, the tone arrogant. "I detest large cities but unfortunately am required to visit here on business, and my uncle, the Comte de Montereau—who is a member, suggested I dine here tonight."

317

"The Comte de Montereau! Of course ..."

"He unfortunately is occupied elsewhere. Your food, he assures me, is not too bad. My uncle entrusted me with that ridiculous coin, which he said would get me past the Cerberus who guards your entrance." He still did not turn to look at the *commissionnaire*. "I presume he meant you! Although you appear to have only one head, instead of three."

"The Comte always makes his amusing jokes."

"I trust it was a joke, and this is not the entrance to Hades. The underworld of lost souls ..."

The *commissionnaire* looked startled.

"Because I do not have a honey cake in my pocket to placate you, and unfortunately I am not Hercules."

"No, Monsieur." His eyes betrayed his puzzlement. "Would you prefer to dine in the large dining room or perhaps one of our smaller rooms on this floor?"

"The large dining room, by all means! I dislike small rooms where everyone whispers."

"Certainly, Monsieur." He motioned for one of the uniformed attendants waiting in a line, to escort him upstairs.

The attendant bowed and ushered him toward the double marble staircase curving up to the first floor.

The young man followed the attendant up the dark-green-carpeted steps, through pools of soft light from candelabra. Then a second, smaller flight of shallow steps to a broad high-ceilinged corridor, past pairs of closed doors, toward the marble-columned entrance to a spacious paneled dining room. He heard a murmur of masculine voices, along with the discreet music. At the entrance he removed his hat, dropped his gloves into it and handed them to a brass-buttoned garçon.

A cold-eyed headwaiter led him to a table near a row of open windows. Pulled out a comfortable armchair and, as he sat down, placed a menu on the table and signaled for the sommelier, who bowed and asked, "Your pleasure, Monsieur?"

"Perhaps a bottle of champagne ..." He glanced around the elegant room. Men, middle-aged or older, eating dinner. No loud voices, although there must be thirty or forty alone or in pairs at the luxuriously appointed tables.

The music came from a balcony at the far end of the room. Five musicians, all male, playing stringed instruments.

318

He didn't recognize the melody, although it sounded like one of Grétry's tunes.

There was a large garden below the open windows, which seemed to float in the moonlight.

The sommelier brought the wine in a silver bucket of crushed ice. Bowing as he rested it on the table. Opened the bottle and poured a little of the champagne gently into a stemmed crystal glass.

The young man picked it up and took a tentative taste. Nodded his approval as he held the glass out to be filled.

The sommelier poured the wine carefully, returning the bottle to the ice. Bowed again and moved away.

As he drank the wine, the young man noticed the *commissionnaire* from downstairs talking to the headwaiter near the marble entrance pillars. Finished his wine and poured a second glass, aware that the *commissionnaire* was coming toward his table.

"Pardon, Monsieur . . ."

He looked up, glass in hand, showing surprise at the intrusion.

"The director of the Midnight Club would like to see you in his private office for a moment."

"Indeed? I don't believe we have ever met. What could he want with me?"

"Monsieur de Plessis regrets interrupting Monsieur's dinner . . ."

"He can't interrupt what I haven't begun!" Raising his glass and draining it before rising.

"If you'll follow me, Monsieur . . ." The *commissionnaire* led him out of the dining room and down the corridor, hesitating before a pair of closed doors and knocked.

A man's voice responded. "Enter!"

The *commissionnaire* grasped the heavy bronze knob and swung the door open.

The young man stepped inside to face the searching black eyes of a man in a black evening suit, seated behind an impressive desk.

"You are the Comte de Montereau's nephew, Monsieur?"

"That is correct." He heard the door close behind him as he crossed the paneled office.

"I am Monsieur de Plessis. Chairman of the board of directors, in personal charge of the Midnight Club. Sit down, Monsieur."

He relaxed in an armchair facing the desk.

"It is always my unpleasant duty to prevent imposters from intruding here."

"Indeed? And how does that concern me?"

"I know, for a fact, that the Comte de Montereau does not have a nephew. Who are you?"

"I am Vidocq."

"Impossible!"

"My previous visit last evening was not satisfactory, Monsieur." He saw de Plessis's face pale. "I decided we should have another conversation."

"I've heard you could disguise yourself, but this is beyond disguise. You are another person."

"I am still Vidocq, Chief of the Sûreté Nationale. Since my previous visit I've learned several rather surprising things about the Midnight Club. And about you, Monsieur . . ."

"What, precisely, do you mean by that?"

"Yesterday I questioned you about one of your members. Narcisse Tessier . . ."

"I assured you that I knew nothing about Monsieur Tessier's private life."

"You did, however, acknowledge that he was a member of your club."

Vidocq casually removed the wig and pulled off his mustaches and beard, resting the wig on the desk and dropping mustaches and beard into it, knowing de Plessis would be confused and distracted. "I also asked you about a man who called himself Tessier's administrator. Who apparently had been in charge of his business affairs. Guardian of the jewels and keeper of the vault!"

"I told you I'd never heard of such a person. I don't even remember his name!"

"Alcidor Drumont."

"Drumont?"

"Drumont's dead. A knife through his throat."

"That is no concern of mine."

"All the jewels he guarded for Tessier are missing. The ingots of gold and silver . . ."

"I know nothing about such things."

"You lie, Monsieur."

"How dare you!"

"You did know Drumont. You knew he'd taken those jewels after Tessier was murdered. Knew that he had a private suite of rooms. Here in the Midnight Club!"

"This is nonsense!" De Plessis's face reddened with a sudden rush of blood.

"I want to see that suite of rooms."

"I cannot allow you to enter any of our private suites. We have a limited number of suites, which our members are permitted to occupy should their families be absent from Paris, or when one of our members from the provinces prefers to stay here instead of at a hotel. But I must approve their living on the premises. Even for a night. This person— Drumont—was not a member and, to my knowledge, never entered this building . . ."

"Then I must have every room searched. My men are waiting outside."

"You have no right!" He straightened in his chair. "I shall inform my dear friend, the Minister of Interior."

"Ah, yes!" Vidocq smiled. "Your friend the Minister sent me a note this morning, in which he informed me that you had complained about my previous visit."

"The Minister would never countenance your returning, in disguise, and threatening me in this fashion."

"I intend to see that suite of rooms which Drumont occupied. I'm inclined to think you're telling the truth when you say he wasn't a member of the club . . ."

"Now, Monsieur Vidocq, you're being sensible!"

"I suspect that Alcidor Drumont was in your employ. I've learned, for a fact, that the mansion on rue Taitbout was leased. Not by Tessier but by Drumont. Probably acting as an agent for you! And I've discovered that you have other criminals employed here."

"Criminals?" His hands clutched at the edge of the desk, like a drowning man grasping a plank.

"Last evening I noticed a waiter whose name is Goron. Also known as Crépuscule, the owl who only comes out at twilight. He is notorious. A moment ago, in your dining room, I saw him again with several other familiar faces. Your headwaiter, for instance, has a long police record as a jack-of-all-crimes! Why does the Midnight Club have criminals on its staff, Monsieur? Are they the brutes you send out to threaten and rob? And perhaps to kill!"

"Is this an official accusation?"

"It's a statement of fact. You arrange for *les grandes courtisanes* to persuade their loves to purchase jewelry for them from supposedly reputable jewelers—including Tessier—which they must return to the jeweler who then gives them a worthless copy. You lease the mansions where these prostitutes have their apartments. Charge exorbitant rents, which their wealthy lovers pay. Encourage them to redecorate their apartments whenever they take a new lover, and the old furniture turns up in some other *courtisane*'s apartment. One of these women—Maya—has been murdered."

"I know nothing about any of this!"

"Did the Midnight Club arrange her death through one of the criminals on your staff?"

"I must consult the other members of our board immediately before I reply to these insinuations." He rose unsteadily, pushing his chair back from the desk.

"I've also learned that Alcidor Drumont strangled Tessier's major-domo, Marpon. So Drumont was a murderer, as well as a thief. But who murdered Drumont? I'm sure you can tell me that."

"The Midnight Club is the finest private club in Paris!" de Plessis declared, as if to reassure himself.

"Is it, Monsieur? I understand that you and the other four directors are known as The Five." He saw de Plessis pull back, as though from a blow. "Five of the city's most respected businessmen! Who, in secret, have been involved with theft, prostitution, and murder!"

"I will confer with my associates . . ."

"By all means, Monsieur." Vidocq got to his feet.

De Plessis moved toward the wall unsteadily, as though his legs had lost their strength. "I will bring them in here. So that you may question all of us together . . ."

Vidocq watched as de Plessis pulled back a carved wooden panel.

He looked at Vidocq again. "They too will deny any knowledge of what you say. I'll only be a moment." He slipped through the opening, closing the panel behind him.

Vidocq smiled, visualizing the scene in that conference room. The faces of those four other men as their leader gave them some sort of explanation. Their panic. If they tried to flee, they would be held by his assistants who were waiting in the courtyard and on rue Royale.

He would give them another minute before he . . .

A shot exploded, echoing through the mansion.

He didn't move, but a faint smile crossed his lips.

For a moment there was no other sound. Only ominous silence.

Then, far in the distance, a man could be heard shouting.

Vidocq sprang toward the wall, but found that the panel was closed and secured.

Turning, he ran to the doors and flung them open.

There was no one in the corridor; the shouting came from below.

He rushed to the closed doors of the conference room and flung both open. Hurried in and stood at the foot of the long polished oak table. Four men sat there, two on each side, staring at the fifth man at the far end. All five remained silent. Four were paralyzed with fear. The other man would never answer any more questions.

De Plessis was slumped in an armchair, a small pistol clutched in his right hand resting on the table, a hole under his chin spouting blood.

Vidocq pulled the silver whistle from a pocket of his waistcoat. Held it to his lips and sounded a blast.

The unexpected sound caused the four living men to turn and stare at him with undisguised terror. Their mouths were slightly open, eyes blank with shock.

One of them was the owner of Galerie Marchadier.

Vidocq continued to blow his whistle until he heard someone pounding on the entrance doors downstairs and heard other whistles shrilling in the distance.

He slipped the whistle back into his waistcoat pocket and bowed. "Gentlemen, I am Vidocq."

Two of the men attempted to rise but fell back, collapsing and gasping for breath.

"Remain where you are, please. I am told that you were called The Five. Now you are only The Four . . ."

There was no response.

"Your director, Monsieur de Plessis, has avoided a rendezvous with Madame Guillotine. If you gentlemen have been involved with murder—and, for a start, I suspect you ordered the deaths of Narcisse Tessier and Alcidor Drumont—you will not be so fortunate. The Widow

323

will be waiting to caress your throats one morning at dawn . . ."

They appeared to be unable to move or speak.

"I had no idea, Monsieur Marchadier, that you were involved with prostitution and murder. I thought your only interests were those fine paintings and rare furniture you sold in your gallery. Your prices are so high, I never suspected you might be involved in a scheme with our most famous *courtisanes* to cheat some of the wealthiest men in our city! What do you have to say, my friend?"

Marchadier's eyes were glazed, but he tried to speak. His mouth moved. The only sound that came forth was like a giggle.

"My assistants will interrogate each of you while I direct a search of this building. From roof to cellars! You must be anticipating with dismay what we are going to find here. Unfortunately that pistol in your friend's hand held only one bullet. No escape for you there!" He glanced from face to face. "I must warn you. Some of the criminals in your employ—Goron, for instance—are certain to tell what they know about the workings of the Midnight Club in an effort to save their own worthless heads. Criminals have a deserved reputation for confessing everything when they find themselves cornered. As you four gentlemen are now cornered! Will you tell what you know about each other? Of course you will. Tomorrow all Paris will learn the secrets of the Midnight Club and hear about The Five who controlled its operation from this room. Monsieur de Plessis, the banker, with a bullet in his throat! Monsieur Marchadier who owned a fashionable gallery on rue Saint-Florentin. Monsieur Clouard the jeweler. Baron Philipon, whose bank will surely suffer from this scandal. And Vicomte Legandre! I know of your extensive property holdings, of course. Had heard rumors about how you obtained some of them, illegally, when our governments changed. But I'd no idea you were also the landlord for all our expensive prostitutes." He smiled. "My assistants will be happy to inform your families, perhaps tomorrow, that you are all being held in the Conciergerie!"

Baron Philipon, the oldest at the table, leaned forward and buried his stricken face in his hands.

The unmistakable voice of Fouché could be heard, rumbling orders in the corridor.

Vidocq looked toward the open doors as Goury hurried in. "Escort these four persons to Number Six."

"Yes, Chief."

"Question them separately. They're involved with theft, prostitution, and murder." He faced the silent figures. "Gentlemen! This is my assistant, Inspector Goury. I will see you later." He turned and strode out of the room.

Fouché was in the corridor roaring orders to groups of men from Number Six. Ronquetti was beside him, looking like an intruder in a black silk evening suit, his sharp eyes missing nothing.

Vidocq smiled. "Monsieur le Duc! Where's the American?"

"I told him to remain at our table and finish the wine. We saw you come in, but he didn't recognize you."

"And I suppose you did?"

"But of course! A magnificent disguise."

"Did you tell the American that you work with me?"

"I thought it would be wise."

"Bien! You can permit Monsieur Penny-packaire to return to his hotel. This matter's no concern of his, although I may wish to see him tomorrow." He turned as Allard joined them. "Pierre! Question the employees while I search through the building with Fouché. One of the waiters, by the way, is Goron!"

Allard grinned. "That's a fine catch!"

"And I recognized several other known criminals, including that headwaiter. Question everyone. Down to the smallest garçon. If anyone has a record or seems suspicious, take them to Number Six."

"That basement room, on a night like this, should melt their tongues!" Ronquetti exclaimed.

"Come, Charles!" Touching Fouché's sleeve. "We'll have a look at the director's office first." Leading him toward the open doors. "His name was de Plessis . . ."

"Was?"

"He put a bullet in his head."

"That body in the conference room? I saw him through the door as Goury went in and immediately sent a man to bring the local gendarmes."

Vidocq went ahead, into the office. "We weren't expected here tonight." Going straight to the desk. "So this shouldn't be locked. I would guess de Plessis kept his keys in one of these drawers." He pulled out the top drawer on the right, but there were no keys among the

325

clutter of small objects. "I want our men to go through every room in this building. If the drawers are locked, break them open and remove all documents. Aubé will sort them out tomorrow." He pulled the center drawer open. "Ah! Here we are." Holding up a cluster of keys on a golden ring and handing them to Fouché. "Open everything in this office. See what you can find while I look through this desk." He sank into the armchair de Plessis had occupied and began to examine the contents of the middle drawer on the right, as Fouché searched for a key to fit the lock of the antique cupboard.

The drawer contained letters from members of the club. Complaining about the food, suggesting some friend for membership, objecting to the rudeness of a waiter.

The bottom drawer, on the right, held unpaid bills. Wine merchant, baker, butcher . . .

"Look here!" Fouché shouted.

Vidocq turned to see that his assistant had unlocked the cupboard and opened two large leather bags on a shelf. "What have you found?"

"See for yourself!"

Vidocq rose from the desk and joined him.

He peered into one of the bags but at first saw nothing. Then, as he leaned closer, there was a cold glitter of reflected light from the candelabra. Reaching inside, he grasped a handful of stones. Held them up and let them trickle between his fingers. Loose diamonds, a string of emeralds. "These are the jewels from Tessier's vault." He glanced down at the floor of the cupboard, "And these are the ingots—gold and silver—piled underneath."

CHAPTER 53

Number Six was silent after several hours of uproar and tumult.

The prisoners had been questioned briefly and escorted to temporary cells in the depths of the Conciergerie for the night.

Vidocq sat at his desk, naked to the waist and perspiring, facing the open windows and staring at a dazzle of moonlight on Sainte-Chappelle.

He had stripped in his upstairs dressing room, after returning from the Midnight Club. Sponged his body and splashed himself with eau de Cologne. Had given instructions to Goury, as he pulled on his trousers, that the four survivors from The Five along with Goron and the other criminals discovered among the staff—there were more than thirty—should be handcuffed and marched across the courtyard to the Conciergerie. Every man on his staff who participated in tonight's raid was guarding that silent procession. Fouché and Goury would sign the commitment papers, which should prevent their being released during the night as a result of frantic efforts of lawyers and families. For the moment at least nobody knew they were there. They had been listed by numbers as they were admitted—an old police trick—and a spy from Number Six was waiting in each cell, disguised as a prisoner, to hear what they said during the night.

The Midnight Club would never open its doors again, and the sinister rule of The Five was finished, their evil power destroyed. Four were now within the shadow of the guillotine. Nothing could save them. Neither wealth nor influence . . .

He had been the last to return to Number Six after a lengthy search of Drumont's suite. It was surprisingly richly furnished and comfortable. Expensive clothes in an armoire but everything else of a personal nature was missing. Two of the club's attendants acknowledged, under questioning, that they had cleaned the suite earlier under the supervision of Monsieur de Plessis, whom they observed removing several objects. They were unable to say what had been taken except for a large sheaf of what appeared to be letters and documents.

The Five had very likely examined them in the conference room and destroyed them. There had been fresh ashes in the fireplace. So Tessier's papers had been burned.

Vidocq had discovered only one hiding place in Drumont's suite. He noticed that a wooden panel in the bedroom wall was unlike the other paneling—carved from a darker wood—and located a metal catch at the side. When he released the panel and swung it open, he had found a shallow space with three shelves. On the two lower ones a battalion of golden louis was arranged in precise stacks. The upper shelf held small parcels wrapped in oiled parchment, which gave off the unmistakable smell of raw opium. He had closed the panel and placed a chair in front of it.

Fortunately, he'd entered Drumont's suite alone, telling Fouché to search the other suites.

The two leather bags holding the Tessier jewels—and the metal ingots—were now in a locked vault downstairs. All those precious stones had been bought and paid for many times. Tessier must have sold them again and again. He would have them brought up here to-morrow. Only Drumont could have known how many diamonds were in the two bags and Alcidor Drumont was dead . . .

Vidocq smiled.

He was certain that The Five had ordered the death of Drumont, but that must be proved.

Aubé was at his desk, sorting piles of papers and documents removed from the Midnight Club by the light of a single candle. He was always the last to leave Number Six when there was a special investigation in progress.

Ronquetti had left the Midnight Club first, escorting Monsieur Penny-packer out through a side entrance. The other guests had been allowed to depart after having their papers checked. Allard had made a list of every name, and many of them would be called as witnesses during the trials . . .

Vidocq glanced at the clock on the mantel and saw it was past eleven-forty.

Only a few hours since he yanked that bell at the Midnight Club. Sounding its doom!

One suicide within a matter of minutes, and now a parade of hand-cuffed men marching through the moonlight to the Conciergerie.

Tomorrow, after they were questioned again and the final papers filled out and countersigned, they would be taken to smaller cells in La Force where they would remain until brought to trial.

Before that, after all his assistants' reports were complete and he'd written his own summary of tonight's events, he would carry a copy in person and hand it to the Minister.

He chuckled, visualizing the Minister's apoplectic face.

When Fouché questioned Goron he had blamed Drumont for every-thing. It was Drumont who hired Goron and all the other criminals for the staff of the Midnight Club. And Drumont had boasted to Goron that he had strangled Marpon. Goron, of course, was spilling information to save his own neck, but he had denied any knowledge of those other three murders. Tessier, Maya, and Clochette . . .

Drumont had been Monsieur de Plessis's surrogate in all criminal matters and carried out orders for The Five. He was the invisible sixth man!

Vidocq's gut growled unexpectedly.

He hadn't eaten any dinner. Only those two glasses of champagne at the Midnight Club.

Another five minutes, and he must force himself to his feet. Go up to the dressing room for a fresh shirt. He should be in bed before midnight.

His attention was drawn to the figure of a man lurching in from the corridor, boots pounding on the floor, heading toward Aubé's desk.

Young Damiot, still in the uniform of a customs inspector.

Aubé waved him on.

Vidocq got to his feet as Damiot came toward him. "What is it?"

"Another farm cart at the barrier! With a different driver."

"Which barrier?"

"Same one. This cart's loaded with roses. When the inspector took the driver into his office, I poked among the pots and found two large paintings in gold frames."

"They're holding him?"

"Until you get there. Cauler's with them."

"Ride straight back." He was already heading toward the corridor, Damiot at his heels. "I'll follow. Soon as I change."

Aubé got to his feet as they hurried past his desk. "You're not going to that barrier tonight?"

"I am. But you can go home. That's an order!"

"Yes, Chief . . ."

CHAPTER 54

The farmer's cart was filled with pots of white rose trees in full bloom.

Vidocq waited, astride the stallion, in deep shadow. Watching the clumsy charrette lumbering off up the long street, its enormous wooden wheels creaking and groaning. As it disappeared into the night, he was engulfed by a wave of perfume, drawn from the roses by the heat.

When he arrived, young Damiot had hurried from the customs office to report that the farmer was complaining because he would be late making his delivery in the city.

They had not questioned him about his destination, following Vidocq's orders, knowing he wouldn't tell the truth.

Vidocq had dismounted and inspected the cart briefly, pushed the roses apart and saw the covered paintings between the clay pots. Told Damiot to have the inspectors release the farmer after he mounted his stallion.

When they escorted him back to his cart, Vidocq saw that it was an older man than he had followed last night. This one had a gray beard.

He touched the stallion with his knees and started in pursuit, holding him to a trot two streets behind the lumbering cart.

Damiot and Cauler would remain as far behind as he was staying from the cart. If he needed them, he would wave them forward with a white scarf, one of several varicolored scarves in his saddlebag.

The roses were now only a faint blur, but they were more visible than the flame of the lantern swaying on the charrette.

His stallion's hooves touched the cobbles lightly. Intelligent beast! Always sensed when they were pursuing someone.

He had warned Damiot that after a few streets he would ride ahead, past the cart, in order to get a closer look at the driver's face. Tonight he was wearing soft leather boots, worn and cracked, on the chance he might need to move quickly or even do some running.

The top floors of the houses on his left were washed in bright moonlight, which made the middle of the street, already in deep shadow, seem even darker. On his right the rooftops, silhouetted against the sky, were like buildings in a medieval Paris.

He could still see the ghostly mass of white roses filling the cart and sniff their fragrance but, glancing behind, was unable to glimpse his assistants or their horses. No matter! They would come galloping after him if needed.

As he goaded the stallion to a faster trot, the roses and flickering lantern flame became more visible. He pulled the brim of his cap down as he came abreast of the cart.

The farmer looked up apprehensively as the stallion passed.

Vidocq rode on, but he'd seen the man's face.

Pulling the stallion's head right, urging him into the next cross street, he circled the block at a canter.

As he rode, Vidocq removed his cap, rolled it up, and thrust it into the saddlebag. Pulled out a blue cotton scarf, which he secured around his neck. Appearance slightly changed, he took his position behind the cart again.

He looked behind him but still couldn't see or hear the others.

Holding the stallion to a slow trot, he watched the mass of white roses in the distance, the lantern's flame barely visible.

It was near here that Balzac had slipped from his horse last night, and the other cart had escaped. Easy for it to turn into any of these side streets and reach another avenue leading to one of the bridges. Unless he was close enough to see what direction the charrette took, he would lose it in the maze of streets near the river.

He realized that, even as he watched, the roses had disappeared.

Halting the stallion, he snatched the white scarf from his saddlebag. Shook it free and waved for the others to join him. Listened briefly, but heard no sound of their horses. Damiot and Cauler must have dropped behind. He stuffed the white scarf back into his saddlebag. No time to wait. That cart would be gone. He kneed the stallion and felt his great bulk spring forward.

Several side streets flashed past before he picked up a scent of roses again.

He slowed the stallion and peered in every direction, sniffing the warm air, but there was no sign of the charrette. No sound of creaking wheels.

As he rode on up the long street past another cross street, the smell of roses faded completely.

The cart must have turned into that last side street!

He pulled the reins hard and galloped back, turning east into the other street. Into a glare of moonlight. The enormous orb appeared to rest on top of the distant houses.

The scent of roses was stronger here.

He had no idea which streets these were. Everything looked unfamiliar by moonlight. Impossible to glimpse any street signs.

As he rode, the sweet smell of roses slowly vanished again.

He turned the stallion north up a street leading toward the river then left in the next side street and north again at the first cross street.

The farmer must have become suspicious when he slowed beside him and taken the next side street to escape, but he would certainly be heading for one of the bridges.

Vidocq recognized a building. They were on rue Saint-Jacques near the Petit Pont. The bridge was straight ahead.

The stallion pounded across the bridge and up rue de la Cité.

They were passing between Place du Parvis, with Nôtre-Dame black against the eastern sky, and the familiar stone walls of the Préfecture, looking blue in the moonlight.

If he shouted, Aubé might hear him through the open windows of Number Six. He hoped Aubé had gone home but knew he would, as usual, be waiting for his return. No matter how late the hour.

Continuing on, he glanced at the solid mass of the Conciergerie in the distance. By moonlight the ancient prison was even more ominous.

Only a few carriages passed him as he rode, and nobody was walking. The scent of roses didn't return as he clattered across the Pont Nôtre-Dame to the right bank of the Seine.

Rode back and forth from street to street, until he picked up the scent again in rue du Renard.

He goaded the stallion, and within moments a strong aroma of roses filled his nostrils again. Riding on eagerly, he glimpsed the white roses straight ahead.

He leaned forward as he slowed the stallion but was unable to see the lantern flame behind the cart.

The farmer must have covered it! Approaching his destination, he wanted the lantern dark in case anyone was following.

Keeping his eyes on the roses, Vidocq held the stallion to a walk. They were within a few blocks of the sprawling markets, and now there were other farm carts clattering in the same direction. He eased between them, avoiding their huge wooden wheels. Saw that one cart was piled with cabbages. Another held crates of chickens whose complaints shattered the night. As they came closer to their destination—now there was a glow of light in the distance—he saw the charrette loaded with roses swerve into a narrow side street.

When the stallion reached the mouth of the street, Vidocq glimpsed the cart briefly, moving through the light from a lantern suspended above the entrance to a café that would remain open all night, feeding people who worked in the markets.

Easing the stallion down the street, he was in time to see the roses swallowed up by darkness beyond the café. He passed empty carts with horses munching oats from feed bags, waiting for their owners to finish supper before turning back to the country.

As he rode on, Vidocq saw a high stone wall enclosing a windowless warehouse of gray stone. There were many of these surrounding the markets. In the moonlight this one looked like another prison.

He was moving through a heavy scent of roses again. That charrette must be just ahead.

Slowing the stallion, he saw they were approaching a pair of entrance gates as tall as the stone wall.

The wooden gates were open.

Holding the stallion to a walk so that his hooves were barely audible on the cobbles, Vidocq crouched low and peered into a large open courtyard.

The bearded farmer stood beside his cart in bright moonlight, close to the entrance. Two ruffians were unloading the pots of white roses. There were several empty carts, without horses or attendants.

He eased the stallion into deep shadow beneath a tree, jumped down, and secured his bridle around a branch. "Be quiet here," he whispered. "Not a sound."

The stallion snorted faintly, as though he understood.

Vidocq stroked his neck and crept back to look into the courtyard.

The two ruffians, squat and muscular, were lifting one of the large framed paintings down from the charrette. Slowly and carefully. Then each of them picked up a single painting and, trailed by the farmer, carried them up some stone steps into the warehouse, leaving the door open.

The pots of roses had been left on the cobbles. To be replaced in the cart no doubt and sold to a dealer in the markets.

Vidocq darted across the courtyard, avoiding the moonlight, keeping to dark areas between the empty carts. Grateful for the lightweight boots with soft soles, which made no sound on these cobbles.

The white roses filled the courtyard with their fragrance. They had led him here like Ariadne's thread, their perfume following him now, as he bounded up the stone steps and through the open door.

Ducked to one side so he wouldn't be visible against the moonlight in the courtyard. Waiting in the dark briefly, getting his bearings.

He was in a broad corridor with a vaulted ceiling supported by thick stone columns. Iron lanterns hung from spikes driven into the walls.

Their light revealed the farmer hurrying after the men with the paintings. As he watched, the farmer went ahead and opened a door. In the light spilling from inside, he saw the two ruffians carrying the paintings through the door followed by the old man.

Vidocq started after them, moving lightly and quickly down the corridor. Past several closed doors. From the crude carving on them, he guessed this warehouse must be several hundred years old. Reaching the open door, he pressed his shoulder against the wall and eased his face forward until he could see into the room. It was a large chamber—wide and high-ceilinged, stone walls partially covered by tapestries—filled with antique furniture. No sign of the farmer or those men with the two paintings.

He entered the silent room where the only light came from more lanterns hanging on the walls. The antiques were arranged in rows, so one could move between them to inspect each piece. They were rare and beautiful. Several pieces he would like to own.

He had found the stolen treasures.

The only open space of any size was a single passage between the furniture, which he now saw led to another open door.

He continued through the maze of antiques. Ready, if anyone appeared, to drop between the furniture and scuttle out of sight.

As he approached the open door, he saw a long room bare of furniture and, as he entered, realized it was a gallery. The paneled walls were hung with fine paintings.

His eyes darted from canvas to canvas. Barely visible in the soft light from candelabra placed on tables set against the walls. Each of the canvases, elaborately framed, appeared to be a masterpiece. He recognized a Rembrandt and two Fragonards.

Moving forward to take a closer look at a beautiful peasant girl—obviously a Chardin—distracted by her lovely face, at the same time noticing a closed door at the far end of the gallery.

At that instant a heavy cloth dropped over his head and was held securely at the back of his neck.

Vidocq reached out with both hands but grasped nothing. He made no outcry, in order to conserve his breath. Clutched at empty space as his head was jerked back and powerful hands grasped his arms and legs. Felt himself lifted and carried through the air.

He had walked into a trap! They expected someone to follow that cart after last night's attempt, thanks to Balzac, was bungled.

Their footsteps thudded on the wooden floor.

His body relaxed as he waited, in anticipation, for what was to come.

He smiled under the cloth, amused by the comic spectacle he must be making. At least no one was witnessing it, and he certainly wouldn't include this unfortunate scene in his report tomorrow.

If he survived to make a report!

His body stiffened at the thought, and he attempted to kick, but both legs were firmly held.

He waited for whatever was about to happen. Must save his strength for the unexpected.

Then, faintly, he heard a door opening.

As he was carried forward, he was no longer aware of footsteps. They had brought him into a carpeted room.

Now they were hesitating.

"Where do you want us to take him?" Man's voice, behind his head, harsh and deep.

There was no reply to the question, but he felt his body being lowered. He began to struggle, without success, until he realized they had placed him in a chair. A cushioned chair!

He didn't move. All senses alert now.

Had they left him?

He listened for a moment. Not a sound.

Then, very slowly, he raised his right hand toward his head. Stopped it in midair, waiting for a voice to order him not to move any farther.

Only silence.

He lifted his arms suddenly and reached with both hands toward the cloth covering his head. Touched it, analyzing the texture. It was unmistakably velvet. Grasping the cloth abruptly, he pulled it from his face and lifted it off his head.

Then, as he found himself facing a seated figure across an enormous oak table, he let the velvet cloth drop to the floor.

The man wore a coarse black blouse with a black silk scarf tied around his head, a black mask hiding his face.

Vidocq smiled. "Le Diable Noir! I did not expect you in Paris."

"And you are Vidocq. I was hoping it would be you tonight. They told me someone trailed last night's delivery, but the driver managed to lose him. I ordered them to fill tonight's cart with roses, hoping their scent would lead you here."

"You wanted me to find you?"

"The doors were left open for you, and I've been waiting to welcome you. When the cart was late again, I knew the driver had been detained. I hoped, when they released him, you would be following."

He noticed now that Le Diable's hands rested on the surface of the table without moving. They were muscular hands, dark-skinned, the fingers short, thick, and hairy. The hair was black. He peered at the mask but was unable to glimpse the color of the eyes behind the twin openings. "Why have you come to Paris? As long as you remained in the provinces, you were beyond the jurisdiction of the Sûreté. The local gendarmes have been unable to find you. Much less capture you or any of your band! Why have you risked coming here?"

Le Diable shrugged his powerful shoulders. "Vanity, perhaps."

"Vanity has resulted in the capture of many criminals."

"The local police are idiots. Their own stupidities defeat them. I come to Paris at least once each month—not masked, of course, but disguised—hoping one day to encounter the great Vidocq."

"Hoping to meet me?"

"Always looking forward to matching wits with the only man in France who, I suspect, is as clever as I am."

Vidocq laughed. "I'm not certain whether you mean to flatter me or yourself."

"Both, I suppose."

"And you've been coming here every month!"

"Ever since I organized my Black Band, as the newspapers have christened us. At first I was the only one dressed in black, but after one newspaper called us the Black Band, I thought it might be a good idea if everyone wore black. Knowing it would frighten the locals even more! I recruited most of my so-called band in Paris. Many came from the back alleys of Montmartre with their families. They've settled in one village—I won't tell you which—but it's become like a part of Paris."

"I've noticed during the past two years that several of our better criminals have disappeared. I thought perhaps I'd driven them off to South America or the United States."

"They've probably been with me. You have in recent years made crime a risky trade to follow in Paris."

"Risky perhaps, but it continues to flourish."

"Curious! Our sitting here, facing each other. Mortal enemies. Talking like old friends."

"Enemies? Friends? Is there a difference? Several of my best friends have become my worst enemies." Vidocq chuckled as he lifted one leg over the other, reaching down to adjust the edge of his boot, making himself more comfortable. "I have recently been giving considerable thought to you and your activities. And I decided you would have to dispose of your plunder not too far from where you and your band operate."

"That's right!"

"The obvious place was Paris."

"Very true. When that cart was followed from the barrier last night, I was certain it was you. But I was surprised when the driver evaded you so easily."

"That was because I was accompanied by two others. Tonight I rode alone. And I was right! You do bring your loot to Paris."

"I arranged a market for it before I recruited my band. The market was waiting for us. Eager to handle everything we took. Prominent men who had never been involved with stolen goods before but headed an organization they could use as a base for the disposal of everything we brought them. The most expensive pieces of antique furniture! Priceless masterpieces! Many of the rarest items go to Russia or South America. These are wealthy businessmen who never become involved personally with me or my men. I've never met any of them. Only their leader. Before he contacted me, through an old friend in their organization, they had put together the most perfect plan ever devised to cover and protect a large criminal operation . . ."

The words snapped into place in Vidocq's mind. "The Midnight Club!" The name escaped, hardly more than a whisper, from between his lips.

"You've guessed what I'm talking about! Which means I've talked too much!" Le Diable straightened slowly in his chair. "But then, of course, whatever you've learned, you'll never have a chance to repeat a word of it to anyone."

Vidocq had a feeling that, behind his mask, Le Diable was smiling. He looked away from the twin dark holes in the mask and glanced around the room. Barely noticed the rich furnishings, the curtained windows, and framed paintings. The walls seemed to float in a rosy glow from an ornate pair of candelabra. The air was comfortably cool, which meant that thick stone walls were keeping out the heat. His mind at the same time was concerned with what Le Diable had just said. He faced him again, across the table. "I suppose you plan to hold me here."

"It would be stupid of me to think I could do that. It's well known that, in the past, you've escaped from many prisons."

"Which leaves a single alternative."

"That's true." One of Le Diable's hands disappeared briefly below the table and returned holding a pistol, which must have been waiting on his knee.

Vidocq shrugged. "What about a pair of dueling pistols? Or, better still, rapiers?"

"That might give you too much of an advantage. Although, I must warn you, I've killed a dozen men in duels."

"I killed twenty before I reached the age of twenty."

"I don't doubt that. Give or take one or two? You're a clever fellow, Vidocq. The first to guess I provide the Midnight Club with the treasures I take from those castles. They are the most powerful group of men in France! With more influence than any politicians. Their board controls dozens of important commercial and private companies . . ."

"Bankers, jewelers, dealers in rare paintings and furniture? All ruled by a group of men who called themselves The Five?"

"You've heard about them! Doesn't surprise me. However there's nothing you can do. The Five are more powerful than the Chief of the Sûreté!"

"I suppose Monsieur de Plessis was your only contact. Or was it Alcidor Drumont?"

"You know about Drumont? We met, years ago, in Corsica . . ."

"Drumont is dead."

"I don't believe you." He rested his pistol tentatively on the table.

"A knife through his throat. Last night in an attic on rue de la Lune. And Monsieur de Plessis this evening put a bullet into his head at the Midnight Club."

Le Diable smiled. "You're lying!"

"Send someone to the Midnight Club, and you'll find out. My men guard the premises, but there'll be citizens in the street who will know what happened. All Paris will learn the truth by tomorrow. I raided the Midnight Club tonight."

Le Diable reached out and casually put his right hand on the pistol.

"The four surviving members of The Five have been locked in the

Conciergerie along with every man from their staff who has a criminal record. Including Goron."

"Crépuscule?" Le Diable hissed the name. "He's never been behind bars!"

"He will never, I assure you, know freedom again. And you, Monsieur le Diable, no longer have the Midnight Club to protect you or dispose of your booty." Glancing around the room at the rare antiques. "I suppose this warehouse is also owned by The Five. The spoils from those châteaux are stored here until they can be disposed of through the dealers of Paris. They selected this building because it's close to the markets. Those farmers bring their vegetables and flowers here, unload what's hidden underneath, and deliver their roses and cabbages elsewhere."

"I said you were clever!"

"Only your murderous plundering is finished. As the Midnight Club is finished."

"But I am not finished." Smiling again.

Vidocq shrugged. It was impossible to reach the pistol thrust into the waist of his trousers. He would be dead before he could pull it out. Perhaps he might be able to distract Le Diable with flattery. "Talking to you like this, I am surprised to discover that you are an educated man."

"You think so?" Diable laughed, the sound muffled by his mask.

"Your speech is not that of a criminal."

"My education was behind bars. I read every book I could find."

"That's more than most prisoners bother to do."

"I always found someone, like you, who had a book. I would take it from them. Read it over and over until I understood every word. Learned everything I could from each book. You were the first to teach me that."

"Are you saying we've met before?"

"I once took a book from you. Many years ago."

"Where?"

"We were in prison together. You were always reading. The other convicts made jokes about you, but they learned, to their sorrow, that you were a wild man. Fighting everybody. Always winning. They soon found out you were stronger and smarter than any of them."

"I was in many prisons when I was young. Where was this?"

"It was the old jail in Lille."

"Lille?" Vidocq felt a cold breath pass across his forehead.

"I swore that one day I would kill you. For what you did to me there. But at the same time I've always had respect for you. Even admired you. Knew I was a smarter man for the reading I'd done because of you. For years I couldn't believe you were the Vidocq who was Chief of the Sûreté Nationale. It wasn't possible! Then I saw an engraving of the famous Vidocq. It was your face."

"And you are Calamatta." He said the hated name quietly.

"I am Calamatta. Yes . . ."

Vidocq watched with fascination as the muscular brown hands reached up and slowly lifted the black mask away from the dark Sicilian face. He saw the thick sensuous lips and long ratlike teeth, then the hole where a nose had been, the ridged scar down the left cheek, and the ear with most of it missing. Finally the lidded reptilian eyes.

"You see! What you did to my face in that Lille jail. When you managed to steal a cleaver from the kitchen."

"I remember."

"You are the first to know I am Calamatta. The members of my band have never seen my face." He dropped his mask onto the table, near the pistol, then whipped the black silk handkerchief from his head.

Vidocq saw that the hairless brown-skinned skull had a deep indentation running down the center of the forehead where he had embedded the cleaver with a single blow. "Calamatta . . ."

"I've remembered you whenever I see a reflection of my face."

"And I've thought of you. Every day of my life."

"Have you?" He smiled again.

"Do you recall another prisoner in the Lille jail? A young man called Lavedan?"

"Lavedan . . ."

"Baptiste Lavedan."

"No."

"A farmer who'd been given six years sentence for stealing grain to feed his family. I forged a pardon and had it delivered to the warden. Lavedan was set free."

"So his name was Lavedan!"

"You told the warden what I'd done."

"Yes, I did."

"Informed him that I'd forged the pardon. I was ordered to stand for a new trial. That's when I attacked you and, in the riot that followed, managed to escape. My only crime was that I had fought with a man in Lille when I found him with my mistress. For that I was serving a sentence in the Lille jail for three months."

"So that's all you'd done! I never knew . . ."

"I forged that pardon so Lavedan could return to his family. Because of you I was recaptured and brought to trial for forgery. Sentenced to eight years in the galleys and sent to Bicêtre. I tried to escape, again and again, without success. So many times that they moved me to the galleys in Brest."

"A foul hole! I've been there."

"I escaped and signed on with the crew of a French privateer, which swept the North Sea for British merchant ships. Until one night in port, I was recognized and arrested. My sentence was doubled to sixteen years, and I was sent to the Toulouse galleys."

"From which there's no escape."

"But I escaped. Managed to reach Lyon, where I was picked up again and faced a return to the galleys. This time sentenced for life! Fortunately, the head of the Lyon police believed my story. He investigated what I told him and discovered I was telling the truth. The only crimes I'd committed were attacking that man in Lille and forging a pardon for an innocent man. He offered me a job with the Lyon police, and I accepted. But until the King confirmed me as Chief of the Sûreté, I had no papers. No passport . . ."

"And you were working with the police?"

"That's the irony! It was two more years before the Douai court removed that forgery charge from the official records. And all those years I was in danger of being returned to the galleys at any moment. Because of you!" He fingered the top of his boot absentmindedly as he talked. "I lived in the constant shadow of prison because you informed the warden in Lille that I had forged that pardon for young Lavedan. You caused my parents years of misery. You nearly ruined my life!"

Calamatta shrugged. "Which is worse? What I did to you or what you've done to me?" He touched his face. "These scars are more visible than yours. Because of them, I swore I would kill you if we ever met."

"And I vowed to kill you."

Calamatta snatched up his pistol from the table. "Now it is even more necessary that I do so. You are the only person who knows that I am Le Diable Noir!" He cocked the pistol, the click of metal slashing like a knife through the silent room.

Vidocq leaned back, prepared to dodge. Every muscle tense.

"You are a brave man, Vidocq. To come here alone." He slowly raised his pistol. "Tomorrow your body will be found in the Seine. No man will ever know how or where you died. Only I . . ."

"And you will end on the guillotine. If not for my death, for another. Or one of your own gang will kill you."

"You've been a worthy enemy, Vidocq. I will miss you. Farewell!" He pressed the trigger, and the pistol fired.

Vidocq ducked and at the same time pulled out the small pistol he had been fingering in the top of his boot. Cocked it, aiming carefully.

The look of shock on Calamatta's face as he saw the pistol turned to horror. He tossed his own pistol aside and fumbled under his blouse for another.

Vidocq pressed the trigger, and there was a roar of sound.

Calamatta clawed at his chest with both hands.

Vidocq thrust the pistol back into the top of his boot, his eyes never leaving the face of the dying man.

Blood was seeping between Calamatta's fingers, and the pupils of his eyes had disappeared beneath the lids.

To Vidocq's surprise, Calamatta didn't slump forward onto the table, instead he straightened and, with a final herculean effort, appeared to expand his broad shoulders.

There were shouts in the distance. Feet pounding on stone floors.

Calamatta's damaged nose was like an open hole in a skull.

The door crashed open.

Vidocq turned to face Damiot. "My friend! You are indeed a most welcome sight. The gentleman you see seated across the table is all that remains of Le Diable Noir . . ."

CHAPTER 55

The moon had dropped behind a row of distant trees.

Vidocq, perspiring, climbed the familiar marble steps and pulled out his keys as the carriage headed back to Number Six. Fingering his keys until he found the right one, he thrust it into the lock and opened the door. Even the door seemed unusually heavy tonight. He was tired.

Turning before entering, he looked up at the sky.

No clouds and not a breath of air.

Tomorrow morning dozens of documents must be prepared for those two investigations completed tonight. Or was it one? The exposure of the Midnight Club and the capture and death of Le Diable Noir.

Sighing as he thought of more hot weather with so much work to be done, he went inside and bolted the door.

There was a note waiting beside the lighted lamp.

Unfolding the sheet of paper, he smiled as he read.

Another hot day!

This weather would depress me if it were not for Fleuride. Her sweet laughter fills the house. Even Jeanne-Victoire seems much more cheerful.

Fleuride wrote her mother to inform her that she is spending another two weeks in Paris. To which I added a few words of my own.

I've arranged for us to have a little picnic, day after tomorrow, in the country. You can select the spot. Fleuride's looking forward to it, and so is Jeanne-Victoire.

Couldn't you find a nice field beside a stream? Fleuride tells me she enjoys fishing.

We'll discuss this at breakfast.

Sleep well . . .

He folded the note and slipped it into a pocket as he went toward the staircase.

Driving home just now, he'd heard the distant bells of Saint-Séverin ringing the hour. It had been two o'clock.

He hadn't been this late at the end of a day since last winter when there was a rash of curious murders in Faubourg Saint-Germain.

As he climbed the steps, he thought of young Damiot again. Too bad he would be returning in a few weeks to his native Provence. To-night, at that warehouse, he'd done an excellent job. When he asked how he'd found him there, he had smiled shrewdly.

"That was easy! When I lost you, I followed the smell of roses until I saw the farmer's cart in that courtyard. Then I noticed your stallion tied to a tree. I sent Cauler back to Number Six for more men, but when I heard that first shot I went in alone. There were some rough types on guard, but when they saw my pistol they fled. Then I heard a second shot and knew where to find you. I only did what you've always told us. Observe, listen, and move quickly!"

He would give Damiot a present before he left Paris to show his ap-preciation. Perhaps an expensive watch with a personal inscription . . .

Vidocq hesitated at the top of the staircase, but there was no sound from his mother's suite or Fleuride's room.

At this late hour both of them should be asleep.

Only Jeanne-Victoire might be awake.

He started down the silent corridor, thinking of all those reports he must read tomorrow morning. The summary he would have to write . . .

He opened the door to his wife's suite, making no sound, and crossed the foyer into her bedroom.

Tonight she had tossed the sheet back and was lying on her right side, facing the open windows.

Crossing toward the bed, he was unable to see her eyes because strands of golden hair covered the side of her face.

"Who are you, Monsieur?"

"Your weary husband, Madame." He kissed her forehead and was surprised by the coolness of her flesh.

"You are very late."

"It was a busy night. Sleep well, my love . . ."

"And you. I will see you in the morning?"

"Not tomorrow."

"No?"

"I must be in my office very early. Tell Maman I couldn't wait for breakfast."

"I will tell her. And Fleuride . . ." Her voice faded.

He strode across the bedroom, out of the suite, and down the corri-dor, eager for bed. But as he walked he remembered that he still had three unsolved murders on his hands. He'd completely forgotten about them in tonight's excitements. Clochette, Tessier, and Maya . . .

No! There were four. He still had no idea who killed Drumont.

Four murders . . .

He would get back to them as soon as those reports were finished, each suspect questioned. Everyone he'd ordered into the Conciergerie must be properly admitted under their true names. So much to be done before he could even think about those four murders . . .

Reaching his door, he glanced down the hall again and wondered if Fleuride might be awake.

He swung the door open and saw that the maids had forgotten to leave a lighted lamp in his bedroom.

No matter! It would be cooler without a light.

He closed the door and, loosening his cravat, started across the foyer. Someone was in his bed!

Moving closer, careful not to make a sound, he saw her black curls.

He undressed quickly in the reflected moonlight coming through the open windows, tossing his clothes onto a chair. Stretched out beside her.

Leaning close, he saw that her eyes were closed, and she was snoring softly. He inhaled her perfume as he sank back onto the pillows.

His mind returned immediately to those four unsolved murders.

He would never get to sleep tonight. Thinking about them . . .

Clochette, Tessier, Maya, and Drumont . . .

Fleuride turned in her sleep, moving closer to him, snuggling against his side.

Vidocq smiled, mind and body relaxing, and fell asleep.

CHAPTER 56

Birds were singing in the trees on rue Royale and diving down to the pavements for their breakfasts.

The quiet street was empty except for a gardener filling buckets with water from a big cask on wheels and sluicing down the sidewalks in front of one private mansion, to cool the air.

Vidocq pulled out a silk handkerchief and dried his perspiring face as the fiacre reached the Midnight Club. As they entered the courtyard, the horse startled several pigeons that shot into the air with a soft thudding of wings. Except for them the courtyard was deserted.

Jumping down before the horse slowed to a halt, he glanced up at the driver. "I'll only be five minutes."

"Yes, Monsieur."

The entrance door of the Midnight Club swung open before he reached the top step. It was one of his younger men.

"Morning, Chief." Touching his forehead in an eager salute.

"Anyone here this early?"

"One other man from Number Six." Closing the door and trailing after Vidocq through the lobby.

"No outsiders are to be admitted today. Turn everyone away unless they have written permission from Aubé. There'll be representatives from the newspapers later, when they learn what happened last night. Keep all of them out."

"Yes, Chief."

"This should only take a moment. I want to have a look at some of the upstairs rooms by daylight." Bounding up the curving marble staircase, he wondered if the house on rue de l'Hirondelle was coming awake. He'd left a note for his mother, explaining his early departure.

When he opened his eyes this morning, he had been alone. Fleuride had slipped away during the night.

He'd left without disturbing anyone and found a fiacre to bring him here.

Instead of going from room to room on the first floor, where all the doors were standing open, he continued upstairs and went straight to Drumont's suite.

It had not been disturbed.

He removed his hat as he crossed the luxurious small salon and set it on a table. Pushed the chair out of his way and opened the wall panel.

The golden coins gleamed as they caught the light from the windows.

He didn't touch the parcels of opium but counted the stacks of coins. Fifty piles with ten louis d'or in each. Moving quickly, he removed one coin from each pile until he held ten, five in each hand. Carried them to a table and arranged them in two piles. Brought out a pair of small gray velvet pouches from his pockets. Extended their mouths and placed five coins in each. Repeated this until he had removed fifty coins. Placed twenty-five in each pouch and slipped the pouches into separate pockets.

He closed the wooden wall panel, pushed the chair in front of it again, snatched up his hat, and went down to the first floor, where he briefly inspected each room. The restaurant was a shambles, and plates of unfinished food on several tables were attracting flies through the open windows. Continuing on, down the dim central corridor where he had first glimpsed Goron, he glanced into the director's office but did not enter. Paused in the doorway to the conference room and looked down the long table toward the chair where Monsieur de Plessis had died. Saw the dried blood, a dark blot on the polished wood.

Then, abruptly, he turned on his heels and strode toward the front staircase. Saw the two guards from Number Six waiting below. Held himself erect as he went down the curving steps so the coins made no sound in his pockets.

The guards saluted as he crossed the lobby.

"I've just discovered something upstairs. A hiding place full of gold coins. Don't know why we didn't find them last night. I'm leaving now."

One of the guards sprang ahead of him to open the door.

"I'll send someone later to remove all that gold. We'll hold it at Number Six until legal ownership can be established. If that's possible. Otherwise those coins become the property of the government." He was smiling as he went down the steps to the waiting fiacre. He would send Fouché to get the coins. Meanwhile nobody would be able to find that secret panel in the wall. He hadn't told them which room it was in, but he was certain those two young guards would search for the coins.

When he reached Number Six, he paused in the outer office and told Aubé to have the bags of diamonds brought up from the vault. Young Revol would be arriving with that goldsmith.

"Will you want breakfast?" Aubé asked.

"My usual. Didn't have time for any before I left home."

"I'll tell Madame Babelay." He rose from his desk.

"I paid an early visit to the Midnight Club. Found a cache of louis d'or hidden in Drumont's suite that we overlooked last night. Fouché

347

can pick them up later. Be sure to count them before you lock them in the vault."

"I'll make an inventory. Still have to count those diamonds."

"You can do that after the goldsmith sees them."

"Everybody's in early today. Writing their reports on last night's raids."

"I'll read each one as they finish." He went through the antechamber into his own office, placing his hat upside down on the table behind the door.

Glancing back through the antechamber, he saw Aubé heading for the corridor.

Vidocq removed the velvet pouches from his pockets and locked them in a secret drawer of his desk that even Aubé didn't know about.

He made several notes on a pad, then swiveled his leather armchair to face the open windows and saw that hot sunlight was already edging down the facade of Sainte-Chapelle, making black shadows between each carved buttress.

After he read those reports, he would turn them back to Aubé, who could combine them into a summary. He would add his own brief comments. That completed, he would personally take the first copy across the street to the Minister. He looked forward to that.

Then, while his assistants supervised the transfer of last night's prisoners from the Conciergerie to La Force and signed all the necessary forms, he would have Goron—Crépuscule—brought here. He would question the Twilight Owl himself.

Goury and Fouché could handle all details this morning relating to the Midnight Club and Le Diable Noir. Those two investigations would be combined into one report.

His own immediate and most urgent project was to solve those murders.

He scowled as he stared into the glare of sunlight.

Four murders. Clochette, Tessier, Maya, and Drumont. In that order . . .

Was there only one murderer involved? Or a different murderer for each? Four murderers to be caught and unmasked!

At least the Diable Noir dossier would be closed when he wrote his report on their meeting in that warehouse.

His enemy was dead! He had achieved his long-sought revenge . . .

Vidocq had a sudden thought that made him smile.

When he reported his face-to-face encounter with Le Diable Noir, he wouldn't mention the fact that he was Calamatta. Even his band of ruffians didn't know his true identity. That would deny Calamatta the fame he would receive if it became known that he was Le Diable Noir. He would never tell anyone! This would complete his revenge . . .

"Good morning, Monsieur."

He turned his chair to see Madame Babelay with a breakfast tray. "Madame! I am in desperate need of black coffee."

"I brewed a fresh pot." She placed the silver tray in front of him. "Everybody's drinking coffee this morning. You must've had a busy night!"

"One of our best." He picked up the silver pot and poured steaming coffee into the Sèvres bowl.

"I can always tell from the amount of coffee drunk each morning what sort of night everyone had. As well as being kept awake by all the goings and comings. I'll bring more coffee later."

He watched her scurry through the antechamber as the Nun appeared in Aubé's office. "Good morning, Mademoiselle!" he called. "I'm having breakfast." He observed her tiny figure pass buxom Madame Babelay, who briefly put her in complete shadow.

The Nun was wearing a gray and white dress with a plain gray bonnet, like a novitiate's habit. As she came closer, her pale face reminded him, as always, of Jeanne-Victoire's.

"I think I may have information for you," she murmured.

"Sit down!" Buttering a piece of brioche and chewing a mouthful of omelette. "You've had breakfast?"

"Hours ago!" She sank into the armchair facing him, resting her white-gloved hands on her lap. "I made a tour of fences yesterday."

"Did you learn something?"

"You wanted to know if anyone, particularly a nun, had tried to dispose of loose diamonds or diamond jewelry . . ."

"Within the past week."

"I talked to two fences—one on rue Pigalle, the other rue Blanche—who'd been visited by nuns this week. One wanted to sell a diamond necklace, the other had a small cross. From their descriptions, I would say it was the same nun each time."

"They took her name?"

349

"No. And they didn't report her to the local police."

"But every fence in Paris was ordered to report anyone who offered them diamond jewelry."

"These diamonds were false."

"Of course! When we sent out instructions to all fences, we thought they were genuine."

"Both fences told this nun they were imitations, worth no more than a few francs, and the settings were gilt!"

"Clochette's cross and Maya's necklace. Both false . . . When did this nun try to sell them?"

"The cross five days ago, the necklace day before yesterday."

"What did the nun say when she was told the diamonds were worthless?"

"She appeared to be shocked. Informed both fences that the jewelry was given to her convent by a wealthy patroness and they needed the money from the diamonds to help the poor."

"Did these two fences give you a description of the nun?"

"Only that she seemed to be young. Spoke quietly, with no sign of nervousness. Slipped the jewelry into a pocket of her robe as she left."

"Was there a carriage? Or did she walk?"

"I asked that, both places, but neither fence followed her to the door."

"Damn . . . Where's the Rat this morning?"

"She sent her youngest daughter to tell me she's not feeling well."

"Too much red wine again?"

"More likely the heat." She smiled tolerantly. "She suffers more from it than I."

"I want you to visit secondhand clothing shops and costumers this morning. Find out if a young woman has bought or rented a nun's habit in the past ten days."

"I was going to suggest that. You can still find every sort of religious habit for sale. From the years when all the convents were closed and most nuns fled France, leaving their possessions behind. I've bought several habits myself."

"I'm sure you have."

"They're made of the best materials." The Nun rose from the chair. "I hear you caught Le Diable. Congratulations!"

"We caught several unexpected fish last night."

"I'll try and catch you a nun."

"Take one of the carriages! It's too warm to walk." He finished his omelette as he watched her leave, passing a guard standing near Aubé's desk clutching the two leather bags. "Bring those in here!" he called.

The guard turned, as Aubé waved him on, and crossed the antechamber with the bags.

"Morning, Chief. Where you want these?"

"Behind that door," motioning toward the table. "Leave them there, beside my hat."

"Yes, Chief." He hefted the bags onto the table and departed.

Vidocq saw that Damiot was handing his morning report over to Aubé, whose desk was piled with documents and papers confiscated from the Midnight Club. "Damiot!"

He turned, grinning, and hurried toward him.

"You the first to complete your report?"

He shrugged. "Don't know."

"Yes!" Aubé called. "He is."

Damiot laughed. "Guess mine will be the shortest."

"Shortest is frequently the best." He studied Damiot's square-jawed peasant face. "Still determined to leave us?"

"Yes, Chief."

"Why couldn't you marry that girl and bring her to live in Paris?"

"She's happy in Courville. Never wants to see Paris . . ."

"Your job will be waiting if she changes her mind. Women do, you know. I want you to go over to the Conciergerie and start arrangements for all our prisoners to be transferred to La Force. Enter them with their legal names this time, not the numbers we gave them last night. Goury and Fouché will be there later. You can get things started."

Damiot turned to leave, moving with purpose.

Vidocq checked to see that Aubé had begun to copy Damiot's report. That should keep him occupied for several minutes.

He rose from his desk silently and went to the leather bags resting on the table. Unfastened the cord wrapped around the neck of each and opened the bags. Reached inside and scooped up several diamonds. Selected five of the largest and set them, carefully, on the table. Dropped the others back into the bags, closed them and wrapped the cords around their necks again. Snatched up the five diamonds and hurried back to his desk. Pulled out the secret drawer and placed the five diamonds between the velvet pouches. He would give those fifty louis d'or to Coralie tomorrow. For Clochette's baby. Fifty golden louis, courtesy of Alcidor Drumont! But he would take the five diamonds home tonight. Lock them away in the hiding place behind a panel in his picture gallery, with all those other valuables he'd collected through the years.

Voices from Aubé's office.

Closing the secret drawer, he saw Goury handing his morning report over to Aubé and waved for him to enter. "I've just sent Damiot over to start moving our prisoners into La Force. Told him you and Fouché would take charge."

"Was on my way there now."

"As usual, I prefer not to show myself, but I want to personally question Goron and make that Twilight Owl sing. Last night was a great success for the Brigade. We showed all the Préfectures of France that we could catch Le Diable. After they had failed."

"The King should give you a medal."

"Not a chance. Two of his friends were involved with the Midnight Club. On the board of directors. Louis doesn't like his favorites caught, their follies exposed. That's why I had them imprisoned anonymously. By the time their names are known, it will be too late for them to be rescued. Even by the King!"

Goury laughed. "I realized last night what you were doing."

"They won't, any of them, be able to escape from justice. Or from the scandal. Have you heard from Ronquetti this morning?"

"He's in his office."

"At this hour!"

"Making out his report, like the rest of us."

Vidocq chuckled. "It was quite a night. Have someone bring Goron over to see me later."

"I'll tend to it."

As Goury left Vidocq saw Revol crossing the anteroom. "Come in, my young friend!"

Revol approached, smiling. "You see before you a happy man!"

"Indeed?" He motioned toward an armchair.

"Last night after dinner I hired a fiacre, and we—Mademoiselle Belinda and I—drove out through the Bois." He sank onto the chair. "There was a moon . . ."

"There was, indeed!"

" . . . and the lady agreed to become my wife."

"Congratulations!"

"Her father gave us his blessing this morning at breakfast. I'll be leaving next month, with the Penny-packaires, for the United States of America!"

"America . . ." Vidocq sighed. "I wish you every success."

"Monsieur Penny-packaire told me he came to Paris this year hoping to find himself a new wife, but instead Belinda's returning home with a husband. We're to be married in Paris, but there will be a more elaborate ceremony in the cathedral of New Orléans. Monsieur Penny-packaire is also very happy today. He received some good news of his own. Asked me to tell you he would see you, here at the Sûreté later today."

Vidocq smiled, knowing what that meant. "Everyone's having good news! What happened to that goldsmith you were bringing to look through those sketches?"

"He's studying them now."

"Splendid! You see those two bags on that table?"

"Yes . . ."

"They contain the jewels, as well as jewelry, which Drumont removed from Tessier's vault. Take them and let this goldsmith . . . What's his name?"

"Pierre Thanot."

"Have him match each piece of jewelry with its design."

"Right away." He rose and went to get the velvet bags. "I'm very grateful, Monsieur. Your many kindnesses . . ."

"What have I done?"

Revol hesitated in the doorway, a bag swinging from each hand. "Without your help, Monsieur, I would never have been able to marry Belinda! You've made my fortune. I'm going to America!"

"Meanwhile, let me know what Thanot discovers . . ."

"Yes, Chief."

As Revol left with the velvet bags, Vidocq picked up a quill and resumed work on his own report. Keeping it brief, each word precise. Continuing to glance at the activity in Aubé's office as more reports were turned in. Aware of their two quills scratching, his and Aubé's, in the brief periods when they were alone.

Fouché's deep voice made him look up. "Charles. I have a job for you." Setting his quill aside as Fouché joined him. "I went back to the Midnight Club this morning . . ."

"Did you expect to catch Goron there last night?" Fouché asked, towering above Vidocq's desk.

"Matter of fact, I did. I'd seen him the previous evening when I paid a more casual visit. This morning I discovered a secret hiding place in Drumont's suite, which we overlooked last night. Had a feeling there must be one. It's a wooden wall panel in the salon. I suspect it's more visible by daylight. There's a slightly different color of wood, and I left a chair in front of the panel. I want you to open it and remove the contents."

"What's there?"

"Rows of louis d'or and packages of what appears to be raw opium."

"The twin desires of man! Happy dreams and golden coins!"

"I didn't count the coins or touch the opium. Take one of our men with you in a carriage and bring everything here."

"Yes, Chief." He turned, eager to carry out his instructions.

"Store it in our vault after Aubé has counted the coins and signed for them. Then you can join Goury at the Conciergerie!" he called after him. Smiling as he watched him hurry through Aubé's office, wondering how many coins he would take. He waved as Ronquetti appeared from the corridor, passing Fouché but pausing to drop a sheet of paper on Aubé's desk before continuing through the antechamber.

"Monsieur le Duc! Was that your morning report?"

"Unfortunately I had very little to report. Which, of course, always takes much longer." Ronquetti collapsed into an armchair, hat tilting back from his forehead. "I could only say I was dining with the American gentleman, Monsieur Penny-packaire, when I heard a shot. Followed by several blasts on a whistle, which I suspected came from the Chief himself. I recognized your silver tone."

Vidocq chuckled.

"Our table was engulfed by a stampede of waiters. Fleeing in every direction! Pursued by fellow members from the Sûreté in various disguises. The dinner guests for the most part remained seated, but there were a few gentlemen who were swept up into the panic. I suspected they too might be involved in what was taking place, so I pointed them out to young Allard, whom I had recognized in spite of his false mustache."

"How was the food last night at the Midnight Club?"

"The soup was too thick. That's as far as we'd gone when we heard the shot. No food served after that. Monsieur Penny-packaire, of course, realized—from my reactions—that I'm working with you."

"That doesn't matter anymore."

"I told him you'd assigned me to observe him and his daughter because of the disappearance of that diamond bracelet. For their protection. He was delighted to learn I'm with the Sûreté. However, he still thinks I'm a real duke, and I didn't disillusion him. We finished dinner at the Régence and, from there, walked over to the Palais-Royal for cards."

"How much did the American lose?"

"We both won! Monsieur Penny-packaire learned to gamble as a youth in the bordellos of New Orléans. Even taught me a few tricks! He was in a happy mood all evening. Although disturbed by your raid on the Midnight Club."

"Was he?"

"Seems he has in the past made many contacts there. Business deals. Buying merchandise for his American emporium . . ."

"I'm sure he has!" He saw Aubé hurrying toward him with a sheaf of papers. "Have you finished the first copy?"

"Except for your personal report."

"I have that here." He handed it across the desk as he took the papers from Aubé. "When you make a copy of that I'll deliver it to the Minister."

Aubé peered at Vidocq's writing. "In ten minutes." He turned, still reading, and hurried back to his desk.

Ronquetti got to his feet. "You have much to do, and I've not had breakfast. By the way, I wasn't able to learn anything about Baron de Chabrillat. He seems to have disappeared from the boulevards in the past year."

"So I've learned."

"There are rumors about his health. One gentleman thought he had died."

"Not yet. But soon, I suspect."

"Will you require my services later?"

"Don't think so . . ."

"Perhaps I'll see you tonight." Tapping his hat onto his head more securely as he departed. "On the boulevards . . ."

Vidocq began to read Aubé's summary of all the reports on last night's events. The raid on the Midnight Club, Monsieur de Plessis's suicide, the capture and death of Le Diable Noir. Everything brief and clear, nothing omitted, his assistants' reports condensed and every member of the Brigade who had been involved was listed at the end.

He set the sheaf of papers aside. The copy of his own report would be placed on top of the others and Aubé would put them in an official folder for him to present to the Minister.

Today when he faced the Minister, he would pay off many old debts and insults . . .

"Monsieur! I've found something!"

He looked up to see Revol with Thanot, whose face he recalled from the morning he met Tessier's staff for the first time. "Come in!"

Revol led the frail old man into Vidocq's office.

He saw diamonds glittering in Revol's hand, and Thanot was carrying several sketches. "What have you discovered?" Bowing to the old man. "I wish to thank you for coming here this morning."

But it was the excited younger man who answered. "We've found the Penny-packaire bracelet!"

"What?"

Revol held up the bracelet as he took the drawings from Thanot. "You can see! Here's my design." He spread four sketches on the desk and arranged the bracelet on top of one.

They were identical.

"But what was Belinda's bracelet doing in that bag?" Revol asked. "With those other pieces of jewelry and all those loose gems?"

"I hope Monsieur Thanot can tell us that." Vidocq saw that the old man appeared to be startled. "There are only two letters—RE—at the end of this line of letters and numerals under the sketch of the bracelet." Looking up at the old man again. "I learned from Monsieur Ponsard that RE means returned and DE destroyed. This bracelet was returned but had not been destroyed. Why?"

"That is my fault, Monsieur." The thin voice quavered. "Tessier ordered me to destroy it, but I hadn't gotten around to doing it. The letters DE mean that an item of jewelry has been taken apart. The jewels are always saved to be used again, but the gold is melted down."

Vidocq remembered Coralie saying there was nothing wrong with the jewelry Tessier had given her to wear. They had been returned but not yet destroyed! He glanced at the other sketches. "This cross ordered by Baron de Chabrillat for a whore—Clochette—is also marked RE and DE. Like Maya's necklace. This other sketch . . . Do you have any idea how they were returned to Tessier? By whom?"

"No, Monsieur . . ."

"Was it Alcidor Drumont?"

"I—I couldn't say . . ."

"Clochette and Maya gave them back to Tessier in exchange for a copy."

"That's right."

"Someone had to be the go-between! Who?"

"I never knew who it was. Tessier explained why the jewelry was returned one evening when he invited me to have a bottle of wine with him. I'd been wondering about the returned pieces for years, as well as the copies. You see we made a copy of every design that was sold. False jewels in settings of imitation gold. Exact replicas of the original pieces. He said that some rich men who bought expensive jewelry for their wives wanted duplicates for them to wear in public places where they might be robbed. They, of course, kept the original pieces. The *courtisanes,* on the other hand, returned every piece of jewelry in exchange for a copy, which they wore. And the gentlemen who gave them the original never suspected it had been given back to Tessier."

"So! The gems were sold over and over? Only the settings were destroyed."

"Some of the diamonds were sold dozens of times!"

Vidocq looked at the fourth design. "This necklace . . . There's no RE or DE at the bottom. So it was never returned or destroyed."

Thanot looked closer, squinting and frowning. "You are right, Monsieur. That necklace was not returned."

"Do you know the name of the fortunate lady who received it from Baron de Chabrillat?"

"No, Monsieur. Tessier never told me."

"And it was never returned . . ." Something stirred in Vidocq's mind. "I believe I know who received that neckalce. *Mon Dieu!* Her life may be in danger . . ."

"I've finished the report for the Minister."

Vidocq turned to see Aubé with a black folder in his hand. "Good! I'll take it to him."

Aubé passed the folder across the desk.

Vidocq opened it and inspected the copy of his own brief report attached to the summary of last night's events. More than a dozen pages. "You've done a fast job, my friend. Make the usual copies. I'll sign them later." He reached for a quill, dipped it into the inkwell as he talked, scrawling his name—larger than customary—across the bottom of his own report, as Aubé returned to his office and Revol picked up the bracelet and gathered the sketches together. "Put that bracelet in your pocket, my friend."

Revol looked startled. "Monsieur?"

"My wedding present for your bride! Tell Mademoiselle Belinda we managed to find it just in time. But don't ever explain how."

"I'm very grateful."

Vidocq rose from his desk. "Now I must see the Minister!" He thrust the black folder under his arm and headed for the corridor, past Aubé's desk. "Today I shall do all the talking so my meeting with Monsieur le Ministre will be brief."

CHAPTER 57

"Monsieur Vidocq!" The grim-faced assistant looked up from a note he was writing as Vidocq strode past him toward the inner office. "I was just penning a message to you. Monsieur le Ministre wanted to see you again."

"More important, I want to see Monsieur le Ministre!"

"But, Monsieur . . ."

He knocked sharply on the heavy door.

"Monsieur le Ministre sometimes takes a nap at this hour . . ."

"Does he? I shall rouse him." He flung the door open and burst in, aware that the Minister was blinking his eyes as he straightened his angular figure behind the desk. "Sorry to wake you, Monsieur!" Slamming the door and striding toward him.

"I—I seem to have dozed . . . It's this wretched heat." Selecting a letter from the pile of opened mail. "You received my message? This communication concerning you arrived by hand . . ."

"No, Monsieur, I did not receive your message. Your assistant told me he was writing it, as I came in."

"Did he? Well, I . . ."

"I'm here to personally give you a brief report of last night's surprising events."

"Last night?" The Minister looked startled. "What events? What're you talking about?"

"I want you to know the true facts. Before you receive false information and rumors from your spies downstairs in the Préfecture."

"What happened last night?"

"I tracked Le Diable Noir to Paris . . ."

"Le Diable? In Paris!"

" . . . trapped him in a warehouse near the central markets."

"Mon Dieu! I've had no word of this . . ."

"When I confronted him, he fired a shot at close range, but his aim was faulty. I fired once in return and killed him."

"But he should've been imprisoned! Tried for his crimes and sent to the guillotine!"

"I saved the government the cost of his trial."

"Ah yes! Perhaps, after all, it's for the best. How did you manage to trace Le Diable to Paris? None of the provincial police were able to find him."

"That's in my report. You can read it later."

"Who was Le Diable? Did you find out?"

"I killed him before I could learn his identity."

"Perhaps we can question members of his band. If we ever find them."

"I caught several of them last night in a warehouse filled with loot they've taken from those châteaux."

"You will interrogate them?"

"As a matter of routine, but I doubt that any of them will know who he was. The important thing I did learn, from Le Diable himself, is that everything they took was brought to Paris and delivered to this same warehouse—which, I suspect, was owned by the Midnight Club."

The Minister straightened, his silver hair seemed to rise like the crest of some exotic bird. "What did you say?"

"Monsieur de Plessis—it seems—was a member of a secret group that called itself The Five."

"Secret group? I can't believe this!"

"They composed the board that ran the Midnight Club."

"What?"

"Your friend, de Plessis, was their chairman. Were you ever a member of the Midnight Club, Monsieur?"

"Certainly not! I was invited to join, several times, but never accepted."

"Never went there?"

The veinous nose appeared to redden even more. "I have of course dined there." His voice quavered. "Always as a guest of some member . . ."

"I will want a list of their names."

"If I can recall them . . ."

"The Midnight Club, guided by The Five, has been in collusion with several prominent businessmen, as well as some of *les grandes courtisanes,* in a scheme to swindle many of our wealthiest citizens!"

"Impossible! Not de Plessis . . . He would never be involved with— *courtisanes!* His family is one of distinction. I knew his father . . ."

"My men and I raided the Midnight Club last night."

"By whose order?"

"I obtained all the necessary legal documents yesterday afternoon. This was an exclusive operation of the Brigade de la Sûreté. The Préfecture was not involved."

"Why wasn't I informed?"

Vidocq disregarded this question. "Some of the club members who were dining there last night are being held in Saint-Pelagre. All known criminals—I recognized several among the restaurant staff—are in La Force. The Five apparently hired them for their own private purposes. Including the notorious Goron!"

"You caught Goron?" The Minister whispered the evil name.

"He will, I suspect, go straight to the guillotine after his trial."

"What about de Plessis? You aren't holding him . . ."

"Four members of The Five are, at this moment, being escorted to La Force. The fifth, their leader—de Plessis—put a bullet into his own head." Vidocq saw that the erect figure appeared to be sinking into the massive armchair. He held out his report in its official black folder and let it drop onto the desk. "You will find everything explained in my official report."

"I am shocked, Monsieur. Terribly shocked . . ."

"I believe Monsieur de Plessis and his fellow members of The Five were instigators of theft and murder. I suspect they were also involved with the Parisian underworld."

The Minister shuddered.

"They apparently controlled some of the most famous jewelers, art dealers, and bankers. Arranged apartments for *les grandes courtisanes*. Furnished with priceless antiques and paintings they obtained from Le Diable Noir. Ordered them to persuade their admirers to pay for everything. Expensive jewelry from famous jewelers, which they returned in exchange for a cheap duplicate. The buildings in which they live are probably owned by the Midnight Club. So they—The Five—were involved in prostitution, pandering, and robbery. As well as murder."

"Murder! I was never a member of the Midnight Club . . ."

"So you said, Monsieur."

"And I barely knew de Plessis! You do believe me?"

"Of course, Monsieur le Ministre. You would never associate with such a group of villains."

"Please, my friend! Sit down for a moment . . ." The long fingers fluttered toward an armchair. "We should discuss this further."

"I must return to my office. Much remains to be done. You say there's a letter that concerns me?"

"Letter? Ah, yes!" He reached for it again. "This arrived, from the Marquis de Luynes . . ."

"The Marquis?" He saw that the Minister's hand, holding the note, was trembling.

"I had no idea that you were his friend."

"I performed a slight service for Monsieur le Marquis last week . . ."

"So he writes." Glancing at the note. "He pays you many compliments for the ease with which you solved a certain 'unpleasant incident.' Which, by the way, he fails to elaborate or explain. He writes that you handled this matter, which concerned a member of his family, with 'intelligence and discretion' . . ."

"The matter is closed, Monsieur le Ministre. It was of such delicacy that I did not make a report and have placed no record of the incident in the files of the Sûreté. There was no crime involved. I, frequently, receive personal requests for help from residents of the Faubourg Saint-Germain."

The Minister seemed to be regaining his poise. "As Chief of the Sûreté, Monsieur, you have become one of the most important men in Paris. Which, of course, means of all France! Your power extends into every corner of our city. You know everybody! From the lowest to the highest!"

"I certainly know many of the lowest."

"Your friends in the Faubourg Saint-Germain are, I suppose, the single most influential group in this nation. They have access to the King and to every top official in our government. I envy you!"

"Envy me, Monsieur?"

"Your position as Chief of the Brigade de la Sûreté Nationale has become, I suspect, impregnable."

"My goal remains simple and unchanged. It has always been to protect the good citizens of Paris from the evil citizens—the criminals. Nothing more. That is my job. Good day, Monsieur le Ministre!" Vidocq bowed and, smiling now, strode to the door. Flung it open but neglected to close it as he departed.

The Minister's assistant looked up, scowling, from the documents he was sorting on his desk.

Vidocq did a little dance step as he passed, aware that the assistant was hurrying to close the Minister's door again.

CHAPTER 58

Vidocq realized, as he signed the stack of finished reports, that he was perspiring, the white quill had become slippery between his fingers.

He was conscious of people passing in and out of Aubé's office but had warned him, as he returned from his visit to the Minister, that he would see no one.

For the moment he could waste no time on Alcidor Drumont's death. He'd assigned a man to ferret out the details of Drumont's past. That might turn up something important.

He must work out a plan for Ève's protection. She was apparently the only *grande courtisane* who had received expensive jewelry from Baron de Chabrillat and hadn't returned it to Tessier. Her life was certainly in danger.

He must prevent anything happening to Ève.

Three people involved with Baron de Chabrillat had been murdered. Clochette, Maya, and Tessier. The Baron, slowly dying in his desolate mansion, was thus far the only link connecting them.

The windows behind him were open, but the heat in his office became even more intolerable as the sun moved across the city.

He wondered if his mother was planning that picnic for Fleuride tomorrow. Would Jeanne-Victoire feel well enough to accompany them? He could carry her down to the carriage in his arms . . .

"Excuse me, Chief . . ."

"I'm just signing the last of these." He finished writing his name and closed the final cover. Rested his quill on the silver rack before handing the stack of reports to Aubé. "There you are, my friend."

"Wasn't trying to hurry you. There's a visitor I thought you'd wish to see."

"Oh?" He glanced past Aubé through the open doors and saw a tall figure waiting in the outer office. "Monsieur Zeb! Welcome!" Rising, as Aubé carried the pile of reports back to his desk. "My spies tell me you've had good news."

"Your spies are everywhere!"

"Only the more important places." He held out his hand.

"Like the Hôtel Belvedere?" Laughing as he shook Vidocq's hand across the desk.

"The Duc de Modena tells me you discovered last night that he works with me." Motioning toward an armchair.

"It was unavoidable in the confusion not to notice that the Duc was a friend of what was obviously a group of policemen in disguise who were raiding the premises like a New Orleans brothel." Resting his hat and cane on the desk as he sank into the chair. "It was a fascinating evening."

Vidocq resumed his seat at the desk. "I observed you dining, from a table across the room."

"The Duc told me later that you were the gentleman with the elegant blond beard and mustaches, but I didn't recognize you. Only glimpsed you during the confusion, after you'd removed your disguise."

"Your news from the country, I hear, was satisfactory."

"Thank God! The Marquis de Lafayette has agreed to make an extensive tour of our major cities. Making speeches of course at every stop."

"So your visit to France is a success!"

"A complete success for the mission I performed for our President.

Not so successful, unfortunately, in terms of my own personal business, and as yet I've found no charming French lady to become my wife. I've met several delightful creatures, but they all appear to be happily wed."

"French wives are not always quite so happy as they seem. They are consummate actresses—in public—but you can discover the truth from the way their eyes wander at the dinner table."

"I wouldn't dare risk a duel with a jealous husband. However, my dear daughter will be returning home with a handsome husband. Thanks in part to you, she tells me. I'm very grateful, Monsieur. In fact, you've provided me not only with a new son but an authentic jewel expert from Paris who will create the most elegant designs exclusively for me. He is, as you assure me, a fine young man! Penniless, of course, but I will soon change that. A member of an old and honorable provincial family. Which is more important than money! These are the only successful endeavors of this summer's visit to France. Persuading Lafayette to visit America and Belinda finding a husband. My business affairs are less promising."

"Indeed?"

"Since the opening of the Midnight Club five years ago, I've made many important deals through its members over dinner. Louis de Plessis was influential in my meeting these gentlemen. New ones every year! This morning I heard rumors that Louis is a suicide, the other directors of the club are behind bars, and the Midnight Club closed."

"All quite true." He studied the American's face as he explained. "The club was controlled by a secret board known as The Five. Composed of de Plessis and four others. They appear to have been involved with every sort of crime. From plundering the castles of the Loire Valley to murder."

"Murder? This is indeed shocking!"

"They obtained rare antiques and paintings, stolen by Le Diable Noir and his murderous band, which they sold through some of the finest and most respectable dealers in Paris."

"I may have bought some of those treasures! Shipped them to the States. But I swear to you, before God, I never knew they were stolen. Every item had a document guaranteeing its authenticity."

"I'm sure they were authentic, Monsieur. Yet, unfortunately, they had been stolen."

"Dozens of other American and British merchants come to Paris on similar purchasing expeditions. None of us had any notion that we were buying contraband. Everything passed through customs inspections before being placed aboard our merchant ships. Their bills of sale were never questioned."

"The customs officials had no suspicion they were stolen."

"Will your government want everything returned? Speaking for myself, it's all been sold and scattered throughout the United States."

"The French government would never attempt to get any of those items back. That would be an impossible task. Fortunately, there's a warehouse filled with treasures stolen by Le Diable that will be returned to the châteaux where they belong."

"This is obviously going to cause a scandal."

"Only for those persons who controlled the Midnight Club. They will be tried and sentenced. The four surviving members of The Five and the criminals they employed. You told me the other day you were not a member."

"I don't know of any American who ever became a member. We were invited there for dinner by members—given a guest card—and introduced to other members. That's how deals were made."

"I believe you, Monsieur, and I promise your name and the name of those other American and British gentlemen will not be involved. The French government would not wish to embarrass respectable businessmen who bought stolen property."

"I am relieved . . ."

"Furthermore, I will see that all records of foreign buyers will never be found. I shall personally destroy them, to prevent an international scandal. Only a Parisian scandal! In Paris we enjoy our scandals. They make life more amusing." He glimpsed Revol coming through the antechamber. "Here's your future son-in-law!"

Pennypacker looked around and sprang to his feet. "Lucien! My dear boy . . ." Placing a paternal arm around Revol's shoulder. "I had no idea you were here."

"Been checking through Tessier's designs for Monsieur Vidocq."

"And what have you learned?" Vidocq asked.

"Monsieur Thanot has written a name under each sketch when he knew who had received them as gifts."

"Did he find any other jewelry that was sold to Baron de Chabrillat?"

"Nothing."

"Thank Monsieur Thanot for me."

"Will you need me again today?"

"Not today or any other day, my friend!"

Revol looked surprised. "But, Sir . . ."

"I would suggest you guide your future father-in-law to find new sources of merchandise for the United States. Your knowledge of Paris should be invaluable."

"Of course! My pleasure . . ."

"What a splendid idea!" Pennypacker exclaimed.

"I've something to show you, sir." Revol pulled the bracelet from his pocket, diamonds glittering.

"Belinda's bracelet!" Snatching it from his hand. "Where did you get this?"

"Monsieur Vidocq found it."

"Where?"

"I can only tell you this much," Vidocq responded. "The bracelet, I believe, was stolen from Mademoiselle Belinda in your hotel or on the street by a professional. I gave it to Revol as a wedding present for your daughter."

"She will be very pleased." Returning the bracelet to Revol. "Why don't we take Belinda somewhere for lunch to celebrate the return of her bracelet?"

"And I will present it to her!" Revol slipped the bracelet back into his pocket.

Vidocq got to his feet. "Tell Aubé to send Monsieur Thanot home in one of our carriages."

"Yes, Chief."

"Thanks again, Monsieur." Pennypacker shook Vidocq's hand vigorously, then snatched up his hat and cane. "Come along, my boy! I have a fiacre waiting."

As Vidocq sank into his leather armchair, his thoughts at once returned to Ève.

Her life was in danger! She had refused to return that necklace to Tessier, and those diamonds were genuine . . .

He must, this afternoon, plan how to save her. Find the man who had shot Clochette, Maya, and probably Tessier. It had to be one man. One pistol . . .

If he could discover the identity of that nun who had been seen before Clochette and Maya died! She might lead him to the killer before he showed up at Ève's apartment . . .

"Chief?"

He looked up to see Aubé again.

"I've counted those louis d'or Fouché brought from the Midnight Club."

"How many?"

"Exactly four hundred."

Vidocq smiled. Fouché had also taken one coin from each pile! "Have them locked in the vault with a label saying they were found in Drumont's suite at the Midnight Club."

"You wanted to question Goron . . ."

"Is he here?"

"Three guards are holding him in the downstairs lobby."

"I'll question him in the interrogation room." Rising from his desk. "You'd better come along and take down what he says . . ."

CHAPTER 59

The interrogation room was dark except for a lantern hanging from the ceiling near the door, casting a pool of light on the chair at the end of the long table.

Vidocq stood at the other end, beyond the light, facing the closed door.

The airless room held a familiar sour smell of fear and guilt, left behind by thousands of criminals who had been questioned here.

As the knob turned, he faced the wall so that his face would not be revealed by the light from the anteroom.

Footsteps of three men entering.

"Sit down."

He recognized the voice of a guard and heard the prisoner's leg chains as he collapsed onto the wooden chair.

"Why'd you bring me here? I've told you everything I know!"

The guard didn't respond.

Vidocq heard the guards departing.

"You're leavin' me in this hole?"

The door closed, and a key turned in the lock.

He faced the table and slowly moved closer to it.

Goron was seated at the far end, in the light from the lantern, looking over his shoulder toward the closed door. He hadn't been given a prison uniform yet, and his black waiter's jacket looked rumpled. Goron turned, head twisting birdlike on his scrawny neck, to squint into the darkness, but his eyes hadn't yet adjusted, and he was unable to see anything. Then, surprisingly, he began to pound on the table with his fists without making a sound. The Twilight Owl was caged and frightened.

Vidocq whispered one word. "Crépuscule . . ."

Goron blinked his eyes, uncertain that he had heard his name.

"Crépuscule—the Twilight Owl . . ."

He knew now that someone was here and leaned forward trying to see.

"The gray owl who is never seen in daylight. We meet again."

"Vidocq!"

"You disappeared, and none of your cronies knew what had become of you." He felt the edge of the table press against his thighs. "And all this time you've been working at the Midnight Club!"

"It was an honest job."

"You've never had an honest job in your life! Certainly not working for The Five."

"Don't know what you're talkin' 'bout . . ."

"The Five are now only The Four. Monsieur de Plessis put a bullet into his throat when he realized the game was finished."

"So it's true! I heard rumors last night, as they put us in our cells, but I didn't believe it."

"Your leader's dead, and his accomplices are in La Force. They will talk, all four of them, in the hope of saving their own precious necks! I would suggest you do the same."

"I don't know nothin' . . ."

He studied Goron's face briefly, the sharp beak of a nose that had very likely been the original reason for his being called the Twilight Owl. Or had it been the sparse gray hair, like feathers, that partially covered his skull? His face was gaunt and the hands, resting on the table, were gray-fleshed with nails like talons. They were the sensitive fingers of a master burglar and pickpocket.

Goron seemed to sense that his hands were being inspected, because he withdrew them from the table and dropped them out of sight.

Vidocq raised his voice abruptly as he asked his first question. "Was it you who strangled that old man—Marpon?"

"I didn't touch him!"

"Killed him in his attic room on rue Taitbout . . ."

"Drumont did that!" His voice became shrill. "Told me so himself. Doesn't matter, me tellin' you, now Drumont's dead. He went back to the house on rue Taitbout alone. I had nothin' t' do with it!"

"Why would Drumont kill the old man?"

"He had guessed too much. Threatened to tell the police what he suspected."

"Then it was you who killed Drumont!"

"No!"

"As he lay in an opium stupor in that other attic room on rue de la Lune . . ."

The hooded eyes became crafty. "Nobody'll ever be able t' prove I did. That wasn't my knife in his throat."

"How do you know it was a knife? Only the murderer would know that."

Goron's face revealed his guilt.

"You took those bags of diamonds and jewelry from the attic in rue de la Lune to your boss—de Plessis—at the Midnight Club. After you stabbed Drumont. Along with the ingots of gold and silver. So you had somebody helping you. And they will talk."

"I don't know nothin' 'bout no diamonds . . ."

"We found them last night, hidden in Monsieur de Plessis's office. Everything Drumont removed from rue Taitbout. The Five had a habit of taking jewels back, even after Tessier sold them to a customer. Tessier was a part of that arrangement. Sold his jewels again and again!"

Goron's eyes reacted to this, narrowing and blinking.

"Did you know Drumont had a hiding place in his suite at the Midnight Club where he kept a hoard of raw opium as well as a cache of louis d'or?"

"What?" His eyes widened in surprise.

"You must've searched that suite many times without finding it."

"I never set foot in there!"

"Was it you—in your youth, the cleverest pickpocket in Paris—who took that diamond bracelet from Mademoiselle Penny-packaire's arm when she was walking on the boulevards with her father?"

"I never heard of these people!"

"Or was it while she was with young Revol in the gardens of the Palais-Royal?"

"I didn' touch her bracelet!"

"But you know who did. Better start talking, or the Widow will see that you never talk again."

Goron's eyes darted from side to side. "That bracelet was taken from the American girl at her hotel. Removed from her dressing table while she slept. Next morning she never noticed it was gone . . ."

"And by that time it was back in Tessier's vault."

"I was never told what became of the jewelry . . . Suppose I tell you what I do know? Will you go easy? See I get a short sentence . . ."

"That might be arranged. I'm sure you've heard that I'm sometimes lenient if a man agrees to talk. The truth could save your neck, if you're wise. Or you'll pay your first and last visit to the Widow."

"What d'you want me t' tell you?"

"If you didn't take Mademoiselle Penny-packaire's bracelet, who did?"

"It was a valet at the Hôtel Belvedere."

"A valet?"

"Placed there by The Five! They had at least one man—or woman—in every first-class hotel. Where the rich foreigners stay."

"And I suppose you instructed each of these persons in the fine art of thievery. That was part of your job, wasn't it?"

Goron shrugged, accepting the accusation as flattery.

"You taught them your skills. Robbing without detection."

"Most times the victims thought they'd lost or misplaced their jewelry. Of course, many of them couldn't report their loss to the police. That English milady last year didn't discover her diamond necklace was gone until after her husband arrived from London. Since it had been bought for her by a lover, she couldn't say anything to the husband. And that German prince who lost those diamond bracelets didn't want his Embassy to find out he'd had them made for himself!" He peered at Vidocq down the length of the table. "You're goin' t' help me, aren't you? See I don't get a long sentence?"

370

"You'll have to tell me much more than this." He rapped on the oak table sharply with his knuckles.

Goron straightened, startled by this unexpected sound. "I still say I never killed nobody! And you can't prove I did."

The door swung open, silhouetting Goron's seated figure against the light as the guards hurried into the dark room.

"Take him to his cell," Vidocq ordered. "I'll talk to him again tomorrow."

"Yes, Chief."

They seized Goron's arms and lifted him from the chair.

"You want a short sentence?" Vidocq snarled. "Unless you tell me everything you know, I'm sending you to the Widow!"

"I'm innocent!" Goron screeched, as they pushed him toward the open door. The shrill cry was that of a doomed bird caught by a hawk.

Vidocq followed slowly, along the edge of the long table.

"You didn't learn nothin' from me! You got no witness t' what I said. I'll deny everything!"

The guards pulled him out of the interrogation room into the light and closed the door.

Vidocq paused beside the hidden opening in the wall. "You have all that, my friend?"

"Every word," Aubé responded, on the other side of the wall.

"Let's go back upstairs . . ."

CHAPTER 60

Vidocq sank into the armchair at his desk and considered what he'd learned from Goron.

The Twilight Owl had certainly killed Drumont, who had strangled Marpon, and a valet at the Hôtel Belvedere had stolen that diamond bracelet from Mademoiselle Belinda. Crépuscule obviously was involved in the theft of many pieces of jewelry . . .

He would question him more carefully tomorrow about the operation of the Midnight Club and get the names of every criminal on their staff . . .

"Will you want some lunch?"

He looked up to face Aubé across his desk. "That might be a good idea. I'll be here all afternoon. I'm going over everything we have on those three murders—Clochette, Tessier, and Maya. Has anything more come from the Préfecture on Clochette's murder?"

"Nothing. They've closed the case."

"And you can close one of those doors so I won't be too visible. I don't wish to see anyone this afternoon." His eyes darted across his desk, over fresh piles of reports and dossiers waiting to be read. Noticed for the first time three yellow rosebuds Madame Babelay had left in the small vase this morning.

Ève was the only one to receive a necklace of diamonds from Baron de Chabrillat who was still alive! Had refused to return her jewels.

Clochette and Maya had returned theirs for worthless copies, and they had been murdered.

Was Tessier killed by the same person? Or was his death a coincidence? Why didn't the killer strip those diamond rings from his fingers? And why had the false diamonds been taken from Clochette and Maya? Because the murderer thought they were genuine. He wouldn't have sent that nun to a fence if he'd known the diamonds were false . . .

That woman disguised as a nun must be the murderer's wife or, more likely, his mistress. If he could locate her, she would lead him to the murderer.

Ève! His thoughts kept returning to her. She was most certainly in mortal danger. But from whom?

He reached for the two piles of drawings young Daumier had made in Maya's apartment and the mansion on rue Taitbout. Pulled out the sketches of Tessier and Maya with the twin black holes in their foreheads.

That could happen to Ève next!

Ève was his favorite of all *les grandes courtisanes!* Of course there would be many beautiful young women hoping to take her place. New ones each year! Except no other woman could ever replace Ève. The thought of anyone killing her angered him. He had to prevent that!

His thoughts were interrupted by Madame Babelay with his lunch.

"I've brought you cold ham and fresh bread I baked this morning.

As well as potato salad with anchovies." Resting the tray in front of him. "The wine's from that bottle you didn't finish. Will you want coffee later?" She was heading for the door.

"Just the wine." Unfolding his napkin.

He ate everything and drank all the wine, then pushed the tray aside and resumed his examination of the two sketches. Maya and Tessier . . .

Sat there a for a long time, unaware of the clock on the mantel striking the hour or the chiming of distant church bells. Barely aware of Aubé sticking his head in to announce he was going upstairs for lunch and, fifteen minutes later, reporting that he was back.

It was the middle of the afternoon when he sensed an intruder's presence and looked up to see the Nun's tiny figure poised in the doorway. "Did you learn anything?"

"I think so . . ." She glided toward him and sank into an armchair. "I went to two of the better known costumers before I tried that hag on rue Neuve Saint-Marc."

"Madame Nourisson? I know the witch."

"She told me right away she'd sold a nun's habit to a woman several months ago."

"What sort of woman?"

"Thin. In her sixties, perhaps older. White hair . . ."

"That couldn't be the woman who was seen before those two murders!"

"She told the hag it was for a young niece in the provinces, who hoped to become a nun."

"Did she ask for the habit of a particular order?"

"No, she didn't. That's what made the hag suspicious. She sold her a black habit and veil with a white wimple."

"It's our nun! Did this old woman seem to be educated?"

"She looked like somebody's servant."

"Buying the nun's habit for a young woman who, I would guess, is the killer's mistress. She watches the residence where a murder is being planned. Discovers which hours he can enter with the least likelihood of being observed. At least we know now for a fact that there is a nun, and she isn't genuine! And the false nun who came to Clochette's door and the other one who watched Maya's windows were the same person. You've done a good job."

"Will you need me later?" The Nun rose from her chair.

373

"Take the rest of the day for yourself." He watched her leave as he settled down to consider what she had reported.

A young woman disguised as a nun had been seen before Clochette and Maya were murdered. Surveying the scene before the arrival of the killer?

Ève could be the next victim.

He wondered if the false nun would be lurking on rue de la Chaussée-d'Antin at this moment, observing the building and watching Ève's windows ...

Tessier had been killed around noon, but the two courtesans were shot in the evening. Clochette sometime between eight and nine. Maya between seven and nine ...

So the killer entered their apartments between seven and ten.

Most likely around eight when daylight would be fading. The hour when all *les grandes courtisanes* would be relaxing after their baths. Drying their plump bodies or stretched out on a chaise. Resting before they sat at their dressing tables to prepare their faces for the night ahead.

Ève, at that hour this evening, would also be alone ...

"Aubé!" he shouted.

"Yes, Chief?"

"Come in here. Quickly!" He heard Aubé's footsteps, moving faster than usual, crossing the antechamber. "I have a plan to catch that murderer!"

"Which murderer?"

"Madame Ève's murderer!"

Aubé stood in front of him, eyes wide. "Madame Ève? Has she been ..."

"Before she's murdered. I'm going to set a trap when the murderer shows up at her apartment. The same killer who shot Clochette and Maya ..." Leaning forward as he explained. "I shall be waiting there myself! Guarding the beautiful Ève! Tell Goury I want to see him at five o'clock."

"Yes, Chief."

"Along with Fouché and young Cauler. Also La Belle Violette! I want all of them here. Promptly at five!"

CHAPTER 61

The high-ceilinged apartment on rue de la Chaussée-d'Antin was silent.

Vidocq stood in the deep window embrasure nearest to the head of Ève's bed, his back turned to the pair of open windows, but he would be invisible to anyone below in the garden because of the tree branches heavy with leaves. He was leaning against the paneled wood of the embrasure, facing the partially closed inner curtains. Able to observe the bedroom through a small hole he'd cut in the heavy fabric.

The murderer couldn't see him, but he would be able to watch the intruder from the moment he—or she—entered Ève's bedroom.

He was facing the white and gold framed mirror that formed a screen beyond the foot of her bed, covering the entrance. He could see a reflection of the bed with the scaled serpent holding the golden apple between its fangs. Directly beneath was an exquisite pink-fleshed body with a mass of red-gold hair flowing over the shoulders onto the pillows. She had tossed the sheet aside and was twisting about restlessly on the bed. He had warned her not to talk. She would by now be getting bored.

The only illumination came from a candelabrum on a table at the far side of the bed, but the light was too faint to reveal his hiding place.

From time to time there was a burst of laughter and giggling from the distant kitchen. Only Madame Sidoné knew what was happening. He had warned her to see that the servants acted as usual and remained with her in the kitchen. They had not been told that he was here.

If anyone rang the doorbell, Madame Sidoné would tell them Ève was dining out this evening but would return home at eleven.

Not a sound from the garden. Cauler was on watch there, hidden in the shrubbery, and would give warning if he glimpsed a dark figure stealing through the dusk.

He suspected the murderer would appear from that back alley and enter through the greenhouse. Come up that private staircase he had always used. The killer would have to reach up and silence that bell on its wire spring above the door.

Madame Sidoné had escorted Goury and Fouché to separate rooms on either side of the boudoir, where they were waiting, also hidden in window embrasures behind the curtains.

His trap was set.

Now he could only wait. And hope for success . . .

His meeting with staff members had taken an hour, and when they finished each had known what he must do tonight.

Madame Babelay had served him a light supper, including more of her cold ham. He regretted that now, because he was getting thirsty.

His mind as he ate had been on the evening ahead, and he realized that Ève should be warned of his plan in advance but he hadn't wanted to visit her apartment before dusk in case the false nun might be watching the street.

There was only one place he might be able to find Ève away from her apartment.

He had ordered a carriage and instructed the coachman to drive to the open glade in the Bois where he had frequently seen Ève gossiping with her friends. This evening there had been two other landaus, as well as Ève's. Blond Apolline in her white landau and brown-haired Fifine in a pale tan one. Each with its uniformed coachman and footman. Ève's scarlet landau faced the others, and they were talking quietly as he drove out of the forest. Conversation stopped as they turned to inspect the intruder.

He had tapped on the overhead window with his cane and instructed the coachman to pull up beside the scarlet landau facing Ève.

She had been startled to see him. "Vidocq?"

"I must talk quickly," he explained, as his carriage came to a halt beside her, keeping his voice low. "Your life, I believe, is in grave danger tonight . . ."

"What are you saying?"

"It has something to do with the diamond necklace given to you by Baron de Chabrillat."

"So you know, do you!"

"I believe both Clochette and Maya were killed because of the Baron's gifts to them."

"But they had returned the originals to Tessier. Their diamonds were false. I was just telling Apolline and Fifine . . ."

"Their murderer, I believe, thought the diamonds were genuine. I'm certain the killer will visit you next. Perhaps tonight."

"Mon Dieu!"

"But I have a plan to protect you. Save your life . . ."

"How? What must I do?"

He lowered his voice to a whisper as he explained, so that the others were unable to hear. Finally he ordered her to return to her apartment and follow his instructions.

While his carriage was circling the open glade, he heard Ève shouting directions to her coachman.

As he headed back toward Paris through the twilight, Ève's red landau had shot ahead of him, followed by the other two *courtisanes*, laughing and squealing. He ordered his driver to pass them, and there was a wild race through the twisting lanes of the forest. His carriage moved in front of them as they left the Bois and headed for the Étoile de Chaillot barrier.

The customs officer, hearing the pounding hooves, hurried out from his office and, recognizing Vidocq, ordered the barrier raised.

His carriage passed through first, followed by the three swaying landaus. He could hear Apolline and Fifine shrieking, above the clatter of hooves, afraid their horses were out of control.

As he raced ahead of them down the broad avenue, he glanced at the crumbling stone wall in front of the Baron de Chabrillat's estate. Impossible to see the mansion beyond those trees, but he glimpsed the decaying garden through the open gates.

Was the Baron sitting inside facing those same windows?

He had returned to Number Six where he remained until darkness covered the city, when he'd taken a fiacre to Boulevard des Italiens, then followed side streets and alleys to join his associates at the gate to Ève's rear garden.

That was half an hour ago.

It must be after eight o'clock now.

He wondered where Monsieur Pennypacker was dining. One of the expensive boulevard restaurants with the Duc de Modena? Or had the American been invited to another private party where he would inspect every attractive woman, hoping to find himself a new wife?

There was a brief but distinct birdcall from the garden, above the murmur of birds settling down for the night.

Young Cauler prided himself on his ability to imitate more than a dozen birds. That had sounded like a nightingale.

Vidocq leaned closer to the inner curtain, adjusting his eye to the opening he had cut.

He squinted at the left edge of the white and gold mirror frame. The murderer should appear around that side from the anteroom. He waited impatiently, aware of the silence.

Then, very faintly, he heard an almost inaudible clink of metal.

The intruder had reached for that spring to silence the bell as he cautiously opened the door at the top of those rear steps.

He wondered if Goury or Fouché had heard it.

Certainly the beautiful woman on the bed hadn't. She was sitting up now, leaning on an elbow, studying the reflection of her breasts in the mirror. Smiling faintly, pleased with what she saw. But suddenly, as he watched, her expression changed to fear.

"Who are you? What are you doing here?"

Vidocq barely heard her questions as his eyes moved back to the edge of the mirror.

A black-robed nun was standing there, a small pistol in her hand.

Baron de Chabrillat's daughter! It was unmistakably her face.

"I was told you had red hair." The nun was moving, very slowly, toward the foot of the serpent bed. "Your servants are eating their dinner in the kitchen. They always do at this hour. They won't hear a shot from this distance . . ."

"You're not going to kill me!" She had pulled up the sheet, protectively, over her breasts.

"I've already shot three worthless people. Two whores and a stupid cheat of a jeweler . . ."

Vidocq realized that the nun's voice, barely a whisper, was hoarse with excitement. Her face was pale, but the hand holding the pistol was darker. Darkened by the sun, no doubt, while working in the convent garden.

"I want your necklace."

"What necklace?"

"The diamond necklace Baron de Chabrillat gave you. The one he ordered from Tessier . . ."

"You murdered Maya and Clochette! My friends . . ."

"For a cross and a necklace that proved to be false. They were scum! Both of them. And so are you . . ."

Vidocq was aware that the nun's voice had sharpened, but it still wouldn't be heard as far as the corridor. He pulled his pistol from the waist of his trousers. The instant she took more precise aim, he would

378

shoot her. Wound her in the arm but not kill her. He must do that with one bullet or the woman in the bed could die.

"Why are you doing this? For what reason?"

Vidocq smiled. He had told her to ask these questions, and she hadn't forgotten. Now if the nun would only answer . . .

"My father is the Baron de Chabrillat."

It *was* the Baron's daughter.

"But you're a nun. You've taken a vow of poverty. What would you want with a diamond necklace? Why did you kill those other people?"

"To avenge my father's honor. He was cheated by Tessier! Robbed by you and those other whores. Now he's dying from disease you and your filthy sisters gave him! You have blinded him, and his brain has rotted. He is penniless because of the fortune he squandered on you and your kind! He lives in the only room of our ancestral home that's furnished. I've sold all the heirlooms and paintings. One after another. To provide for him. Then last month I had an idea! I would get back the jewelry my father gave to you and those other harlots. I questioned him, but his poor mind remembers nothing. He couldn't even tell me your names. The one name he recalled was Tessier. I wrote Tessier a note, asking to see him about a matter concerning my father. Told him it must be at an hour when no one would observe my presence. I received a reply, saying to come at noon. He would watch from a window and admit me. When we talked, he scoffed at returning any of the money my father had paid him. All I was able to learn were the names of three whores to whom he had given diamonds. Tessier said only one of them still had the jewels, but he wouldn't tell me which. I didn't believe him. He laughed at me, and I shot him. I didn't take the diamond rings from his fingers because I only wanted the diamonds my father had bought."

Vidocq saw that the pistol was almost imperceptibly being raised.

"You're the one who still has my father's diamonds in your possession. I want them. Now . . ."

"But you will kill me, even if I give them to you."

"Not if you swear never to tell anyone I shot those others."

Vidocq smiled, knowing that once the nun had the diamonds she would kill again.

"Where is the necklace hidden? Get it for me."

The pistol was lifting higher, but the black-sleeved arm was not yet aiming.

"Quickly! If you don't get the necklace at once, I will be forced to kill you and search for it myself."

Vidocq could no longer see what was happening. He moved slowly toward the edge of the curtain as he listened to their voices.

"You can't find my necklace! And I shall never give it to you."

"This pistol is small. Your servants won't hear it. But it has already killed three people. And now . . ."

Vidocq swept back the curtain and aimed his pistol.

The nun sensed the movement of the heavy curtain and turned, confused, her pistol wavering.

Vidocq fired.

The nun's pistol went off as it dropped from her hand.

La Belle Violette hopped from the bed and, completely nude, dashed across the bedroom to disappear behind the mirror.

Vidocq moved toward the nun who was clutching her wounded arm. "I aimed carefully, sister, because I didn't want to kill you."

Goury and Fouché appeared from around opposite sides of the mirror, each holding a pistol.

The nun, seeing them, whipped off the black veil and starched white headdress with her left hand.

Vidocq saw that it was a young man with curly black hair.

"I am Flavian de Chabrillat!" he exclaimed proudly, pulling at the black robe and ripping it from his body, kicking its black folds out of his way.

Vidocq saw blood dripping from a wound in the youth's right forearm. He was naked to the waist, his trousers tucked into boots, medium height with powerful shoulders tanned by the sun.

"The last male de Chabrillat!" He straightened, facing Vidocq. "I attempted to avenge the honor of my family, but I have failed."

Fouché bent to retrieve the pistol from the carpet.

Vidocq thrust his own pistol into the waist of his trousers. "I suppose you got the idea for this disguise from your sister . . ."

"The fact that she's a nun gave me the idea perhaps, but she knows nothing of what I've done."

"I'm sure she doesn't." He realized that the young man's face was powdered to disguise his features and give him a nun's pallor. He had the de Chabrillat nose, and beneath the powder there was evidence that he had once been handsome, but like his father's the face was marked by debauchery. "You wanted those diamonds for yourself. Not your father."

"And you, I suspect, are Vidocq!"

"That is correct."

"At least it required the great Vidocq to catch me!" Glancing toward the bed. "Another moment, and I would have destroyed this creature who bled my father and doomed him to an early death."

"The lady in the bed was not Ève, but a substitute. She was bait in the trap I set for you. What did you plan to do with the money you'd have gotten from selling the real diamonds?"

"You're quite right. I was not going to give it to my father. That old fool!" He sneered. "I needed it for passage to America to set myself up in business there. I have failed."

"You will shortly be given the solution to all your problems. It will be brief and not without mercy. The blade is so light, you hardly hear it falling. So sharp you'll barely feel its bite."

Surprisingly, young de Chabrillat straightened and held both shoulders back. "I shall die like a hero. But no one will weep for me."

"Who was the old woman who bought this nun's costume for you?"

"You know about her, do you? The good woman looks after my father. Madame Bette has no knowledge of what I've done. I knew that as a nun I would be able to walk the streets of Paris unnoticed."

"You've been living in that empty mansion with your father . . ."

"He never suspected. I've hidden there for more than a year. What happens to me now?"

Vidocq glanced at Goury and Fouché. "See that a doctor attends his wound."

They each grasped one of de Chabrillat's arms.

He shook himself free. "I shall offer no resistance, gentlemen." Facing Vidocq again. "It took the most brilliant policeman in France to arrest me. I salute you!" He bowed and marched out of the room followed by Goury and Fouché.

Vidocq smiled, amused by his arrogance. He pulled a silk handkerchief from a cuff to mop perspiration from his forehead.

"You caught the murderer?"

"Yes." He turned as Ève, dressed in white satin for the evening, swept in from the other side of the mirror. "Your life and your diamonds are safe."

"And I am grateful!" She flung her arms around him and kissed him delicately on the lips. Careful not to spoil her makeup. "I saw them escorting him toward the rear stairs. Who is he?"

"Baron de Chabrillat's son."

"The old boy never told me he had one. How was Violette's impersonation?

"In this light he barely saw her face."

"All whores look alike in bed!" She laughed as she moved past him, with a rustle of satin, toward her dressing table in the alcove.

Vidocq watched her. Scarlet hair looped with pearls and emeralds, exquisite shoulders and breasts revealed by the décolleté of her white gown. "Tell me, my love. Have you ever thought of marriage?"

"Constantly!" She turned and looked at him. "If only I could meet a rich gentleman who would ask me. Any suggestions?"

"Not a suggestion. A candidate. How would you like to live in the United States of America?"

"America!" She came back across the boudoir. "I've always wanted to go there."

"Would you consider New Orléans?"

"I've heard it's like Paris! What are you getting at?"

"Your husband would be one of the richest men in the United States. A friend of the President . . ."

"You devil! You're teasing me again."

"This is not a joke."

"You're serious?" She looked into his eyes. "Yes. You are . . . When do I meet this American prince?"

"Tomorrow night? I will bring him here for supper, and you can study him. Just the three of us?"

"I promise you there will be no other guests."

"I want nothing to distract you as you make your decision."

"But it's already made. I'll marry him, even if he has two heads and two of everything else!"

"He's very handsome . . ."

"I shall wear my diamond necklace! For the first time this year." She went toward the head of her bed and leaned down. Touched one of the gold-rimmed scales of the serpent with a fingertip.

There was a soft whirring sound, and the jaws of the great snake slowly parted.

Vidocq saw that, at the same time, the huge golden apple was revolving.

"Now, *chéri,* you know all my most intimate secrets."

"I doubt that."

She pulled a thin golden chain from the bodice of her gown with a gold key hanging at one end. Reached up to insert it into the apple. Turned the key and stepped back.

The apple opened and a shower of louis d'or cascaded down. As they dropped onto the pillows, there was a flash of jewels twisting among them.

Vidocq looked down and saw the diamond necklace curled in the nest of golden coins like a glittering snake.

CHAPTER 62

He swung the door open and turned, as was his custom, to watch the fiacre roll on down rue de l'Hirondelle, returning to the boulevards.

A faint breath of air touched his face and moved through the trees.

He would welcome the first snowfall when the shade of François Villon would return—he never glimpsed the rascal in the summer—to steal through the dark alleys of Paris.

Slipping the keys into his pocket, he went inside before the fiacre disappeared around the corner, closing and bolting the door.

He was earlier than usual tonight, but even so he was tired and eager for sleep.

The old mansion was silent, but the air held a trace of his mother's lilac powder. She must have come downstairs to leave him a note before retiring.

As he went toward the lighted lamp on the console table, he wondered if Goury and Fouché had finished their duties at the Conciergerie. Young de Chabrillat would be in his cell, the formalities completed.

He hadn't returned to Number Six—although he'd meant to bring those diamonds home tonight and lock them in the vault—but had come straight here after leaving Ève's apartment where a bottle of champagne had delayed his departure.

Those three murders solved! Maya, Tessier, and poor little Clochette . . .

One murderer and one gun.

Tomorrow he would pay another visit to the Minister. He smiled. Take him a report on his capture of young de Chabrillat. The Préfecture had said Clochette was killed by a prowler!

As he reached the table holding the lighted lamp he saw his mother's folded note and picked it up.

> *Such a warm day!*
> *I only hope tomorrow will be cooler*
> *for our picnic.*
> *And I hope you haven't forgotten it!*
> *Both Jeanne-Victoire and Fleuride*
> *look forward to our outing.*
> *I thought we could drive to one of*
> *those pleasant spots where we used*
> *to picnic when dear Annette lived*
> *with us. One of them had a stream*
> *full of delicious fish.*
> *Sleep well . . .*

He thrust the note into a pocket and continued on toward the staircase.

Tonight he had saved Ève's life . . .

And tomorrow night he would take Monsieur Zeb to meet her. He would observe them during dinner. Would Ève be willing to give up life in Paris for a wealthy American? Would Pennypacker marry a *courtisane?* Why not! Nobody in the United States would ever learn about Ève's past. Must remember to destroy her dossier at Number Six with any documents they might have filed at the Préfecture. Aubé could take care of that . . .

Climbing the steps slowly, he considered tomorrow's picnic. He would go to Number Six for a few hours in the morning but return home around eleven, in time to leave for the country.

Vidocq paused at the top of the staircase, but no sound came from his mother's suite or Fleuride's bedroom.

He continued on to his own suite and swung open the door. Through inner doors he saw moonlight flooding the bedroom.

Fleuride was stretched out, invitingly, in his bed.

He smiled as his eyes rested on her firm brown flesh. She was asleep, but he would wake her after he visited his wife.

Leaving his hat on a chair, he continued down the corridor to Jeanne-Victoire's suite. Crossed the little foyer into the bedroom. Glimpsed her pale body against the white sheet.

Approaching the foot of the bed, he heard the nightingale singing in the garden.

"Who are you, Monsieur?" She turned on the pillows and held out her arms.

He smiled. "I am . . ."